THE SCENT
OF BETRAYAL

Historical Fiction Published by McBooks Press

BY ALEXANDER KENT
Midshipman Bolitho
Stand into Danger
In Gallant Company
Sloop of War
To Glory We Steer
Command a King's Ship
Passage to Mutiny
With All Despatch
Form Line of Battle!
Enemy in Sight!
The Flag Captain
Signal–Close Action!
The Inshore Squadron
A Tradition of Victory
Success to the Brave
Colours Aloft!
Honour this Day
The Only Victor
Beyond the Reef
The Darkening Sea
For My Country's Freedom
Cross of St George
Sword of Honour
Second to None
Relentless Pursuit

BY DUDLEY POPE
Ramage
Ramage & The Drumbeat
Ramage & The Freebooters
Governor Ramage R.N.
Ramage's Prize
Ramage & The Guillotine
Ramage's Diamond
Ramage's Mutiny
Ramage & The Rebels
The Ramage Touch
Ramage's Signal
Ramage & The Renegades
Ramage's Devil
Ramage's Trial
Ramage's Challenge
Ramage at Trafalgar
Ramage & The Saracens
Ramage & The Dido

BY DAVID DONACHIE
The Devil's Own Luck
The Dying Trade
A Hanging Matter
An Element of Chance
The Scent of Betrayal
A Game of Bones

BY DEWEY LAMBDIN
The French Admiral
Jester's Fortune

BY DOUGLAS REEMAN
Badge of Glory
First to Land
The Horizon
Dust on the Sea

BY V.A. STUART
Victors and Lords
The Sepoy Mutiny
Massacre at Cawnpore
The Cannons of Lucknow
The Heroic Garrison

BY C. NORTHCOTE PARKINSON
The Guernseyman
Devil to Pay
The Fireship
Touch and Go

BY CAPTAIN FREDERICK MARRYAT
Frank Mildmay OR *The Naval Officer*
The King's Own
Mr Midshipman Easy
Newton Forster OR *The Merchant Service*
Snarleyyow OR *The Dog Fiend*
The Privateersman
The Phantom Ship

BY JAN NEEDLE
A Fine Boy for Killing
The Wicked Trade

BY IRV C. ROGERS
Motoo Eetee

BY NICHOLAS NICASTRO
The Eighteenth Captain
Between Two Fires

BY W. CLARK RUSSELL
Wreck of the Grosvenor
Yarn of Old Harbour Town

BY RAFAEL SABATINI
Captain Blood

BY MICHAEL SCOTT
Tom Cringle's Log

BY A.D. HOWDEN SMITH
Porto Bello Gold

BY R.F. DELDERFIELD
Too Few for Drums
Seven Men of Gascony

The Scent
of Betrayal

DAVID
DONACHIE

THE PRIVATEERSMAN MYSTERIES, NO 5

McBooks Press
ITHACA, NEW YORK

Published by McBooks Press 2003
Copyright © 1996 by David Donachie
First published in the United Kingdom in 1996
by Macmillan London, Limited

Cover painting by Geoff Hunt

Library of Congress Cataloging-in-Publication Data

Donachie, David, 1944-
   The scent of betrayal / by David Donachie.
      p. cm. -- (The privateersman mysteries ; no. 5)
   ISBN 1-59013-031-6 (alk. paper)
   1. Ludlow, Harry (Fictitious character)--Fiction. 2. Great
Britain--History, Naval--18th century--Fiction. 3.Louisiana--History--
To 1803--Fiction. 4. British--Louisiana--Fiction.
5. New Orleans (La.)--Fiction. 6. Privateering--Fiction. I. Title.
PR6053.O483 S34 2003
823'.914--dc21

                                                 2002012357

Distributed to the trade by National Book Network, Inc.,
15200 NBN Way, Blue Ridge Summit, PA 17214
800-462-6420

Additional copies of this book may be ordered from any bookstore
or directly from McBooks Press, Inc., ID Booth Building,
520 North Meadow St., Ithaca, NY 14850. Please include
$4.00 postage and handling with mail orders.
New York State residents must add sales tax. All McBooks
Press publications can also be ordered by calling toll-free
1-888-BOOKS11 (1-888-266-5711).
Please call to request a free catalog.

Visit the McBooks Press website at www.mcbooks.com.

Printed in the United States of America

9 8 7 6 5 4 3 2 1

I dedicate this book to

NIGEL LOVE, GLENN COULL & ALAN BURRETT

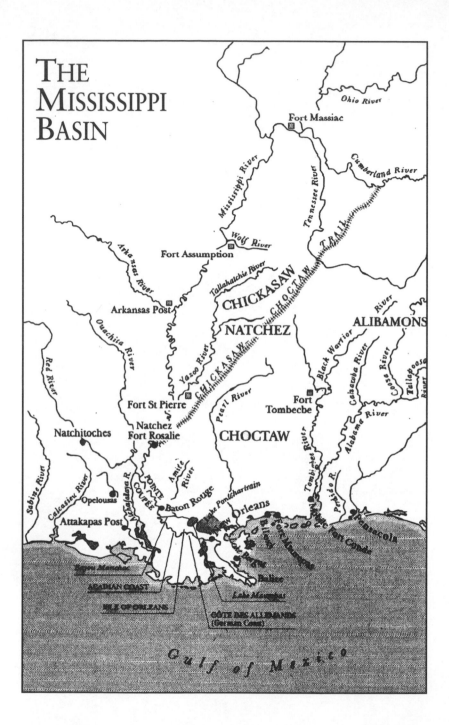

THE
MISSISSIPPI
BASIN

Ohio River

Fort Massiac

Mississippi River

Cumberland River

Tennessee River

Arkansas River

Wolf River

Fort Assumption

TRAIL

Tallahatchie River

CHICKASAW

CHOCTAW

Arkansas Post

Ouachita River

NATCHEZ

ALIBAMONS

River

Red River

Yazoo River

CHICKASAW

Black Warrior

Coosa River

Tallapoosa River

Cahawba River

Fort St Pierre

Pearl River

Fort
Tombecbe

Natchitoches

Natchez
Fort Rosalie

CHOCTAW

Alabama River

Tombigbee River

Sabine River

Calcasieu River

Opelousas

Amite River

POINTE
COUPÉE

Atchafalaya R.

Perdido R.

Attakapas Post

Baton Rouge

Lake Pontchartrain

New Orleans

Pensacola

Fort Condé

Bayou Manchac

ACADIAN COAST

ISLE OF ORLEANS

Balize

Lake Maurepas

CÔTE DES ALLEMANDS
(German Coast)

Gulf of Mexico

HISTORICAL NOTE

GENERAL James Wilkinson did exist, as did his gold. Someone once said of him that "He was a man so careful in defence of his honour, it was clear that he had none." He conspired, at Valley Forge, to remove George Washington from the command of the Continental Army, the first but not the last of his underhand dealings. Personal advantage was his prime motive, though it was cloaked in statements relating to all manner of high-sounding causes. While a serving soldier in the army of the United States, he sought to serve both Spain and his own country, while deceiving them both regarding his aims for Kentucky. He did solicit a bribe of $200,000 from the Governor of New Orleans, this to act as a paid informant against his fellow Americans. The gold was shipped, in secret and by a circuitous route, up the Mississippi. But before it could be handed over, those carrying it, and their escorts, were ambushed and robbed. No trace of the money, or of the identity of those who stole it, has ever been established.

CHAPTER ONE

HARRY LUDLOW wasn't one to get inebriated often. But celebrating Oliver Pollock's birthday had led to a bout of drinking that got out of hand, and an extended period of sleeping ashore in this cramped lodging house had dulled the sixth sense that every ship's master needed as a guard against sudden danger. Pender, who'd expected his Captain's eyes to open as soon as the door creaked, was obliged to throw the shutters wide, allowing the first bright streaks of Caribbean sunlight to stream in through the window and fill the sparsely furnished room. That wasn't enough, it didn't even break the rhythm of the loud snores. He had to shake the recumbent figure very hard before he got any kind of response. Half awake, and confused, he was slow to comprehend what Pender was saying.

"Who?" Harry croaked.

"Your American friend, Pollock," Pender repeated slowly. "Who was matchin' you jug for jug last night. The drink didn't seem to affect him in the same manner as you. He set sail in the *Daredevil* at the full and not a hint as to where he was headin'. I don't recall him saying anything about shifting out of here in the middle of the night."

Harry shook his head very slowly.

"Coffee, I think," said Pender, making for the door.

Harry tried to say *gallons*, but the word wouldn't come. He lay back on the wide double bed and closed his eyes, rubbing his temples in a vain attempt to dull the ache of what promised to be a serious hangover. His brain was slow to clear, the events of the previous night, as well as the last few weeks, unfolding in a series of confused, non-chronological images. Five men; great quantities of food; endless toasts. The scarred face of Nathan Caufield, native of Sag Harbour and former Loyalist, bridling at any reference to the American Revolution. The Long Island sailor's seeming indifference when his son, Matthew, in the company of James Ludlow, slipped away to yet another assignation at Madame Leon's bawdy-house.

The impression existed that for all he'd consumed in food and wine, which was considerable, he shouldn't be feeling this bad. Harry Ludlow would never claim to be a trencherman of the first rank, but in a world where no meal was considered memorable if it wasn't huge, where drink was taken regularly and copiously, he could recall few occasions when he'd felt as weak as he did now. His next attempt to speak died as Pender returned, no more than a rasp in his bone-dry throat. Handed a pitcher of water, he drank from it greedily, allowing a fair quantity to spill over the front of his shirt. He looked down.

"God in heaven," he sighed, at the realization that he'd probably been carried to bed, "I'm still in my breeches and boots."

Raising his eyes he observed that he wasn't alone in his distress. Pender's face was tinged with grey. The eyes, steady as they contemplated his plight, had a red, bloodshot rim round each pupil, and his voice had a weary quality.

"Since you was dead to the world, I decided to partake of a bit of a gargle on my own account. I was on my way back here when one of the fishermen told me about Mr Pollock."

Another image floated into his mind. Of Pender, cold sober in the background, stepping forward only occasionally to top up a tankard that wasn't full to the rim. It must have been some "gargle" he'd crammed into the time he had left.

"Beats me how Pollock managed it," Pender added, "given what he put away. He must have been the very devil to rouse out. There's no way he could have walked to the quayside, that's for certain."

Harry, with a deliberate air, swung his feet onto the floor, an action which produced an alarming stab of pain in his head. His

nostrils picked up the odour of coffee long before the serving girl
set the tray she was carrying on the table. Pender had a cup poured
and in his master's hands before her footsteps faded. He drank
the coffee gratefully, then hauled himself to his feet. By the open
window he could see out over the whole of St Croix harbour. Several ships, including *Daredevil,* had slipped their moorings during
the hours of darkness. He struggled to recall the names of others
but his hangover defeated every effort in that line and he turned
his attention to his own ship, *Bucephalas,* knowing that the mere
sight of her clean lines would lift his spirits.

No man sailing as a privateer could ask for a better vessel.
Over a hundred foot long and well armed, she lay by the quay,
still handsome despite the staging round her stern. The work he'd
ordered done on her was all but complete. Today he intended to
set about removing the mess the shipwrights had made of his pristine deck. Normally a man who harried such people, he'd been
content to let them work at their own pace. The topsail schooner
Ariadne, which he'd escorted here, was in need of greater repair:
as well as substantial damage to her upper works, her timbers had
suffered from worm and weed. Hauled over by the nearest stretch
of beach, she looked forlorn in the clean morning light. Both ships
had been damaged in a recent battle with two French frigates and
here, safe in the Danish harbour, the local shipwrights were making perfect the temporary repairs that had been undertaken at sea.
In less than a week from now they'd both be ready, with Harry
determined that they should part company as soon as they'd
weighed.

"Odd that Pollock didn't let on he was leavin'," said Pender.

"He'd have informed us if he'd known."

As much a question as a statement, it produced no response
from his servant. Pollock must have left because of some unforeseen emergency. Despite many conversations, he still knew little
about the American's reasons for calling at St Croix. He was just
about to make this observation when both the Governor's signal
guns boomed out over the harbour. Raising his eyes, he saw much

commotion on the parched lawn in front of the residence. Both guns boomed out again. The Danish flag rose and dipped as someone sought another method of alerting the inhabitants. All of which could mean only one thing: serious danger, which in this part of the world tended to mean an attempt to take the island. Painful as it was to make any sudden move, his response was immediate.

"Get the crew aboard *Bucephalas* and make ready for sea. Send someone to drag James and young Caufield out of that damned whorehouse and tell Matthew to rouse out his father. He's to turn him into the trough if necessary, but get him aboard ship."

Pender was hanging out of the other window, trying in vain to see what the fuss was about. His Captain's sharp tone brooked no argument, nor did it invite questions. Harry Ludlow had his own well-developed sense of impending peril, honed by years at sea, that was proof against a mere hangover, and when he spoke in that manner he expected obedience. Pender was out of the door before Harry had grabbed his sword, pistols, and papers from the sea-chest by the side of the bed.

The commotion in the street was tremendous, the harbour worse, with every ship firing off some kind of weapon, adding to the air of panic. Men in the tops of each vessel, sent to make sail, were pointing towards the west, clearly the source of whatever threatened, while below their masters were attempting to haul the ships over their anchors. With no clear idea of what lay in the offing, Harry pushed his way through the throng towards the quay. He found his way blocked by a heavy crowd milling around outside the locked door of the Børsenen house, with those in the front banging on the thick wood. The leading banker in the town, he held money for the majority of the traders in St Croix and in a crisis all wanted their funds in their own hands. The buzz of conversation, in a dozen tongues, engulfed him as he fought his way through. There was a great deal he didn't comprehend. But he understood enough.

His original supposition, made at the first boom of the signal guns, proved accurate. There was a fleet in the offing, flying the French flag, beating up towards the island, intent on a landing. How much was this a threat to a neutral Danish possession? Then the expedition leader's name was mentioned, and that stood out no matter what language was used. Harry's already delicate stomach heaved with apprehension. There was no way of knowing how the crowd had come by the information, or indeed if it was true, but a voice had named Victor Hugues as the man leading the French expedition. As soon as he heard it Harry ran twice as hard. Hugues had arrived from France two years previously. He came with troops, a message telling the slaves they were free, and a guillotine. Having retaken Guadeloupe, he'd shown little hesitation in using the symbol of the Terror on white and black alike. On its own, that made little difference, since whoever commanded the invasion force, the security of neutrality did not apply to a British ship's Captain sailing as a privateer.

But if it was indeed Hugues, Harry's case was made much worse because of the Frenchmen he'd escorted here. While not by nature Royalists, the Ariadnes had taken up arms against the forces of the Revolution, first on their home island of St Domingue and secondly against Hugues himself when he'd invaded Guadeloupe. Once that ogre was ashore, on an island without a Danish garrison, there could be little doubt where power would lie. The Governor would have no say in what took place. If this emissary of the Terror discovered their identity he'd certainly take his revenge. A man who'd brought a guillotine all the way from France, who had shot hundreds of his enemies in cold blood, wouldn't hesitate to ship it from one Caribbean island to another. A similar fate could well befall the crew of the *Bucephalas:* his name and that of his ship must be known to every Frenchman in the Caribbean. In the company of a British fifth-rate and the *Ariadne,* he'd fought two French frigates within sight of Guadeloupe, taking one and severely damaging the other.

All these thoughts chased around his throbbing head as he barrelled his way along the crowded quay towards his ship. He shot up the gangplank and onto the deck, there to be greeted by a scene of utter confusion. Pender, by means that didn't bear thinking about, had got the men to work. Normally his crew could be relied upon to perform efficiently, but judging by the way some of them were staggering around he wasn't the only one who'd spent the night drinking—and this surprising development had robbed them of the power to see what must be done. His dehydrated shout emerged as a harsh croak, but enough of his crew turned to allow him to issue some orders. The primary task was to cut the stout ties that attached the staging on his ship to the quay, then he wanted everything not belonging to *Bucephalas* thrown overboard.

The deck was a mess of carpenters' tools, shavings, pieces of timber, and lumps of unsawn wood; ropes hung loose everywhere, left to swing, rather than coiled in the manner in which he normally insisted; what sails he had aloft were haphazardly slung, and certainly insufficient to get him out into the approaches off the harbour mouth; his guns, which he might need desperately in the next few hours, had been struck below so that the shipwrights could repair the damaged gunports. It was as if everything on board made a swift departure impossible. And it was his own fault. The ship had needed so many minor, scattered repairs he'd relaxed his own strict standards, learned when he was a naval officer, and allowed his crew to take their pleasure ashore in numbers that left *Bucephalas* practically unattended.

"Harry!"

The call made him swing round. His brother James stood at the gangway. Elegant as ever, his face was shaved and his hair combed, that in sharp contrast to the Captain, whose obvious stubble allied to his grey face and general state of undress undermined his natural air of authority.

"Where in the Devil's name have you been, James?"

The furious tone, accompanied by a bloodshot glare, really a reflection of his own anger at himself, was immediately mistaken as a rebuke. Whatever James had been about to say died on his lips, his look of concern replaced by one of defensive hauteur. His words carried that quality of icy disdain he could so easily adopt when ruffled.

"My God, brother, you looked wretched. Had I encountered you on the quay I might have slipped you a beggar's coin."

"Where is Matthew Caufield?" snapped Harry, in no mood for jokes or condescension.

"Gone to try and raise his father." James sidestepped neatly as a trio of sailors rushed past him with a load of planking. "I hazard that given his love of the bottle he looks worse than you."

"Victor Hugues is just offshore, preparing to take over the island." The shocked look that produced, even if it was only rumour, cheered Harry somewhat. "Do you know the whereabouts of our Frenchmen? I should tell them, if you do, that it might be in their interest to unbolt that chest of treasure from the deck of the *Ariadne* and fetch it aboard *Bucephalas*."

"What about their ship?"

"She's halfway up a beach. She'd probably sink if we tried to float her." He looked towards the harbour mouth, to the few vessels that had managed to weigh. They were beating out of the narrows hoping to take the Trade wind on their quarter. In their haste some of the slower vessels impeded the more efficient ships and judging by what was happening in the rest of the harbour, matters were likely to deteriorate rather than improve. "I'm not even sure we'll be able to get away ourselves. But it's their only chance. They either come with us or . . ."

Harry had no need to finish the sentence, nor was he given the opportunity. James was already out of earshot. He gave more instructions to Pender then ran for the mainmast shrouds, reflecting on the words he'd said to his brother, which were nothing but the plain truth. But he had no real idea if they'd even be given the chance to escape. If the French were here in strength, and gained enough time to block the approaches, he was wasting his time. Yet if the others were trying to flee, a chance must exist. *Bucephalas*, compared to them, was a much better sailer, and being merchantmen, quite possibly fully laden, they presented the enemy with tempting targets. That in itself might suffice to aid him, despite the odds against success. Harry Ludlow was determined to sail through any gap that presented itself rather than wait in the harbour for an inevitable surrender.

He was halfway aloft when a thought struck him: Pollock's sudden departure might not be unconnected with what was happening. Yet surely if he'd known the American would have sent word to warn him: he knew all about Hugues, whose behaviour had become a byword for brutality all over the Caribbean. And even if he hadn't heard the story of Harry's action against the French ships from the horse's mouth, there were enough loose tongues in St Croix to give him fair outline of what had happened.

Harry didn't often come across people with whom he struck up an immediate rapport. Oliver Pollock was that rare creature, of an age and jaundiced outlook on life with him, one that allowed them to take few things too seriously, including the recent past. A slight feeling of isolation had probably helped, with James more interested in painting Madame de Leon's mulatto girls than his company. Barring regular discussions with the Danish banker, Børsenen, at whose house they'd first met, Pollock seemed just as unencumbered by duties as Harry. Meeting regularly at a tavern overlooking the harbour, their friendship had matured rapidly until they'd seemed inseparable.

As he climbed the ladder of ropes, Harry conjured up an image of his ruddy face, generally half-covered by the rim of his tankard, eyes twinkling and cheerful under his close-cropped white hair; in drink he sang loud songs or recited patriotic poems, mainly compositions relating to the defeat of the British army by the forces under Washington. Both men were old enough to see that conflict in perspective, and with the gift of hindsight to reflect that for all the animosity it had created, all the blood and destruction, the outcome had been beneficial for both countries. A lieutenant at the time, Harry had missed that war: not an occasion of happy memories for him. He'd lost his commission after the Battle of the

Saintes because of his refusal to apologize for duelling with a superior officer. The fact that the man was a martinet didn't count, since Harry had put a ball in his shoulder. Even the son of a serving admiral had to be disciplined for such an offence. Normally reticent on that subject, he'd opened up to Pollock, prepared to admit just how much such a loss had disappointed his father, even hinting just how much it had hurt him. The American could not know just how that rated him in Harry's estimation: it was a subject he never talked about, even to his own brother, James.

The thought that someone like Oliver Pollock, to whom he'd bared his soul so comprehensively, had deserted him at such a time induced a wave of depression that did nothing for his overall wellbeing. His hangover, which he'd temporarily forgotten, suddenly returned with a vengeance.

CHAPTER TWO

AT THE GOVERNOR'S mansion, people were still milling about in panic. The signal guns kept up a steady rate of fire, which added to the air of confusion that gripped the whole town. As soon as he reached the crosstrees Harry was overtaken by a wave of nausea. It needed a tight grip on a stay to avoid falling and several deep breaths to bring back some form of normality, allowing him to concentrate on the difficult task he faced. From this elevated position, he could see with the naked eye why some ships had got under way. The French, clearly identifiable by their tricolour battle flags, were some distance away. The "fleet," with one exception, was a collection of small brigs and barques. But that exception was significant. A proper warship, a frigate he recognized immediately as the *Marianne,* survivor of the pair he'd fought off Guadeloupe. Certainly enough to subdue St Croix, this small armada was not enough to beat off any serious attack at sea. This lack of strength was very likely the reason they'd chosen to approach from the west.

The Trade winds coming in from the east would almost certainly have made the descent on the island a complete surprise, but such a course would have taken them through a zone regularly patrolled by Royal Navy warships. The second option, the direct route from their base on Guadeloupe, was just as hazardous. Shaving St Kitts and Nevis, as well as the Spanish-held island of Santa Cruz, would have provided his intended victims with an early indication of his intentions, if not a clear idea of his actual destination. Small boats plied continuously between the various settlements in the Virgin group, all able to outsail a fleet that needed to stay in close order for mutual protection. But the French, once ashore, would be relatively safe. It would be months before the Danish government, with scant resources to respond, would even know they'd landed. The British, if they saw these actions as a threat to their security, would need to undertake a properly mounted invasion to dislodge them once they'd garrisoned and fortified the island.

Obviously, if it was Hugues, he'd come in a wide arc. Detected *en route,* it would appear that he intended to take his ships up through the Mona Passage. This ran between Hispaniola and San Juan and was the route for a possible descent on St Domingue. Once in sight of the mountain tops behind Ponce, he'd simply turn due east to gain the element of surprise. While his approach made tactical sense, it forced his ships to beat up into the wind, difficult when he was obliged to proceed at the speed of his slowest. But full daylight, the sight of his objective, and a clear unthreatening sea released him from that constraint. Captain Villemin, in command of the *Marianne,* had separated and was doing everything in his power to come up, tack upon tack, his aim to close the gap and seal the harbour mouth.

Having engaged the man twice Harry Ludlow knew certain things about him. Villemin was no great shakes in the sailing line and was indecisive at critical moments. More important still, he knew his ship was no match for *Bucephalas* on a bowline. So if Harry could clear the harbour he had, sailing into the wind, a fair chance of getting clean away. Set against that, Villemin knew just as much about his opponent. They'd first skirmished in mid-Atlantic, with Harry, by some deft manoeuvring, foxing his opponent. Off Guadeloupe they'd participated in a proper battle. Villemin had seen his superior officer forced to strike to a British frigate, in the main due to Harry's actions. What would go through his mind if he saw the outline of an enemy who'd bested him twice? Would that induce caution, or such a strong desire for vengeance that he would outdo himself?

The solution would have to wait. The signal guns were sending shock waves across the harbour that made his head ache. At the crash of falling, breaking timber he looked down, just in time to see most of the elaborate scaffold of the shipwrights' staging tumble into the sea. That reinforced the pain in his temples, and he rested for a moment against the rough wood of the topmast. Quickly the images in his mind changed from solid thoughts to disjointed dreams. His head, falling forward, jerked him awake, and he took a more secure grip on the mast. For probably the first time in his life, Harry Ludlow didn't relish the thought of being so high in the air. Nor did he want to look down to the deck below.

But like it or not, he knew he must. He had a clear view of progress on deck and he forced himself to consider in a logical sequence what he would need to do in the next half-hour. Most of the objects interfering with his ability to sail the ship had been cleared away and his boats, left in the water so their seams stayed sealed in the heat, could be used if required. There was enough wind, even in this sheltered part of the harbour, to allow his topsails to draw, and once out into the bay he might be able to let fall the main course. So he could try the entrance, but he could only clear it if Villemin was too far away to try a broadside. With his own guns still below, he had nothing with which to oppose the Frenchman if he got within range.

Some of his men were already aloft, preparing the yards to take the canvas being hauled out of the sail room. It wasn't as swift as he would have liked, the sharp edge of a crew who'd been continuously at sea was missing, but they were working with a will that would not be improved by shouts from a sore-headed commander. A glance towards the point where the quay met the beach showed James approaching fast with his party of French-men—the heavy brass-bound chest with their combined wealth needed four men to carry it. They represented another conundrum altogether, not least because they were going to be forced to abandon their ship. Taking a firm grip and several deep breaths he slid down a backstay to the deck, landing heavily. Pender, having seen him begin his descent, was there to help. His Captain favoured him with a wan smile, gave the orders to set sail, sent a lookout to the cross-trees to keep an eye on *Marianne,* and turned to him.

"Get a pair of swivel guns and some grapeshot onto the quarterdeck. I want you and a strong party, with muskets, in the barge. Stay just ahead of us as we cross the harbour. If anyone disputes our passage fire a volley over the head of the man conning the ship. I'll follow up with a dose of grape."

Pender, seemingly quite recovered from his own drinking bout, grinned at the mention of muskets. His white teeth stood out sharply in a face that already dark skinned and weather beaten had received a spell of West Indian sunshine. The deep brown eyes, still bloodshot, fixed on Harry's grey face.

"I put the cook to lighting the galley fire, Capt'n. He's a useless sod on deck in any case and I reckon that you're not alone in needing somethin' hot to keep you going."

"The *Marianne*'s out there, Pender. If we don't shift Villemin'll be across the harbour mouth and we'll get something much too hot for our welfare."

The grin stayed there. "After what we've done to him in the last bout, your honour, I reckon he'll take one look at us an' turn tail."

"Not if he realizes that our guns are down in the hold."

Even that couldn't dent his faith in his Captain. James, hurrying aboard as Pender went off to collect the barge crew, adopted the same tone, one which regardless of the difficulties always assumed that his older brother had a solution. This was based more than anything on Harry's own sanguine temperament, plus a not inconsiderable ability to give a sudden piece of inspiration the air of a deep-laid plan. Ordinarily he would have played up to this image, but tired and burdened with the effect of the previous night's debauch he wasn't his normal self. He couldn't begin to appear positive. Even his voice lacked the usual confident note.

"Have you explained things to our Frenchmen, James?"

"As much as I can, Harry. But even with the possibility of

Hugues in the offing they're worried about losing their ship."

"First things first, brother. They must realize that if he gets his hands on them he'll lop off their heads. I'd be obliged if you'll ask them to go below and prepare the guns. I can't haul them up while we're setting sail but I want to as soon as possible. If they've already been shifted into position with slings on, it will save a lot of time."

"What in the name of God is the French for slings?"

"Damned if I know, brother," Harry replied, wearily, "but they've all served aboard ship, so they should respond if shown what to do. Take Dreaver with you if you wish."

Aloft, order was emerging out of near chaos, with his topsails bent on and ready to let fall. A shout to the lookout told him that *Marianne* only needed two more tacks before her broadside would seal the harbour mouth. What he had rigged wasn't perfect, but enough to give *Bucephalas* steerage-way; Pender, efficient as ever, had his party armed and in the barge. On his command those on deck ran to man the braces, and he turned to order the shore party to cast off when a hail distracted him. Emerging from the crowd milling around by the last of the warehouses, half-carrying his father, he saw Matthew Caufield. He sent two sailors and after an interminable delay they were bustled aboard. Nathan Caufield collapsed in a heap by the bulwarks. Matthew, gasping for breath, didn't have the wind to apologize. But the glare from Harry Ludlow gave him enough energy to assist in hauling in the gangplank.

The cables were cast off and men used capstan bars to push them free. Pender had dropped a cable out of the hawse-hole to the barge and Harry could hear him shouting at his crew to bring the ship's head round, allowing the sails to take the wind. Their efforts paid off handsomely and with the bows no more than ten feet from the quay, *Bucephalas* had life. Harry took the wheel himself to con her through the mass of shipping still anchored in the bay, surrounded by boats as those masters who knew they couldn't get clear worked furiously to remove anything of value. Then, with an unimpeded view of the harbour mouth, his heart sank. The whole narrow exit was blocked by a tangle of merchant vessels. Men were stabbing at each other with poles and pikes, trying to fend off so that they could get to the open sea, some of the ships had run aground on the sandy western shore, with boats over the side struggling to tow them off, and all the time the signal guns boomed out from the Governor's lawn.

"Matthew, get your father below. There should be a chart of the harbour on my plotting table. Fetch that, then come and take charge of these swivel guns. I want them loaded with grapeshot."

Harry was racking his tired brain, trying to remember if he'd left the chart where he said, and more importantly what it told him about the soundings. Most Caribbean islands were extinct volcanoes, with the natural harbours formed by the sea's incursion into the dead core. This often meant that deep water ran right up to the very edge, where the shoreline shelved sharply even where it turned to white sandy beach. The tide entering the harbour mouth, aided by the wind, was pushing the tangled mass of shipping to the western edge of the entrance, leaving a slight gap by the eastern shore. That appeared to be his only chance of making an escape, but everything depended on having enough water beneath his keel.

"There's no sign of any chart, Captain Ludlow," said Matthew, coming back onto the deck. "The plotting table is covered with shipwrights' drawings."

"Damn!"

Harry dropped his head forward, again overcome by a wave of nausea. Matthew's voice, asking if he needed help, brought him back to life, and he called for a man to assist him at the wheel. The boy's father, who'd spent his life in the West Indian trade, had probably sailed out of St Croix dozens of times. He must know it well. Distracted momentarily by the need to set more sail, he returned to the thought once the main course and outer jib had been sheeted home. Matthew, by then, had loaded one of the swivel guns that nestled in its mount on the gunwale.

"Do you think your father is in a fit state to tell me anything about the soundings by the eastern shore?"

"I'd say not," replied Matthew sadly. "What the deuce did he have last night? I ain't never seen him in that condition."

Harry felt his stomach heave at the thought. Bile filled his throat and he rushed to the side, sending a fount of vomit into the greasy waters of the harbour. He felt the acid from his guts burning his throat as he replied to the young American's question.

"Whatever it was, it has affected me as badly. Be so good as to replace me at the wheel. Hold the present course and keep the bowsprit pointed towards the small gap by the eastern shore."

Matthew's eyebrows shot up as he looked towards the blocked entrance. "Are we going through there?"

Harry positively snapped his reply. "Unless you can provide us with wings, Matthew, I'd be very grateful if you'd just do as I ask!"

Making his way forward he saw that the cable attached to the barge had been cast off. Using a speaking-trumpet he called to Pender, requesting that he come alongside. As he did so Harry dropped a leaded line into the boat, then pointed straight ahead.

"We're going for that gap and I don't know if we've got the depth of keel to get through. I want you right ahead of me catching the line. The rest of your men to play their muskets on that pile of fools who've got themselves in such a mess. Make sure they stay out of our way. And Pender, remember this. If it is Hugues, and he takes them, they risk losing their cargoes. If he takes us we'll end up on his guillotine. Should they show any sign of disputing our passage, you are to shoot to kill."

The faint voice from the masthead was just what was needed to emphasize his point. "*Marianne*'s come about on another tack, Capt'n. She'll have her guns athwart the entrance in no more'n twenty minutes."

Harry was still not his usual self, but that recent evacuation had made him feel slightly better. There was a mass of things to be done and no time to do them. He must get fenders over the side so that if he did run into another ship he would suffer no

damage; he needed some crew in the bows with capstan bars to
fend off; more men with muskets to frighten those merchantmen
if they got that close. Once he'd cleared the entrance he'd need
different sails aloft to get the best out of his ship as she sailed into
the wind, canvas that was not yet out of the sail room. It was a
time for clear, sharp thinking. Instead every decision had to be
dragged from what seemed like a deep, dark well. He shook his
head violently, but that only produced pain. At the water-butt by
the binnacle he ducked his head right under. As he lifted it out,
eyes still closed, he heard the quiet voice by his side.

"After you, friend."

Harry hoped he didn't look as bad as Nathan Caufield. The
American's lips were like scarlet slashes on his chalk-white face.
The eyes, under his pale lashes, had a distant quality, seeming not
to focus on anything.

"I won't ask you how you feel."

"Death can't be worse."

"It could be that you're about to find out," said Harry, standing upright and pointing towards the entrance. *Marianne*'s upper
masts were clearly visible now, with the Tricolour flag streaming
back from the mizzen. Caufield blinked once or twice, his fuddled
brain trying to make sense of what he saw. "I've no time for the
finer details of our predicament. What I need to know is the soundings around the eastern arm of the harbour."

"Deep water right up to twenty feet off the shore," he replied,
without hesitation. "I've bumped the odd rock as I drifted but
never sustained damage."

"Do you feel up to conning the ship?"

Caufield nodded towards the French battle-flag. "Do I have a
choice?"

"You do. Both you and your son, being Americans, have nothing to fear from the French. You may take any boat you wish and
row ashore."

Caufield didn't reply. He merely turned away and headed to
join his son. Relieved of the need to steer, Harry gave orders to

break out more canvas then went forward to direct the men in the bows. The cook, Willerby, his wooden leg tapping on the planking, came striding up to him with a steaming pewter tankard in his hand. As he reached his Captain he thrust it forward.

"Fire's a-lit, your honour, but it'll be an age before my coppers get hot. I did this over a spirit stove."

"What is it?" asked Harry, taking the tankard. The smell that emanated from the top produced a renewed feeling of nausea in his stomach.

"There's two things as regards that there mixture, Capt'n," said the cook, looking him straight in the eye. "One is that knowing what's in it will do you no good, while sticking it down your hatch in one go will."

Harry tried to give it back to him, looking aloft to see how the men were faring. But Willerby wasn't to be put off by authority or procrastination. He pushed the tankard hard towards his Captain.

"I've been at sea since before you was breached, your honour. An' that is a brew that was given to me by the greatest man with the bottle I ever knew. An' he had more sense than to argue with a cook when his head was sore."

Harry looked at him as hard as he could, but he was not to be deflected. He just pushed the tankard against Harry's chest. There was no time to argue: Willerby was in what every member of the crew would have recognized as his paternal state. So he did as he was ordered. Whatever the old man had put in the tankard was foul, and halfway down he gagged, nearly spewing it back onto the deck. But somehow he managed to swallow it, his face reddening from the effort.

"Damn it, Willerby, what was in there? Not even Macbeth's witches could come up with something as bad as that."

Willerby took the tankard as he turned to stomp away. "As I say, your honour, best you don't know. Though I will own there's a lot of neat rum. Nothing like the dog's breath to cure a sore head."

CHAPTER THREE

THE SITUATION at the mouth was deteriorating rapidly as *Bucephalas* crawled across the harbour. All the efforts at disentangling produced more chaos rather than less. Merchant ships lacked the men to cut the skein of tangled cordage as well as push against the run of the tide and their fellows, to be far enough away for their sails to draw. Beyond that mass of hulls, masts, and ropes, Harry saw that one ship's master who'd reached the exit first had got clear and was heading south. He called aloft to ask if he was being pursued, only to be answered with a resounding no. That momentary pleasure was soon dashed as the lookout informed him two small brigs, both showing French colours, were approaching from the east. Despite everything which needed to be organized on deck, that called for his undivided attention. He was halfway up the shrouds before he realized that his stomach had settled and his head had cleared. Whatever Willerby had put in that drink was doing the trick. A glance over his shoulder showed the cook, belligerently pushing forward on his wooden leg, forcing another tankard into Captain Caufield's chest. It was received with similar reluctance, making Harry laugh out loud and adding vigour to his climb. Unbeknown to him his reaction aided his crew. If their Captain was laughing now, instead of being glum like he had since coming aboard, then things might not be as serious as they'd supposed.

Once aloft and settled, it was immediately obvious that exactly the opposite was true. Very likely the two brigs coming in from the east had not met their proper rendezvous. Surely they should have been off the harbour mouth, ready to enforce a blockade at

first light, so ensuring that no ship could escape? It was small comfort that they'd failed, since their presence complicated Harry's
slim hope of evading capture: they sat right across the course he'd
intended to adopt. Fully armed he might have brushed them aside,
the mere threat of his cannons enough to cause them to sheer off;
without anything but a pair of signal guns he was toothless. But
pressing as that problem was, it would have to wait. Looking
down into the clear blue water beneath the keel he could see, by
the change of colour, how rapidly the bottom was shelving. Ahead
Pender was casting the lead, calling off the soundings in a loud
hail. Four men manned the oars, while the remainder sat amidships, muskets at the ready.

He called out suddenly for them to open fire. They couldn't
see from their waterline position, but as Harry had feared, the
crew of the nearest merchantman finally untangling their rigging,
were poling off from the others. He could still get through the
narrowing gap, but if they spun their yards to take the wind they
would certainly foul his own. At the crash of the barge crew's
muskets the armed men in the bows did likewise, and their fire,
aimed from their higher elevation, had a greater effect. But it was
the swivel gun that really made the merchant sailors desist. Loaded
with grape, a gun of that calibre posed little serious threat, but
the small balls, whistling over their heads, must have sounded like
mortal danger. The Captain, who'd been directing their operations,
and who'd turned to shake a fist at the fusillade of muskets, threw
himself to the deck, cowering behind the wheel. His men dropped
their poles and headed for the nearest companionway. The ship,
freed from the pressure of their efforts, began to drift back into
contact with her neighbour. *Bucephalas,* steadily gaining speed,
was now committed to the space that left. Pender realized that
given her pace the time for soundings was past. In fact he was in
some danger of being overhauled and driven under. He dropped
his leadline and ordered the firing party to put aside their muskets and join the remainder in rowing. In dead calm water,
sheltered by the nearby shore, the barge shot forward and was
swiftly out of danger.

The water beneath *Bucephalas* was no longer even pale blue. The colour of the sandy bottom had turned it to something approaching milk. Fronds of weed bent and twisted in the current, occasionally revealing the black jagged shape of a rock. Others, even larger where the undersea vegetation was thicker, would remain hidden from view. Whatever Caufield said about deep soundings, this was going to require a degree of good fortune. A ship drifting sedately into this part of the harbour stood in little danger of damage, but that did not apply to one running at speed. *Bucephalas* was barely making three knots, but that was enough to rip her bottom out if she made contact.

The bowsprit inched over a particularly dense patch of greenery. Harry, counting off the seconds till the deepest part of his keel made contact, was suddenly aware that he was holding his breath. It seemed like an eternity as all other sounds around him faded. His heart nearly stopped as the topmast swayed forward, until he realized that it was merely the effect of the thick weed slowing the ship, something barely noticeable on deck but very exaggerated aloft. Lifting his eyes he saw another patch dead ahead, and for reasons that added up to nothing but guesswork, called down to Caufield to change course slightly to avoid it. This took him too close to the other vessels and forced the men below to haul the yards round so that they lay nearly fore and aft. The pressure of the wind pushed *Bucephalas* over and she juddered as her bulwarks grazed into the side planking of a merchantman.

Here the fenders proved their worth, even if they were ripped off by the pressure of the rough wood as his men fought to pole their way past. On the merchantman's deck every member of the crew was shouting imprecations and abuse in a language he couldn't understand. He would have paid them no heed even if they'd cursed him in English. All his attention was directed to those using the capstan bars, calling orders to pole hard and create a thin strip of blue water between the ships so he could trim his sails to take a bit of wind. That and the efforts of the men fending them along the merchantman's side finally pushed them past its high forecastle. The sight of the empty outer roadstead spurred them to even greater efforts. *Bucephalas* rose, then dipped forward as she breasted the first gentle wave, telling Harry that they'd cleared their first hurdle. The sandy bottom receded and now the bowsprit swayed over a mass of deep blue water. Within half a minute they were clear and Harry turned his attention to the next problem.

There was no time for a leisurely examination. He'd never stay out of range of Villemin's guns with what he had aloft, so thirty seconds were allotted to an impression of the two brigs' sailing qualities. A sudden deep thud made him look down in alarm, but it was only Pender, who'd brought the barge alongside. Hooked onto the chains, he'd allowed the sea to swing his boat into the ship, yelling all the while to those on deck. Lines were thrown over the side, one to lash the boat, others to provide an escape for the barge crew. Once the men were clear it was eased towards the stern till it spun into position just ahead of the other boats. All this took place while Harry slid to the deck. He landed, this time steadily, on the piled canvas that had been fetched out of the hold, some of it already being bent onto the lines that would carry it aloft. His brother's head appeared just above the companionway and he shouted to tell him that all the guns were in slings, ready to be hauled up when he needed them. Harry waved in reply, with a pleasure that was pure fiction. He still needed all the pulling power at his disposal to get his sails aloft. There would be none to spare for guns.

As soon as he approached Caufield surrendered the wheel. Pender, back aboard, took station behind him. The feel of the ship in his hands, the way she responded to every move he made, a sensation he'd not had in weeks, restored some measure of confidence. But it was short lived as the myriad difficulties reasserted their dominance on his thinking. He must bear up into the wind. But there was little point in doing that without the canvas that would carry him out of danger. Sailing large he could set it with greater ease, but such a course took him straight towards the guns of the *Marianne*. Having spent so long ashore, his crew were not as sharp as they'd been when continuously at sea, which meant an added risk in the loss of valuable seconds. The Frenchmen could not be used as extra hands: on this unfamiliar deck, working alongside men whom they could neither understand nor blend with, they were a liability. They would only be a help if it came to hand-to-hand combat. Suddenly he turned to look at Pender. The sight of his servant made him smile, a gesture which was returned in full measure. It was partly Harry's natural optimism, partly the continuing effects of Willerby's potion, that kept his spirits buoyed. But it was also necessary to look confident, to reassure his men that all was well. He knew in his heart that they were in desperate straits, but he also felt that if any vessel, and any crew, had the sailing qualities to get him out of it, he had them under his direct control.

"Pender, get round the men. Tell them we'll be taken if one of them fails to perform to the very best of his ability. Ask my brother to put his Frenchmen as extra hands on the upper deck capstan to get the topgallant yards aloft." Willerby's observation about the beneficial effects of the dog's breath came into his mind and he added, "And if you think a tot of rum will help either party, then dish it up."

Pender needed no second bidding. With a proper sense of priorities he went straight below to fetch a barrel of rum. He knew the men didn't need encouragement. A drink would do them much more good, with the same probably true of the bearer himself. Not that Harry intended leaving them much time to consume it. Hungover they might be, but these men knew their place in the scheme of things and they concentrated hard on the tasks they had to perform. Not one raised so much as an eye to look at the frigate ahead, now swinging round to present her broadside. Harry wondered what would be going through Villemin's mind. No doubt, seeing the nature of the trap his enemy was heading into, he'd be a happy man, finally in a position to exact the full price for his previous failures. As an added bonus, this would occur in full view of the rest of his countrymen.

Hugues's fleet at least represented no danger. The close order had been abandoned, but none had made enough headway to interpose itself into the coming engagement, and with his men now fully occupied, Harry had a few moments of relative peace to seek some way of confounding the Frenchman. He couldn't manoeuvre, nor could he reply to any cannon fire. Villemin would have a telescope to his eye, and would, at least, be well aware of part of Harry's predicament: the need to get canvas aloft with maximum speed. There was little doubt that he expected to trade broadsides. He'd already swung round, so that he could bring all his guns to bear on *Bucephalas*. Yet that was only one side of the damnable equation. Even if Harry could escape that trap, there were those two brigs waiting across his path, their sole task being to slow him down. Even if they achieved only partial success the *Marianne* would have all the time in the world to come up in his wake and close the trap. Once Villemin was within close range nothing could stop him from taking the ship and its crew as a prize.

His eyes, ranging along the deck, took in Matthew Caufield and his father, standing by the bulwarks, their eyes fixed on the rapidly approaching frigate. But they also took in the fixed carriages which normally held his carronades in place. Bolted to the deck, they had runners that allowed the guns to recoil, rather than the normal breechings. Carronades, short-barrelled cannon that fired a huge ball, were called smashers because of the effect they had on an enemy hull, but they were useless at long range. The relative positions of the French ships barred his preferred method of confounding the enemy, by doing the unexpected, and heading right into the arc of Villemin's fire he knew that something must be done about guns, even if the sight of them being rigged only served to cheer his men. A glance aloft showed him that though rapid progress was being made, he could not escape one or two broadsides. But assuming nothing vital was wounded he should then be able to bear up into the wind and use his superior sailing ability to put some distance between them.

That would very quickly bring him into contact with the two

brigs, an altogether different problem. They couldn't know he was unarmed, and that alone, if he manoeuvred aggressively, would induce caution, especially if they'd exchanged any information with the Mariannes. They must have discussed the previous battle with either Villemin or his officers, giving them a very clear idea of the accuracy, and power, of their opponent's gunnery. *Marianne* had felt the effect of the carronades when Harry had removed great chunks of Villemin's bulwarks in mid-Atlantic, and aimed at the hull of a smaller ship they would do correspondingly more damage. Yet time was against him still. There was not enough of it to arm more than one side of the ship. Even that might prove impossible and it certainly wasn't a task he could entrust to his brother.

Pender was back on deck, dishing out his tots, and Harry called for him, as well as both the Caufields, to join him by the wheel. Once they'd assembled, he explained what he wanted.

"Do you really think that will do any good?" asked Matthew, glumly.

"All I know is that it will do no harm," replied Harry sharply. "If it makes just one of them sheer off a trifle . . ."

The boom of the *Marianne*'s guns killed the rest of his sentence. Great founts of water shot up, well forward of the starboard fore-chains, which seemed to indicate that the enemy had fired at too great a range.

"That was a wasted shot," said Matthew, aiming a rude gesture in the Frenchmen's direction.

"Don't underestimate him. That was deliberate, a mere warning, an invitation to strike."

"Guess he would rather take us in one piece if he can," added Matthew's father.

Caufield senior gave Harry a look that said, quite plainly, that if no one else on deck had the sense to see how bad things were, he certainly did. But whatever thoughts he had he kept to himself. The calls from aloft, telling the Captain that his sails were ready, began to float down, first from the foremast, then from the main. Looking up to check Harry saw the pennant which identified him as a British letter of marque.

"Pender!" Harry snapped. "Get on the mainmast halyard. Shiver our pennant a trifle as though you're trying to get it down and it's stuck."

"Aye, aye, Captain."

Such a ploy was too late for the second broadside, which was certainly well within range of Villemin's longer cannon. But the way the guns were aimed confirmed that the Frenchman wanted him whole. They could see the balls quite clearly, arcing through the clear blue sky, fired from cannon set at maximum elevation. Although everyone on deck was drenched by flying water, not one of them struck the hull. Captain Caufield gave him a wry smile. As Harry gave the orders to let fall, sending others to man the braces, he pulled at his son's sleeve and both men ran to carry out their allotted task. Pender tugged away at the halyard as the commands rang out. The slight dip of the flag would make his enemy wonder. Likewise the men running to their places on the deck. They could be about to let fly the sheets, rather than haul round on the braces. There would be no avoiding one proper broadside when Villemin realized the truth. But it might be just the one, since by the time he'd reloaded *Bucephalas* would be sailing out of range. Harry yelled the requisite commands and as the men began to haul, he threw his weight on the wheel to bring her round into the wind.

This was the moment when Villemin proved, once more, that he was a poor commander. Anyone with any sense, having an enemy ship at such a clear disadvantage, would have timed his salvo for maximum effect, taking care to aim each gun to wound the target where it mattered, in the rigging. Not Villemin. Surprised or angered by Harry's action, he fired at once. The resulting broadside was ragged, as the slower crews sought to change their aim, and it was executed partly on the downroll, so only a small portion hit home. *Bucephalas* shuddered nevertheless, as the great balls skipped over the water and smashed low into her hull. But she was coming round handsomely, presenting a proper target to the *Marianne* when the enemy guns were unloaded. By the time they were ready and run out, Harry was heading away from an enemy who was practically still in the water. The calculated risk this involved, in presenting his vulnerable stern to his enemy, was vindicated by another ragged, poorly aimed salvo, every ball of which missed completely.

CHAPTER FOUR

JAMES CAME on deck, intent on making his way towards the wheel, only to find himself dodging several groups of running seamen, all hauling like heathens on the thick hempen ropes, forced to skip nimbly to avoid being mown down. He joined his brother with a rush that left him flushed from embarrassment and exertion. The boom of the French guns, fired in a more orderly fashion, gave him a moment to regain his breath. He opened his mouth to speak just as the balls landed in an even pattern right in their wake. Several great founts of water shot into the air. Even with the wind carrying the majority away, enough came inboard to drench everyone abaft the mainmast. Harry hoped it would be the last broadside for a while. The range was increasing rapidly and the Frenchman would be forced to abandon his gunnery and send his crew to man the braces in order to take up the pursuit. James flicked at his coat with an elegant hand, as though it was stained by a few specks of dust rather than ten gallons of sea water.

"I've left Caufield *pére et fils* to sort out the guns you want. I thought I'd better come and tell you, brother, that while they are working with a will our Frenchmen are beginning to show distinct signs of edginess."

"You may tell them we are safe for the moment, James."

"I think they'd be happier on deck, where they can see what is happening for themselves."

Harry held up a pleading hand. "Keep them below, please. Our crew are used to each other. They'd merely confuse things. I think you've just observed how even the most well-intentioned soul can get in the way."

James ignored the gibe. "Then you'd best tell me how we lay, so that I may pass it on."

Harry explained what had just happened, as they both cast anxious eyes towards the frigate, now coming round into their wake. Then, without pause, he turned to include the two brigs, as though the mere wave of a firm hand was enough to brush them aside. Freed from pressing duties, and seeing Harry conversing with his brother, several of the more curious members of the crew had edged towards them. Harry would have been economical about the true peril of their situation anyway. Their presence made him doubly so. Yet those with the wit to see would not be fooled.

The brigs were doing exactly what Villemin required of them, sailing large and holding the advantage of the weather-gage. They would never surrender that, no matter what he did. A close engagement would force Harry inshore, where manoeuvre was impossible. Alternatively they could stay ahead, blocking his path, obliging him to come off his best point of sailing to try and slip past them. That would take him, every time he tacked or wore, right into the teeth of the wind, the inevitable effect, playing on the bulk of the ship, acting to slow him down.

"I won't pretend the situation is rosy, brother. It's not. We are in some peril. But it depends on those two fellows in our path. Can they coordinate their actions to near perfection?"

"I take it, by your tone, that they must?"

"Most certainly," Harry replied, forcing himself to sound cheerful. "*Bucephalas* represents a superior force. On the face of it I could inflict terminal damage on one, or even both, as long as the *Marianne* is too far away to intervene."

"Will she be?" James boomed.

Harry smiled, even if it had a bitter quality. This was typical James, asking questions in a voice loud enough to be heard by those of his crew standing close, questions that they dare not pose themselves.

"Briefly. And only if I don't lose one ounce of speed."

"A tall order, brother, since we have no guns."

"They don't know that."

"Will they not guess? A man in their tops will see all of our deck."

"It's possible. But that's all it will be, a guess." Harry pointed towards the Caufields, who'd now manoeuvred the first of the carronades onto the deck. "The real question is this. Given the damage they think we can inflict, is either Captain prepared to make the ultimate sacrifice to stop one ship when they're about to take possession of a whole harbour full of rich prizes?"

James gestured towards the waist. Several French heads had popped up and were looking hard at the pair by the wheel. "This is going to require a deal of explanation."

"It's not a task I would entrust to anyone else," replied Harry. He only realized once he'd spoken that really James had no other function to perform. But if he'd wounded him by pointing that up, he had no time to repair the fault, and that made him sound more harsh than he truly intended. "Now, if you'll forgive me, brother, I must change tack."

"Now there, Harry, is an expression that suits you to the letter."

Harry favoured his brother, for just a second, with a black look. Then, remembering they were under observation, it was instantly replaced by something more sanguine. Perhaps if James had been content to carry on a private conversation he would have been more forthcoming, admitting their true situation, but he'd been forced to speak in a way that would bolster the crew. Things were bad enough without them giving up hope. He was sure that they trusted him to get them out of this scrape, as he had got them out of so many others. Perhaps luck would favour him. Perhaps one of the two Frenchmen ahead would indeed throw away the total advantage provided by his lack of sea room; fail to use even one of their guns, or sacrifice the all important weather-gage and leave him a clear escape route. Perhaps one of them was a complete and utter fool!

All that stuff about superior force was hogwash. If they played their cards right they didn't even have to fight him. They had time on their side, which would allow Villemin to close the range. And he wouldn't fire off long shot this time, he'd want to get close and inflict real damage. Once that happened, Harry knew, he must strike his flag immediately. The Frenchman might harbour a deep desire to take *Bucephalas* intact, but the previous signs of resistance would put paid to that notion. There'd be no second chance at subterfuge. Everyone aboard the ship would find themselves helpless victims of the full force of the *Marianne*'s uncontested broadside.

The dull boom of distant cannon rumbled in the air. Having heard so many that morning Harry paid the sound no heed. Nor, since he'd looked back to check on the frigate's progress, did he see the founts of water that rose high in the gap between the two ships ahead.

"Them two brigs are shortening sail, Capt'n," called the lookout.

"Shortening sail," Harry said, snapping his head round to look.

"You sound surprised, brother."

"So would you be if you were a sailor, James. That is the very last thing they should be doing. Later, yes. Now, most certainly, no!"

The lookout called again, this time his voice full of excitement. "Ship off the larboard beam, Captain. It's them that fired the shot."

"What shot?"

The lookout either didn't hear the question or was too excited to answer it. "Dead ahead, Captain, just clearing the headland. I can see her tops. She's got an American flag aloft. I think she's the *Daredevil* barque that was in St Croix harbour."

Harry snapped at his brother. "James, take the wheel and hold her steady."

He rushed forward, grabbing a telescope from the rack. The *Daredevil*'s bowsprit, rounding the point ahead, came into view.

The Stars and Stripes streaming forward from her masthead stood out clear above the loom of the land. As she came into plain view he could see that she was heeled over at a steep pitch, a full suit of sails aloft and clearly seeking to make maximum speed. Harry had no way of deciphering what this meant, but the mere sight of the American barque making such a supreme effort lifted his depressed spirits. They had no reason to crack on so unless they intended to take a hand against his enemies. Why that should be so, he couldn't say. A puff of black smoke spewed forth from the barque's bow. This was followed a second later by the dull boom of the gun. The salvo that had been fired posed no real danger to either of the brigs. But it left them in little doubt of the *Daredevil*'s intentions.

"That's their second go, Capt'n," said Pender, who had come to join him. "I reckon you missed their first one."

Harry merely nodded, his mind racing. This completely altered the nature of the engagement. With a ship to windward of them which looked likely to do battle, the two French brigs had lost their advantage. They could no longer act with impunity, since to pursue Harry Ludlow as required would put them at a distinct disadvantage *vis-à-vis* the American. And given the *Daredevil*'s position and course, any effort to pen Harry inshore rendered their situation more dangerous. The proof wasn't long in coming, and the brigs changed course away from the land. Not that he was in the clear. His opponents were only showing due caution. Something had to be done to make them believe that matters were a great deal worse than they had supposed if he was to actually escape.

"Stand by to go about," yelled Harry, rushing back to the wheel to join James. "Captain Caufield, if you can get that one carronade ready to fire, I think we can now confound those two ahead of us."

"What do you intend, Harry?"

"I want them to think I don't care about Villemin. I want them to believe that I intend to sink them before I strike." Harry turned his back on his brother, cutting off the next question. "Pender, get below quickly. Inform the gunner I want powder and shot on deck in two minutes, for no more than two rounds of the carronade. And tell him that what I require most from his cartridges is a great deal of smoke."

"One gun, Harry?"

Harry glared at his brother, a look which softened immediately. It wasn't James's fault. He didn't understand, any less than Harry had trouble comprehending the most rudimentary skills required to paint, and what seemed like a negative question wasn't anything more than a request for clarification. Harry raised a hand, forcing James to look up at the sun, now fully risen in the sky.

"We'll open all the ports, James, and they will be shaded. He won't be able to see if they contain guns or not, and if we can produce enough smoke he might think we fired off more than one ball. They probably didn't relish a fight with us in the first place, since they could be put in the situation of sacrificing themselves so that Villemin can claim the glory. They certainly won't engage on his behalf against two enemies, one of who appears suicidal. But they'll never let us pass if we don't show some teeth. All I need is one shot for the sake of their honour. If I give them that they can sheer off with a clear conscience."

Caufield had grabbed several seamen, regardless of the need to change tack, and was working furiously to rig the carronade. Realizing that he didn't have enough time to attach it properly to the carriage he'd set two men to rig a temporary breeching that would go some way to holding the massive recoil when it was fired. *Bucephalas* came round onto the starboard tack with absolute precision, moving away from the shore into more open water, taking maximum advantage of the space provided by her enemies' shortening sail. The *Daredevil*'s bow chasers spoke again. This time, with the range shortened, the balls skipped very close to the nearest Frenchman's hull, which caused the Captain to shy away. But they did no actual damage.

"When you're ready, Captain Caufield," Harry shouted. He then addressed the entire crew. "Take station behind the gunports as though they have cannon rigged and ready. I intend to come back onto the larboard tack and make straight for the enemy. Once within range I'll show him our side. Gunports to remain closed till we come round. I don't want them to see the true state of our armament."

As the men ran to their places Pender came on deck carrying a precautionary length of slow-match, just in case the flintlocks failed to ignite the charge. He was accompanied by the gunner and two Frenchmen. They carried the great metal balls that would hopefully induce caution in their fellow-countrymen. The gunner bore the cartridges in a solemn fashion, like some votive offering. His servant called to the gun crew to step forward and load and the men who worked that particular cannon took their accustomed places. Meanwhile Caufield had passed a stout cable out through the bulwarks on either side, looped round marlinspikes for extra purchase, before fetching them inboard again and lashing them to the tompion of the gun.

"No one to stand behind the cannon, Captain Caufield, if you please. Aim it a touch forward and fire as soon as she bears."

Caufield waved just as *Daredevil* fired off another salvo. Harry looked up to observe the fall of shot, slightly alarmed that with the shortened range they'd still inflicted no damage. He himself was so close the faces of his opponents were in plain view. They'd maintained their position in relation to each other and still had the capacity to snuff out what he was about to attempt. If the American had wounded them, perhaps they'd have shown more caution. But there was no time to speculate on the reasons for *Daredevil*'s lack of accuracy or the nature of his enemy's attitude. He gave the orders that would bring them on to the larboard tack, and took a firm grip on the wheel.

Bucephalas came round handsomely. Using the pressure of the rudder, Harry let the wind carry her to a few points more than his previous course. At his command the gunports flew open. Every

sailor who normally manned the guns crouched at his usual position, as if they were about to deliver a broadside. Visible only
from the upperworks of the Frenchman, with the guns themselves
hidden in shadow, this would add a degree of verisimilitude to the
picture that he was seeking to create. The only gun captain with
work to do, standing perilously close to the carronade, pulled at
the lanyard. Nothing happened. He immediately dropped the slow-
match to the touch-hole and jumped backwards. It was as well he
did. The carronade belted out a great cloud of smoke which at
maximum range billowed back over the deck. The gunner had
done Harry proud in the mix of his powder. Not only did it produce a deafening roar, but the quantity of smoke swirling around
on the side of the ship gave credibility to the idea of more than
one cannon being used. It was merely fortuitous that *Daredevil*
fired off another pair of guns at the same time. The combination,
with water churning about their hulls, was enough for the two
Frenchmen. Both put up their helms and headed to the south, leaving Harry Ludlow a clear passage between them and the shore.
Villemin fired off his signal gun repeatedly, presumably ordering
them to change course and resume the engagement, all to no avail.

As soon as the *Daredevil* saw the engagement being broken
off, she put up her helm and set a course due north. Harry fetched
her wake and they sailed out of danger in company. The two ships
weren't alone. Cutters, avisos, and even wherries had put off from
every bay on the island, each one full with those who for their
own reasons had no desire to wait and test the reputation of Victor Hugues. Once news got out every island in the Virgin group
would be constructing a makeshift defence, blocking their harbours to anything other than small boats.

The American Captain made no attempt to enter any of them;
instead he used up nearly the whole of the day heading for the lee
of Tortola. Having found a secluded bay, he anchored there. Harry
did likewise. By the time he secured himself fore and aft, a boat
had pulled off from *Daredevil* carrying his rescuer over to meet
him.

CHAPTER FIVE

"DAMNED if I knew where I was," said Pollock. "Didn't even know I was aboard a ship till the sun woke me."

His normally ruddy face was pale and grey, even if it was split with a weak smile. Harry had grabbed the American as soon as he came aboard, enveloping him in a welcoming bear-hug. The heartfelt plea to be released had struck a chord, and when Harry looked into his friend's eyes he could see that he was still suffering mightily from his birthday celebrations.

"Pender, my compliments to the cook. Say that we require another one of his potions in double quick time."

"Aye, aye, Capt'n."

Harry took Pollock by the arm and led him towards his cabin. As they passed each member of the crew, he was given a hearty thanks. The Frenchmen, finally allowed on deck, were more restrained, but they also showed a proper level of gratitude for his timely intervention.

"Hell's teeth, Harry," Pollock whispered. "What are they doing aboard?"

"That's not just a French fleet attacking St Croix. They say it's Victor Hugues, Oliver. I could hardly leave them and their fortune to him."

"Fortune?"

"Another time," said Harry, hurriedly, looking anxiously into Pollock's grey face to see if his slip of the tongue had really registered.

His French passengers were indeed in possession of a fortune, the proceeds of a period of successful buccaneering in the

Caribbean. Harry had avoided the temptation to relieve them of their money. This was partly due to the circumstances in which they'd acquired it, but more out of respect for their Captain, who'd lost his life fighting his own countrymen. His arrival had been every bit as timely as that of the *Daredevil,* though he'd taken a more positive role in the action, an act which Harry knew had saved *Bucephalas* from certain destruction. He had accepted their offer to pay for his repairs as well as their own, and watched with satisfaction as they'd settled a decent sum on Nathan Caufield, who, trading illegally into the West Indies, had through no fault of his own become one of their victims. Their heavy treasure chest now sat out of sight in Harry's sleeping quarters. While it had been aboard the *Ariadne,* its presence had been a carefully guarded secret, one that they'd all tried hard to keep from the realms of gossip. Judging by Pollock's mystification, they'd been successful.

"Let's get you sat down, before you fall down."

The American responded to Harry's solicitous tone. Pender entered bearing the steaming tankard. Pollock's suspicions were similar to those of Harry and Caufield, and lacking the element of danger it took a great deal more pressure to get him to drink it. But he complied eventually, taking half a dozen reluctant gulps. Slowly, as he talked, the colour returned to his cheeks, making him look like a human being instead of a corpse. Judging by his endless yawning, he was a very tired man.

"Two of the *Daredevil*'s crew laid some crayfish baskets last week. They were heading out to check on them when they were nearly run down by a Hanseatic trader. He'd spied the Frenchies' topsails at dusk and was heading out of the area for safety. By the time their Captain got the information I was dead to the world. They didn't even try to wake me, just loaded me aboard and weighed anchor."

"They didn't think to tell anyone else?" said James.

"So it seems," Pollock replied, though he had the good grace to blush at their lack of regard for the inhabitants of St Croix. "Naturally when I came to I insisted that we return. When we saw those two brigs with their guns run out, then you with that frigate on your tail, firing off a salvo seemed the only neighbourly thing to do."

"Without hitting anything," added Harry.

The American just grinned. "Damned right, Harry. We aimed to miss and thank God we did. Can't go starting a war with the French now, can I? Wouldn't be right after what they did for us in '78."

"And if they hadn't sheered off?"

"Don't rightly know, friend. But I can tell you this. Cabot, the *Daredevil*'s Captain, was loath to risk his ship in any way whatever, and I lacked the will to force him."

"You did enough, Oliver. We'd have been taken without your intervention."

There were holes in the tale and all present, including Pollock, knew it. As an American he had nothing to fear from an attack by anyone, including the French, who would always take care never to wound the pride of a potential ally against Britain. In fact, thinking about it now, there were gaps in everything to do with Oliver Pollock. A man who claimed to be in trade but seemed singularly disinclined to do any, who sailed in an armed barque not a merchant vessel. But only a churl would have the gall to speak when Pollock's actions, however confined, had just saved them from the wrath of Victor Hugues.

"You're tired, Oliver, and so am I. We're safe here. I suggest we all get some rest, then we can have Captain Cabot join us for dinner."

Harry drifted in and out of sleep, rudely awakened from time to time by the clang of metal on metal. Willerby wasn't pleased when he was ordered to cook a dinner for the Captain and his guests. As he pointed out, noisily, they'd left St Croix "in their smalls" and though they might be "well found in the article of wine" he'd not taken on the kind of stores to produce a meal that would reflect credit on the ship. The noise from the galley, as he used every utensil in his armoury to beat on his coppers, was enough to wake the dead. Pender finally lost his temper and told the one-legged cook that they'd be eating shark meat if he'd didn't "stow it," with the old man used as bait. There were fishermen in the bay, happy to sell their catch, adding some lobsters from their pots. But Willerby wasn't happy. He might have quelled his banging, but he could still be heard muttering to himself, as the sweat dripped off his triple chin, that "a dinner with no red meat was no meal, at all!"

Even without Willerby's banging, sleep would have been difficult for Harry Ludlow. Too many thoughts were chasing each other round his head. He went back to the first dinner he'd shared with Pollock, provided by the Danish banker Børsenen. Harry made no secret of the fact that he was a successful privateer, and was proud to inform the American that James, despite his modest protestations, was a well-known portrait painter. Pollock might claim to be no more than a run-of-the-mill businessman, yet a great deal of what he'd subsequently said, when drink had loosened his tongue, indicated that he was someone of substance, a man who was highly regarded by the United States government, perhaps even some kind of envoy. His anecdotes were peppered with references to such luminaries as the brothers Morris, Alexander Hamilton, Jefferson, Jay, and Adams. Even Washington himself was mentioned, all spoken of with a familiarity that implied a degree of intimacy. He undertook to introduce them to James should he choose to visit New York, with a recommendation that they sit for him. Deliberately or otherwise, Pollock left no one at the table, quite particularly their Danish host, in any doubt as to the strength of his connections.

His passion was his country. Pollock loved everything about America; its political system, its people, and its vast landscape. Yet he himself lived in New Orleans, which was under Spanish control. Harry had listened with an extra degree of attention when he described his home city; the climate, language, and some interesting opportunities. With no desire to have to explain either his own recent behaviour or theirs, Harry gently pumped the American on behalf of the Ariadnes. He knew they were experiencing some difficulty in deciding on a destination. Indeed the only point on which they seemed to agree was a desire to leave the Caribbean. A return to France or settlement in Quebec were the preferred options, but many were after their previous experiences fearful of unbridled French rule. Others harboured deep suspicions of the British, who ruled Canada.

The Louisiana Territory had a strong French presence, and it seemed a vast area ready for exploitation. Harry wondered if it might provide a destination for them. Everything Pollock told him, in their subsequent meetings, he passed on. Seeing that this had an effect, he undertook to speak to his new friend, if they decided in favour of Louisiana, and ask him to look out for their welfare. But with a caution born of experience, he avoided mentioning the subject to Pollock until matters were settled.

That love of country had led to their one and only disagreement, and thinking about it now Harry could see just how many questions had been left hanging in the air at the conclusion of what seemed at the time something quite minor. Pollock, again having consumed slightly more drink than was good for him, was describing the blight that had struck America in the years after they'd separated from the British Crown.

"I never thought to see my people in danger of dying of starvation. But, thanks to your navy, and your Navigation Acts, we couldn't ship anything out of the country, and had no one to sell them to if we could. The wharves were heaped with goods that just rotted. We had an army disbanding that expected to be paid, and nothing to pay it with. We were near to anarchy."

"But matters have improved."

"They have, Harry," he replied, the bitterness, for once, still in his voice, "though Albion's arm seems mighty long and sticky. General Wilkinson was still negotiating to get your soldiers out of Detroit when I left. And the commercial treaty we just signed had British green written all over it. It was so pernicious that getting it ratified was a close-run thing."

"Then why did you do it?"

"Had to, friend. Four-fifths of our trade is with your ports and Billy Pitt knew it. The umbilical cord remains to strangle us." Pollock picked up his drink and proposed a toast. "Damnation to Albion, Harry."

"Sorry, Oliver," Harry replied good-humouredly.

"You should shift out of that land of corruption, Harry."

"I'm happy as I am, believe me."

"Nonsense! If only you'd seen half of the things I have."

Harry grinned. "I don't have to. You never stop telling me about them. I feel as though I know every mountain, tree, and river in the whole continent. In truth, given your love of the place, not to mention your admiration for the Constitution, I can't fathom why you live in a Spanish colony. Nor have you explained it. I sense that you might be the possessor of some dark and dangerous secret."

This was no more than the plain truth. But the remark, intended humorously, produced a deep frown, an abrupt change of subject, and a definite chill in the mood. Pollock leant forward in a slightly threatening manner, his eyes cold.

"If your King's officers don't stop whipping any man they choose out of our ships, I can see a day when we might be at war again, cousin versus cousin."

"Then I'd best stay this side of the Atlantic, Oliver," Harry replied with a grin, trying to keep the conversation in a jocular vein. "If we go to war I shall have some very profitable fun with your merchant ships."

That he'd failed was very evident in the sharp reply that sally received, one that in its bellicosity made him wonder if Pollock had been at the bottle before they met.

"Perhaps you'll bite off more'n you can chew, Harry Ludlow. They ain't all lacking in the means to fight."

"The *Daredevil* certainly isn't," Harry replied, finally showing

a trace of the same impatience. "Nor is she designed to bear cargo.
A more sceptical soul might enquire what a man who says he's in
trade is doing aboard such a ship."

"Convenience, Harry," Pollock said swiftly, his eyes narrowing. "Nothing else but convenience. She was heading this way and
I hitched a ride."

Said with force, and given the frosty way the words were spoken, it was not something Harry felt inclined to pursue.

When Captain Cabot came aboard from the *Daredevil* Harry realized that since he'd never come ashore in St Croix, no one from
Bucephalas had ever met him. Suspecting a misanthrope, Harry
found him to be an amusing companion who shared his love of
wine and conversation. The food, if Willerby thought it plain, was
fresh and delicious, and since neither Ludlow brother believed in
stinting himself in the vinous line, the drinks that accompanied
each remove were excellent. James was the first to propose a toast
to American ships in general, and the *Daredevil* in particular.

"Hear him," cried Cabot, happily.

"Mind you, sir," James continued, "how will I recognize such
fellows when I see them? Every time I spy an American ship the
flag has changed."

"Stars, sir," said Matthew, with an enthusiasm that earned
him a glare from his father, "represent each additional state. One
day you'll see a whole lot more. Kentucky, Vermont, and Tennessee are already in, as you know. But it won't stop there."

"What about New Orleans?" said Harry, turning to Pollock.
Again the question bothered his guest, producing the kind of
expression that Harry remembered from his daydreams.

"Pigs might fly, Harry. A Spanish colony with a French population, sitting right across the best river route out of the interior?
Damned if anyone can make sense of things there, even me. The
Spaniards won't give it up, even though it drains their treasury
and the French if they want it back aren't saying. Meanwhile their
people seem intent on getting rid of King Carlos and installing

some kind of Republic. Thank God they're too small in number to have their way. The last emigration was the influx of refugees from the Terror. I hope it was the last. The more Frenchmen we have there the more unstable the place becomes."

Harry blushed slightly, making a mental note to avoid alluding to his recent discussions with the Ariadnes. Pollock talked on. He clearly had mixed views about the French as a nation, quite prepared to admire them as individuals, while deploring their collective inability to find a political solution that didn't involve fratricidal bloodshed. That good opinion did not, however, extend to the Creoles of New Orleans, who he saw as nothing but a nuisance.

"The form of government don't matter much, just as long as it's French. I half suspect that if Spain doesn't give it to them they'll try and take it back by force, then ask Paris for recognition."

"And what will the Americans do then?" Harry asked, with just a trace of malice. Pollock looked at him keenly. "Come along, Oliver. The solution is obvious. The last thing you would welcome, after all the trouble it caused us, is France back on your borders. And what about the Mississippi delta? When we still controlled the colonies there was many a voice raised on both sides of the Atlantic, advocating that New Orleans should be taken by assault."

"That's speculation," he replied sharply, "which I won't indulge in. Right now there's no need for such talk. Things have improved since Senator Pinckney signed the recent treaty. The Dons have given us free navigation and rights of deposit at New Orleans for twenty-five years. They make more money and, given a method of shipping their goods out of the interior, we hear less from the frontier states about secession from the Union."

"Secession?" said James. "According to Matthew, they've only just joined your great enterprise."

"Games. The Kentuckians in particular play the Spaniards off against us, all intended to extract some concessions from somebody. A trading privilege from the Dons or a bit more Indian land grabbed with the approval of Congress. They are, without doubt, the most ill-bred set of low-lifes it has been my misfortune to encounter. They drink to excess, fight without any cause other than an ill-timed look, and seem to have affection for only one thing, their damned long rifles. If there's one thing worse than a French Creole, it's those godforsaken Kentuckians."

CHAPTER SIX

THE CONVERSATION moved on, since any talk about Louisiana seemed to upset Pollock. They speculated for a while on what the Royal Navy would do about Hugues, and then moved on to the question of whether the Spanish, having made peace with France, would stay out of the war.

"Rumour has it they're talking of a pact already," said Pollock. "After all, Harry, they've allied themselves with France against Britain most of this century."

"A different France," observed James.

Cabot pulled a wry face. "They trust John Bull less, Mr Ludlow. And given the way your politicoes behave, who can blame them?"

"Not to mention your naval officers," added Matthew Caufield.

"Might I remind you," said Harry, smiling, "that this is a British ship."

"Not with all those Frenchmen aboard it ain't," said Pollock. "Since I can't see you keeping them as guests, what do you plan to do with them?"

"It's not up to me, Oliver. They will choose."

"Kinda drops you in a quandary though, Harry. Having fetched them out of St Croix you've taken on the responsibility."

Harry replied thoughtfully: "That's not as much of a problem as it first appears. They have several options."

"What did you mean when you said they had a fortune?"

"Not a fortune, Oliver. I said good fortune." Pollock's eyes narrowed, as though what he'd heard didn't square with what he knew. "It's a long story, Oliver, which I won't bore you with."

"There was a buzz around the harbour, gossip that you and those men had been engaged in a bit of no good. That they'd made a pile, which you had a share in, by less than honest means. I paid it no heed, since I don't see you that way. Perhaps I was wrong to do that?"

The way Harry ignored that was both blatant and somewhat insulting. He carried on as if Pollock hadn't asked anything about piracy or gold. And what he said was offensive in its own right.

"I didn't say this before but I've been advising them that since they can't decide on Europe or Canada, they'd be better off heading for Louisiana, quite possibly New Orleans."

"What!" Pollock snapped.

"All, I must say, due to your glowing description of the place, which I was happy to pass on. The language is right and I think the climate will suit them."

"You're proposing to take Frenchmen to New Orleans?" asked Cabot.

Since Pollock still looked unhappy Harry spoke to him. "Thirty new colonists won't make any difference, Oliver."

"They will to me, Harry. And let's get back to this good fortune you seem so keen to avoid talking about. Just how much of that particular commodity have they enjoyed?"

Harry waved a hand airily. "A few thousand of your American dollars. I'm not certain of the exact amount, but it's no more than that, I'm sure. Enough to ensure that they're no burden to anyone when they land."

James had to turn away at that point, so Pollock wouldn't see his smile. He'd seen this trait in Harry before. Sometimes it angered him. At other times, like now, it was a cause of much amusement. Harry had been quite vocal about his liking for this particular American. Yet even with people he purported to trust and admire he was inclined to dissimulate, never telling them a truth they didn't absolutely need to hear.

"I rather fear that after what I'd already said they were going there anyway once their ship was repaired. Now that they are in my care, I don't see that I have much choice."

"You do, Harry," said Pollock, coldly.

"We can hardly take them back home with us," said James.

"I don't think you understand, sir," Pollock replied. "The Spanish are the most nervous race on God's earth. They have as much love for French colonists as I have. And I might add that the sight of an armed British ship at a time like this in the Mississippi delta won't help cheer them either."

"But we're not their enemies," James added. "They're neutral."

"Can any English ship be truly neutral to the Dons?" said Cabot.

"That is a truth that is particularly relevant in this part of the world," added Pollock. "They still scare their children with tales of *El Draco!*"

"Drake and Hawkins are long dead," said Harry, with a pleading look in his eye. "And if that's where they want to go, either I take them there or I hire someone to do so."

"You were going to ask me?" said the American quickly.

"It had occurred to me, yes."

The sarcasm was very thinly veiled as Pollock replied. "Much as I'd like to oblige you, my business precludes it."

"But you live in New Orleans, Oliver. You must be going there. And the sight of your ship must be familiar to the Dons. They won't even ask who you've got aboard."

"The *Daredevil* doesn't hail from New Orleans," said Cabot. That remark earned him a sharp look from Pollock that made the Captain flush with embarrassment.

"They still know you, Oliver."

Harry saw the same look as Pollock turned to face him. But it disappeared swiftly, to be replaced by a blank expression. "True. But I don't know when I'll return. Captain Cabot and I are heading for Chesapeake Bay. I have places to go and people to see."

"Pity."

"Harry," said Pollock, leaning forward eagerly, a friendly smile on his face, "do me a favour. Take them somewhere else."

"I'll see what I can do, Oliver."

"Thank you," the American replied, his smile turning grim. He must have been aware from Harry's tone that his efforts to deflect the Frenchmen to another destination would be limited. Did he understand that it wasn't entirely his choice now?

"So, who are you off to see, Oliver?"

Pollock's eyes narrowed slightly, and the smile on his face became still harder. "Tell me, Harry Ludlow. How would you like it if someone started quizzing you about your business?"

Harry's face reddened just a touch. "Forgive me. I had no intention of prying."

Having put Harry firmly in his place, Pollock's voice softened. "Truth is, I don't know where I'm going. Business is like that, which is something I don't have to say to you. And I have learned over the years never to discuss my doings with anyone. I've seen too many propositions fail because the man contemplating them talked too loud."

"You must forgive Harry, Mr Pollock," said James, with wicked and evident pleasure. "His curiosity is endemic. And your tone of apology is quite wasted. If ever I've known a man who was reluctant to show his cards it is my brother. Not even I am privy to his innermost thoughts."

They watched the *Daredevil* depart with mixed feelings. James and the Caufields were still full of gratitude for the American ship's intervention, but Harry was subject to different emotions. He would have laughed at anyone who even intimated that he was wounded. Yet Oliver Pollock's behaviour had troubled him. The close companionship of St Croix had quite evaporated. But emotion, of necessity, was soon put aside, as he began to contemplate the needs of his ship. *Bucephalas* couldn't go anywhere without wood and water. Then there was food, which presented more of a problem. Harry's men were sailors to their fingertips, and they had a very strict idea of what they should be fed. He needed salt pork and beef, flour in the sack, ship's biscuit in the cask, gallons of beer and kegs of rum. Since Tortola was not over-endowed in the chandling department, time was spent as the stores were gathered from the nearby islands. Nathan and Matthew Caufield, who'd decided to leave the ship and head home, agreed to organize the supplies, as a small recompense for the way he'd helped them in the past.

What he didn't realize, as they went ashore to find accommodation in Tortola, was that in Nathan Caufield he'd lost his main interlocutor with his passengers. James, who might have taken his place, having a limited love of shipboard life, went ashore with them. Initially Harry welcomed this as an opportunity to get on closer terms with his Frenchmen, the main object finding a way of ridding himself of them. There was nothing personal in this, just the need to regain his freedom of action. Since their Captain had been killed he'd maintained limited contact: they'd stayed in the main aboard their own ship, while he was on *Bucephalas,* so they were very nearly strangers. The only two men he'd dealt with on St Croix, Lampin and Couvruer, spoke some English and were pleasant enough. It was to them he'd imparted Pollock's glowing account of Louisiana life. Lampin was of medium height, balding, with a lively expression, bright blue eyes, and an almost permanent smile. Couvruer was taller and darker, with deep brown eyes that rarely left Harry's face, clear evidence that he listened intently to what was said.

Asking them to come to his cabin, Harry quickly discovered that there was still no consensus at all amongst the group about where they should go next: Europe, Quebec or Louisiana. And thanks to Pender, he was soon made aware that his own crew were less than enamoured of the Frenchmen's presence aboard ship. It was impossible, in a vessel the size of *Bucephalas,* to keep the two groups apart, and since he didn't call upon his passengers to undertake any tasks to do with running the ship, they were quickly labelled as idle loafers. Added to that, since most of his men had at one time in their lives served on men-of-war, and had fought the French as the enemy, they were ill disposed to suddenly accept them as friends and equals. This didn't apply to all the crew, of course, but it only took a few, aiming well-rehearsed insults, to infuse both parties with a mutual antipathy, that, unchecked, could lead to violence.

Nothing demonstrated this more than the second meeting Harry had with Lampin and Couvruer. No doubt suspected of being too soft on the *Rosbifs,* they were accompanied by two other men, neither of whom deigned to give his name. They were a surly pair who insisted on the conversation's being carried out in French. Their first demand was that their brass-bound chest be transferred from Harry's cabin to the section of the berthing deck where they messed. This Harry flatly refused to do. In vain, he tried to point out that a chest known to be full of gold and silver coins in plain view of his crew would do nothing to ease the tension. Privateers' ships were not manned by people of a saintly disposition. Quite the reverse. Harry had recruited them to fight, and if necessary kill, and while the selection had been careful, leaving out sodomites and hard bargains, they were as greedy as any other crew, quite possibly more so. Clearly Lampin and Couvruer, just by their expressions, agreed, but could do nothing in the face of their fellow-countrymen's intransigence. They clearly didn't trust the Ludlow brothers with their wealth, or, it seemed, their future. The meeting, when it broke up, left him in a foul mood.

"It's damned galling," said Harry. "If we hadn't take care of them they'd be rotting at the end of a gallows' rope in English Harbour."

"I don't see why you don't just sling them ashore here, your honour," said Pender. "Let's face it, they've got the means to survive."

"I started to suggest that very thing, but then I was reminded of my own undertaking. I'm hoist upon a promise I made to see them to their destination. The one thing they're adamant about is that they don't want to stay in the Caribbean." He noticed Pender frown. "It seemed a simple thing to do, since they were underwriting the repairs to *Bucephalas*."

"Well, I've said it more'n once, Capt'n. If'n you don't get them off the barky quick, one of 'em might get a knife in the guts."

"It doesn't help," Harry snapped, "to have you adopting that attitude."

Pender grinned, not in the least bit cowed by Harry's outburst. He might be termed a servant, but both the Ludlow brothers, and Pender himself, knew he was more than that. To Harry, especially, he was a friend and confidant, as well as a man who could on occasion act as his master's conscience.

"I don't care one way or the other, Capt'n. But I don't want to see you in the post of judge and jury over one of our crew. Specially since, if one man gets hurt, others are bound to follow. An' there ain't no good pretending it won't go that way. Them Frogs is no better than our lot."

"Do you think I should put them to work?"

"That'd just make things worse. The baiting will get louder the more they see of each other. At least half the day the Crapauds are out of sight."

"I'll have to talk to the crew," said Harry wearily.

"In the main they don't need it, your honour. It's only the odd one that hates them Frenchmen enough to bait them. And you could talk to them till your face turns blue an' it wouldn't make an ounce of difference."

"Then, damn it, I'll lock them up."

"Which will upset the rest of the crew. No, Capt'n, the only way is to get them ashore as soon as you can."

James, accompanying some stores that the Caufields had gathered, was quizzed for his opinion.

"And, brother," said Harry, gravely, "if Pender says it's that bad it cannot be anything less than serious."

"Then I suggest you get them to make up their minds, Harry."

"Easier said than achieved. If I try to give them advice it's likely to rebound on me. Apart from Lampin and Couvruer I doubt any of them trust us at all."

"That cannot be the case with thirty men. Most of them will be sheep, with two sets of views vying for their support. And even if they are sheep they're not necessarily without the wit to see that it will be them who suffer if matters come to a head."

"You're suggesting that I talk to them directly?"

James nodded. "Give them the options, Harry. Point out that the more time they spend aboard *Bucephalas* the more likely it is that one of them will end up as a victim. Then list the different distances between their various choices."

"You think they'll plump for New Orleans?"

"I can't say that with certainty. But if you put it the right way then I think you'll get the result you want."

"I have no interest in the result, James," said Harry.

"That is not true. Unless you harbour a deep desire to satisfy the reservations of Oliver Pollock regarding French colonists."

The use of the name raised two emotions. The first was a fond memory, but the other was a feeling of slight betrayal, as though by minding his own business Pollock had been callous.

"Rest assured, James, that he doesn't come into it at all."

"He should, if he was right."

"About colonists?"

"No, Harry. About the reactions of the Spaniards. If they're thinking of coming into the war on the side of France, New Orleans would be a bad destination."

Harry shrugged. "I don't see we have to worry about that, brother. There's no news come to any of the islands of such a event."

"Would it come here first?"

"It would certainly get to the Caribbean before it reached the Gulf of Mexico."

James frowned. "He did say we wouldn't be welcome even in peacetime."

"I doubt they'd throw us a celebratory ball. But they won't dare interfere with a British ship, James. There's no country in the world more careful of her maritime rights than Britannia. There is one way to guarantee a war with King George. Infringe them! The War of Jenkins's Ear was begun for that very reason and a race that remembers Drake will remember that. Besides, we'll only be touching at the mouth of the delta. We can drop our passengers and head straight back out into the Gulf. As long as they see we're not going to hang around in their bailiwick, they will be happy."

"Well, that's fine," said James gaily. "Since the only problem left is to persuade our passengers."

Harry glared at him. "I'll try persuasion first, James. But if the sods don't agree, I'll damn well tell them."

"That's the spirit, Harry. Quiet diplomacy. But just as a precaution I should sound out Lampin and Couvruer first."

That was a piece of advice Harry was happy to take, though implementing it without causing suspicion proved to be difficult. Examining the problem objectively, he could see that James was right. It wasn't malice that was keeping them from a collective agreement, but pure indecision. They'd been through a lot in the last few years, turfed out of St Domingue by the slave revolt, then out of Guadeloupe by the arrival of Victor Hugues. As a group they'd come to rely on their late Captain to decide everything for them. Now they must do so for themselves, and the method of leaving St Croix had done little for their self-confidence. His talk with the two Frenchmen was of necessity brief. But he secured what he needed, a definite agreement that Pender's assessment of the situation was correct: that animosity and fear were growing, with violence not far below their surface calm.

For a man who'd set out to persuade rather than dictate, Harry showed scant patience. Faced with a sea of surly faces, and being a person who preferred to command rather than plead, his voice soon lost the tone designed to gently nudge them in the right direction. Instead, made worse by his less than perfect French, he became harsh, practically accusing them of ingratitude, especially in the matter of their treasure.

"Do you think I'd touch a sou of your money?" he growled. "I wouldn't. Every coin that's in there now will be with you when you go ashore, you have my word."

Faced with his angry glare, several heads dropped. Harry sensing the opportunity, and guessing that they liked to be led, told them he was going to the Mississippi delta; that he would put them ashore there; and if any of the party didn't like it, they certainly had the means to proceed to the destination of their choice.

CHAPTER SEVEN

THE HURRICANE, so early in the season, caught out more ships'
Captains than Harry Ludlow. There would be a heavy toll to pay
all over the Caribbean and the Gulf of Mexico when it finally blew
itself out. Not that the men lashed to the wheel of the *Bucephalas* had any thoughts to spare for the plight of others: all their
attention was concentrated on keeping their own ship before the
wind. The two scraps of heavy storm canvas on the topsail yards,
secured by extra braces, all that they had to maintain steerage-
way, stood between them and disaster. That and the Captain's
ability to read the flukes in the wind and weather. The tempest
screamed through the rigging at a steady ninety knots, but the
mountainous waves, with their cable deep troughs, called for constant vigilance, since the full fury of the hurricane eased in the
valleys they created, only to return with renewed intensity as the
ship crested each rise.

Running before the storm at least kept the spume out of their
eyes, though their entire world was water. *Bucephalas* shipped
great quantities amidships as the ragged top of each wave broke
under her counter, so much that it appeared impossible that the
ship should float. But it did, groaning as each deluge was sloughed
overboard, rising with an effort and a rending sound that seemed
almost human. Not all the sea water went over the side. Despite
every precaution, a great quantity found its way through both the
planking and the hatches, turning each companionway into a temporary torrent forceful enough to carry anyone who'd not taken
a firm grip all the way to the bilges. Down below, under those
very same hatches, the men on the pumps slaved to send the flood

back into the sea. Too much water in the well and *Bucephalas* would lack the buoyancy to keep afloat. If that happened no amount of seamanship would save her.

Harry Ludlow, who'd been on deck for the last eighteen hours, had the central position at the wheel, body lashed to the spokes and feet jammed into the looped ropes he'd stapled to the deck. Pender stood to his right and a giant bearded Frenchman, Brissot, to his left. Even with a full complement of his own Harry wondered if they could have ridden out the storm. The extra hands provided by his French passengers had not only provided assistance at the wheel, they had allowed him a continuous relay of reasonably fresh men on the pumps. Reasonable because no one could rest properly in a situation where the slightest easing of concentration would see a man thrown right across the lower deck, slammed into the side with a force that flesh and blood couldn't withstand. The cockpit, once more a temporary sick bay, was already overflowing with sailors who'd fallen victim to the storm. James Ludlow, battered and bruised himself, sought to ease the pain of deep cuts and broken bones, his main aid being liberal quantities of undiluted rum.

Not that Harry had any communication with those below decks. He'd issued them their orders hours before; pump hard, then pump even harder. It had been an age since anyone dared to venture up from below. To come onto this deck was to invite certain death. Not even the man ropes rigged all over would have allowed anyone to keep their feet. What human grip could withstand the pounding of such a sea? To the trio conning the ship no world existed outside the confines of that little patch of disturbed water. Even at the crest of a wave the spume whipped to the tops from the rear cut off all view of the surrounding sea. Above their heads the black clouds seemed to bear down on them, pushing their puny human frames into the waterlogged planking. They were all alone in this nightmare world, where the slightest error would see *Bucephalas* broach to and founder, before a wind that would push her under within a matter of seconds, a furious drowning that would leave no trace of the ship or the men who'd sailed her.

The odd word could be exchanged with those beside him at the bottom of each trough, where the howling decreased just enough for a man to be heard by a close neighbour. There was little to say, barring the odd message of reassurance. Repetitive they might be, nevertheless Harry gave them constantly, since the least hint of despair in either man could produce a lapse in effort. Brissot, whose English was extremely limited, nodded every time Harry spoke, even if he barely understood what was being shouted into his well-wrapped ear.

"Bring her head round to larboard again."

"How we doing, Capt'n?" gasped Pender, through salt-encrusted lips.

"I reckon the gale has eased just a fraction," Harry shouted, as he fought to turn the wheel. The party on the relieving tackles below, seeing what they were trying to do, would take some of the strain on the ropes that led to the rudder, helping to bring the ship round onto the course their Captain desired. Care had to be exercised, so that the instruction to belay as the bows began to rise was readily obeyed, ensuring that the control of the ship lay with those who could see the bowsprit and feel the weight of pressure this hurricane was exerting on the hull and the masts.

"I dunno how you can tell that, your honour. But I'm minded to believe you out of hope alone."

"Stand by!" screamed Harry for the hundredth time, his head back, eyes fixed firmly on the twin scraps of storm canvas. High enough to be above wave height they'd never lost the force of the wind, which gave him valuable steerage-way, putting sufficient speed on *Bucephalas* to ensure that as she breasted the next enormous cap, the slight forward motion of the ship, added to the pressure of the wind coming in abaft her larboard beam, would, by forcing her head round, carry her over into the next patch of relative safety. The flash of forked lightning, followed immediately by the deafening crack of thunder, made all three men duck involuntarily. But, even half-crouched, they strained as one to turn the ship's head once more. Then as she rose they let the wheel slip slowly through their fingers as *Bucephalas* was forced to pay off on to her original course.

"Listen hard the next time we crest," shouted Harry, patting his ear as he turned to repeat the message to the Frenchman. Brissot nodded, to say he understood. More of a sailor than Pender, he'd noticed the slight drop in the tempest's angry note, the first sign that they might, at last, be steering into calmer waters. Not that he could be sure. He knew as well as Harry how deceptive a hurricane could be, that seeming diminution merely the prelude to a startling increase in wind power, the precursor of the tempest's maximum strength, a wall of air blowing so hard that no seamanship, however cunning, no wooden vessel, however sound, could hope to survive. Harry held his breath as they crested the next wave, every nerve stretched to breaking point lest the wind had increased. The relief that this wasn't so was compounded when he turned to look at Pender. Not much of his servant's face showed, but those dark lively eyes were creased like a man smiling, evidence that he too had noticed how things had eased.

"Are we safe now, your honour?" he croaked, as *Bucephalas* spilled over the highest point of the wave, shipping tons of water, before careering like a dropped stone down into the well of the trough.

"Not safe, Pender. But the danger has eased for the moment. If we're lucky then we're on the edge of the hurricane." He had to stop so that they could deal with the next rise of the bowsprit, but he continued as soon as they returned to the relative quiet. "Either that or we're close to the eye, which means that we'll have a short period of total calm then be forced to face the storm all over again."

"And I thought thieving had risks," Pender yelled, his eyes screwed up with effort as he hauled once more on the wheel.

It was Harry's turn to grin under his soaked muffler, which

brought instant pain as the rough wool rubbed against skin made raw by friction and hardened salt. Pender didn't often refer to his previous life as a thief, certainly never when others were around. A man who could pick even the most complex lock in seconds, he was nicknamed "Pious" for the time he spent, so occupied, on his knees. Having come into Harry's service by accident, he'd proved so much of an asset to him and brother James that life without him now seemed unthinkable. Just as unthinkable as that Pender should behave like any normal servant, and fail to tell both brothers, in no uncertain terms, when he thought they'd overstepped the mark. Barred by the exigencies of the task at hand from his desire to pat his servant on the shoulder, Harry turned to look at Brissot. The idea of putting him on the wheel instead of one of his own men had paid off. With one of their own number responsible for conning the ship, the rest of the Ariadnes had worked with a greater will. The giant Frenchman's sea-soaked beard, straggling over his chest, made him look more vulnerable than usual. But it also exposed the smile that told Harry that he too thought they were out of the woods.

The storm died away as suddenly as it had arrived, leaving an ocean full of heaving waves which, without the wind, had *Bucephalas* wallowing in the most uncomfortable manner. Men who'd survived the tempest now succumbed to the ship's motion, retching over stomachs that had long been empty. In such a sea the galley fire stayed unlit, which meant that the succour which might have been provided by hot food or Willerby's potions was unavailable. But after hours of this, as the sky cleared to bring forth a welcome burst of warm sunlight, the motion began to ease. Harry, finally convinced that the worst had passed, allowed himself to be unlashed from the wheel.

His hands, which had held on to the spokes for so many hours, seemed permanently set in the gripping position. Any attempt to move them provoked an agonizing response. His eyes were like two drops of watered blood in his chalk-white face. Stiff from his ordeal, he had to be helped below. His cabin was a shambles of sodden clothes and broken furniture. James, Pender, and Brissot slept where they lay, impervious to the water that still lapped around their recumbent frames. Harry croaked his last instructions as he was helped to lie down, orders to be awakened at the first hint of danger from whatever source. Then, still wrapped in his oilskins, he fell into a deep sleep, grunting and groaning as in his tortured dreams he recalled every moment of the ordeal he'd so recently survived.

The same tub of fresh water had to be used for the entire crew, since sailing in the Tropics precluded extravagance in that area. But brackish as it was it served to wash the salt from their clothes and bodies. The water in the scuttlebutt, meant for drinking, was splashed liberally over eyes, noses, and ears, allowing all to return to something approaching their normal state. The pleasure of survival had some effect, keeping previous tensions below the surface for all of that day and most of the next. But soon they rose again, with the French passengers returning to the surly behaviour that had so characterized the voyage. No amount of smiles, or of spoken reassurance would convince them that every member of the English crew, particularly their captain, wasn't scheming to cheat them; that the course they'd set, supposedly for New Orleans, wasn't some kind of trick. James remarked on it, after observing a particularly sour exchange of looks between the two nationalities.

"I tried to thank all of them," growled Harry, "for the help they rendered during the storm. Most refused to meet my eye and Brissot, who'd smiled at me like an old friend not 48 hours previously, just grunted. I could very easily have left St Croix without them and their damned chest."

"Perhaps another one of your lectures is required," said James.

"I did not lecture them," Harry replied, guiltily.

"You most certainly did, brother. Still, we'll soon be shot of them, won't we?"

"Damn it, I hope you're right. But I can't even be sure of our true position. If one of them comes and demands another look at the chart, it will be all bluff. I wouldn't be able to tell them, truthfully, where in hell's name we are."

The hurricane had not only thrown him off course, it had thrown his chronometers from their bulkhead, damaging them. Without these timepieces, one set to Greenwich and the other to local noon, he was unsure of his exact location. *Bucephalas* could be just off the mouth of the Mississippi or two hundred miles to the south, west, or east. All he knew was this: he was heading north towards a certain landfall. And that once he touched he would be able to reset his chronometers and shape a true course for his destination.

"Still, it would be wise to speak with them again, Harry," said James.

"And not just them," added Pender, in a doom-laden tone.

The unwelcome thought had barely registered in Harry's mind when the cry from the masthead came clear. "Ship, your honour."

"Where away?" he replied, automatically reaching for a telescope.

"Twelve points off the starboard bow. Merchantman, for sure."

Harry was halfway to the cap before the lookout finished the sentence, the fatigue of his recent ordeal dropping away as the excitement of a potential chase coursed through his veins. He fairly raced the path of the upper shrouds.

"Something odd about her, your honour," the man said as Harry focused his telescope. "For a start she's mighty low in the water, specially by the head. Her sails are set, but they don't appear to be drawin' much."

"I have her," Harry said as the ship leapt into view.

He swept the glass fore and aft, taking in the lowered bows and the correspondingly elevated stern, before concentrating on the deserted quarterdeck. A merchant vessel, built like an old-fashioned caravel, with the high poop and forecastle denoting her

build, either Spanish or Portuguese. Then he took in the sails, alternately drawing and slacking as the wind caught them. There was
nothing there that hinted at a ship in danger, more a suit of
unstained canvas that would carry a vessel along comfortably in
a steady breeze. With no hand on the rudder the ship was drifting before the wind. He raised his glass to the masthead, there to
check for the flags that might warn of disease aboard, but the ship
carried no pennant of any kind. Harry called for an increase in
sail, then made his way back to the deck to take over the wheel.

"We have a mystery on our hands, James," he said, passing
the telescope to his brother. "A ship that has no crew, no flags,
and no apparent destination."

"I take it we are about to investigate."

"Most certainly," Harry replied, as Pender handed him a
sword and his pistols.

"Perhaps they all perished in the recent storm," said James.
"Swept overboard."

"No, brother. That fellow has not been in any storm. In fact,
given that he has new canvas aloft that's in a pristine state, I doubt
he's been made to suffer even a serious blow."

"How could he avoid it?"

"Easily, James. He may not have been at sea for very long.
Perhaps, for instance, he's just set sail from the security of a well-
protected harbour."

Harry changed course immediately. But he made sure before
he did so that the lookout understood his dual responsibilities. He
must keep an eye on that deserted deck. But just as much of his
concentration should be set to watching the horizon, to ensure
that this ship, wallowing in the water, was not some elaborate
form of bait.

CHAPTER EIGHT

HARRY APPROACHED the high-sided caravel with excessive caution, guns loaded and run out and men in the tops with muskets to cover the deck. The whole ship creaked eerily as the light wind and the leeway of the Gulf waters inched it along over the gentle swell. The unmanned wheel spun back and forth, jerking occasionally as the sails took the wind, only to ease back as the vessel, lacking a firm rudder, payed off. His shouts through the speaking trumpet elicited no response. He ordered Pender to lower a boat so that he could be rowed round for a thorough inspection along the waterline. Close to the lowered bows the list to starboard was more evident. He also observed the dark red line that ran from one of the forward scuppers, staining the ship's painted side. And here and there on the bulwarks the wood showed clean and bright where a sharp instrument had hacked at it. Had this caravel recently been in a fight? A call to *Bucephalas* saw a grappling iron cast that lashed tight brought the drifting ship to a halt. Pender then brought the barge in under the main chains. There was no need of a rope to get aboard, the chains being so close to the waterline, and Harry jumped up as soon as she touched. Scrabbling over the bulwarks he threw himself onto the deck and drew his sword. Pender was beside him before he'd cleared his scabbard, followed by the rest of the barge crew.

The sight that greeted them was the stuff of sailors' deepest superstitions. A vessel devoid of human life, with no indication where the crew had gone. The planking was spotted here and there, in some kind of square, with dark, dried blood, but it was insufficient for any fierce contest and the rest of the deck was merely untidy in the manner to be expected of a merchant vessel. The four small-calibre guns the ship carried were bowsed tight against their ports, with no indication that they'd even been loosened from their breechings. The chicken-coop, set amidships on the foredeck, was empty, feathers weaving to and fro on the breeze. Harry examined the cut marks on the rail, touching the slight drop of blood that lay at the centre of a few of them. All seemed confined to a small area, as though they'd been part of some concentrated task. But the deck by the scupper was different, showing much more evidence of bloodletting. He knelt beside the largest stain, one deep enough to have resisted the warm Tropical air. It retained a slightly tacky feel and a corrupt odour, which had Harry sniffing at the ends of his stained fingers.

Pushing himself upright he stood for a moment in silent contemplation before making his way to the wheel to take control of the ship. The orders he issued to his boarding party had them easing the braces so that by backing and filling he could bring her under his own control. From his position by the wheel, looking along the canted deck, the list was very obvious, though he reckoned it posed no immediate danger. Wooden ships were hard to sink and, given that there was no sound of any pressure on the bulkheads below, this one had a long way to go before the water threatened to make it founder. Handing Pender his sword, he turned towards the cabin door and drew one of his pistols. Gingerly, he pushed it open and entered the shaded interior. The master's day cabin, off to his right, had an open chart on the table, with a quill pen standing ready in the inkwell and a pair of dividers, accompanied by a ruler, on top. The course penned on the chart indicated that this ship had been bound for the Keys, no doubt intent on using the Florida Channel to exit into the Atlantic. A faint odour of recently cooked food assailed his nostrils as he passed what would have been the steward's quarters. This increased the moment he opened the main cabin door, though in the Captain's quarters it had a stale quality.

The cabin was, in the nature of such ships, exceedingly spacious and well appointed. The dining table, set across, bore the remains of a feast, all of it in a heap where it had slid as the vessel wallowed in the swell. A huge silver tureen occupied the centre of the confused mass of dishes. The rack of decanters, half full, sat atop a wine cooler, gleaming as the sunlight streaming through the casements to play upon the delicate crystal. Pender, hard on Harry's heels, examined the side cabins, shaking his head to indicate that they too were devoid of humanity. Meanwhile Harry separated the dishes on the table. Set for three, the half-finished food on two of the plates was cold. The other plate was clean and Harry noticed that only two chairs had been brought to the table. The soup in the tureen had congealed. All three glasses, locked into slots and thus still upright, carried a residue of wine at the bottom. He spotted the chronometers as he walked round the table towards the Captain's carved desk, beautiful pieces encased in fine mahogany. Silently he studied them. But being set to a different time than those he used himself, they told him little regarding his actual position.

The centre of the bulkhead behind him was dominated by two portraits, one large and imposing, the other much smaller. Harry assumed the dominant one to be the Captain. He was florid of complexion, dressed in a dark burgundy velvet coat, a thick red band bearing a diamond-studded star across his waistcoat. One leg was set forward and in his hand he held what looked like an Imperial Roman baton. The eyes gazed over the artist's head at some unseen but decidedly puissant destiny. His back was to a set of small-paned windows, hung with blue damask drapes edged with gold, through which a white wake stretched endlessly off into the deep blue sea. His other hand, fingers splayed out, rested on an elaborately carved desk, beside a large globe. Turning to look behind him, Harry was confronted, over the laden table, with the very same setting, lacking only the globe and the ship's wake. Clearly, when he'd stood to be immortalized he'd done so in this very cabin. The smaller portrait showed a rather bland-looking female, whose eyes lacked any expression, leaving Harry to conclude that the male portrait was the far better picture.

A quick search of the desk drawers produced the usual detritus of a Captain's life; writing materials, manifests, sealing wax, the personal pieces that any travelling man hoards. One drawer contained a brace of expensive pistols still in their case, the brass plate on the top of the box stating that they were the property of one J. B. Rodrigo. In another, papers, marked with the same name, that looked like some form of commission, judging by the flowing officialese of the writing and the heavy embossed seals at the base—not that he could make any sense of them. But the Captain's log, once he'd opened it at the most recent page, told him all he needed to know.

Spanish was not a language Harry was overly familiar with, having just enough to make himself understood in an Iberian port, but the odd word made sense. The names, dates, and courses he could decipher. These told him that this ship, the *Gauchos de Andalusia* under the command of one Juan Baptiste Rodrigo, had left New Orleans five days previously, and had only cleared the Mississippi delta at Fort Balize in the last 36 hours. He thought he recognized the words that indicated Rodrigo had, in fog, followed the wrong channel out of the delta, and ended up stuck on a sandbank for his pains.

Harry knew Pender was watching him, dying to ask questions, but he merely looked at him as if he had the answer to this mystery. Pender shook his head to indicate the opposite and his Captain turned to finish his examination. The foot-lockers revealed little except that whoever had occupied this cabin was masculine and a fussy dresser. They were full of fine garments, coats, waistcoats, breeches, and shirts, all carefully packed and smelling of camphor. The sleeping cabin, with its double cot, appeared to have been occupied by a couple, though there were few female garments. Lastly he examined the main door to the cabin, which had a lock but no key. He was just about to institute a search for it when he remembered Pender's skills in that department.

"Please secure the door behind us," Harry said as he made to leave. "I don't want anyone in here just yet."

There was a slight pause before Pender responded with the obligatory, "Aye, aye, Capt'n." Harry heard the rattle of picks as he made his way up the corridor to emerge once more onto the sunlit deck. *Bucephalas* was now alongside, with James leaning nonchalantly on the rail. Harry, a great deal higher up than his brother, leant over and called to him.

"What have you found?" asked James.

"Apart from the fact that she's Spanish, and was Captained by a fellow called Rodrigo, there's nothing that would make any sense, as yet."

"The ship is empty, then?"

"So far. I've yet to look below."

"Will she float?"

"I think so," Harry replied. "Why?"

"I just thought we might solve two problems in one by requesting that our French guests take this ship to New Orleans themselves?"

"No, brother. I can't put that many men aboard without making her more secure. That means frapping the hull with a tarred sail, which would take for ever. With the hold full of cargo and water we would be hard pressed to come at the source of the leak even if we pumped ship all day. And doing that could move whatever it is that's kept her afloat this long. The odds suggest that matters would be best left as they are. Besides, even frapped, we'd need to go with them as far as the delta just in case it failed. And then there's the salvage value to consider. Nothing would induce me to hand that over to them as well."

"If they were on this deck while our crew are on their own it would lessen the danger of an ugly incident."

"Not if our crew thought we were enriching them even more."

"Captain!" Harry turned to see Dreaver standing by the companionway, his sharp, foxy features screwed up in apparent confusion. "There's something mighty odd down below here that I reckon you should see."

Harry followed him down the steps into the waist, then on down to the lower deck. The caravel, being a cargo ship, had deep holds below the crew's sleeping quarters. These, cramped and filthy, were arranged round the sides of the vessel. The hatches were open and piles of pungent tobacco lay strewn around each lip. As Harry approached he stepped on a brown substance spread about on the floor. It was the colour of hard sand, yet it glistened slightly and made a peculiar scrunching sound underfoot. He bent to touch it, picking up a faint odour of molasses. Gingerly he pinched some in his hand and raised it to his nose, sniffing like a nervous animal. Then he put some on his tongue.

"What is that stuff, your honour?"

"That I don't know, Dreaver. But it tastes and smells just like sugar."

"Ain't like no sugar I ever saw."

Harry shook his head slowly, then looked around him. The empty boxes that had contained the mess had been thrown carelessly into an untidy pile. Dreaver lowered a lantern into the hold to reveal that all the containers still inside had their lids torn off, with deep indentations in the contents as though some of each had been removed. A great deal had spilt down the sides of the bales of cotton which formed the next layer of cargo, and where it had come into contact with damp it formed an unpleasant sludge. Harry could hear the water sloshing around at the lower levels, but it was clearly confined, since a quick calculation of the total number of barrels he could see, added to what he suspected still lay below, showed that the *Gauchos* had left port with a full cargo. It was a thoughtful Harry Ludlow who examined the empty bread room and the barren meat and dry goods stores. Returning to the main deck, idly casting an eye towards the forepeak, he observed that the manger was empty. No pigs, cattle, or goats filled the space, though the odour from the disturbed straw bore witness to their recent presence.

"Dreaver, a word to my brother, if you please. Inform him

that we will be towing the ship. Ask Pender to take charge of a party aboard to secure the cable as well as a man to ease the rudder. If my brother wishes to come aboard himself, he may do so."

James, having learned all about the layout of the main cabin from Pender, joined Harry in the set of cabins immediately below. There were two on each side of a large oak table. Harry was in the one furthest from the door, fingering the garments that he'd laid out on top of some crisp linen sheets. The smell of camphor was quite strong. A sea-chest lay open before him, the bright colour of expensive material gleaming in the fitful light that filtered through the salt-encrusted casements.

"A woman?" said James.

Harry nodded. "It may be that you will know more than I about this. But my guess is that these are the property of someone reasonably young. The garments are exceedingly vivid, though not what I would term fashionable."

James took the piece that Harry was holding, fingering the elaborate embroidery that edged the upper part of the dress. "This is made of some form of very fine animal skin, Harry. No trace of any kind of struggle?"

"None. I can't even say for certain that this cabin was occupied. The cot is made up but appears unused."

James looked around, noticing the mirror above the chest, with combs, pins, and some lace hanging beside it.

"There was certainly a lady next door, but I think she's older, judging by the clothes. Certainly she was untidier and may well have been sea-sick." James needed no telling about that. A cabin occupied by someone who'd suffered that affliction had a smell all of its own which lasted for days after the event. "And we're overburdened with art. There are two paintings in the main cabin, and a case containing a portrait in the cabin opposite. It would be interesting to know if it was painted recently."

"Shall I have a look?" asked James, curious to know why, but prepared to wait for an answer.

"By all means."

He was gone less than a minute. The crumpled, sick-stained

sheets in the corner overbore the vinegar which had been used to contain the smell. Returning with the round leather container, an object specially designed to carry rolled-up works of art, he pulled the portrait out gently and opened it. The light wasn't good but both could see the pale features of a young woman who was quite a beauty. Her eyes, modestly cast down, indicated rigid Spanish decorum. The chair in which she sat had a high back with an armorial carving at the top. A dog wearing a jewelled collar sat at her feet, while in the background a white wooden mansion stood surrounded by trees draped in moss.

"It's of a tolerable quality, Harry," said James, "and not very old. There are no cracks in the surface at all."

"That bed has been used and the chest in there contains garments which are rather more grand in style, certainly more Spanish. There were several mantillas like the one in her portrait."

Harry put the things he was holding back in the chest and took the seamed edge of one of the white, folded sheets, peering at it. "The cot was remade with the same linen after the occupant was sick. If you look closely, you will observe that it carries an embroidered message."

James took the sheet from Harry and carried it to the grubby window, but there was insufficient light to read by.

"Anything in the other cabins?" asked James, as he handed the sheet back. Harry folded it untidily and stuck it under his arm before replying.

"The master, probably. The other was unoccupied."

"Just the single officer then, barring a Captain?"

"That's all that a merchant vessel requires. They don't stand watches with the same rigidity as we do, and they shorten sail at night. In a Spanish ship the Captain does very little of the actual sailing. He considers himself too much the gentleman. Such things as navigation and sail plans are left to the master and his mates, who double up as common seamen to save on the wage bill."

James turned to leave, followed slowly by Harry. "What did Dreaver find in the hold that was so interesting?"

"Come and have a look."

James examined the brown granules, which had some of the feel of coarse, rough gunpowder. Like Harry he thought the taste and smell reminiscent of sugar. "But what it's called, heaven knows. I thought all the plant discoveries had been made decades ago in this part of the world."

"A mystery substance to go with a mystery ship."

"Are you in a position to speculate?" asked James as they made their way back up to the main deck.

"Only very slightly. They've abandoned ship for no discernible reason, so I have to assume another vessel. Having said that, the ship that approached them was known to the Captain at least, since he clearly anticipated no danger. If he laid down his fork to go on deck and greet them I'd be surprised. Those who took him wanted neither the vessel or the cargo it seems, since they have tried to sink her."

"Without success."

Harry, now back on the upper deck, stated that the list had not increased while he been aboard. "It's almost certain that some of the cargo has shifted and blocked any gaps they made in the planking."

"How permanent is that?"

"Without knowing what's in the lower holds I couldn't even begin to form an opinion. We just have to hope that it's stable. But the water could penetrate at any moment. We'll get some warning if it does, so I don't consider it dangerous."

"You were speculating, I recall." James took the sheet from under his brother's arm and let it fall open.

Harry smiled at his brother's singlemindedness.

"Whoever approached the *Gauchos* wanted something and it's my guess that they had a very clear idea of what it was. It certainly wasn't that sugarlike substance we've just tasted, because that was all over the deck. Yet each cask was open and disturbed. Did they succeed in finding what they wanted? I can't say with absolute assurance, but the chest that contained the sheet you're holding was open but undisturbed, just like the other cabins, including the Captain's foot-lookers. That indicates the answer is yes. But I do know one thing. Whoever came, in whatever vessel, though not starving, was in need of stores. I would also advance the theory that the ship that came alongside was rather small."

"How can you tell?"

"One thing at a time," Harry replied, holding up a hand to count off the points on his fingers. "There are the remains of a fully cooked meal on the Captain's table, practically untouched, with more in the steward's gallery. Not something a hungry man would turn away from. But every storeroom on the ship has been cleaned out and both the manger and the hen-coop are bare. That blood by the bulwarks forward is where they slaughtered the animals."

"Just the animals?"

Harry shrugged. "You know the odour of pork as well as I do. It smells like animal blood, but of course I can't be sure."

"And what does that indicate?"

"That whatever else they sought they decided to take the food. But their ship lacked the space to accommodate live creatures."

"Piracy?"

"Possibly. Certainly theft." Harry fingered the edge of the sheet and held it up. "And, very likely, with women aboard, an abduction."

"Or murder," said James. "After all, you're not absolutely sure about the blood."

"No. But with no evidence of even a minor struggle . . ."

James pointed questioningly to the spots of blood on the deck that formed a square on the deck.

"You haven't been in a lot of fights, brother. But you've done enough in the cockpit to know that a fighting, or even a struggling man, once wounded, sends blood in all directions. And a man and two women, leaving a meal, either in panic or because of force, tend towards creating a mess. There's not a drop of food on the cabin floor, no sign of wine spilt or chairs tipped over."

"A small boat?"

"Yes." Harry nodded slowly. "It would be helpful to know how far she drifted, of course. But at a guess I'd say that whoever took over the ship could easily have come this far in an inshore type of vessel."

"Which adds up to what?"

He shrugged, then smiled at James. "Nothing more than I've already said. But the *Gauchos* sailed from New Orleans, and passed Fort Balize, which is our destination. The least we can do is try to take her in with us. Perhaps those in authority there will know more about such matters than we do, and by taking her in we will at least convince them of our peaceful intentions. Certainly, if there are pirates operating, they'd know who they are, and where they berth."

James thrust forward the sheet, indicating the thin blue embroidery that was not the usual initials. Instead it was a name, or perhaps a word, *Hoboi Hili Miko,* which made no sense. Unfolding it, he saw that the embroidery continued, this time more recognizably.

Harry leant forward to read it. *"Vent!"*

"'That's "wind" in French," added James.

"Which is what we're whistling for," replied Harry, with a grin.

"You're sure, of course, that it was another ship?"

"Don't tell me that you believe in ghosts, James?"

"I don't. But you've referred to the gullibility of sailors many times. I might as well tell you now that there is hardly a man in your crew who is not muttering darkly about that very thing. And our Frenchmen have gone very silent indeed."

Harry grinned and fingered the linen sheet again. "Shall I don this and come aboard in the dark?"

"Not without all the boats over the side, brother. The sight of you in that sheet will cause them to abandon ship."

"No one should be exposed to such temptation."

CHAPTER NINE

THE DECISION to tow the ship only deepened the crew's curiosity, and that was heightened when they heard Harry order the party he put aboard to take their own rations and touch nothing, either on the deck or below. Lanterns, rigged at the ends of the yards, caused several sailors to speculate on which particular kind of banshee feared the light. Harry, who knew the answer to be much more prosaic, couldn't bring himself to tell them the true reason, since his men seemed to derive so much pleasure from their superstitions. The dark mutterings increased as they ran a stout cable out of the tier, all the men who handled it fearful, and quite convinced that whatever had seen off the crew of the Spanish ship would have little trouble in walking along the thick rope to seal their fate. Some strong words were required to counter their reluctance.

Once in place it ran from the bitts below decks on *Bucephalas,* out through the aftermost porthole and came aboard the *Gauchos* forward, there to be lashed to the capstan. Towing was never easy, but of all the ships ill designed for the purpose, a caravel, with its old-fashioned design and high forecastle, could be numbered amongst the worst. This was a situation made more troublesome by her condition—she was forever yawing to the side at the slightest pressure of wind or water—so a journey that had taken *Gauchos* little more than one day looked set to take Harry at least two.

He'd gone to bed and was sound asleep before danger threatened. Called from his cot he knew as soon as he reached the deck that *Gauchos* was in trouble. The angle of the lanterns he'd rigged on the yards told him that, by towing the ship, he'd opened up whatever was stopping the water from coming inboard. *Gauchos* was further down by the head and had definitely increased her starboard list. But what was peculiar was that Pender, with whom he'd left specific instructions to cover such an eventuality, seemed to be still on board. Neither had he signalled to say he was coming off.

"Dreaver. Man the barge. And put a party ready to cut the cable, just in case the tow sinks suddenly."

The moon was up, a thin sliver low in the cloudy night sky. Uncovered, it barely illuminated the seascape. But once behind a cloud total darkness descended, leaving the ship a ghostly shape lit only by the faint lanterns still on the yards. It was at such a moment that they approached the side. His calls to the party on board went unanswered, which caused him to wonder and the barge crew to suddenly cease to row.

"Pender!" he shouted again.

"They've been got to," cried a voice behind him, as the clouds cleared to reveal the silhouette of the bowsprit dipping towards the warm blue water.

"Belay that nonsense and head for the side," barked Harry.

"Don't, your honour, or we'll be taken."

He tried a more soothing tone of voice. "There's nothing there to be afraid of."

"Then where's Pender?" said another oarsman.

Harry snapped then. "He's probably below, damn you, carrying out my instructions. Now stop behaving like a bunch of old women and put the barge alongside."

No one moved. Looking back at them Harry could see the terror in their eyes. To him it was absurd. If the merchantman had been manned by a hundred wild-eyed pirates he could have called upon them to advance and they'd obey. Right now he wasn't sure. But he knew he had to try, and opened his mouth. Just then an ethereal voice, which seemed to come from the lower decks of the ship, started singing a strange and haunting refrain. This was followed by hideous screaming.

Cries of "Oh my God!" mingled with more blasphemous oaths as the barge crew reacted. Some grabbed their oars and tried to row. Others threw themselves into the bottom of the boat, cowering in terror.

"Get us outta here, Captain."

Harry, whose own certainty was shaken, and who'd nearly fallen back as the boat jibbed, couldn't respond with his normal commanding voice. So when he called them to order he sounded as nervous as the crew, which did nothing for their morale.

"It's Old Nick hisself, your honour."

That set off a bout of wailing in the barge, which only increased the noise coming from the ship.

"Ho! ho! ho! ho!" boomed the voice. "You're all for the chop now, you fornicatin', loose-livin', pox-ridden buggers. I'll suck the blood out of you afore this night is out, just like the lot that I saw to this very afternoon."

"Pender!" Harry yelled, this loud enough to carry over the screams of his crew. "Belay that this second, or half these idiots will jump overboard."

Pender stood up, probably quite forgetting that he'd covered himself in a white sheet. The cries of terrified seamen rose in a new crescendo and the barge tilted as some indeed sought the dubious safety of the surrounding sea. Only the loud laughter of the rest of Pender's party averted what could have been a disaster.

"Got you there, daft sods."

Terror turned quickly to anger and the whole night was full of foul-mouthed insults, as those aboard the *Gauchos* jeered at the barge crew, who responded with dire threats. It was quite some time before Harry could make himself heard above the din, and a good deal longer before he could issue any orders that would be obeyed.

"Cutter's loaded, your honour," replied a breathless Pender to his Captain's shouted enquiry. "Just as you ordered. Had to cut that big painting out of its frame to get it out the cabin door."

"Have you looked below?"

"I have. She's a goner, I reckon. Water's up above the forward
hatches. I'd say there was a rate of tobacco in the hold to begin
with, an' that's what kept her up. Now some of it's near the top
of the hatches."

"Then cast off the tow, for God's sake."

The humour was still in Pender's voice when he replied, "Just
as you wish, Capt'n."

They stood off in their separate boats as the *Gauchos* went
down. It was a slow demise, with much groaning and cracking of
overburdened wood which ended in a final hiss as the last air was
forced out through the open companionways. Then the masts tilted
suddenly as the sunken hulk heeled over. They held their buoyancy for a minute, then slid below the water, sinking through a
morass of those brown granules mixed with tobacco leaf and cotton. Harry said a silent prayer, part of the burial service that he
knew off by heart. He didn't think anyone had died aboard the
Gauchos. But it was something he needed to do just to ease his
own mind.

Back aboard *Bucephalas* he tried to remonstrate with Pender,
but having James in the cabin made that impossible and it wasn't
long before all three were helpless with mirth. It was some time
before Harry could check that Pender had brought aboard all the
things he requested be saved. He had the ship's papers and manifests, the chart showing her course, some dried blood scraped off
the deck into an oilskin pouch, the beautiful chronometers, and
the dinner service from the Captain's cabin, plus the rolled-up portraits. All these were piled on top of the sea-chests of everyone
who'd been aboard and a box of the strange granules. Quietly he
examined them, before instructing his servant to stow them somewhere safe.

The sky had cleared and was now a mass of stars, which
allowed Harry a chance to establish, within reason, their position.
Once he was satisfied that he'd taken a reasonably accurate fix he
ordered the men to increase sail then stayed on deck till the first
hint of grey touched the eastern horizon. Satisfied that *Bucepha-*

las was alone on the vast expanse of the sea he went below. By the time the sun rose above the rim of the earth he was asleep again, snoring gently.

Harry knew he was close to the delta area long before he sighted land. The discoloured water, faint at first, became darker by the hour. This was a clear indication that he was approaching the mighty watercourse that ran from the Gulf of Mexico right into the heartland of the American continent. Some of the mud he was observing had travelled from the headwaters of half a dozen huge rivers, all of which joined with the Mississippi at various stages on its 2,500 mile journey to the ocean. The thought of such a natural wonder clearly affected his imagination, though his evident enthusiasm produced little reaction in James.

"It only requires a minimal canal network to have a river system that would run all the way from Canada to the Gulf," said Harry, seeking to draw his brother's attention to the map in his hand.

"And what advantage would that produce?" asked James, who barely spared a glance. He was occupied with his pad, drawing a copy of the embroidery that they'd found on the linen sheets aboard the *Gauchos*. The portrait case, now containing three pictures instead of one, lay beside the desk, on top of the two chests of clothes that Pender had fetched aboard.

"Rivers are the best way of shipping trade goods out of the interior. Such a network would open up a vast area of virgin land to development. Don't you remember what Pollock said?"

James stifled a slight yawn. "Indeed I do."

"I have the distinct impression that this doesn't interest you, brother."

"What doesn't interest me?"

Harry waved a hand towards the northern horizon. "The American continent. The sheer size of the thing. The vast area of wilderness that lies beyond the Cumberland Gap and the Appalachian mountains. Fort Pitt and Ticonderoga, the Great

Lakes; a land teeming with wild game and Indian tribes."

"You are right there, brother. These names which you trip so glibly mean nothing to me. Besides, I prefer teeming civilization."

"So the great forests and plains, mountains and rivers hold no fascination for you?"

James laid aside his pad. "None whatever. The thought of an endless wilderness, full only of savages and animals, has no attraction at all. At least none to compare with the glories of Italy. Grandeur is all very well. But some of the most tedious paintings I have ever seen are those in which such vistas dominate."

He picked up the portrait case, undid the catch, and tipped out the three paintings, taking one and holding it up for Harry to see. It was Captain Rodrigo in all his imperial splendour.

"Let this be part of your artistic education."

That brought forth a groan from Harry, and another less than pleasant memory of St Croix. His brother's nautical ineptitude never ceased to amaze him. He could not fathom why the retention of even the most basic fact of wind, weather, or sail seemed to slip in one ear and out of the other. Forgetting James's tendency to overstate his ignorance, Harry had made a rather waspish remark on the subject. James responded by setting up his easel and inviting Harry to learn to paint. Never one to duck a challenge, and with little to do once the ship had been handed over to the repairers, Harry set to with a will. He'd listened with tremendous concentration as James gave him a lesson in the basics; the divisions of the human frame, preliminary sketching, light and shade, and how to mix and apply paints. It was, by the very nature of the subject and the pupil, a crash course. The resulting display of temper from Harry Ludlow, as James turned the tables on him, had amused the whole crew. And nothing hurt Harry more than the gentle way his brother would say, when he encountered some technical difficulty, "But Harry, I explained that to you, in great detail, only yesterday."

If James heard the groan he ignored it, and aimed his pen at the casement windows and dark blue drapes of what had been the

Gauchos. "The task of a landscape is the same as that of background, to set a dimension to something of more interest."

He picked up the second portrait, the one they'd found in the case, this time indicating the white mansion and the dark chair in which the subject sat.

"That house, being white, sets off the darkness of the dress and the deep brown of the furniture. Likewise the source of light playing on the heavy carving helps to concentrate the eye. Do you understand, Harry, on its own, a ship's wake, the blue sea, the snow-capped mountain or an endless plain is of little appreciable value."

"Well, at least it makes the thing interesting," said Harry, grabbing the small portrait. "Look at this, it's as dull as ditchwater."

"I rather like it."

"In God's name, why?"

James took it from Harry and looked at it closely. "It's by the same artist as the one of Rodrigo. But in this the man executing it cared for his subject."

"How can you tell?"

"The brushwork is similar, and the way he approaches various parts of the anatomy. But instead of throwing his brush around as he did for that foolish painting of the Captain, he's taken care to try and see into the mind of his subject, rather than provide mere surface arrogance."

"And this one?" asked Harry, picking up a corner to show the mantilla-crowned face.

"Very different."

Harry looked closely at two of the pictures, but unable to say what the difference was, or that he preferred the one James termed arrogant, he took the subject back to where it had begun.

"So America and noble savages do not inspire you?"

"Noble savages, Harry?" replied James, with an arch tone. "I fear that the estimable Benjamin West, along with John Singleton Copley, have quite exhausted that *oeuvre.*"

"These things of which I speak are not merely on canvas, brother. They are real."

James put down the small painting and picked up his pad with a dispirited air. "They will be, Harry. Some fool will be seduced by them and seek to record them with the brush."

Harry opened his mouth, about to deliver a sharp retort, but a sudden tap on the cabin door halted him. Dreaver poked his head round the jamb. "Lookout's spotted a small raft in the water, Capt'n."

"A raft," Harry said, sharply, giving Dreaver the same look he'd aimed at James. The sailor stuttered the next words.

"S—says it's a raft for certain, but there's s—something odd about it."

"I'll be up on deck shortly."

"If we don't put our helm down, your honour, we'll have to come about."

"Very well. Steer a course for the raft." Dreaver's head disappeared and Harry turned back to James. "Do you wish to view this, brother?"

"Thank you, no."

As soon as Harry saw it through the telescope he sent for him. James came on deck to be greeted by a grim expression that was not confined to Harry. The whole crew looked troubled. James took the proffered telescope and trained at the spot to which Harry was pointing.

"You will need to look closely, brother."

James did as he was asked, his eyes screwed up in concentration.

"Is that a body lashed to the timbers?"

"It is," Harry replied sadly. "And if you look further afield, you will see some casks in the water."

"I've got them!" James exclaimed. "Six of them, on edge. They seem to be tied to the raft."

"They are payed out to leeward. You are witnessing two of the worst punishments ever invented by a sick nautical mind. They combine hope with futility. Unless, in either case, a rescuer happens to come across the victim, it always ends in death, and with the right conditions that can take days."

"Are these such conditions?"

"I doubt it, brother. If you look at the way those casks are rocking on the swell, the bodies that were attached have gone."

"Bodies!" James replied, struggling to keep his tone and expression calm.

"In the foreground you have the raft. Tie a man to that above salt water, especially in a warm climate, and you have a very refined form of hell. All he can see, if the sun isn't burning his eyes, is the sky, and the birds circling that will, when he dies, take them out."

"What about the casks?"

"With those you take the victim and lash him, seated, to a near-empty barrel. I say near empty because a certain amount of ballast is put in the bottom to act as a counterweight to his bulk and ensure that it doesn't tip on its end." As Harry explained his men moved forward to listen. They'd all seen this particular form of pirate punishment done as a joke. But none, including their Captain, had ever seen it for real.

"Some humorous souls even provide the victim with a piece of driftwood as an oar, to give him the illusion that survival is possible. They have not done so in this case, but that raft represented salvation, except that with the run of the tide there was probably no way that anyone, hands tied, could reach it."

Bucephalas was very near the raft now. Close to they could see the remains. The skin was blackened by the relentless sun, the eyes, as Harry had said, picked out by birds. The victim had no hands, and the blood that stained the planking was close in colour to the burgundy velvet of the garment he wore.

"The coat, Harry?" said James.

"Captain Rodrigo, I think," Harry replied.

They lifted their gaze to the row of casks. All were empty, with ropes lashed to them that Harry informed him had once held feet.

"Have you ever tried to sit on a greasy pole at the village fair, James? It is easy compared to a barrel in the sea. But because you're tied to it, when you fall sideways you must try to get upright again, otherwise you will drown. That's where the ballast comes in, to prolong the agony and add to the spectacle for those watching. That is, until the victim becomes too tired. Then the ballast works against him. And once he's under water, it is designed to keep him there."

"There's no way that the victim could have pulled his own legs out, is there, Capt'n?" asked Pender, standing by with a boathook. "I was just wondering if'n there might some poor soul in the water."

"You're a sailor. Called upon to tie a knot that would keep a man secure, could you do it?"

"Then how come they ain't there now?" asked one of the crew.

"They've been pulled out bodily by a shark, I should think." The crew shuddered at this information. "Let's hope the poor sod had already drowned by the time it happened."

The voice from the tops distracted them just at the point when Pender got his boathook under the rim of the cask.

"I think we might be close to land, your honour, but I can't be sure. There's birds an' the like, too many to be scudding round a ship, but nothing solid for 'em to set on."

Harry cast his gaze over the side again, deliberately avoiding looking at the blood-stained platform as Pender hauled it close. The dark brown, impenetrable soup that ran down the ship's side told him more than his lookout's eye could observe.

"As soon as you can, cut those casks loose," he said.

They got a line around one of the timbers and hauled the raft onto the deck, cutting the ropes that streamed out from one side as they did so. Harry, on his way to take over the wheel, ordered Pender to cover it over.

"It's that cove in the picture right enough, Capt'n," said Pender, on his knees beside the body. "His shirt's torn and there are a rate of wounds on his chest. It's as though he's been tortured. Looks as though his tongue has been sliced out."

Harry deliberately didn't look. He walked back to the wheel and then informed James that they were, if his reckoning was correct, approaching the south-eastern passage into the Mississippi, guarded by the island of Balize.

"That is if it is still there," he added.

"Is this island another mystery, brother?"

"No. But I heard that the whole thing was washed away by a hurricane in '68, including the lighthouse the French built to indicate the river mouth. But the silt, plus the detritus from the Mississippi, recreated the island. I suspect they've rebuilt the fort, since it provides the best protection for the whole delta, but we're obviously still without the lighthouse."

"Shall we land there?"

"No. There is little that will be of any use to us. It will suffice to offload our passengers at Fort Balize. They can hitch a ride in the next merchantman going upriver. Break out a British flag to let them know that we are neutrals. I'll shorten sail so that they can send out a boat if they feel the need to question us."

CHAPTER TEN

THEY SAILED on in a light breeze that hardly ruffled the canvas on the yards, eyes straining forward to catch the first glimpse of the low-lying banks that lay at the eastern side of the delta. Waves were breaking over the confused mass of sand bars and islands to larboard. It was the wide gap, the exit channel, intermittently marked with buoys, that first alerted them to its presence. But there was no sign of any building, and little of the vegetation that had come into view earlier, lining the shore of the archipelago of islands to the west. Harry guessed that any buildings would be to the north of the island, at the very mouth of the Mississippi. He spent his time studying the chart he had, constantly looking over the side for some evidence that the channel he was following was the correct one.

"It is at times like these, brother, that you pray for up-to-date soundings. The sands shift alarmingly round here. This chart was printed by Jefferson in '94 and could well be useless."

"Sail ho, Captain Ludlow, directly to larboard. Two, three, five."

Harry swung his telescope round swiftly, his eye immediately catching sight of the row of single square sails, set nearly fore and aft, high on the mast of a line of ships. The vessels, close to the low, heavily overgrown, western shore appeared to be making good speed through the water, even if they had neither the wind nor enough aloft to justify it. Without any certain knowledge of their numbers, there had to be pirates operating in this part of the Gulf. Unsure if they represented any danger, he was just about to order the ship to go about and clear for action when the flag at the mainmast on the leading vessel, hitherto an indistinct blue, swam into focus as it turned into the wind. He couldn't see the coat of arms on the pale cream background. But the two blue bars, top and bottom, readily identified the whole.

"Spanish!" he said, dropping the telescope to take in the faint outline of the leader's hull. With it now out in a patch of open water, he was momentarily perplexed by the series of white flashes along its side. Then, when two others had pulled out from behind the sandbars, he recognized them for what they were, the spume from oars being dipped rhythmically in and out of the blue water.

"Good God, James, it appears we are in the presence of a fleet of galleys."

"Galleys? Have we found Atlantis?"

"These are close to the kind of ship a Barbary pirate would use, small, manoeuvrable, and exceedingly handy in a close encounter, with guns set to fire fore and aft. They're the very devil to handle in any kind of sea. The Americans manned something similar during the war against us. They used them in the inshore waters."

Harry watched as the line of ships edged its way through the sandbanks that lined the Louisiana shore. The topsails weren't so much drawing as acting like a lateen staysail, set to keep each vessel's head steady. For the area in which they were operating, they were perfect. With all those oars and a shallow draught they were capable of working inshore without the need for a breeze. Even a lee shore presented no problem in light airs. Likewise, given the strong currents of the Mississippi in spate, they were ideally suited for making their way up such a formidable river.

"I've got sight of what I reckon to be the fort now, Capt'n," said Pender, who had another telescope aimed over the bowsprit. "If'n it can be called that. My cousin's cowshed stands higher. There's a boat puttin' off, armed cutter, and the cove climbing into the thwarts has a bit of braid on his shoulder."

With the galleys a long way off, Harry turned his attention to the approaching cutter and the island behind. From the deck of *Bucephalas* they could barely see the rampart that formed the walls of the fort, it being nothing more than a low wooden palisade. This seemed to be the only part of the island that could truly be said to exist above sea level. Indeed, to call Balize an island at all was a serious misnomer. Harry had the distinct impression that if any kind of swell got up, those inside the fort would soon see it lashing against the walls, threatening by its action to sweep the sand from beneath their feeble human construction.

Inside the palisade, its roof just showing above the spikes, stood a single long building which obviously provided the entire accommodation for the garrison, little enough shelter from the near-Tropical heat and the ferocious storms that blew up frequently in this part of the world. He dropped his telescope and the face of the braided officer swam into Harry's focus. Dark-skinned and moustached, he had a doleful countenance which befitted his surroundings. Harry took in the oarsmen, noting that they too were of a dark complexion, before raising his glass to re-examine the fort. As a posting it stood close to being a nightmare, especially with the knowledge that it had already, in recent times, been swept away. With no way of foreseeing what the weather would produce, the garrison would have little time to evacuate the island and find a safer shore. His mind turned to the tempest they'd so recently survived. They must dread such an event, since in a hurricane they'd have nowhere to run to. The whole delta was low lying and prone to flooding. Harry could only surmise that any officer assigned to such a duty was, along with his men, serving out some kind of punishment.

"Head for the channel marked ahead. If we don't make it, we'll heave to when he comes close."

The boom of the gun made everyone on deck spin round towards the Spanish warships. The leading galley had fired off a signal gun, judging by the puff of black smoke which wafted away to leeward. A set of flags broke out at the masthead and the cutter, which had been heading for *Bucephalas,* immediately swung round on to a new course, its bows now aimed for the shallows.

"He seems to have lost interest in us," said James.

Just then they heard a grinding sound. The bows lifted slightly and the masts swayed as the ship lost all forward motion. That sound of sand on wood told Harry all he needed to know and he ran forward. It was impossible to see anything in the muddy waters, but they'd run aground. Not badly, since they'd hardly had steerage-way, but enough to bring forth a stream of curses from the Captain. It was, to his mind, typically Spanish, to maintain a marked channel that was no longer clear. Under normal circumstances he wouldn't have been too troubled by such an event, knowing that the boats, given such a soft sandy bottom, could tow him off. But this particular incident immobilized him at what might prove to be an inconvenient moment.

"Get a party over the side with the kedge anchor," he shouted, "and a cable to the capstan. Pender, drop the best bower to make it look as though we've hove to, at that distance the Dons won't know if we still have way on the ship."

He made his way back to the quarterdeck, observing that the cutter had closed a great deal of the distance. The lead galley hove to as it came alongside and the officer climbed aboard. Behind him the men were already rowing away from the ship to drop an anchor that he could use to haul himself clear. It was in place before the galleys got under way again. The leader, towing the Fort Balize cutter, was heading straight for him. The others were taking a more southerly course which would bring them across his stern. Still stuck fast, there was nothing he could do about it. As the range between the Spanish ship and *Bucephalas* shortened, Harry examined the galley's lines. Over-elaborate in the Spanish manner, she was nevertheless a formidable instrument in any situation which suited her build. He calculated that she carried four heavy-calibre guns, two in the bows and two in the stern. Long habit made him wonder about her Captain and her crew. He was aware, more than most, that even the finest, best-armed sailing ship was only a fraction of the equation. Success depended on a decisive and competent officer on the quarterdeck, in command of a well worked-up crew that acted as one unit. The French Navy built better ships than the British, the Spanish generally carried a superior number of guns on their line-of-battle ships. But both

nations lacked the uninterrupted sea service that, forming everyone aboard into a single entity, made the Royal Navy so formidable
an instrument.

"Galley's putting a boat over the side, Capt'n," cried the lookout, unnecessarily, since they could now see the other deck quite
clearly. "And there's a well-dressed party that's about to get
aboard."

"Well, let us break out some decent wine," said Harry. "And
Pender, raid our stores for the very finest cold collation."

"Are we seeking to impress him, brother?" asked James.

"Not really. But if he's anything like the Spaniards I've come
across, he'll be as proud as the proverbial peacock. Anything less
than our best will offend him. In fact, given the number of galleys in this little fleet, let's give the fellow a commodore's salute."

The first of the guns boomed out before he was halfway across
the gap between the ships, the white smoke drifting away in the
soft breeze. Gun followed gun until the full entitlement of thir-
teen was complete.

"*Navarro,*" called the Spanish coxswain from the bows of his
Captain's barge, boathook extended to hook on just aft of the
gangway. The name of the ship was followed by the name of her
commander, just in case these Englishmen needed to be over-awed.
"El Señor Felipe San Lucar de Barrameda."

"The length of his name is certainly impressive," said James.
"Almost as gorgeous as his attire."

His clothing was more than that, a fact very evident when he
came aboard to the sound of the boatswain's whistle. El Señor
Felipe San Lucar de Barrameda was a very tall man, unusual in a
sailor of any race, though his build was of sufficient girth to avoid
any hint of lankiness. The coat he wore was of mid-blue watered
silk, set off by an equally fine cream waistcoat in the same material. His linen was as white as the wig on his head and the dark
eyes flashed with a hauteur that made his gold-fringed tricorne
hat, swept elegantly to one side as he bowed, seem appropriate
rather than theatrical. His skin was of a sallow hue, carefully kept
from any exposure to the sun; the moustache and beard a thin

black carefully barbered line around the full red lips of his mouth.

The man behind him was very different, more suited to their location off Fort Balize. A doleful Captain of infantry, he was as sad as the place itself. The dark skin that Harry had noticed while he was still in the cutter was even more marked when set in contrast to that of his superior officer. His heavy black moustache trailed at either side of thick purple lips and the braid, like the buttons on his uniform, was tarnished and green. The cloth of his linen coat, which had once been a beige colour, was now so stained that it resembled the muddy Mississippi water that slid by the ship's hull. There was a mildewed air about him, as though while not in any way wet he was never actually completely dry. Harry stepped forward to introduce himself, speaking French and making as formal a bow as the Spaniard.

"I've prepared some refreshments in my cabin, Don Felipe San Lucar de Barrameda. A humble repast, not fit for a man of your illustrious station, but the best that a poor ship like mine can do."

The Spaniard took this rubbish at face value, which was more than James could manage. Unaware of Harry's motives for such grovelling, and lacking his experience with the notoriously stiff-backed Dons, he quite failed to see his brother's words for what they were: outrageous flattery to a man who looked as though he would settle for no less. His subsequent remark, delivered in English, might have gone unnoticed, but James, likewise, had decided to speak French.

"Nonsense, brother. I dare say our guest has been on short commons the whole commission and will welcome a square meal."

The Spaniard's eyes only opened a fraction. But on such a haughty countenance it was enough to convey a measure of the shock James had achieved.

"Allow me, Señor, to name my brother, James," said Harry, giving the younger Ludlow a glare of such intensity as to melt ice. "A man renowned, I might add, for his wit."

"Delighted," the Spaniard replied in English, with just the right intonation to let James know he was anything but.

"You speak English, sir?"

"I was a prisoner for three years, Captain Ludlow, during the last war."

"My condolences, Señor. That is rarely a pleasant experience for any man, let alone a man bred to fight. I can only hope that those who had charge of your confinement left you with a good impression of my country."

San Lucar de Barrameda didn't answer that, which left Harry looking both concerned and rather foolish. James grinned as the Spaniard stepped to one side, exposing the officer who'd come out from Fort Balize.

"Captain Pasquale Fernandez, a native of Havana. Commander of the Cuban regiment which provides the garrison at Fort Balize."

Fernandez did his best to appear elegant. But the condescending way in which San Lucar de Barrameda had referred to his Cuban origins, plus his own complete lack of natural grace, undermined him. And in the presence of his immaculate superior the attempt at a deep bow looked comical.

"Please follow me, gentlemen," said Harry, leading the way towards his cabin. "Pender, something to drink for the barge crew and Captain Fernandez's men in the cutter."

The party walked just far enough away from Harry to allow him to whisper more orders. "Get Dreaver to man the capstan and see if he can ease us clear. One pawl at a time. I don't want our guests to know."

Progress to the cabin was agonizingly slow, as San Lucar de Barrameda examined each one of Harry's guns. He was particularly taken by the squat carronades, and spent an inordinate amount of time studying their outline. Clearly he longed to ask about them in detail, these being a type of cannon he could only have heard of and never seen, but good manners forbade him to do so. And just so that he would get Harry's previous flattery in context, the Captain of the *Bucephalas* didn't oblige him. Finally he dragged himself away and followed Harry into the day cabin.

This boasted a table laid out with everything of quality, in silver and plate, that the Ludlow brothers owned. If the food, the best that Tortola could offer, wasn't perfect, the wines were exceptional, a fact that actually registered on the masklike face of their guest.

"Pender," said Harry softly, after drinks had been poured, "get that stuff from the *Gauchos* on deck, so that our Spanish peacock can examine it. Put it beside that raft."

Pender left a scene of restrained conversation. Direct questions were avoided. Even James knew that there was a protocol in these things: the polite exchange of conversation regarding each sovereign's health, larded with flattery as to the numerous virtues of the two nations; the enquiries regarding the nature of each other's task, without in any way indicating unseemly inquisitiveness. Even if the word privateer surprised him, it would have taken a very observant onlooker to notice the effect on San Lucar de Barrameda, determined to abide the rules. And, as befitted a man of his station, he ate and drank sparingly. Not so his fellow officer. Fernandez, presented with an opportunity to eat and drink things he rarely saw, slurped and munched away, taking no part in the exchange of pleasantries. Indeed, his indulgence forced his superior to continue with his gossip for some time, until, finally losing patience, he said a sharp word in Spanish that had the infantry Captain sitting bolt upright in his chair. Then having served notice of a change of mood, he turned to Harry.

"I am, sir, curious as to why an English privateer should be in these waters, which I would remind you, are wholly the province of His Most Catholic Majesty."

Harry stood up abruptly, turned, and reached into his desk drawer. His hand emerged holding the packet that contained the log and papers of the *Gauchos*.

"Would you return to the deck with me, sir? I have something very unpleasant to show you."

CHAPTER ELEVEN

THE SPANIARD was surprised by this suddenness and he recoiled slightly. With an evident expression of distaste at such unseemly behaviour, he pulled himself to his feet in preparation. Then, with his mask of indifference firmly back in place, he followed Harry to the deck. The *Navarro* had now come quite close, and like *Bucephalas* had dropped anchor. She lay bow on, her oars now shipped. There was some form of cage on the foredeck but Harry was so busy shepherding his guest that he couldn't spare it a proper look. The items that had been fetched off the sinking ship were laid out on the deck. On seeing them, San Lucar de Barrameda stopped dead, clearly perplexed. After a moment of examination he raised his eyes to meet the steady, sad gaze of his host.

"It is never a pleasant duty to tell a fellow sailor that one of his country's ships has been lost." Harry handed him the packet. "These are the ship's papers of a merchant vessel we came across called *Gauchos de Andalusia.*"

Harry got no further. This time San Lucar de Barrameda reacted as if he'd been slapped. His eyes held a startled expression and what little blood he had in his face drained away.

"*Gauchos?*" he whispered.

"We came across her drifting, with not a soul aboard, about a day's sailing to the south of the delta." The Spaniard couldn't help it. He looked at the guns lining the side as Harry continued quickly, "It was no act of ours that left her so. Nor was she fired on by any other vessel. Apart from an attempt to open her planking below the waterline, she was undamaged. Indeed we tried to tow her to Fort Balize. I'm sorry to say we didn't succeed."

"Where did this take place?" de Barrameda snapped.

Quite clearly, in his shock, he'd failed to hear all that Harry had said. The explanation which followed was complex, since he could only guess at the precise location. Certainly, the chart showed the Spanish merchantman's course, but lacking an accurate position of his own, Harry couldn't say with any conviction how long she'd been drifting and at what point they'd intercepted her. His reference to soup tureens and some sticky blood on the deck brought a growl of impatience, which Harry reacted to with stoical forbearance. He couldn't advance a full explanation of what had occurred, even if he did list the thoughts he'd had, and this was frustrating his guest. But as he tried San Lucar de Barrameda recovered some of his composure, only the pressure of his lips now betraying the depth of his anxiety. James was watching him closely, and he was probably the only one to see the skin tighten around his cheeks when Harry mentioned the sweet-tasting granules. By the time he'd heard about the top layer of boxes in the hold being opened such evidence of discomfort had disappeared.

"Naturally, unable to save the ship, we took out as much as we could in the way of personal possessions, plus everything that might provide a clue to what actually happened. Then we set course for New Orleans."

"That may account for your presence off Balize, Captain Ludlow. But it does not explain your presence so far north in the Gulf of Mexico. Just where were you headed when you came across the *Gauchos?*"

James, when he saw Harry's face, with that tightness a man adopts when suppressing a curse, suddenly understood what he was up to. Harry knew full well that Pollock was telling the truth. The Spanish might not welcome French colonists with any greater degree of enthusiasm than the American. The plan to drop them at Fort Balize having gone awry, his brother was trying to sneak the Frenchmen upriver on the back of this unfortunate discovery. Worried by the possibility of a refusal, he was keen not to ask that they be allowed to stay. A firm *no* would leave him with the unpleasant alternative of putting them ashore surreptitiously or even worse taking them elsewhere. De Barrameda had spotted the flaw and Harry was about to be forced to explain himself.

"I think there's one other thing you should see, Captain." Harry nodded to Pender, who was standing by the tarpaulin that covered the raft. "We found this as well, just before we raised Fort Balize. It was drifting on the tide. There were half a dozen casks tied to it, all empty, which we suppose had been used to dispose of the crew."

De Barrameda stared at the body impassively, which was more than could be said for Harry's crew. Denied the chance for a close look when it came aboard, they pressed forward as much as decency allowed.

"I'm sure you will recognize this form of punishment as one usually confined to pirates."

Harry's crew were not alone in their curiosity. Fernandez had actually walked up to the raft, and, like man who coveted them, knelt down to finger the victim's boots. To look at the state of his own footwear, scuffed and practically worn through with exposure to sea and sand, it wasn't too fanciful a notion. Suddenly he crossed himself. Then he stood up and resumed the stance he'd adopted since coming on deck, shoulders hunched, sucking his teeth, the picture of indifference. Hardly surprising since the entire conversation had taken place in a language he didn't comprehend.

"This was not the work of pirates," said de Barrameda.

"Naturally," Harry replied, "I bow to your superior knowledge. But I'm at a loss to know how you can be so certain."

"If you cast your eyes over my ship, you will observe that there is a caged man on the deck."

Harry turned to look, as did James and everyone else aboard. The *Navarro* had swung round slightly, giving a clearer view of her foredeck. The cage was easy to see now. Just as obvious was the man hanging by his wrists from the roof.

"Henri-Luc Charpentier, who claims to lead the vermin who occupy Barataria Bay. I burnt four of their vessels and chased the crews into the swamps. There have been no pirates at sea for days."

De Barrameda suddenly rapped out a series of orders that

made Fernandez jerk to attention. Harry only understood a fraction of what he said, but little genius was required to guess the rest. Once he'd received his instructions, Fernandez was over the side and into his cutter at the pace of a scalded cat. The rowers caught his mood and grabbed their oars. De Barrameda waited till they'd pushed off from the side, frowning at the untidy nature of their efforts, before composing his features once more, in order to address Harry.

"How can we thank you, Captain? You say it is sad to tell a man of the sinking of one of his country's ships." He nodded in the direction of the desiccated body. "How much worse to know that friends have suffered such a dread fate at sea."

"Captain Rodrigo was a friend?" asked Harry, solicitously.

Out of the corner of his eye Harry could see the Spanish cutter heading for the *Navarro*, not Fort Balize or the mouth of the river. Given the proximity of de Barrameda's ship any orders could easily have been shouted, which could only mean that the Spaniard didn't want him to hear them. That made him uneasy.

James, less distracted, was concentrating on this hidalgo sailor, observing the effect of Harry's question. He saw the skin tighten around the mouth again. Clearly the grief that the Spanish officer was about to convey made him uncomfortable.

"He was, indeed," de Barrameda replied. Then, as if aware of the discomfort this would cause his hosts, he waved an elegant hand towards his ship.

"As you will observe, I have sent Captain Fernandez over to the *Navarro*. I have given orders to my master to signal the galley with the best oarsmen aboard. They will row upriver at speed. The Barón de Carondelet must be told what has happened."

"And who, pray, is the Barón de Carondelet?" asked James.

"He is the Governor of Louisiana," snapped the Spaniard, as if such ignorance was inexcusable. "You, of course, must make your way there too. And as soon as my present mission is complete, I, along with the rest of my fleet, shall accompany you."

"Your present mission?" said Harry.

"I am here to rendezvous with two transports carrying troops from Havana."

Harry still didn't give the Spaniard his undivided attention. Part of that was focused on the *Navarro*, with him quietly wondering what orders Fernandez had imparted which caused so much activity along her decks.

"They are a day overdue," the Spaniard said, looking to the south, where his galleys now formed a line that blocked the route.

"I expect they have been delayed by the same weather that slowed our voyage," said Harry, a remark which earned him a cold look.

Fernandez put off from the *Navarro* and headed back to the fort, his eyes firmly fixed on the quarterdeck of *Bucephalas*. He was hardly ten feet away from the side before the signal broke out at the masthead. One of the galleys immediately dipped its oars and headed for the river mouth at an impressive pace.

"Do you wish to take these things aboard your own ship?" asked Harry, indicating the sea-chests and the box.

De Barrameda shook his head emphatically. "No, Captain Ludlow. I would rather you kept them. The Governor will want to question you himself. It is better that everything you took out of the *Gauchos* stays with you aboard your own ship."

"Sail, Capt'n," called the lookout, "due south."

De Barrameda, having looked aloft, first at *Bucephalas'* tops, then at his own, aimed a hard look at *Navarro*'s quarterdeck. He was upset that these ships should have been spotted by an *Inglese* first. This wasn't helped when the lookout added: "Two sail, your honour."

The five seconds of embarrassed silence that followed seemed like an eternity as the Spaniard continued to glare, first at his own ship, then at the rest of his little fleet. Finally a cry came from one, which was immediately taken up by the others. This was followed by a bustle on deck of the *Navarro*. A man appeared at the bows and informed his Captain, in Spanish, what he'd already learned in English. Aloft, Harry's lookout continued to reel off information about the approaching vessels, identifying them to de Barrameda's satisfaction as the ships with which he was to rendezvous.

"I must return to *Navarro*," he said abruptly.

Harry waited for him to call across the intervening water for transportation, only to find himself on the receiving end of a cold stare.

"The barge, if you please, Pender."

"Well, Harry, we are to be granted our wish, it seems. If we tell our Frenchmen we are going to New Orleans with them, they will jump for joy."

Harry didn't even drop his telescope, nor did he respond. James concluded he had cares he was loathe to share, since, as usual, most of the crew had stayed as far aft as they dared. The Spanish ships were hull up now, closing the distance slowly, the wind having dropped considerably with the heat of the day. Occasionally Harry would turn his glass to look at the fort, now a distorted image in the haze. With the accommodation so low in relation to the wooden walls there was no way of telling accurately what was going on inside. Yet enough activity showed, with men running to and fro on the firesteps, to indicate some form of bustle. He could see the deck of the *Navarro* with his naked eye and there was nothing there to reassure him of San Lucar de Barrameda's peaceful intentions, especially with the other three galleys still anchored across his stern. He stayed like this until the ships, broad-beamed merchant vessels, dropped anchor.

Various signals were exchanged between the Spaniards, with the odd one including the garrison of Fort Balize. After several of these, each emphasized with a signal gun, the cutter put off from the island, with Fernandez again sitting in the stern. Two boats had been lowered from the merchantmen and all three converged on the *Navarro*, where a party of marines had lined up to do the honours. De Barrameda was on deck to greet the arrivals and Harry watched to see how they stood in relation to each other. It was all revealed in the bowing, with only one individual, in a buff military coat and a braided hat, of enough stature to get by with a mere nod of the head to the Spanish Captain. They then approached the cage on the foredeck. A bucket of water brought some life to the man inside, but not much, and after trading a few insults with him the whole party went below.

"I dare say that we are a ripe topic of conversation, brother," said James. This time Harry turned to grin at him, as if to compensate for both his past and his continuing silence.

"You may whisper to me if you wish, Harry."

The clash of metal as the marines presented arms made both men turn their heads sharply. De Barrameda was back on deck with the military officer. Fernandez followed in their wake. The two senior officers got into one boat while the garrison commander went aboard his own. A signal gun banged and Harry saw one of the merchantmen begin to weigh anchor. The master hauled round his yards and started to edge in towards the island, a leadsman in the chains. Boats were lowered from the other three ships and slipped into his wake. Fernandez was ahead of them all, on course for the fort. But the two senior officers were taking no part in this. They were heading straight for the side of *Bucephalas*.

"El Señor Cayetano de Fajardo de Coburrabias."

"Brevity is not only the soul of wit," said James, so quickly and softly that only Harry picked it up. "A plainer appellation would do these men good."

"The military commander of the Louisiana Territory," added San Lucar de Barrameda, without warmth. "I have informed him of the unfortunate fate of the *Gauchos*. He has particularly asked to look at what you have discovered."

On being shown the raft, de Coburrabias examined it closely, all the while carrying on a heated conversation with de Barrameda. Even if he couldn't understand it, Harry was listening hard, trying to establish the relationship, in terms of rank, of these two individuals. Clearly, judging by the icy tone of the exchange, there was little love lost between them. But neither one backed down to the other, which led him to conclude that they were equals. Finally, subjected to another pointed enquiry, de Barrameda threw up a hand in angry disgust and walked back towards the Ludlow brothers. As he spoke to them, he adopted the same tone as he'd used to his fellow countryman.

"You have yet to tell me what you were doing in these waters."

Harry had to bite his tongue again, something that was hard for him judging by the look on his face. If the Spaniard noticed the effect of his condescension it didn't show. And the mention of the Frenchmen and their desire to land at New Orleans had no effect either. De Coburrabias had joined the party and listened, seemingly without comprehension, to the exchange. Eventually, bored, he barked a question. De Barrameda actually flushed, to James's mind showing for the first time that his body contained blood.

"Captain Ludlow, you will have observed that one of the transports is approaching Fort Balize. We are about to change the garrison and Captain Fernandez will be coming upriver with us. I am about to request that he and his men travel aboard your ship."

Harry's raised eyebrows forced him to adopt a faster mode of speech than suited his demeanour. "It is a request I have told El Señor de Coburrabias that you will be happy to comply with."

"That was rather presumptuous, sir," said Harry.

"No more than the idea that we will welcome any more French immigrants. The troops can bed down on your deck, and will only be aboard for two days at most. I must tell you that I am the senior naval officer in these waters and it would not please me to insist."

Harry walked to the rail and looked toward the fort. The boats that had accompanied the merchant ship, with the addition of several flat-bottomed affairs from the Fort, were busy off-loading men, who were being rowed ashore. A queue had formed by a small jetty as those who were being taken off the island waited to fill the newly vacated craft.

"Since the wind is fair for a passage upriver, Captain Ludlow, both Don Cayetano and I will go back to our ships. As soon as Captain Fernandez and his men are aboard you can get under way."

"Would I not do better to follow you? After all, you know the river better than I."

"Never fear, Captain Ludlow," said de Barrameda, quickly. "The current is sluggish at this time of year, with the sandbanks plain to the naked eye. And I have to escort the other two vessels and be available to provide a tow if required. If you wish for a pilot, I can certainly provide you with one of my master's assistants."

"That would be most kind," Harry replied.

Another florid bow followed, before San Lucar de Barrameda shepherded his companion through the gangway. Harry waited till his gold-braided hat disappeared before turning to Pender.

"Man the boats and get us off this damned sandbank. Clear the deck forward, as well. As soon as the soldiers are aboard stand by to get under way."

"Something tells me, Harry, that you're not a happy man," said James.

"I'm not, brother."

"Then let's turn our helm and head south."

"Have a look at the deck of the *Navarro,* James. Observe how crowded it is in the bows."

"Particularly around the cannon."

"Quite. El Señor Felipe San Lucar de Barrameda intends that we should go to New Orleans, and take his soldiers with us, even if he has to persuade us to do so against our will."

"Did you see his face when you named the *Gauchos?*"

"I did, James. And given that he's such a cold fish, I have the distinct impression that it was carrying something more important than that poor wretch lashed to the raft."

"Is that the reason for the soldiers?"

"It might be. But I could be worrying for nothing. Maybe it

is that other peacock, de Coburrabias, who doesn't want the men who've been here for a while mingling with his new draft from Havana."

"Must we obey him?" James asked.

"We are in shallow water, stuck on a sandbank, without charts I can put my trust in, with only light airs to fill our sails. Added to that we are stationary in the presence of four galleys that can not only bring to bear a great deal of firepower, but can get up speed immediately. And three of them are between us and the open sea. No, James. If I was going to defy our Spaniard I wouldn't do it here and in these conditions."

The men clearing the foredeck had to move the raft, and one asked Harry where he wanted it stowed.

"Break the damned thing up and throw it over the side," said Harry testily. "And stow the poor sod in canvas. But don't touch his clothing."

James looked over the side again at the *Navarro*. "Does it occur to you that he might suspect us of being responsible for the sinking of the *Gauchos,* as well of the death of her Captain?"

"Boat puttin' off from *Navarro*," called the lookout.

Harry paused for a second, to check that information, before replying to his brother's question. "Then he's a fool. What man in his right mind would sink a ship, sail towards its home port, show the evidence of his action openly on deck, then consent to an armed escort up a river like the Mississippi?"

"So we establish our innocent credentials by compliance."

"Precisely. And as a favour for letting them know of Captain Rodrigo's fate, and carrying the garrison of Fort Balize, they will allow us to disembark our Frenchmen."

"I wonder what it was aboard the *Gauchos* that was so important?"

"I hardly think," said James, "that it was brown, sweet-tasting granules reminding you of sugar."

Harry replied gravely, as he felt *Bucephalas* rock gently as she floated clear of the sand bar, "Let's hope that it wasn't the women."

CHAPTER TWELVE

JAMES WIPED the sweat from his brow, then eased his linen shirt to take advantage of the breeze. "Why in God's name, Harry, did they settle so far upriver? There's no wind around here at all and any number of places to build a settlement."

"You're seeing the Mississippi at its most benign, brother. I've never had experience of it myself, but I've been told it can be fierce. In the spring those sandy banks over yonder are under ten feet of water and there's a time when the current is so strong, and so full of debris, that any attempt to get upriver is fraught with peril."

"I rest my case," James replied.

Perspiring himself in the humid atmosphere, Harry turned to the young man beside him at the wheel, a master's mate from the *Navarro*. He, it seemed, suffered no ill effects from the humidity. In a combination of halting English, indifferent French, poor Spanish, and sign language, Harry repeated what he'd just said to James. The youngster was a native of northern Galicia, his mother tongue Basque. That gave him a strong accent which didn't help matters. But both being sailors they managed to communicate, and a discussion confined to eddies and currents, sandbanks and submerged hazards, given the time available, didn't tax them too greatly. Such a commodity as time was not at a premium. *Bucephalas* was making slow progress. The width of the river, a mile in some places, took most of the force out of the current. The wind, acting on his topsails, was enough to give him steerage-way, though not strong enough to cool the deck. Slight as the breeze was he was grateful for it. He knew that any drop in the southerly wind would mean he'd either have to put his boats out and tow, or heave to and wait. Even then it was flukeish, with the watercourses on either side, dark, moss-strewn caverns, providing vents that played tricks with the wind's strength and direction. The high vegetation, if Harry sailed too close to the bank, could kill it altogether. If it turned foul he'd need to kedge his ships all the way to New Orleans, using his boats to drop an anchor upriver of *Bucephalas,* then putting his crew onto the capstan to haul them the length of the cable, a manoeuvre repeated time and again as he inched his way north.

He looked towards the bowsprit, to the filthy Cuban soldiers lounging in the shade of an awning. As a group they gave the impression that they hadn't washed for months. Not one of their uniforms was clear of patches, all of which had begun life as different colours, and because of the climate the dye from these had seeped into the surrounding cloth. Had those colours not been so universally faded some would have looked like Harlequin. Harry wondered if their state was more to do with their last posting than any natural inclination against cleanliness. But then he saw Fernandez, with his hang-dog air and a uniform that was only marginally better than those of his troops. Their commander did nothing to elevate them as a group. Harry promised himself if the wind dropped then he would get hold of Fernandez and tell him to man the boats and tow. Harry'd discovered, from his Galician, that the reasons they were aboard *Bucephalas* were much as he'd suspected. Fernandez had got into trouble for beating one of his men near to death and was now in even hotter water because he'd allowed several men to desert from the island. Both in appearance and morale they were certainly not the kind of troops any sensible commander would want mixing with a new draft.

Behind him the merchantmen, with their broad beam and inelegant sail-plan, were finding things even harder. Bringing up the rear, the advantage held by the *Navarro* and her consorts could not have been more obvious. They put out their sweeps at every point where the river's course made the use of sail difficult, and manoeuvred round the sandbanks with an ease that made Harry

jealous. At least they'd cut down their pirate prisoner. Not that
he was afforded any protection from the elements, being still confined, now comatose, to the foredeck cage.

Looking around, and imagining the flood waters in spring, it
was obvious why so few people settled here: the lack of any high
bank plus the marshy nature of the low-lying delta islands. Each
island would certainly have elevated ground at the centre, but in
this part of the world that was measured in inches, not feet. Sometimes these mounds would be by the water's edge. Where that
happened the riverbank had generally been cleared to build a
house. In the main these were sad affairs, tumbledown and surrounded by squalid outbuildings, all showing signs of the
decrepitude such a sub-Tropical climate induced. But the further
north they went the more successful the planters, and some had
built substantial mansions. They were singular in their design, a
compromise between the memory of European dwellings and the
requirements of a wholly different climate. Where the houses had
an element of grandeur, the owners had taken trouble with the
land between them and the river, laying lawns. Given the rich alluvial soil, the grass that this produced was thick and deep in colour,
running down to a thin strip of sand where a jetty would pro-
trude over the muddy brown water of the river.

Naturally, since nearly all local transport was water-borne,
they passed a mass of small craft using the Mississippi as a high-
way. In the main these were pirogues, whole trees dug out to form
canoes, with one or two Europeans in the middle and blacks at
each end to work the oars. The more substantial boats, in width
and length the dimensions of an armed cutter, carried both humans
and freight; their blunt prow and position, generally inshore at
the point where the current was weakest, showed clearly that they
were flat-bottomed affairs, perfectly suited to the moss-strewn
waterways, termed bayous, that ran off the main rivercourse on
both sides. Harry climbed into the tops to get a better view as
they passed the fortifications at Plaquemines. The redoubts were
scarcely whole, the bastions mounted few cannon, and the set-up

had a delapidated air which bespoke of a place that, to official thinking, had outlived its usefulness.

They had to heave to for the night, just to the south of one of the islands—the young Galician pilot insisted on it, so that nothing floating downriver could collide with their hull. Since flotsam could include whole trees weighing several tons, it was a wise precaution. *Navarro,* along with the other galleys, all well lit, lay close by, their decks deserted, barring the watch officers, though judging by the noise from below the crews were in no hurry to get any sleep. The other ships were dark and silent. Fireflies danced in the evening air, which, close to thick vegetation, was filled with the sounds of the night, the cries of the birds mingling with the grunts and calls of animals, all overborne by the slightly sickly smell of a fecund, rotting swamp.

Harry and James, having just finished their supper, ruminated on the Frenchman and the vexed subject of their money. Basically, they were presented with a problem they'd never anticipated. Harry, intent on getting them to Louisiana, had assumed that a time would arrive when he would just hand it over to them, the method of getting it ashore a problem that could safely be left to the owners. That was a reasonable assumption when talking about an uncomplicated landing at a sleepy outpost like Fort Balize, not at all the same thing when faced with the organized customs officials of a major port. The unwholesome vision presented itself of the Ariadnes, artisans and tradesmen without any knowledge or experience of business, standing on the New Orleans quayside with a fortune of dubious provenance at their feet. At best they'd be defrauded by some local shark, at worst awkward questions would be posed about how they'd come by such a sum. That could lead to all sorts of complications. It might even see their money impounded by some zealous official.

"We must see them settled, Harry, with their fortune safely banked. And it has to be lodged with someone who will take a long-term interest in their welfare. It's the least we can do."

"I suppose you're right," said Harry, with an almost weary air.

"I take it we have no intention of hanging about?" asked James.

"None. We'll be off as soon as we've satisfied them about the *Gauchos*."

"And if they don't agree to accept the Ariadnes?"

"Then we'll land them somewhere between here and the delta," growled Harry. Then he saw the look in James's eye and added, with a great deal less passion, "You'll have to be at your most persuasive, brother, or we'll be obliged to take them on to Canada."

James was quick to respond. "This is not something I will allow you to depute to me, Harry. Though I will agree to stay here and give you my backing."

"That's very decent of you," he replied, with a sour expression.

"One of the advantages of being a mere passenger, brother."

The arrival of the very men they were talking about killed any reply of Harry's. Pender opened the door to admit Lampin, Couvruer, and two of their compatriots, who'd been detailed to escort them. Harry indicated that they should sit down, an offer which was declined.

"We shall be in New Orleans by early morning." That didn't elicit much response, since they knew already. "I also have to tell you that, judging by the way we were obliged to come upriver, landing there is unlikely to be a simple matter of picking up your belongings and leaving the ship as you please."

James coughed politely, in a bid to move Harry on, since their visitors could guess that too. They might not have heard what the Spaniard had said, but they'd have to have been dense indeed not to sense the frosty atmosphere.

"There are formalities to observe."

"Bribes might have to be paid," said Lampin.

His voice was flat, emotionless, and deliberately unfriendly. Harry put this down to the presence of his compatriots, but he was grateful to him, since sensible as Lampin was he'd got right to the nub of the problem. Neither the Frenchmen nor the contents of their chest could go ashore legitimately without clearance, and the two were very likely intertwined. They needed someone who was willing to circumvent any customs controls. That meant using their wealth as a lever with some reliable banker. Finding such a person was a task that only he and James had the experience to undertake. If the chest was inspected aboard, or opened by some petty official on the quayside, all hell could break loose. Sharing the money out merely multiplied the risk of discovery; it would quite rightly be interpreted as an attempt at evasion. But customs men the world over had greasy palms. So a few well-placed coins, delivered without haste to the right people, by someone who knew whom to bribe, would do the trick.

"Besides," he concluded, tactlessly, "how could you, thirty homeless Frenchmen, justify having in your possession so much wealth?"

"It would help, Monsieur," said Couvruer, as Harry paused, "if you told us what you intend to suggest."

"My proposal is simple. It will stay in my cabin, as my property, until we can find a place to lodge it."

"*Non!*" snapped one of the escorts, when this was translated.

"It is not a subject of debate," said Harry.

"Why?" asked Couvruer, his dark eyes steady and penetrating.

It was James who answered, his voice soothing and calm, in contrast to Harry's more abrasive delivery.

"My brother and I are accustomed to wealth, to dealing with bankers and money-men. If we ask them to come and see us they will do so readily. And we are in a position to ensure two things: that they are discreet and that they treat you properly in the future."

Harry cut in, his voice still a long way from the tone of gentle persuasion he'd suggested to James.

"I doubt any one of you has ever had possession of more than two gold coins. We carry letters of marque signed by King George. As privateers we don't have to explain the possession of wealth which in your hands would elicit a number of uncomfortable questions, especially since it cannot be said to have been come by honestly."

"Lacking experience in these matters," said James, "you may make an unwise choice that could cost you dear."

Harry spoke again, his impatience becoming increasingly obvious. "When we are satisfied then we will hand back to you what is rightfully yours."

"We have agreed," added James, softly, "that we are responsible for your well-being."

"Some of our men think you intend to rob us," said Lampin, quickly. Judging by the looks he was getting two of them were in the cabin. "I have tried to persuade them otherwise. This plan of yours will not aid me."

"Ask them this," snapped Harry. "If I was going to rob them, why have I come this far? You may also inform them that my brother and I are intending to go to a great deal of trouble on their behalf. If they don't like it, they will be doing us a great service by insisting that we wash our hands of the whole affair."

"It is your property and you will have it," James said, giving his brother a look of despair. "Every sous."

"I'm sorry if this offends you," Harry added, though he signally failed to sound compassionate. "You have my personal guarantee that your money is secure, and if that is not enough then I've no more to say."

"Your personal guarantee?" asked Lampin.

"Yes."

One of the two escorts opened his mouth to speak, but Lampin cut him off. "Very well, Captain. We shall say no more."

He turned so swiftly that Pender had to haul the door open. All four filed out with Harry's servant mouthing "saucy buggers" under his breath.

"Well, you handled that brilliantly, Harry," said James. "I've never seen such a contented bunch."

CHAPTER THIRTEEN

AT DAWN they noticed that one of their escorts had departed; being at the time assaulted by a quite astonishing number of mosquitoes they thought no more of it. Thankfully once out in the middle of the river this nuisance disappeared. Luckily the wind held, but that was soon working against them as, having passed Fort St Mary, they had the task of negotiating Englishman's Turn, named because a British naval Captain had been forced to retreat years before. After a further five leagues they came in sight of the city. The forest of masts lined the inland shore just at the point where the Mississippi, after a crescentlike bend, ran north to south, with the opposite shore half a mile distant. The foreshore had been built up into an embankment called a levee, first by the river, then by man to protect the area behind from flooding. Downstream there was but a single roadway, which crossed a short watercourse, both soon swallowed up by dense undergrowth, probably the sole land route leading to the plantations they'd already passed. Inland the heavy vegetation stopped abruptly, with a clear field of fire between it and the fortifications that had been built to protect New Orleans from attack. A long deep ditch surrounded the town, with a palisade of picketed cypress on the inner edge. Five-sided stone towers, bastions as well as gatehouses, stood at each corner right by the water's edge, the embankment between them providing protection for the riverside. A boat, flying a great Spanish pennant, put off from the shore before *Bucephalas* had passed the downriver bastion. Close to the main chains it swung round, the man in the bows calling out instructions to their pilot, quite clearly an indication that they should berth upriver.

Harry had left the wheel to the young Galician and made his way to the mainmast cap, so that he could see over the levee. From that higher elevation his view took in the whole of the original settlement. Behind the customs house and the shoreline factories the city seemed to be one extended building site. Few of the newly constructed houses and warehouses matched the older dwellings in style, being more Spanish than French. Thanks to the *Navarro*'s pilot, Harry knew that the city had recently suffered from a fire that had destroyed some four-fifths of the homes, workshops and factories, this before the effects of a previous conflagration had been erased. Both fires, it seemed, were a combination of French exuberance and the tinderbox nature of the building material, a mixture of wood, mud, and Spanish moss which caught fire when dry with astonishing rapidity, consuming everything that stood in its way. They came abreast of a large, dusty parade ground, with a group of Negroes dancing to a tuneless fiddle on the levee, an activity which seemed to be accompanied by much drinking. At the rear, to the left of the damaged cathedral church, the first storey of an imposing official-looking structure was nearing completion. Whatever had gone before, they'd learned their lesson, since this was to be entirely constructed of stone.

Harry glanced at the Frenchmen, who'd also come aloft, deeply curious about what could prove to be their new home. If any had heard the Spanish pilot's disparaging remarks about their race they didn't acknowledge it, any more than they now responded to Harry's crew. He suspected that they'd had enough of Englishmen, seeing their presence as a curse, and longed for nothing more than to be once more masters of their own fate. The Cuban soldiers were being hustled out of the bows by the sailors, who were getting ready to anchor. Harry heard many a curse aimed at them both for their dilatory ways and the filthy state in which they'd left the deck.

He turned his attention back to the port, assessing its mercantile status. The low tonnage of most of the seagoing ships was a clear indication that they carried most of their cargo to destinations close to the river-mouth, like the West Indies, Mexico and the Spanish Main. Only two, moored just upriver of the western bastion, had the build necessary to withstand an Atlantic crossing. This squared with something Pollock had said about the city only recently coming to life. The Spaniards had denied the Americans navigation rights ever since the state was founded, but in a sudden reversal of policy, a Senator Thomas Pinckney had persuaded the then chief minister to King Carlos, Manuel de Godoy, to allow them 25 years as an experiment. Because of that, trade was on an upward trend.

He could see no warships, other than the galleys. One, which they'd missed that morning, was berthed opposite the parade ground. The rest, with *Navarro* to the fore, having overtaken the merchant transports were now in his wake. Passing on, *Bucephalas* came abreast of the blunt-prowed riverboats, huddled close to each other at the far end of the levee. He was intrigued by the curious shape of these boats, which, with the exception of the odd trading galley, all had a shallow draught, a high freeboard, and a spacious deck cabin, looking like some form of primitive ark. This impression was reinforced by the single stumped mast amidships, which could carry a square sail. More biblical was the great sweep that jutted from the stern, worked by a man standing atop the deck cabin. One, just arrived from upriver, was steering for the shore. Two men stood in the bow with long poles, ready to fend off the craft already berthed, whose crews stood by the stern, their attitude quite clearly aggressive as they dared these newcomers to take so much as an inch of shaving off their woodwork.

The pilot guided them on to a point by the upriver bastion, some hundred yards short of a sandy beach. Beyond he could see clearly where the city had encroached into the abutting swamplands; some fine houses had been built and more were in the process of construction. Huge rafts, almost like floating islands, obviously used to transport freight downriver, had been pulled out of the water. Men scurried around breaking them up, the timber they provided being used on the houses. These mansions seemed

to have escaped the ravages of the recent fires, no doubt saved by
the firebreak between them and the city walls. All in all, the place
had an air of prosperity, the look of a town that was expanding
rapidly, just the location for a group of enterprising new immigrants, well provided with funds, to make their mark.

Harry slid down to the deck as the pilot swung the wheel to
bring them round and place them close to the two seagoing vessels he'd spotted earlier. Broad-beamed and of similar construction
to the *Gauchos,* they had half a dozen gunports each—no doubt
they carried several small-calibre cannon amidships. Their sides
were full of men, curious to take stock of this newcomer, and on
the nearest a party of soldiers, in smart white uniforms and armed
with muskets, were drilling on the poop, watched by a group of
officers.

The Cubans were gesticulating towards them. Fernandez had
raised his stained tricorne hat and was scratching his head. A sudden feeling of unease gripped Harry Ludlow. Neither soldiers nor
those officers had any place on what was clearly a merchant ship.
Looking back, he saw that the crews of the riverboats on their
sterns were assembled as if to watch a show. Even the prisoner in
the foredeck cage had stood up to see what was happening. The
splash of the sweeps indicated that de Barrameda and his consorts
had put on speed, closing the gap between themselves and
Bucephalas. Men were already by the guns, running them out to
threaten his ship. A sudden rumble had him turning towards the
shore, in time to see the great cannon poke out of the embrasures
in the stone bastion, and when he turned back towards the two
merchant ships, the soldiers had ceased drilling with their muskets, and now lined the side with their weapons aimed at him.

Harry could see San Lucar de Barrameda plainly across the gap.
Standing between his hastily constructed cell and the bows, as
finely dressed as before, he was staring at the *Bucephalas* with an
air that could only be described as malignant. The barge that had
escorted them to their berth was now alongside, with a younger,

less gaudily clad officer preparing to come aboard. Other boats had put off from the shore which he surmised were to be used to remove the Cubans. Some of Harry's crew looked towards him, as if seeking instructions to turf the sod into the river as soon as his head showed by the rail. He shook his head slowly, even if he was tempted to partake of a futile gesture in order to show how angry he was.

He was aware also of the presence of the others on deck—the Cubans, who seemed perplexed, and the Frenchmen and his brother, all looking to him to solve this sudden dilemma. The desire to satisfy them, to engage in something more than a mere gesture, had to be resisted. The muskets, given the range, didn't matter much, nor did the small-calibre guns on the merchant ships, now run out to threaten his larboard side. The Cuban soldiers, even if they showed no offensive spirit, would still need to be subdued, though Harry had no doubt his men could achieve that. Then there was San Lucar de Barrameda sitting downriver, with his guns run out, unlike Harry Ludlow. But that wasn't ultimately what gave him pause. Even if all these problems could be solved, he was still threatened by the guns of the fortress. With ample time to spare, they'd trained their cannon on the point chosen for him. At such close range, the 42-pound balls of those land-based monsters would rip through one side of the hull and come out the other. Probably, given their elevation, below the waterline.

"Pender, fetch the remains of Captain Rodrigo from below."

Once the empty boats were alongside, the officer came aboard, carrying in his hand a small piece of parchment. The Galician pilot was over the side in a flash, clearly desperate to be off so threatened a deck. Fernandez approached him and fired a sharp question, which was answered with equal speed and a complete lack of respect. The Cuban officer then walked over to Harry and spoke to him in halting French. It was hard to decipher, but Fernandez wished the Captain to know that he had no idea of San Lucar de Barrameda's intentions. Given the way the Cuban had been treated every time he'd seen them together, Harry believed him. As they started to disembark, Harry indicated the body sewn into its sack. This was picked up and lowered gently into the waiting boat, in sharp contrast to de Barrameda's captive, Charpentier. He was also going ashore, but with less ceremony or regard than Rodrigo. Indeed, the men of the *Navarro* took a savage delight in practically throwing him into the wherry that had come out to collect him. For the first time Harry was close enough to make out his features, which were handsome if somewhat bloated. But he held his head high, with an insolent cast to his features designed to irritate his captors.

Harry's attention was brought back to his own problems as the young officer stepped forward. The paper in his hand was examined closely, as if the messenger needed to check his facts, before he took off his hat, and bowing, addressed the group by the wheel.

"I am Lieutenant de Chigny. I present the compliments of the Governor of New Orleans, His Excellency Francisco Luis Hector, Barón de Carondelet."

His eyes searched for the response that would identify the man to whom the message was addressed. Everyone looked at Harry. Another small bow followed.

"Captain Ludlow, he respectfully requires that you come ashore with me, and that you answer to him for the fate of the *Gauchos*."

Harry replied sharply. "If the Governor doesn't respect the laws of neutrality, Señor, how can I believe you when you offer to respectfully escort me?"

The young officer looked at his note again, his lips moving silently as he rehearsed his words. Then he waved a reassuring hand at the circle of danger that enclosed *Bucephalas*.

"Please do not take these precautions amiss . . ."

"Precautions!" bellowed Harry, putting as much force into his bluff as he could. "Might I remind you, sir, as if you did not already know, that I came to this berth of my own free will. I required no coercion to make my way upriver, and I require none to make me stay. I have even gone some way to aiding your superior by acting as a troop transport."

The young officer looked confused, aiming a quick glance towards the *Navarro*. But his head snapped back towards Harry as he continued to berate him.

"Spain and my sovereign may no longer be allies, sir. But I have as yet received no intelligence that we are at war."

"We are not at war, Señor."

"Then why the guns?"

De Chigny replied robustly. "Surely you appreciate, Señor, that we have lost a valuable cargo."

"Not to us, sir," said James. "My brother did everything in his power to save your ship."

This seemed to increase the young man's confusion, and in the absence of an answer to that he waved the note at Harry. "I have my orders, Señor."

"And if I decline?" snapped Harry.

That produced an interesting response in the messenger. Hitherto a supplicant, and evidently confused, he pulled himself upright, jammed his hat back on his head, and addressed Harry in a more military fashion.

"That, Señor, would be unfortunate. The Governor has been good enough to issue an invitation. If you do not accept it, I will be obliged, with the considerable means at my disposal, to insist."

James replied on Harry's behalf, his voice even. "I think it would be more fitting, sir, given the nature of the service my brother has done Spain, for the Barón de Carondelet to call upon us."

"Then, Señor, it is plain that you, along with all the others aboard this ship, misunderstand the nature of the summons."

"Ah!" James replied, waving an elegant hand, like a man who'd just nailed a particularly annoying paradox. "It is a summons, not an invitation."

"My English does not extend, Señor, to a recognition of the difference."

"That, young man, may explain a great deal of your country's recent decline. Let me enlighten you to the damning accuracy of the English language. Great Britain invited you to partake in a war against the forces of the Revolution. Due to the incompetence of your armies, those same people summoned your King to sign an ignominious peace. The word you would use in such circumstances is surrender."

Harry, who couldn't fail to see how James's barb had wounded the Spanish officer, cut in. "Well, brother, if I had any chance of a refusal, your desire to exercise your sense of humour has buried it."

"I wouldn't want them to think us intimidated, Harry."

Harry responded to that with a grin.

"Certainly not. And it wasn't much of an opportunity anyway. But just so I don't miss a chance to convince them, I'd like you to accompany me." The grin faded quickly when he turned to address de Chigny. "I will come ashore in my own barge. You may escort me if you wish. But I warn you, sir, lay one finger on me or any of my men, and you will find yourself required to explain your actions to His Britannic Majesty's government. Pender!"

Harry's servant was already moving before he spoke, issuing orders to haul the barge alongside.

"Is there anything you want us to do while you're ashore?" he asked.

"There's nothing you can do."

"And if they try to take over the ship?"

Harry indicated the huge cannon, their muzzles poking out of the stone embrasures. Behind them, smoke drifted lazily into the air.

"You could try to sink her. But I think those shore batteries are better equipped than you or I to achieve that."

CHAPTER FOURTEEN

THERE WAS a fussy, bustling quality about the Barón de Caron-delet. Small, round of face and body, dressed in an old-fashioned way, he moved constantly; sitting down only to stand up again; pacing to his desk to examine a paper that was immediately dis-carded; darting forward to examine his "guests" before returning to stand behind his high-backed chair, every word accompanied by an exaggerated gesture of the hand. His speech was rapid, made very evident in his heavily accented, near-incomprehensible Span-ish. Enough could be gleaned by the Ludlow brothers to be sure that he was questioning de Chigny about what had happened on the deck of the *Bucephalas*. Harry and James were subjected to quick, penetrating stares, rendered more malevolent by blue pro-truding eyes and a flushed complexion, allied to a habit of standing, feet apart, hands on hips, during each curt examination. James, in between these unfriendly stares, indicated to Harry the portrait on the wall behind his desk. Clearly the Governor had sat for it, though the artist had taken care to soften his subject's grosser fea-tures to produce the image of a quite attractive human being.

Finally, having exhausted his interrogation, carried out in Spanish to exclude the brothers, de Carondelet turned to include them. But his voice, even in French, held a sneering quality and he deliberately kept his back to them, rifling the papers on his desk as though such documents were of vastly more importance than these two Englishmen.

"My aide informs me that you claim neutrality; that your jour-ney to New Orleans was made of your own free will."

"Do you dare to doubt it, sir," James replied, his voice cold, slow and deliberate, in sharp contrast to the staccato, derogatory tone of the Governor.

De Carondelet, clearly unused to being addressed in such a manner, spun round, adopting the same aggressive pose he'd fixed them with earlier. "Do you really expect us to believe that you have come all this way on a charitable mission to find a home for a group of displaced Frenchmen?"

"I grant you any man who lacks charity himself would find such a thing difficult to comprehend."

"Might I remind you, Señor, who you're talking to? I am the Governor and Intendant of the entire Louisiana Territory. As such, I command respect."

If he'd hoped to frighten James, either by his look or his haughty tone, he failed abysmally. Harry suppressed a smile as he saw his brother's eyebrows lift in mock surprise, a sure sign that the riposte that was coming would, to the Barón's ears, be even more unwelcome.

"Then I need hardly remind you, a high-ranking subject of the King of Spain, that good manners are a prerequisite both of your office and of your station as a gentleman. I would also observe that the lack of such manners would shock your sovereign, should he ever have the misfortune to hear of it."

"Does someone of your persuasion dare to check me regarding my manners?"

This question was accompanied by a sweep of the hand large enough to encompass the whole territory, before the Barón turned back to his desk.

The languid tone disappeared suddenly. James's face and countenance visibly hardened. "If you continue to behave in such a boorish manner, sir, I will continue to point out to you that it is unsuitable, unbecoming, and rude."

"As well as unproductive," added Harry quickly, as de Carondelet spun round again. His eyes looked set to pop right out of his head, evidence of a temper that could hardly benefit the Ludlows, or their passengers. "Even if you find it hard to accept, it is the plain truth. I have an obligation to these men, who are refugees from St Domingue. Naturally, given a choice of destination, they chose one with a climate, plus an ambiance, that suited them."

"We have no room for more French paupers."

"They are far from paupers, Barón," said James. "In fact I think they will bring more to your colony than they could possibly take out."

Harry cut in quickly, lest James say too much. "Each one is a skilled artisan, Barón, which is something no colony can be over-burdened with."

De Carondelet didn't reply. Instead he fixed his gaze at a point midway between the brothers, for all the world like a Solomon contemplating justice. Harry decided to take the initiative on what he suspected was the true reason for their presence here.

"Clearly the *Gauchos* was carrying something of value, Barón, the loss of which had upset you. While that something is not in our possession, if we can assist you in any way in finding the people who stole it, we will do so. But first you must tell us what it is."

Eyes so bulbous couldn't, in the conventional sense, narrow. But the lids closed enough to give de Carondelet a cunning air. "If you have no idea what it is, Captain Ludlow, how can you possibly know that it is valuable?"

"Because I am, like you, sir, no fool. Captain San Lucar de Barrameda—"

De Carondelet's hand cut down in a vicious gesture as he interrupted Harry. "It is only through his timely arrival at Fort Balize that you are here. If he hadn't turned up you would have dropped off your passengers, left that dim-wit Fernandez with some platitudes to swallow, and escaped into the Gulf of Mexico, no doubt to murder more poor innocents."

"We'd just come from the Gulf of Mexico," said Harry, in a voice that was so loud it was close to a shout. "And let me say that I dislike the implication of some form of culpability for either the loss of the *Gauchos* or the death of Captain Rodrigo."

De Carondelet grunted, clearly not convinced.

"If we were involved, can you explain to me what we were doing off Fort Balize in the first place, having just taken and robbed a Spanish merchant ship, then having committed murder? That, Barón, would be an act of madness."

James cut in, his tone no less sharp than Harry's. "And might I remind you that the only reason you know that the *Gauchos* was lost or that someone is dead, is because we have had the good grace to tell you."

The Governor, clearly agitated, started to dart about the room, very much in the same manner as he had when interrogating his aide. A list of accusations poured forth, each made in a disjointed manner which exactly matched his jerky movements.

"Bluff! Subterfuge! Lies! You wouldn't have been there if our fleet of galleys hadn't caught you." He faced them for half a second before throwing himself into his chair. "Cunning, I grant you. We were bound to find out, in time. No doubt you planned to take other ships; to kill other people. The *Gauchos* was such a rich prize, a man like you would wonder if there might be others. Thank the good Lord that San Lucar de Barrameda smelled a rat. Like all pirates, your cowardice is your abiding trait."

"We are privateers, sir!" snapped Harry.

De Carondelet leapt to his feet again, his voice rising. "A word. Drake, Morgan, Hawkins titled themselves in the same way. But say it to a Spaniard and he will yell pirate, especially when the villain is an Englishman."

He leant forward on his desk with such force that half the papers it contained were scattered on the floor. "You may think you've stolen my gold and silver, but I shall recover it, even if I have to try you on the rack to find out where it is concealed."

"Gold and silver?"

De Carondelet stopped suddenly, his voice softening. "There. You acknowledge it."

"Everything that we found of any value, Barón, is on our ship," said James. He was about to continue when Harry held up a restraining hand.

"Where did El Señor de Barrameda tell you that he first sighted us?" asked Harry.

"South of Balize, of course."

"Not south, Barón. We were off Balize. We were hove to, waiting for the boat carrying Captain Fernandez to come out from the fort."

Harry was bluffing, hoping that since no one had mentioned it the fact that he'd run aground was unknown. De Carondelet started to search the untidy heap of papers. De Chigny, hitherto silent, sensing his mounting frustration, began to clear those which littered the floor. Even unable to find what he sought, the Governor replied to Harry with complete assurance.

"Not true. It was only the sight of the fleet in the offing that forced you towards Fort Balize in the first place. You were made to run, hemmed in by his presence, and of necessity had to concoct this tale."

"I take leave to observe that you are no sailor, sir," said Harry. "But even you must see, by the merest glance, that Captain Fernandez would only approach a vessel that he could both see and reach."

De Carondelet finally found the document he was seeking. He held the paper close to his face so that he could read it. His voice had a note of triumph as he continued.

"You were inshore."

"That is in the report you have?"

"It is!"

"Which came to you from the Captain of the *Navarro?*"

"Exactly."

"If you can explain to me how Captain San Lucar de Barrameda can have us out in the Gulf of Mexico, forced to run, while being inshore at one and the same time, I'd be obliged."

"That is irrelevant, Captain. You openly state you are a privateer, a man whose business is to take and destroy your sovereign's enemies."

"Of which Spain is not one."

The pause was infinitesimal, the actual answer sounding contrived. "Such things are hard to prove out at sea."

"So you choose to believe the obvious contradictions in Captain San Lucar de Barrameda's report?"

"Are you impugning the honour of one of my officers?"

"I have had enough of this," said James. "San Lucar de Barrameda is a liar and this, sir, is a complete fabrication. If you don't withdraw it—"

Harry wasn't quite sure what stopped James. It could have been the absurdity of issuing a challenge to such a man. More likely it was the way that de Carondelet suddenly collapsed, falling backwards into his high-backed chair like a punctured Montgolfier balloon. The Barón put one hand to his forehead, in a clear gesture of despair. De Chigny stepped forward and spoke to him quietly, before turning to the Ludlows and asking them if they'd leave the room.

"I don't think we're destined for the rack," said James, looking along the timbered veranda that ran along the front of the wooden building.

"Don't be too sure, brother," Harry replied. De Chigny came out of de Carondelet's office and, giving them an angry glance, headed off down the passage.

James addressed his retreating back loudly enough to ensure his remark was heard. "I cannot say that I'm overly impressed with Spanish hospitality."

"Damn the hospitality, James," said Harry, walking to the rail and looking out to where the ship's masts showed above the levee. "That old man was in a stew because of the report that San Lucar de Barrameda sent upriver. Clearly the solution the good Captain offered was one he dearly wanted to accept. It's as if, in some way, merely having someone to blame would absolve him of responsibility."

"Which means?"

"It means that whatever was on the *Gauchos* was there by his approval."

"It might even be his own personal property."

"No," Harry replied, his face creased in concentration.

"I wonder how much gold and silver she was carrying?"

"Enough to reduce the Governor of New Orleans to the quivering syllabub we've just witnessed. Do you think the Spaniards could have discovered new mines here in Louisiana?"

"That's perfectly possible, given the size of the territory."

"Think of the implications of that, brother."

"Such a find would do wonders for de Carondelet's prospects."

"What about Spain's prospects? Remember this place was originally French and even King George had his eye on it at one time. The French gave it away because it was costing them money and we, having lost North America, also lost interest in the Mississippi delta. The Spanish are only here because no one else really wants the place."

"Add mines full of bullion and . . ."

James didn't really need to finish that sentence. The Dons had been forced to cease hostilities with France partly through being nearly bankrupt. Despite the wealth plundered from the New World over the centuries, Spain was poor. If France was strong enough to impose peace, it was also strong enough to take back possession of New Orleans.

"It's not the kind of cargo that's normally consigned to an ordinary merchant ship," said Harry. "All the precious metal that Spain mines in the New World is collected at one point, usually Cartagena or Vera Cruz, then shipped home in convoy."

"So that's a good way to disguise the shipment, Harry. Especially if you wish neither to share credit with the Viceroy in Mexico nor alert an overwhelmingly French population to the find."

"True. That might also explain the way it was being transported."

"Enlighten me."

"It was hidden. I have a feeling that even the Captain didn't know it was aboard."

"How can you say that?"

"I can't, James. But if you were carrying a lot of specie, and it has to be a substantial amount to so rattle de Carondelet, you wouldn't let anyone near you, friend or foe, without taking some precautions."

"You didn't with the *Navarro*."

"My choices, in that respect, were severely limited. Also I had no reason to fear them."

"I dare say you know where it was hidden too."

Harry smiled, since James's tone was clearly sarcastic. "Surely it had to be in those casks with those strange sweet granules? Remember, each one had been opened, each one scooped out just below the surface."

That made James pensive. "I was watching de Barrameda when you mentioned those. He went quite green around the gills."

"Which suggests that I'm right. He knew about the cargo. No wonder he didn't shout his orders to the *Navarro*."

"He did more damage by not doing so. But we were with him before the boat set off upriver. How did he write to de Carondelet?"

"He must have sent another despatch by that galley we missed this morning. But I can't fathom for the life of me why he did it. Surely he doesn't actually believe we took the *Gauchos*."

"Is that a question, Harry?"

That produced a wan smile. "Not really, James. But you remember I said to you that whoever overran the ship was known to the Captain, and the crew."

"So it's unlikely to be a pirate."

"Even more so given that de Barrameda had just attacked their base."

"One could have slipped past him."

"Perhaps he did the slipping, James."

"You think de Barrameda might be the one?"

Harry just shrugged. "I'm really not concerned, James. I don't care who it was. Just as long as we can convince the Barón that it wasn't us."

"It's intriguing, though."

"There's another odd thing, brother. No one has even alluded to the rest of the crew, or the passengers."

They were left kicking their heels for a good hour, with James's temper matching the rising heat of the day. The sun was full up in the sky, and he was fuming, before de Chigny returned, hurrying in the footsteps of San Lucar de Barrameda. The Spanish Captain deigned to offer them a small bow, accompanied by a cold stare, before throwing open the door and entering the Governor's quarters. The aide managed a slightly more friendly look, almost a smile, before he too disappeared.

"Something tells me our stiff-necked friend has a little explaining to do. I must say the prospect calms me somewhat. I wonder if de Carondelet will bring us face to face."

"Don't go expecting an apology if he does, brother. Our Spanish peacock is not the type."

The door opened abruptly. De Chigny, his face a mask, beckoned for them to re-enter. The day outside was now hot enough to warm the interior of even the most substantial building, but it would never lift the chill in this room. De Carondelet, who seemed to have recovered a degree of composure, was standing still, hands behind his back, beside a pile of papers on his desk. He gave them a curt nod of greeting. San Lucar de Barrameda was staring at a point just above the Governor's head. He didn't move an inch to acknowledge their arrival. With a show of unnecessary ceremony, the aide picked up the report from the desk and handed it to de Carondelet. The Governor pulled it close to his face again, and examined it for a moment before lifting his protruding blue eyes to address Harry.

"You claim that you cannot fix the position of the *Gauchos* with any accuracy."

"No, I cannot. And if that in your hand has any bearing on the information I gave Don Felipe, then it will tell you why."

"A hurricane?"

"It damaged my chronometers."

"Don Felipe recalls a heavy swell in the Gulf, Señor. But no hurricane."

"Then I would hazard that he was too far north to feel its effects," said James. "And I say that as someone who openly confesses to be no sailor."

"Thank you, James," said Harry, adopting a tone that was sharp enough to convey the message that the less he said the better. Certainly James got the hint, since he flushed slightly to be so openly rebuked. Harry longed to tell him that they were safe, merely going through the motions necessary to assuage San Lucar de Barrameda. "I'm sure the Captain of the Navarro would be the first to admit that a heavy swell in one area can easily indicate a hurricane elsewhere."

San Lucar de Barrameda managed to nod without in any way dropping his eyes.

"When you first signed the Navarro, you were in the act of dropping anchor off Fort Balize?"

"That is so, Excellency," Harry replied, swiftly.

"So a lookout, seeing only your masts, with sails still aloft, might assume that you were still in deep water."

"He might."

"You must understand, Captain Ludlow, that the presence of any armed British ship in these waters is a cause for alarm."

"Which is why, Excellency, I took great precautions to ensure that all should observe my peaceful intentions."

"I'm sure you did, Captain Ludlow, I'm sure you did." Carondelet spoke in a soothing voice. San Lucar de Barrameda sniffed loudly, unable to contain his irritation. "But I wonder if you can truly understand the very natural suspicions that a ship like yours engenders in so sensitive an area."

"I think I've already acknowledged that."

"Then you will readily appreciate Captain San Lucar de Barrameda's quite commendable apprehensions."

"That is not to say that I accept them."

"It would be pleasant to say that those suspicions have been entirely laid to rest. Pleasant, but untrue. You must also understand that, not being a sailor myself, I have to heed the advice of the men who understand these things."

Harry understood perfectly. He was going to be asked to provide a sop to ease San Lucar de Barrameda's wounded pride. So be it, if it was something he could do without too much personal loss, he would oblige. After all, as a *quid pro quo,* he could demand that any obstacles to his landing his passengers should be removed.

The Barón de Carondelet put down his paper and smiled at the Ludlow brothers for the first time.

"This being so, Captain Ludlow, and so there can be no further misunderstanding, I have granted Don Felipe permission to search your ship."

CHAPTER FIFTEEN

BOTH BROTHERS tried not to gasp, but the implications of what de Carondelet had just asked were so obvious that it really couldn't be avoided. Harry's immediate response was to try to bluff, but his voice lacked the necessary assurance to make the required impact.

"That would be to surrender our rights as neutrals."

De Carondelet, who was expecting easy compliance, was quite taken aback by the reaction. "Come, Captain Ludlow. If, as you say, your encounter with the *Gauchos* was fortuitous, and that everything you took out of her hull is already accounted for, what have you to fear from a search of your ship?"

To insist too emphatically was to ensure that the very thing he sought to avoid would happen. San Lucar de Barrameda was no customs official. The image, firmly fixed in his mind, of him standing over the Frenchmen's chest, horrified Harry. He had to say something that would deflect such a possibility.

"That is precisely the point, Excellency. I cannot think what grounds there are for such a search. Either the good Captain accepts that a genuine error has been made or he doesn't."

San Lucar de Barrameda spoke for the first time. "If I didn't, Señor, we would not be standing here now. You would be in the bowels of my ship, in chains."

Harry fought the desire to respond in kind, to tell a man he considered a pompous oaf to go and jump in the Mississippi. Instead he adopted the same overly polite manner he'd used on first meeting de Barrameda, hoping that the strangled tone so very obvious to him wasn't apparent to the Spaniards.

"It shows great nobility to admit to an error, sir, a quality I never doubted you held in abundance. You are welcome to come aboard as my guest. You're more than welcome to dine in my cabin. But my own pride would find a search of the ship demeaning."

San Lucar de Barrameda didn't reply to Harry. He merely looked at his superior, as if to say that by having to withdraw his previous report he understood the consequences of the word demeaning much better than this Englishman. De Carondelet clearly agreed, or at least was not prepared to inflict further humiliation on his subordinate. The words that followed may have lacked conviction, but they made any further protest futile.

"Don Felipe has the safety of the colony at his heart, Captain. If my senior naval officer insists that a search is required, then good sense alone forces me to agree to his request. Besides, there is the very valid point that were you carrying cargo of any kind, you'd be subjected to customs clearance for anything you chose to land. But please do not take it as an insult in any way. As to dinner in your cabin, I for one would be most flattered, and will readily avail myself of that invitation once the search is concluded."

James, when he cut into the conversation, spoke with studied languor, his gaze wandering to the overly flattering portrait hanging behind the Governor's head. Yet somehow, regardless of the lazy tone, his voice demanded attention.

"I seem to remember you remarked that there was a quantity of gold and silver on board the *Gauchos*." San Lucar de Barrameda grunted, de Chigny sighed, while de Carondelet nodded unhappily. Clearly no one relished being reminded. "Though I have to say that I don't recall you mentioning the value."

"That would be because I didn't, Señor Ludlow."

James didn't respond immediately, as if waiting for the Governor to complete his sentence. When this didn't happen he raised a quizzical eyebrow, to indicate that by declining to continue de Carondelet was being obtuse.

"While we were waiting outside, kicking our heels, my brother advanced the theory that your property was hidden in the boxes containing those strange brown granules."

"You mean the sugar?"

"We thought it to be sugar, but were unsure."

"Made with a process invented here," said de Chigny, looking to the Governor to check that his intervention wasn't unwelcome. "One that could help secure the long-term future of Louisiana."

De Carondelet wasn't listening to James or his aide. He shot Harry a look full of enquiry, mild compared to the Captain of the *Navarro*'s. But Harry's attention was on James: busy searching for a method to allay the Spaniard's suspicions, as well as deflect his intentions, he wondered if James had gone mad. But if his brother picked up the look, one that begged once more for silence, he completely ignored it.

"He also reasoned that if it had been so concealed, not even the Captain of the *Gauchos*, Captain San Lucar de Barrameda's old friend Rodrigo, knew of its presence."

"Rodrigo was a friend of yours?" snapped de Carondelet, his head jerking round.

San Lucar de Barrameda, mystified, shook his head slowly. Then like a man recalling a long lost memory, he raised a hand. "I told these people he was my good friend in an attempt to gain more information about what had happened to the *Gauchos*. As for Rodrigo, I never spoke to the man, except to inform him that I intended to follow him downriver."

"You left New Orleans at the same time as the *Gauchos*?" asked Harry, trying to alter the course of the conversation. All he got from San Lucar de Barrameda was a swift display of temper.

"What concern of that is yours, Señor! Do you think you have the right to question my actions?"

Harry didn't get a chance to reply, since James beat him to it.

"None whatever, Captain. But you will just have observed one very obvious fact; that my brother has an enquiring mind and a sharp brain. While that is often a cause for concern, he is, I must tell you, adept at finding solutions to seemingly insoluble puzzles. This, of course, cannot be achieved without asking questions, some of which can, on occasion, border on the impertinent. But he has advanced these theories. So, I am curious to know, having listened to his speculations, if what he says is true."

He turned his gaze towards de Carondelet, who was still looking suspiciously at his subordinate. "And given that he is blessed with this arcane skill, and your treasure is missing, I would venture to suggest that his abilities might be of some use to you."

James's next remark, aimed at San Lucar de Barrameda, was well larded with sarcasm. "I am right in thinking you wish to recover it, Captain?"

The Governor looked at James as though he hadn't heard him properly.

"Was the gold and silver hidden in the sugar boxes?"

"Yes."

"Without the knowledge of Rodrigo?"

De Carondelet nodded.

"And the value?"

"Two hundred thousand dollars."

"And how many people knew it was there?" asked Harry, his mind racing. The money the Frenchmen had in that chest approximated very closely to the amount de Carondelet had just mentioned, something of which James was aware. Yet he gave no indication that it registered.

"Surely that is none of our concern, Harry," said James, without responding. "That is, unless his Excellency seeks your assistance."

That earned him a proper glare, which had no effect at all. Likewise de Carondelet didn't react to what was clearly an invitation to share his worries with this visiting Captain. James shrugged, displaying seeming indifference.

"Well, Excellency, since you insist on searching *Bucephalas,* I suggest it be done quickly. Our crew, as well as your soldiers and sailors, must be suffering somewhat from extended exposure to the heat."

De Carondelet turned to San Lucar de Barrameda. "If you wish to carry on, Captain."

"No!" replied James, sharply. "If you don't mind, Excellency, we must insist that you supervise the search personally."

"Me?"

"You must understand," James continued smoothly, without looking at de Barrameda, "that to explain my reasons for saying such a thing, here in this room, would hardly be a recipe for harmonious relations."

If San Lucar de Barrameda picked up the allusion it didn't show on his face. But de Carondelet and de Chigny understood perfectly. The Ludlows were not about to trust the search to a man who'd already comprehensively lied about them. The Governor looked towards his aide, but before he could suggest that he undertake the task, James cut him off.

"I know you are a man who understands *amour propre*, Excellency, and that you will do everything necessary to maintain our dignity, in the same way that you care for that of your officers. And if such a request seems demeaning to you, then come aboard as our guest."

Harry, while admiring the diplomatic way that James had manoeuvred the conversation, couldn't see what difference it made. It didn't matter who searched the ship. If de Carondelet ordered that brass-bound chest to be opened, which he was almost certain to do, and saw what lay inside, then the result would be just the same.

"And, sir, having practically accused us both of piracy, it would go some way towards restoring our faith in Spanish justice."

"De Chigny," said de Carondelet to his aide, after a moment's pause, "call out the escort and ask my servant to fetch my hat."

"Splendid," said James. "By the way, this gold and silver of yours, how was it made up?"

"What?"

"I was just thinking that even in proper leather pouches, it would be a dangerous thing to do, placing coins in boxes of loose granules."

"We're not fools, Señor Ludlow," replied San Lucar de Barrameda. "The money was shipped in ingots."

The look that James gave Harry was triumphant, which his brother didn't begrudge him at all.

On the way back down to the levee, James chatted to de Carondelet with seeming unconcern. Harry, alongside San Lucar de Barrameda, while gnawing away at the problem presented by that chest, was content to ignore him and take stock of their surroundings. Ashore, the amount of construction work was even more evident, and close to, he could see the shells of those buildings which had perished in the fire and had yet to be demolished. Naturally, given the number of de Carondelet's escort, they were the object of some scrutiny as they marched along. Crowds gathered at each intersection to stare, and had to be restrained from advancing into the Governor's path by his soldiers. Several people hissed at the party, and Harry heard the odd French curse aimed in their direction. But most of the comments, loudly delivered, were a lame play on the Governor's name. They called him *Cochon du lait*. Harry wondered how a native French speaker would translate that; either as a milk-fed pig, or a pig in milk. Whichever, it wasn't flattering. More importantly, the populace who mouthed this insult, though not really threatening, showed no fear of their Spanish masters. This explained the size of their escort, as well as the readiness they appeared to have to protect the Governor. Indeed, some of the soldiers, a much smarter bunch than those from Fort Balize, were more rough than really necessary when pushing back people who'd only assembled because they were curious.

The majority of the population were Europeans, some dressed as if they were walking the streets of Paris. They'd adopted the severe cut of clothes made fashionable by the puritans of the

Revolution, even the totally unsuitable hats, as if wishing to make a statement of their allegiances, and since they were nearly all men it gave them a sombre hue. But there were ample flashes of colour, provided by the majority of the Negroes and mixed breeds. The men, with skin tones varying from pale brown to deepest black, dressed in coloured silk coats, waistbands and scarves, though the women, with fantastically decorated head-dresses festooned with glittering decorations of gold, silver, and glass, really provided the plumage. And their haughty bearing, allied to their elegant carriage, said more about their status than a printed sign.

There were Negro slaves in Louisiana, but it was originally a French colony, with that nation's lax attitude to stratification, and a high percentage of the coloured population were free. There were even Indians walking about, the men selling fruit from trays which hung around their necks. The few women he saw had the more onerous task of carrying great bundles of wood, tied to their backs and held in place by a strap around their head. As a man who despised slavery, Harry was entranced to see the races mixing on equal terms. He'd had many occasions to contest the contrary view in the past. It would be pleasant to have those people here now, to see for themselves the harmonious results that could be achieved by ignoring the colour of a man's skin. Mentally he made a note to request that James sketch some scenes of the free and easy nature of New Orleans life, so that they could be shown not only to the bigots but to Wilberforce and his Anti-Slavery Society. This would provide them with ammunition to silence their critics, whose only claim to racial superiority was wholly based on a desire to grow rich in the lucrative slave trade.

As they crested the levee he looked to see if there had been any change in the predicament of his ship. Someone had moved the awning from the bows to the quarterdeck, which provided shade for those on board; no one had seen fit to provide for those Spaniards who surrounded them. A small group of Indians were by the water's edge, but they moved away swiftly as the soldiers approached. Pender sat in the barge, crouched down under a large sennit hat, ignoring the men guarding him. He looked up at the sound of their footsteps, and seeing the brothers, gave them a huge welcoming smile.

"Man your oars, lads," he said happily. "Captain's back."

"You will, of course, accompany us, your Excellency?" said James to de Carondelet. Then he turned to San Lucar de Barrameda. "You have, I believe, sufficient transport of your own."

"James!" said Harry, with some asperity. He might dislike the man, loathe him even, but this was no time to be making matters worse.

"Forgive me, brother," he replied, all the while looking at the Spanish sailor. "Such a want of manners can occur in the most careful breast. All it takes is sufficient exposure to a certain type of condescension. You may, of course, Don Felipe San Lucar de Barrameda, travel in our barge."

De Barrameda spun on his heel and headed back up the levee to his own ship's boat. With elaborate care, James personally assisted de Carondelet into their barge. As they were rowed out to *Bucephalas* he asked about the process that had turned sticky molasses into those dry brown granules. While de Carondelet knew who'd invented it, and what it meant for the trade in terms of transportation and preservation costs, the actual method was a mystery.

"It is nevertheless, Señor Ludlow, an astounding achievement, which has been attempted by many an inventive planter."

"It occurs to me, Barón, that once we have you aboard, there is something we can show you that will astound you even more."

"And what would that be, Señor Ludlow?"

"As you know, we have just come from cruising the Caribbean. My brother said the pickings would be rich but I doubt even he knew how successful he would be. It will be our pleasure to show you the results of that cruise."

De Carondelet was staring at the open chest with disbelief, his bulbous blue eyes catching the sunlight that streamed through the rear windows of the main cabin to bounce off the mass of heaped coins that had been emptied out of their pouches. He glanced at Pender, who'd dragged the chest from Harry's sleeping cabin and undone the padlock. He now stood back, key in hand, trying to look nonchalant, as if the ownership of such a fortune was an everyday occurrence.

"Where did it come from?" demanded San Lucar de Barrameda.

Harry copied the words James had said to de Carondelet in the barge, which, with reservations, was nothing but the truth. But regardless of the conviction in his voice, it produced an angry reaction.

"How can you expect us to accept that!"

"Sir," said Harry coldly. For all his efforts patience wasn't part of his nature and he'd had enough of de Barrameda. "I have allowed you the liberty of abusing my honour once. But if you make a habit of it I will be forced to seek redress."

"The *Gauchos* goes missing . . ."

"With a cargo of gold ingots," said James.

Both Spaniards looked at him, slightly nonplussed.

"Even a cursory glance will show you that contents of the chest consists of nothing but coins."

"No doubt Captain San Lucar de Barrameda thinks we minted them on the way upriver," said Harry. "That despite the presence of his own troops on board."

The object of this gibe started guiltily, evidence that his mind was moving that way. It was an absurd idea, since the coins that Harry had tipped out consisted of quite a mixture; eight-real pieces, louis d'or, moidores, guineas, American gold dollars, Swedish, and Danish crowns. In fact, nearly every currency available in the world, hardly surprising since they'd been taken from ships of every nationality. Harry, with deliberate sarcasm, drove the point home.

"But then, of course, they'd look brand new, which is hardly the case."

"Why did you not tell me of this off Fort Balize?" demanded de Barrameda.

Harry replied sharply. "I should think, in the light of subsequent events, the answer to that is obvious. Besides, Captain, it is, rather like the movements of the Spanish navy, actually none of your business."

James, seeing de Barrameda swell up with indignation, spoke quickly to de Carondelet. "You are welcome to search the rest of the ship, Excellency, but I can assure you that apart from a decent sum that we keep for the everyday affairs and personal purchases there is nothing of interest to see."

"Which is why we brought you here first," added Harry. "We are keen to assure you that we have nothing to hide, just as we are determined to depart at the first opportunity. My crew have been away from home for a long time, Barón."

"Then it seems strange to me that you came to New Orleans at all," said de Carondelet, wistfully.

"The nature of my obligation to our French passengers left me no option. As we've already told you they want to land here and settle in Louisiana, which they perceive as a haven from the recent upheavals both at home and in the Caribbean. It was my intention to advance them sufficient money to aid their settlement."

That seemed to break his reverie. He responded angrily: "I've told you. We have quite enough Frenchmen in New Orleans." His emotion increased as he spoke. "And the last influx, who fled from the Terror in their own country or her colonies, are the worst. A sane man would think they'd learned their lesson. But no. They agitate for a return to French rule." De Carondelet's eyes seemed set to pop out of his head so great was his indignation. "French Revolutionary rule!"

"These men do not come as refugees, Barón. And I can personally vouch for their antipathy to Jacobin ideas."

"That may not do, Captain."

"Do I have your permission to carry on with the search?" asked de Barrameda.

"There seems little point in any further search."

De Barrameda reacted angrily, his agitation made obvious by the manner in which he addressed his superior. "Don Francisco, you gave me your assurance and I insist that you honour it."

The older man looked at his subordinate for a second before replying. This seemed to take out of him all the anger he'd stoked up. His shoulders slumped, and the air of resignation in a situation where he could easily have slapped San Lucar de Barrameda down was palpable. It was as though all his cares had come together at once to overburden his power of command.

"Then carry on, Don Felipe. I did promise that you would be free to do so. But I must say I believe these gentlemen. I doubt your search will produce anything of interest, certainly nothing that shocks me as much as this."

"Pender," said Harry, with a sideways glance at James, "please relock it and fetch the smaller chest. The one that contains our petty cash."

"Wait," said de Carondelet. "How much is the contents of this chest worth?"

Harry hesitated, as if trying to convey ignorance, but he knew that wouldn't wash. It would be obvious to anyone with half a brain that no one could spend time close to this hoard without knowing its value. What worried him most was the knowledge that the sum de Carondelet had lost tallied very closely with the total of the Frenchman's treasure.

"No doubt you have a list of the contents?"

Harry nodded, then going to his desk pulled open a drawer and produced the scroll of parchment, prepared by Lampin and him. He handed it to de Carondelet, who'd held out his hand impatiently. The Barón unrolled it and scrutinized it quickly, his lips moving slowly.

"A pen, Captain Ludlow, if you please."

Harry pushed the inkstand which stood on his desk towards de Carondelet, then reached into his desk for a piece of paper. The Barón grabbed both and with an occasional glance at the scroll, began a series of sums. Clearly he had a good head for figures, plus a fair idea of the value of varying currencies, since he was engaged in listing his conclusions to each entry into a separate account in the margins. Once he'd finished he dusted off the sheet, folded it into his coat pocket, and handed the scroll back to the silent Harry. Pender then stepped forward and closed the chest, securing it with a huge padlock.

"I will not dine with you aboard ship. Captain Ludlow. Instead, you and your brother will dine with me ashore. The hour will be somewhat later than you are accustomed to but that cannot be avoided."

"That's very generous, but—"

"No buts, Captain. I insist. I will also invite certain members of the *Cabildo*." Observing James's look of incomprehension, de Carondelet explained: "It is the body that advises me on policy. As to this chest, I fear I must take that ashore with me now."

Harry opened his mouth to protest, but de Carondelet gave him no opportunity. "Do not preach to me the laws of neutrality, Captain Ludlow, or squeal about your letters of marque. I have the right, as do any of my customs officers, to require any ship berthed in New Orleans to land their entire cargo."

"With respect, sir, *Bucephalas* is no merchantman."

"That is a point. But it's not one I wish to consider as relevant. I infringe no law when I do this since you did not inform the port authorities of the nature of your cargo on arrival. In that respect you have failed in your obligations. And I leave you with what you choose to call your petty cash so that you may provision your ship as necessary."

"It is also within your rights to declare any goods, so described, as contraband. If you intend to do that, I must warn you that I am not without influence in London. The consequences for both you, the colony, and Spain could be grave."

They exchanged stares for a moment. But de Carondelet held all the cards and knew it. So did Harry Ludlow. London was four thousand miles away.

"I take this chest because I am within my rights to do so. And also for safe keeping."

"Then will you call off your galleys and the soldiers on that merchantman? In fact, do I have your permission to move my ship to another berth? I dislike being under the guns of that bastion."

De Carondelet tried to smile, to make it sound like a trifle. But his lips were too tight and his jaws too clenched to bring off the easy manner he was striving for.

"That, I think, can wait until tomorrow, Captain. Now if you will forgive me, I have instructions to give to my steward. I will expect you and your brother at six o'clock."

CHAPTER SIXTEEN

HARRY LAY in the netting slung in the bows of *Bucephalas* for a long time. Half his mind was concentrated on the reasons why his fears were groundless, but the remainder had him turning his head this way and that, first examining the approaches to the bastion then the looming bulk of the galleys, with their open gunports and crowded decks. Upstream the soldiers who'd lined the side of the merchantman had been stood down. But there were still officers on duty to keep a watch on his ship, ready at a moment's notice to call their musketeers back into position. Occasionally his eyes would trace the line of the levee, eventually ending up at the downstream bastion, a twin of the high stone structure that stood before him. Pender waited close by, just as still, knowing that his Captain needed time to think. Anyone who got too close, their curiosity having become unbearable, was treated to a glare that sent them scurrying away.

As the light began to fade, the furnace for the gunners' hot shot started to glow. Soon torches began to appear on the battlements, complemented by lanterns strewn in the rigging of the straddling ships. As an extra precaution San Lucar de Barrameda had run a cable from his stern to that of the merchant ship upstream. It was not strong enough to stop a determined attempt to breach it, but meant that Harry couldn't try to get away without jerking it and alerting those on duty on the *Navarro*. Finally, assuming that the Spaniard's precautions were complete, Harry stood up, and balancing on the bowsprit leapt back onto the deck. With a nod to Pender, who followed on his heels, he made for the cabin. As he entered James looked up expectantly.

"You've been a long time about your musings, Harry."

"Not dressed, James? We're supposed to be going to dinner."

Harry started to remove his shirt. Pender immediately called forward for hot water, then opened the box that contained his shaving kit. Harry made his way into the quarter-gallery followed by his brother.

"I wasn't sure that we'd accepted. In fact, I half suspected, seeing you examining the defences, to be sharpening cutlasses by now."

"Sorry to disappoint you, brother."

"What? No assault on de Carondelet's vaults?"

"No!" Harry snapped, impatiently.

"You show a rare degree of bad temper, Harry, which is commonly a sign that you are worried."

"Do you know me well enough to say that with such assurance?"

James smiled, recalling that as a youngster he'd seen little of elder brother Harry, away at sea and all the more heroic for that to a boy stuck at his school desk. Such separation had saved them from any form of sibling rivalry and allowed them to be friends as adults. They had a natural respect for each other's privacy, knowing that to both there were areas of their lives that did not invite discussion. But you couldn't be at sea with anyone for nearly three years without even their most intimate traits becoming obvious.

"That, brother, is one of the products of being cooped up in a ship with the same people for months on end. You get to know them very well. Sometimes too well."

"I don't much care for the word cooped, James."

"I can't think of another. But I am right. And I would add that in my experience it's not like you to sit still and let others dictate your actions."

"I'm not sure there's a choice. No more than I am sure that we're actually in any danger. I have been firmly hoist on my own petard in the matter of our Frenchmen's treasure, with little notion of what to do about it."

"We are, I assume, somewhat badly placed to do anything?"

"Understatement. We are, proverbially, like rats in a trap."

"I take it that I wasn't mistaken, that you were examining the options."

"I was, and as to effecting an escape, death and glory ain't in it. It would need a shore party to silence the guns on that bastion, and they'd not only have to get ashore but make it to the firing platform without being detected. We couldn't hang about for survivors, so that is close to being a suicide mission. At the same time, we're given a miracle and we've drifted out of range of the soldiers' muskets and slipped past the four galleys without sustaining real damage. Having achieved such success there are still their stern chasers, probably loaded and ready to run out. San Lucar de Barrameda will inevitably undertake a pursuit and he has a distinct advantage in confined waters. Finally, there's the other battery downriver. That has, I suppose a similar complement of forty-two-pounders and the means to heat their shot. Imagine that, James. They, warned and prepared, sending red-hot metal into our timbers, as we float by with little more than the river current to carry us."

"So we can do nothing?"

"Let's say we appear to do nothing," Harry replied with a grin, as Pender pushed past carrying a steaming jug of water. He sat down and his servant began to lather his face.

"But we are accepting de Carondelet's invitation. If your peregrinations have taken such a turn has it occurred to you that we might not return?"

Harry tried to respond, but Pender confined him to a nod by jabbing at his opening mouth with the soapy brush, forcing an abrupt closure, accompanied by a calm observation.

"It seems to me that one glance at a watch would tell a man that's going to a six o'clock dinner that he's a mite short on time. Upsetting the host won't aid matters one little bit."

Despite the threat of a mouthful of soap, Harry spoke. "There you are. Pender thinks we should go."

"Why?"

Pender made sure that his Captain got no more opportunity to add his opinion, placing the razor before his eyes and waving it about. "It's a mite dangerous to be conversin' when you're being shaved, your honour."

"I didn't ask Harry a question, Pender, I asked you."

Pender crouched, all his concentration fixed on scraping Harry's chin. "You've got to go 'cause no good will be served by not doing so. It'll only give him the notion that you're up to something. Let's face it, your honour, if that there Spaniard wants to come aboard an' clap us all in irons, there's nowt we can do about it. An' if he wants to hang on to the money, then he'll be seeking an excuse. Then there are them Frogs. I don't fancy your chances of getting them ashore without butterin' him up." He peered at James's jaw. "Do you want shavin'?"

James rubbed his chin, and lacking Harry's growth, pronounced himself satisfied.

"Then I'd recommend a cleaner shirt, your honour," said Pender, razor poised to stroke Harry's other cheek. "That one you're wearing ain't been improved by the heat of the day."

James grinned at him before turning away to comply. By the time he returned, in clean linen, Harry was getting dressed. Pender had clearly echoed his Captain's doubts about the safety of the ship, and he was seeking to reassure him. Listening, he thought he could detect a note in his brother's voice, a tone of false confidence that made him sound like a man vending shoddy goods.

"But if he was on the up, he would have let us move our berth," Pender protested.

"Which neatly expresses my own concerns. But I've already said they may be groundless. You have to look at the positive aspects as well as the others. He took the chest by invoking a legality."

"A narrow one, Harry," said James.

"True. But in order to stay within the bounds of legality he knows he must respect our rights. Even with the information given to him by San Lucar de Barrameda he made no attempt to take over *Bucephalas* once we'd berthed. I take that to mean that he's cautious, a very wise policy for a Spanish official in light of past events. How many times in the last fifty years has Albion banged the drum and forced them to back down? De Carondelet knows that they're weaker now; that faced with a British threat, Spain will have to do the same again, with a heap of ordure waiting to be dropped on the man who caused such a stink. And he couldn't keep what he's done a secret, even if he was to throw us all in a dungeon. Being even a fraction in the wrong will be enough to cause an outcry in London."

"I have heard many an outcry in London, Harry, and let me tell you they don't amount to much after a day or two."

"There will be a lot of people at home, especially greedy naval officers, who'll maintain that since the Dons are no longer our allies we should go the whole hog and make them our enemies, whether they infringe on our prerogatives or not. Taking over a British letter of marque without just cause, even stealing what appears to be our profits, would give them ample ammunition."

"They hate us, Harry. We've seen enough of naval officers to know that."

"We're like Jenkins's ear, we'll do as an excuse to start a war. De Carondelet won't want an incident to fan such sentiments. And he'd have more than London to worry about if things flared up. Can you imagine what the French would do if they thought we might try to take Louisiana? Or the Americans, for that matter. Danger would threaten from all over the place. I doubt he has sufficient troops. He's only got a few galleys, which would be too flimsy for a real battle, and you saw the state of the defences at the delta. All that combines to make New Orleans vulnerable."

"So, on balance, we have little to fear?"

"Ask me after dinner, brother."

"And the Frenchmen's money?"

"The same."

"How very enigmatic, Harry."

"It has to be. All I know is this: Pender is right. If we fail to

show up, or make any difficulties, he'll draw unwelcome conclusions, perhaps even become as bellicose as he was on first
acquaintance. San Lucar de Barrameda doesn't have a monopoly
on pride. Denting de Carondelet's cannot be to our advantage.
Our first priority is to try and retrieve that chest. Then we must
gain some freedom of action."

"And our passengers?"

"Provided we get their money back, all will be well. If we
can't get them ashore legitimately, we'll do it another way. There's
endless places to land them along the riverbank."

"Well, then," said James, clearly unconvinced, "let's hope de
Carondelet's perception of the dangers is as acute as you say. But
it seems a slender thread to me."

"How did he strike you, as a man?"

"Excitable," James replied. "Quixotic, even. Under some pressure. Prepared to command someone like San Lucar de Barrameda
only up to a point—which would go some way to explain it."

"Honourable?"

"Not transparently so."

"I didn't ask if he was a saint, James."

"On balance, I think, yes. After all, he backed away from de
Barrameda's report once he'd been shown the contradictions."

"He's certainly not naturally devious, since his attempt to be
cunning about us shifting our berth was painfully obvious. He
might as well have looked me in the eye and said, 'I'm up to something.'"

"That's a contradiction, Harry. In one breath you say he's not
devious then in the next you say he is."

"That may be more to do with his worries than his inclinations. As you say, he's under some pressure. You don't need to be
very bright to detect that his problems here in New Orleans are
manifold. And for reasons we don't yet know, the loss of that treasure has dealt him a serious blow, one that has nothing to do with
its actual value. Somehow it's made matters worse. It's the level
of instability that will dictate his actions, of course. But I'm of the
opinion that as far as he's capable his word is his bond."

"De Barrameda is quite the opposite. And he clearly exerts great influence."

"I think we may find out tonight just how much, brother."

"He would have taken over the ship without hesitation."

"True," Harry replied. "De Barrameda's the worst kind of Spanish officer; prickly and proud, without an ounce of common sense, who got his command because he's a hidalgo. He's probably totally useless at sea."

"Would that also apply to his crew?" Harry looked at him questioningly. He smiled in return. "Just in case we were thinking of attempting the impossible."

"Impossible just about sums it up," Harry replied grimly.

"Bad officers don't run good crews, your honour," said Pender. "Even if they've got good men in amongst 'em."

"Let's hope you're right," said Harry, with feeling.

Pender looked at Harry keenly. "What do we do, your honour, if they try to come aboard while you're ashore?"

Harry put his hand on Pender's shoulder, his face grim. "In the end, that will have to be a decision you take at the time. If you think you can fight them off, do so. But I doubt if you'll be exposed to any assault. Why bother? They've nothing to gain by damaging the ship in a situation where they can call on us to surrender any time they choose."

"I don't like the sound of that word surrender, Capt'n."

"You're right, Pender, and neither do I!" Suddenly he shed what in a man like him looked remarkably like torpor and issued a stream of orders.

"Say nothing to the Frenchmen. They'll not take kindly to any notion that we might queer their pitch. I want the carpenter to make up some small rafts, big enough to carry barrels of gunpowder. He's to drill a hole at the top of each one big enough to take a length of slow-match. No nails, or they'll be heard all over the anchorage banging them in. Tell him they're to be lashed together. Put others to fill our empty wine bottles with turpentine, and jam a bit of soaked tow into the neck. Empty any sea-chests aboard except those belonging to the French. Get the sailmaker to line them with storm canvas. Then the gunner can fill them with gunpowder as well."

James couldn't keep the slight note of exasperation out of his voice. "Harry, you've just spent ten minutes telling us we have nothing to fear, and even if we did there's nothing we can do about it. Now you're issuing instructions for a battle."

"Who was that Roman cove who said that if you want peace prepare for war? I want to be just that in case de Barrameda persuades him to do something at odds with his own inclinations."

James thought for a moment before continuing. "I can see the use for rafted barrels of gunpowder, Harry, as well as the bottles. But the sea-chests escape me."

Harry smiled. "We can't ship gunpowder to the foot of that bastion, without being seen, but amongst thirty Frenchmen's possessions, if we can get them ashore, it's another matter."

"So we're not trapped after all," said James.

"Oh, we are, brother, but cornered rats always try to escape. If it comes to it, so shall we."

The decision to address the entire group of Frenchmen had, at the time, seemed like good sense. But what Harry and James failed to realize was just how exposed that made them. Lampin and Couvruer, trying to intervene, were bluntly told that they were as much responsible for the loss of their treasure as these damned Englishmen, and only a loud threat from Harry stopped Brissot from turning violent.

"If anyone, of any nationality, so much as raises a fist from now on, I'll stretch his neck."

"And I would remind you that the only reason we are here in New Orleans is to help you," added James.

Harry coughed to cover a slight degree of embarrassment, wondering which of the two statements had done more to calm things. Whichever, he was glad, though the buzz of men grumbling was, in the confined space between decks, loud and worrying.

"Because of that," James continued, "our ship, and the entire crew, is under threat."

Lampin, sensing a chance to speak without being shouted down, took a pace forward. "Because of what you said to me, Captain Ludlow, I assured my friends that their money was safe."

"It makes no difference that it was in my brother's cabin," James replied. "The Spaniards would have taken it from wherever it was found."

Couvruer, who'd joined Lampin, spoke in English, which earned him some hard looks.

"You will not convince all of them that is true."

The giant bearded Brissot stepped out of the crowd, grabbed both Lampin and Couvruer by the scruff of the neck and dragged them backwards.

"You are a rich man, Rosbif," he said. "You give us the money you lost and then keep what you get back from the stinking Spaniards."

That was greeted with a howl of approval, and an aggressive surge forward that forced Harry and James to step back quickly.

"You told us that our money was safe in your cabin."

Harry's voice, rebounding off the low deck beams, brought all forward movement to a halt. It also killed off any sound.

"Perhaps you'd like me to tell the Governor where that treasure really came from!" He glared at them for several seconds, then with a slight tug at James's sleeve, he spun on his heel and made his way up to the deck. Pender was standing at the top, the look on his face enough to convince Harry that even if he hadn't comprehended most of the language he'd understood the mood.

"I have to tell you, your honour," he intoned gravely, "that if they start any of that on me while you're ashore, I'll clap them in the cable tier, one an' all."

Harry, still seething, matched his tone.

"Make it so, Pender, make it so."

CHAPTER SEVENTEEN

DE CHIGNY WAS waiting ashore with a strong escort, all armed with long muskets tipped with vicious-looking bayonets; but a closer inspection showed the soldiers to be rather lacklustre in their bearing. Their mere presence had caused a crowd to gather, as usual in these situations, the most disreputable members of the community. Many a question was shouted at them, mixed with a stream of invective aimed at the escort, all studiously ignored as they marched through the dimly lit streets.

"This is rather like going to an execution, Harry," said James.

His brother looked at him closely only to see that he'd made nothing more than a calm observation. As they reached the part of town that had survived the most recent fire, everything became brighter; this was due to gas lamps, a very modern innovation, affixed to the walls of the houses. A question to de Chigny quickly established that de Carondelet was a great improver, digging canals and strengthening the defences; and in installing lamps to replace flaring torches, he not only cut down on street crime, but reduced the risk of another devastating fire.

"Perhaps we should adopt the same solution in London, Harry."

"You'd have to destroy the place first."

"Considering what a sink of iniquity it is, the notion doesn't bother me."

Because of such lights they could see the faces of the crowd that accompanied them, as well as hearing their voices.

"Harry, those fellows on the outer edge, the Indians?"

Harry followed James's pointed finger. "What about them?"

"Do they seem unusual to you?"

"Why should they? This is where they come from. We saw several weary creatures this morning trying to sell fruit."

"These men are different from the fruit sellers, I think you'll agree."

Harry peered at them again. "True. I'm almost sure I've seen them already."

"Where?"

"They're similar to the party that was on the levee when we returned earlier."

"I don't recall seeing them."

"You were busy with de Carondelet."

Both brothers were now concentrating on them as they kept pace with the marching soldiers. Their copper-coloured skin stood out, as did the brightly decorated buckskin clothing, but it was their silence that marked them. While all around them the crowd was yelling imprecations, including that same *Cochon du lait* insult aimed at the Governor, the Indians merely looked on, dark brown eyes studying the Ludlows with stoical indifference.

"They look like the warriors you see at Hoxton Fair."

Any further thoughts on that score were put to one side as the escort, hitherto content to ignore the crowd, suddenly dropped their bayonets. As they entered the square before an imposing building de Chigny had drawn his sword and was issuing orders, while at the same time threatening those too close to him with the flat of the blade. The formation changed as the soldiers, straightening up and adopting a more military bearing, levelled their weapons to form a sort of phalanx. This meant that anyone who interfered with their passage risked serious injury.

"Why the fuss now?" shouted James, craning his neck.

"I think we're approaching the Governor's residence. Our young lieutenant wants to show how zealous he is."

"It doesn't seem to be having much effect."

Nothing proved this more than the way James had to shout to be heard. The attendant crowd, if they'd been loud before, found a new supply of air to fuel their anger, and they showed little fear, continually tempting the guards, darting forward and forcing the soldiers to withdraw their weapons. Harry observed this with some satisfaction. Nothing demonstrated how tenuous was the Spanish position more than the caution of the soldiers: even under their leader's windows they had no wish to be the cause of a wound or a fatality, and the attitude of the crowd was such that he knew they were looking for an excuse to start something. A wound inflicted on a French colonist was just the thing to trigger off a riot. Finally they reached the entrance to the building. Two stories high, it had brick pillars and what looked like the plastered timber walls to be found at home in England. The soldiers formed an avenue, a frisson of bayonets pointing outwards, and de Chigny led the two brothers into the relative quiet of the interior.

It was only when they'd ascended the stairs that Harry realized they were in the same building as they'd come to that morning, having merely used another entrance. The passage leading to the Governor's quarters was lined, as before, with smart-looking white-coated soldiers. Close to, Harry observed that their height, bearing, and dress contrasted sharply with the depressed-looking men who'd escorted them here. They approximated more to Fernandez's Cuban garrison, although their uniforms were in a better condition. Two footmen swung open the double doors that led to a grand salon hung with Flemish tapestries. These depicted ancient, stylized battles, in which mounted knights speared fearful infantry, all the while watched by admiring ladies in court dress.

James was entranced, explaining to Harry the quality of these hangings. His fingers gently brushed against some of the embroidery as he pointed up the most delicate details. Harry, even less interested in tapestries than paintings, was trying to relate the actions portrayed to the more military detail, such as castles and fortified camps. They talked quietly, each pursuing their own interests, until another set of doors opened noisily to admit the Governor and his party.

De Carondelet wasn't alone. Apart from San Lucar de Bar-rameda, de Fajardo de Coburrabias, and Captain Fernandez, three civilians stood respectfully behind him. The two hidalgo officers had tried to outdo each other in the glory of their apparel. Their bright silk coats, one blue, the other scarlet, overshadowed, despite its evident quality, the sober burgundy of de Carondelet. Even Fernandez had made an effort. In a clean, well-cut uniform he looked plain, but more soldierly, though the drooping moustaches on such a dark face somewhat spoiled the effect. At least he had the good grace to smile at the Ludlows, proof that though his antecedents were Spanish his disposition reflected the more relaxed climate of the Caribbean. The three civilians, no doubt determined to establish their sobriety, were dressed in uninspiring grey cloth.

"Señores! Welcome," said the Governor. Harry and James bowed slightly, managing to look at each other surreptitiously. "Allow me to introduce to you to the members of the *Cabildo*. You will recall that they are members of the council that assists me in running New Orleans. They also act as judges in the courts. Señor Ignacio de Lovio, Señor Joseph Xavier de Pontalba, and Señor Pablo de Aquivar."

Each man bowed in turn as the brothers struggled to attach a name to them. De Lovio was small and fat, with piglike eyes set in a pockmarked face. De Pontalba had a flat countenance, a squashed nose, and the scar of harelip. De Aquivar, medium height, pleasant-faced if rather nondescript, was the only one whose lips showed even a trace of a smile. Then, as if he remembered where he was, it abruptly disappeared.

De Carondelet had no sooner finished his introductions than he emitted a stream of apologies. First for being a bachelor, so that the feminine touch was sadly lacking from his arrangements, then for the circumstances that forced him to entertain in a borrowed house. He explained to the two indifferent Ludlows that his own official residence had disappeared in one of the numerous fires that plagued the town. This was followed by a catalogue of misfortunes that had, in yet another conflagration, robbed him not only of his cook, but also of decent plate and crystal on which to serve the poor efforts of his temporary replacement.

"All lost, gentlemen. So instead of fine European cuisine, I am thrown back on the efforts of a local fellow who is not even French."

Both brothers took this gabbling, rather excitable explanation as a ruse to avoid any discussion of their situation. Yet his civilian guests nodded with sympathetic understanding.

"Can there be a shortage of French cooks in New Orleans?" asked James.

De Carondelet's face creased with anxiety. "There are many, that is true. But I fear that to a man they'd try to poison me."

"Surely . . ." said Harry.

"Perhaps if we shoot a few more," said San Lucar de Barrameda, "they'll learn some respect for their masters."

That brought forth more emphatic nods from the councillors. De Fajardo de Coburrabias, whom the Ludlows thought, from their single previous meeting, lacked any knowledge of French, surprised them by speaking it now.

"What a good idea, Don Felipe San Lucar de Barrameda. You can shoot some, then skittle off to sea and leave my soldiers to clean up the mess."

The faint noise of the remains of the crowd floated up towards the slightly open window of the chamber. "If your soldiers showed more élan, Don Cayetano de Fajardo de Coburrabias, we'd have nothing to fear from these French swine."

Had anyone else spoken, it would have been different. But after what they'd just witnessed in the street, James couldn't help himself. He knew, as well as Harry, that they needed to be polite. He did adopt a grave expression, but a close look would have revealed the twinkle in his eye.

"How I heartily agree, Don Felipe San Lucar de Barrameda. We all know how violence cows a Frenchman. They behaved like rabbits on the way here. And I recall King Louis was quite eloquent on the subject. That is, until he found out he was mistaken."

De Fajardo de Coburrabias grinned as much as San Lucar de Barrameda frowned.

"They are a barbarous breed, Señor Ludlow," said de Pontalba, quite missing the point of the sally. "To chop off their own King's head."

De Carondelet coughed. After all, the English had beaten the French to such an act by a good hundred years. De Aquivar filled the silence with a bitter denunciation.

"And none are worse than those who have colonized Louisiana. They are also stupid. So stupid that they set fire, in the name of a search for what they call political rights, to their own city. Not once, Señores, but several times."

"We witnessed their anger on the way."

"Please do not misunderstand what you have observed in the streets, Captain Ludlow," said the Governor, managing a look that wiped the grin off de Fajardo de Coburrabias's face. "We are in control here and intend to remain so. What Don Pablo de Aquivar refers to is no more than the work of a few disgruntled agitators, people whom we are anxious to isolate by giving them no cause for grievance. Patience, not violence, is our watchword."

San Lucar de Barramdea snorted insolently, which, in turn, earned him a glare from his superior.

"They will learn in time that not only is Louisiana Spanish, but that it will remain so; that it is still ruled by a powerful King and a great nation."

That, accompanied by more enthusiastic nodding, caused both Ludlows to emulate de Carondelet in polite coughing. The Governor must know, as well as his guests, that the state he represented was a shadow of its former self. The nation that had dominated Europe and conquered the New World was no more. The King of Spain was a simpleton who cared only for hunting. The real ruler in Madrid was a jumped-up nobody called Manuel de Godoy, recently titled Prince of the Peace for the treaty he'd signed with France. In doing so he had deserted his ally Great Britain in the most shameful manner, and gone some way to legitimizing the

Revolutionary despots in Paris. The Prince, reputedly handsome, had risen from being a humble courtier to having absolute control of the Spanish government by being the simultaneous lover of both the Queen and, it was rumoured, her husband. The treaty de Godoy had signed with France in the previous year had been, as James had so acidly pointed out, a humiliating surrender, one that reflected the true state of Spanish power.

Harry didn't give a toss about de Carondelet's food or his fantasies about his King. Hitherto silent, he now spoke out. He'd been dying to ask about the treasure chest since they'd entered, and given what looked like an opportunity he couldn't contain himself.

"I'm sure we will see how great a nation you represent, Barón, when you return our property and give us permission to depart."

"Señores," he exclaimed in reply, as though both matters were trifling, "it is not the Spanish custom to discuss matters of business when food is on the table."

That earned a grunt from Harry Ludlow. But he knew that he would be wasting his time if he asked again. De Carondelet was not going to discuss what interested the Ludlow brothers until it suited him, and it was difficult not to let it slip from their minds: the Barón might bemoan the loss of his cook but the food they sat down to was quite delicious. Highly spiced, certainly, but made from fine ingredients which represented the abundance of choice available in the delta. Without concurring, both brothers had decided they might as well take what pleasure they could. Conversation, though often stilted, did flow, as when de Carondelet or his councillors were speaking.

De Fajardo de Coburrabias was a particularly witty dinner companion, who could sail very close to an insult without delivering one, which made the civilians and de Barrameda the butt of jokes they barely comprehended. Yet he was careful of his superior, which led Harry to the conclusion that the Governor had a sharp brain, that the soldier respected. Sat near the brothers, he explained, while de Carondelet was being bored rigid by his

Cabildo members, that he'd been in Louisiana for eight years, that he liked the colony so much the thought of ever departing was unwelcome. Though not in the least boastful, he had, it seemed, prospered in his service, and was the owner of several plantations.

"And gentlemen," he whispered quietly, "should you require entertainment while you are in New Orleans, I have connections with quite a good establishment just outside the north wall of the city. The Hôtel de la Porte d'Orléans. A Mademoiselle Feraud runs it for me. I will tell her of my invitation for you to visit. That will assure you of her very best attention."

There were *longueurs,* when the conversation lapsed into Spanish or simply became bogged down in the subject of most interest to their hosts. James, typically, was examining each man in turn, looking for that key to their personality which, transferred to canvas, turned a mediocre portrait into a good one. Harry fretted, gnawing at what had happened in the last two days, searching for ways to have avoided this predicament. Sometimes conversation ground to an embarrassing halt, usually when San Lucar de Barrameda chose to take part. Fernandez had the misfortune to be next to the Captain of the *Navarro,* a position, judging by the look on his doleful face, that required great forbearance.

"Am I mistaken, Señores," said de Coburrabias, "or have Captain Fernandez's moustaches grown longer? It takes great ability to bore mere hair so much that it tries to depart its host's body."

It wasn't certain that San Lucar de Barrameda heard the remark, but he turned to de Coburrabias and started to harangue him in Spanish. The only thing the Ludlows understood was that he'd returned to the subject of the French colonists. De Carondelet spoke sharply to him, which modified his tone. Then, after aiming one more curse in the direction of the settlers, he started to tell them a long and bloody tale about a recent slave revolt, in which he'd been personally involved. This it seemed had been put down with a degree of savagery he clearly relished.

For once, he and de Coburrabias were in agreement. The soldier, having listened to how they'd discovered the revolt, cut in to tell the brothers how it had been concluded.

"We put a stop to it, and warned anybody else contemplating revolt, by hanging all the perpetrators at various landing stages along the Mississippi River. One per post to be left till their bodies rot. The ringleader hangs, at this very moment, outside my northern headquarters at the Manchac Post."

"It does not occur to you, Captain," said Harry, "that if you chain a man up, he will always seek a way to be free?"

Fernandez nodded. But the other four Spaniards, whose faces had held expressions of approval, looked shocked. De Barrameda, as usual wrapped up in his own thoughts, failed to see the connection between Harry's ship and the slaves.

"They lack the will and the means," he barked. "Nor do they have the wit to organize such a thing. They were inspired by the Americans, of course. We had to expel several of them for complicity."

"You might ask, why would Americans do such a thing?" added de Carondelet. "Ask what have they got to gain by causing trouble here? It is particularly galling that this took place after our government had given them 25 years' free navigation of the river."

San Lucar de Barrameda again snorted derisively. "It is a clear demonstration, Don Francisco, that giving concessions to such people only leads to more trouble. We should have gone the whole way and hanged the Americans as well. Those fools in Madrid don't know anything."

That made de Carondelet go pale. The three magistrates looked at the table, as if not wishing to be seen to take sides. The two soldiers had such blank expressions on their faces that they could only be deliberate. The civilians' heads went even lower as the Governor replied in an icy tone, still speaking French to add insult to the injury he wished to inflict.

"I will take care to include such a sentiment in my next despatch home, Don Felipe. I'm sure the King, not to mention the Prince of the Peace, will be most interested."

De Carondelet had delivered the words with a smile. But no one at the table saw it as anything other than a threat. It mattered little, since it was wasted on the hidalgo officer. "I am quite capable of making my own views known in Madrid, thank you."

Ignacio de Lovio, who'd hitherto said little, coughed suddenly. Having been introduced first he was clearly the senior member of the civilian trio. His piglike eyes had opened wide and his fat face held a shocked expression. A jerk of the head in the direction of the Ludlows was designed to remind the others that they were close to quarrelling in public, as though such a thing had not already happened a dozen times. Being junior to the Governor, he couldn't actually say anything. But whatever undercurrents lay below the surface of the conversation, his action had an effect on de Carondelet.

"I think, gentlemen, that you could leave us now. And you, Captain Fernandez."

All four stood up at once. With polite bows they left the table and the room. The Governor watched them depart, waited till the doors closed behind them, then spun round to face the brothers, his face bright red from a combination of the heat and the wine he'd consumed, those huge blue eyes bulging with keen anticipation.

CHAPTER EIGHTEEN

"TELL ME, Captain Ludlow. How did you know that those ingots were hidden in the sugar boxes?"

Harry toyed with the idea of not answering. But partly through vanity, and more for the sake of the treasure, he did so.

"Because they were all opened. Those that hadn't been tipped out completely had a similar amount of the contents removed. That indicated that one or all of them had contained something hidden. Of course, I didn't know at the time what it was."

"Were any other bales or casks opened?"

"Not that I could see, although some cotton and tobacco had been disturbed and floated to the surface as the ship sank."

De Carondelet looked at him keenly. Harry waited to see if he would admit the obvious fact that someone who knew they were there had either removed them personally or passed the information to a third party. He waited in vain, but having the patience of Job when necessary he knew that he could return to that point at any time. Not so James.

"My brother asked you before who knew of the existence of the ingots, Barón, but you declined to answer."

"And I still do, Señor Ludlow."

Harry smiled. "Which can mean only one of two things: that you asked the members of your *Cabildo* to depart because they knew, and are therefore suspects. I'm curious if that also applies to Captain Fernandez. Certainly you knew, and I suspect so did Don Felipe and Don Cayetano."

De Carondelet held up his hands to silence his two officers, and at the same time fought to ensure his expression didn't register any emotion. But Harry took some pleasure from the way he'd surprised them. The thought had occured to him during the meal, simply because there was no other reason for those people to be present. De Carondelet might try to make it look like a purely social gathering, but it was nothing of the sort. Harry wondered if perhaps he'd expected someone, confronted with the men who found the *Gauchos,* to make a slip of the tongue and incriminate himself. If so it was a forlorn hope.

"That is a deduction that you are at liberty to make, Captain Ludlow. It is not one I will either confirm or deny. I'm more interested in what led you to deduce that Rodrigo knew nothing of the cargo he was carrying?"

"Why conceal it, Barón?"

"There could be any number of reasons," said de Carondelet.

"True. But there are other indicators."

"Which are?"

"Did you know that Captain Rodrigo was carrying not only his wife, but another passenger?"

"Why is that significant?" asked de Carondelet.

"If he knew about the gold and silver he was carrying, you would have been concerned that any passengers were not a risk." Harry looked at San Lucar de Barrameda. "When we first met the *Navarro,* Captain, you were clearly upset by the loss. You claimed Rodrigo as a friend but you made no mention of the likelihood of the *Gauchos* carrying anyone else."

The tall Spaniard, too intrigued to be rude, nodded.

"And you, Barón, likewise. Nor did you mention the crew. That was another group of people who would have been carefully chosen if the cargo was known. Your sole concern was the gold. Even the most hard-hearted soul, if only for the sake of politeness, would not fail to ask a solicitous question regarding such people."

"Does your reluctance to answer questions, Barón, extend to the reasons why the cargo was hidden?" asked James.

"I should have thought, Señores, that was obvious."

"Quite the reverse, sir," said Harry. "You must know that the dream of every sailor, of every other navy in the world, is the taking of a Spanish plate ship."

That startled all three of their hosts, since though it was certainly true it was exceedingly rude to speak of it in such terms. Harry's voice grew harsher as he continued. Partly to drive his point home, he was also incensed that these men, who'd blatantly stolen his property, could react as if the sin of greed was an alien concept.

"And one thing every midshipman learns on joining King George's navy is this: that no gold or silver is shipped out of the Americas unless it goes in a powerful armed convoy, its loading personally supervised by the Viceroy of Mexico. He knows, even if the day is a secret, at what time of year it departs from one of the ports of the Spanish Main. He is told, while still of tender years, that this is an edict that goes back to the heirs of Ferdinand and Isabella. It is, in short, a royal command that no Spanish official dare break."

De Carondelet shifted the subject so abruptly that he caught everyone else out. It took them some moments to catch up with him.

"When you came to see me this morning I was in a state of agitation. If that manifested itself in any way unpleasant to you, I apologize. I admit I was even more abrupt when you enquired about the cargo loaded aboard the Gauchos."

"No more abrupt than you were a moment ago," said James.

"I am not prepared to be interrogated by anyone. I am the Governor in New Orleans."

"That must be exceeding uncomfortable, sir, if what we witnessed on the way here is an indication of how you are perceived."

The Barón swallowed hard. Clearly James had got under his skin.

"And really, Excellency, we would rather discuss the fate of our money than of yours."

"Even if what that ship carried was germane to the entire security of the Louisiana Territory?"

"What has that got to do with us?" asked Harry, brusquely.

De Carondelet continued as if Harry hadn't spoken, which made him wonder if he was listening to a prepared speech.

"With the safety of this colony at stake, I will not debate with you why it was so dispatched. But I will say that I cannot describe its loss as anything other than a disaster."

"How very sorry we are," James replied, without the least trace of sympathy in his voice.

San Lucar de Barrameda cut in, his lips set in a smirk.

"It was bullion, Señores. Surely you appreciate, as well as we must, the shortage of such a valuable commodity in this part of the world. Indeed we have been forced to—"

De Carondelet cut across him abruptly. "Please stick to what is important, Captain."

"We are quite prepared to commiserate with you, Barón," Harry replied, ignoring what should have been San Lucar de Barrameda's discomfort at the way he'd been slapped down. He was about to go on to say he knew what was coming; that any idea of his providing a loan was out of the question, even if he couldn't actually say that the money de Carondelet had taken was the property of his passengers, but he stopped when he saw the look on de Barrameda's face. It was one of evident pleasure, which increased perceptibly as he spoke.

"Of course, Excellency. It is so important that the Barón finds it necessary to sequester the contents of your treasure chest."

"That is theft, Captain," said Harry coldly. He turned to Le Carondelet. "And one you may live to regret."

"Do not threaten his Excellency, Señor," snapped San Lucar de Barrameda, "or you will lose more than your money."

"You may very well lose New Orleans, Captain, when this larceny becomes known in London."

"A valid point, Captain Ludlow," said de Coburrabias.

Harry shot him a glance, wondering if he was trying to distance himself from this decision. He didn't get much time for thought as de Carondelet cut in.

"I can understand that you do not welcome this decision. And the shock of what has just been said has caused you to let your tongue run loose. So, I will let your accusation that I am a thief pass. I take no offence, and neither will anyone else on my behalf."

"I'd be interested to know by what other name you call your proposal," said James.

"With respect, Señor, you did not hear properly what the good Captain said. He used the word sequester. Even that makes me uncomfortable, but I have a problem that presents no other solution. It is necessity that forces me to this. I have the safety of my King's possessions to protect, therefore I must act to do so. But I fully intend that you should be reimbursed, in full, for any sum of money we take from you."

"How?"

Both brothers had spoken simultaneously, and for a moment de Carondelet didn't know who to respond to. He ended up looking at the table, rather than the penetrating stares of the Ludlows.

"The first thing I shall do is allow your French passengers to land in New Orleans. They may settle here or go upriver as they wish. As to the money, I can give you a draft on the Spanish treasury for the appropriate sum."

"And would that include your regrets, Barón?"

"Why should it, Captain? Are you implying that my sovereign would not meet my obligations?"

The lack of passion in the Governor's voice was as clear an indication as was needed that he knew, as well as his guests, the problems attendant upon such a course. Certainly his King would not repudiate his request, but it could take twenty years to achieve repayment, with most of the money going to greedy Spanish courtiers, bribed to use their influence on a reluctant and often barren exchequer.

"I cannot say that your proposal appeals to us."

De Fajardo de Coburrabias, who'd been silent, rejoined the conversation. "There is one other method by which His Excellency could repay you. One perhaps that would be more speedy and more certain."

"And what is that?" demanded Harry, suspiciously.

It was de Carondelet who replied, "Your brother referred to your skill at the art of investigation, Captain Ludlow. And I must say that tonight you have proved his assertion. I was impressed with the way that you extracted conclusions from such scant information as that which you found aboard the *Gauchos*."

De Carondelet paused, his huge blue eyes boring into Harry's.

"I thought perhaps you might be tempted to recover the gold and silver I lost, and in the process bring to book the murderer of Captain Rodrigo. I do assure you, should you find it you may take it as payment for what which I'm forced to borrow from you."

The silence that followed lasted a long time. James said nothing, knowing that it was Harry's place to propose any response. In his mind he was wondering if all those things his brother had ordered before they left, the explosives and bottles full of turpentine, were about to be put into use.

"What about me, my ship, and my crew?"

"You are free to depart from New Orleans, Captain," de Carondelet replied. "That is, if you wish to accept my offer of a draft on the Spanish treasury."

"And if not?"

"Then I require your parole."

"Just mine?"

San Lucar de Barrameda gave a wolfish grin, but it was de Coburrabias who replied.

"It gives me no pleasure to say this, Captain Ludlow, but it would, of necessity, apply to everyone aboard your ship."

"What sort of parole?" asked Harry.

"That you undertake no action without my express agreement," said de Carondelet. "That you do nothing on our soil that will harm either the Spanish crown or the Colony of Louisiana."

"And what if that parole clashes with my need to find your ingots? The two may be incompatible."

"I cannot see how," said de Barrameda.

"Then you are, as I suspected from our very first meeting, a fool, Señor."

De Coburrabias couldn't help himself. He burst out laughing. De Barrameda had gone pale, his thin lips compressed so hard that his thin moustaches seemed to join as one, and de Carondelet had dropped his head, clearly not wishing to make eye contact with anyone. James had no need for such restraint.

"Well said, Harry! And about time."

"It is perfectly obvious to even the dimmest creature," Harry continued, "that only those who knew where the bullion was stored, and which ship it was on, could have had a hand in stealing it. If you want my parole, Barón, then I require something from you in return, and that is a complete list of everyone who knew those secrets."

"No!" snapped San Lucar de Barrameda.

"It will do no harm, Don Francisco," said de Fajardo de Coburrabias. "And Captain Ludlow can hardly make any progress himself without such information."

"Am I right in assuming that you knew?" Harry asked the soldier.

"I did. In fact I was present at the moment Captain de Geurin placed the ingots in the casks. Immediately after that I left for Havana to collect my replacements."

Harry looked keenly at de Barrameda, but without eliciting any response, so he turned back to de Carondelet. "Was I correct about the members of your *Cabildo?*"

"I cannot have such upright men under suspicion," he replied evasively.

"That pirate you captured, Charpentier. Would I be allowed to question him?"

"Why?" demanded de Barrameda.

"He is naturally a suspect, is he not?" asked James.

"The pirates never got out of Barataria Bay, that I can assure you."

"Nevertheless, he will know of the location of his ships," said Harry, "since the one fact which is absolute is this: that whoever made that rendezvous with the *Gauchos* did so in some kind of vessel."

De Barrameda's voice rose till it was close to a shout. "It was not a pirate!"

"Perhaps it was a galley of some sort."

"It is not something I wish to decide on the spur of the moment," said de Carondelet, quickly. "I will let you know within twenty-four hours."

"And until then?" demanded de Barrameda, still smarting from what had been said.

"Until then," said Harry, coldly, "you have my assurance that I will do nothing to embarrass you."

"Oh, I think you've done quite enough of that already, Captain," replied de Coburrabias gaily.

De Carondelet slapped the table with the flat of his hand. "Enough!"

"Will twenty-four hours give you the time you need?" asked Harry, not in the least cowed by the Governor's sudden display of temper.

"What?"

"My brother is wondering whether that is sufficient for you to carry out your own investigations," said James. "There is also the question of what happens if you're successful, sir."

"What do you mean?"

"Will you, if you do discover who has stolen your treasure, hand our money back to us?"

"That will depend on who has it," said de Barrameda.

"Why should it depend on that?" asked Harry.

De Coburrabias answered. "We do have to regain possession of it."

"Perhaps," de Barrameda added, with a sneer, "if it's in a very inaccessible place, we can let you get it for us."

Harry, who'd practically lounged in his chair throughout the discussion, sat forward suddenly.

"Then I hope that it's found aboard your ship. Nothing would give me greater pleasure than to come and take it off you."

San Lucar de Barrameda shot to his feet, towering over the table, and his hand reached, several times, for the sword he wasn't wearing—an action which, for all its venom, took a great deal of the sting out of his response.

"How dare you say such a thing!"

James yawned. "You really mustn't react like that, sir. After all, it was only a few hours ago that you accused us of exactly the same offence."

"I am an officer in the Spanish Navy."

"Ah, the poor King of Spain," James replied, "To be so ill served is a great misfortune."

"Sit down, please, Don Felipe," said de Carondelet. San Lucar de Barrameda looked set to argue, which produced another peremptory slap of the table from his superior, which forced him to comply. Then he faced the Ludlows.

"This behaviour may amuse you, but it does not me. You may return to your ship if you give me your parole for the next twenty-four hours. If not, I will be forced to detain you here."

Harry stood up, followed immediately by James.

"Twenty-four hours, Barón. No more."

The first obvious sign of their changed circumstances lay in the lack of an escort back to the levee, and the brothers walked in silence, each occupied with his own thoughts. Harry's mind was working on two levels, tempted in spite of himself to speculate on the identity of the murderer and thief while at the same time angrily plotting his next move. Experience told him to be dispassionate about de Barrameda, but it was hard. He was never more than a day's sail from the *Gauchos* in a galley, and his lying about them could be an attempt to cover his tracks. Against that his ship had a substantial crew and, fresh from New Orleans, no need for food. Could such horrendous murders, which must have involved the women as well, have been undertaken without fear of exposure? Equally his sympathy for the way Fernandez was treated by his fellow officers mustn't cloud his judgement. It was a fact, attested to by his Galician pilot, that the Cuban had nearly beaten a soldier to death. So under that placid exterior was a violent personality which had both the means and the opportunity to intercept the merchantman. De Coburrabias had arrived in one of the ships from Havana, six or seven days' sailing away, so that ruled him out. Or did it? He, like the three magistrates, could easily have informed someone else, and set them on a rendezvous with Rodrigo. That possibility opened up so many avenues of enquiry that any attempt to find the culprit was doomed. And how did that notion square with the fact that the man clearly knew the person he invited aboard—or, Harry wondered, was he wrong about that? His mind went back to the notion of getting his ship clear, discarding one wild scheme after another.

"What do we tell our French guests about this?" asked James, bringing him down to terra firma with a bump.

"As little as possible," Harry replied, emphatically. "Let's just get them off the damned ship while de Carondelet's offer lasts."

"Without their money!"

"If the Barón finds out that it's theirs we'll never get it back."

"Will we get it back in any case?"

"I cannot believe he's going through with this, James. Surely he must realize what a heap of ordure will descend on him from Madrid if the King of Spain is forced to apologize."

"That's a tall order, Harry."

"It's not, James. I've told you, there are people who will use this as an excuse to start a war."

"I take it you were being truthful about the alternative?"

"I've no intention of accepting a bill on the Spanish exchequer, if that's what you mean. I've known people who willed such

things to their children in the faint hope that they might eventually get paid."

"Could it be discounted?"

"Not at a rate that I'd accept. We must assume that our passengers would feel the same. I imagine Madrid is sick to death of
this place. Perhaps Louisiana is less of a drain on the treasury now
that they've granted the Americans rights of deposit, but it's still
not wildly successful. If it was, de Carondelet wouldn't need to
filch our funds. He could borrow it from the leading traders.
There's Mexico City, of course. They will be accustomed to bail-
ing them out . . ."

"The news would certainly have reached London before that
happened."

"It makes no sense," said Harry. "No sense at all."

They fell silent again, striding along on the flat beaten earth
of the roadway. The place was still busy with that air of pleasant
bustle which would continue late into the night, so common in
cities in warm climates. Each intersection had its crowd, occupying the corners in a proprietory way, and again Harry was struck
by the easy way in which the races seemed to mingle: when a carriage forced them to the side of the road it was as likely to be
occupied by a dark-skinned owner as a European. They had to
stop at one of the junctions, well lit by gas lamps, as two traps,
single-horsed shays, disputed the right of passage. A crowd of people, seemingly intent on going in their direction, gathered round
them.

"You are, I believe, Captain Ludlow?"

CHAPTER NINETEEN

THE VOICE was deep, even, and masculine, with just a hint of a Scottish burr. Harry spun round, to find himself looking at the top button of a black coat. He raised his eyes, wondering how this huge interloper who now stood between him and James had got so close without his having any notion of his presence. Now, looking at the face, he was struck by the slightly coppery tone of the skin, and the eyes, as black as the hair, so deep in colour as to seem almost blue. It was dominated by a beaked nose, made more prominent by the shadows of the flickering gaslight. He wasn't smiling, though it couldn't be said that he looked threatening. If anything he had an expression of confident passivity.

"And who are you, sir?"

"You are Captain Ludlow, I'm not mistaken?"

"Harry," said James, who, given the broad shoulders, had to lean well forward to be seen. The man spun round to look at him, then turned back. "No, it is you."

His proximity, the way he towered over Harry, was slightly alarming. He tried to take a pace back, only to find himself hemmed in by the crowd. The giant lifted a massive hand, which made him shy away defensively, but it went above his head and though he didn't see what gesture he employed the crush eased immediately.

"I'm sorry to adopt such a way of meeting. But I can't come out to your ship without attracting attention."

Now able to look him up and down, Harry wondered what he was on about. Given his height, girth, and bearing, this man would attract attention wherever he went. James walked round him to join his brother. The black eyes flicked from one to the other.

"Perhaps if I was to introduce myself first. My name is Alexander McGillivray." There was a slight pause, during which he perceived no reaction, before he continued. "That would mean nothing to you."

"It does not," Harry replied. Now that he was free to do so, he took another step backwards, trying to get this McGillivray into focus. It was only then that he noticed that the two carriages, so disputatious and entangled a moment ago, had passed each other with ease.

"Did you arrange this, sir?" asked James.

"I engineered our meeting, yes. It did occur to me that four of my men, armed, could be induced to bring you to me, but then you might've tried to fight them, and I would not want you harmed."

"Perhaps we would have inflicted harm rather than succumbed to it."

The eyes looked at them both again.

"You might," he said to Harry. Then he turned his gaze on James. "You? No."

"This is damned impertinent, sir," said James.

"It is. And it's also very public. I wonder if you would step this way? One of the de Carondelet's innovations, apart from his gas-lit streets, is the formation of patrols by a paid force of watchmen."

As he indicated the black-painted door that stood on the point of the corner, it opened immediately, revealing a dark unlit passage. Since whoever had pulled it was hidden, it seemed very like a conjuring trick. McGillivray stepped back into the gloom, his eyes momentarily distracted by his need to check their surroundings.

"Why?" asked Harry.

"It was you who found the *Gauchos*. I need to know what happened to that ship." He spoke hurriedly, almost in panic. "My daughter was on board. I must try to find out what became of her. One of my men spoke to the sailors who manned your barge this morning. I know certain things were taken off the ship."

"Does the expression 'Hoboi Hili Miko' mean anything to you?" asked James.

"It does," replied McGillivray. "It is my name in Creek. It means Good Child King."

"You are a King?"

"No, a chieftain, which comes to me by right—since I am a member of the Wind clan."

"*Vent,*" said James, recalling the French word which had been embroidered alongside.

"That is correct. Now, gentlemen. Will you accede to my request?"

"Tell me, sir," said Harry. "Would you, in an unknown port, enter a darkened house with a complete stranger?"

McGillivray's eyes flicked over Harry's shoulder and he spoke rapidly, in what both brothers assumed was the native tongue, before addressing them again.

"I would if I had a knife pressed into my back."

Harry felt the pressure before he'd finished speaking. Not enough to puncture anything, but certainly sufficient to indicate that it was sharp enough to do so in an instant.

"I mean you no harm, Captain Ludlow. But my own situation and my urgent need for information leave me little option. I have no desire to stay where my presence would be noted, otherwise I would have come to your ship."

"You wouldn't have got close, sir, since it is surrounded by Spaniards."

"Had you not, fortuitously, come ashore, I would have been forced to do so. And had that occurred, I can assure you I would have succeeded."

"You have no need of my brother," said Harry, as the pressure in his back increased slightly.

"Forgive me if I disagree, Captain. I have need of you both."

His eyes were now on James. "Clearly, if you ask the meaning of 'Hoboi Hili Miko', you have some knowledge of events."

The sudden noise of a commotion, faint at first but growing louder, carried over the normal babble of the surroundings. McGillivray stepped further back, practically disappearing into the darkened doorway, to avoid detection.

"Soldiers," whispered James.

"No, sir. What you are witnessessing is the unpopularity of the Governor's watchmen, who are approaching. You will be tempted to call out now, Captain Ludlow. Please don't do so. We Indians are adept at disposing of people silently."

Harry stepped forward, taking James's arm to propel him in the same direction, aware that he had no choice. He tried to sound relaxed, even though he felt anything but. "One second you mean us no harm and the next we've expired without so much as a whimper!"

The lantern appeared as soon as the door was shut. Harry, turning, saw that whoever had pressed the knife in his back had stayed outside. Apart from the man with the lamp they were alone with McGillivray.

"Please follow me, Captain," the giant said. He walked up the passage, took the lantern, dismissed the man holding it, and opened the door to a comfortable parlour. "If you'd care to take a seat, gentlemen."

It was James who replied. "I don't think I want to do that until you tell me who you really are."

"I've already done that."

"You say your name is McGillivray, which is clearly of Scottish origin, yet you expect us to believe that you're an Indian chieftain of some substance."

That made McGillivray smile. He had a mouth full of large white even teeth that were near to sparkling. "It must sound strange to your English ears, I know."

"And if I'm not mistaken, sir, you even have a Caledonian lilt to your voice."

James pronounced this with all the dislike that he felt for Scotsmen evident in his tone. Harry considered it was a subject on which his brother was barely rational. Their sister had married an impecunious Scottish lord when James was still a youngster. That brother-in-law, Lord Drumdryan, who'd seen fit to take a hand in his upbringing and dictate matters in their family home, he held to be typical of the race, and since he despised Drumdryan, he allied himself with those Englishmen who, greedy for political favour and seeing the northern interlopers prospering, hated the Scots.

"My father was Scottish," McGillivray replied. "He married my mother, who was half Creek Indian and half French. In the Creek nation the bloodline is female, and my mother was a member of the Wind clan. That is the clan that stands highest in the eyes of our spirits. So I inherited my position from my mother."

"You said your daughter was on the *Gauchos,*" said Harry.

A slight pause. "She was. Sequoy Marchand McGillivray."

"And how old is she?"

The answer didn't come immediately. It was as though McGillivray had to count the passage of time. "Sixteen years by a European calendar."

"Was she alone?" asked James.

"She was on the *Gauchos* with Captain Rodrigo."

Harry cut in. "Were there any other passengers?"

"Not that I was aware of."

Even by the faint light of the candle Harry could see that James was perplexed. "Is it not unusual to send a sixteen-year-old-girl abroad unattended?"

"Perhaps we don't count New York as abroad," McGillivray replied sharply.

"New York!" Harry barked. "Was that the ship's destination?"

"Why does that surprise you?"

"I had assumed that it was bound for Spain."

McGillivray shook his head. "Captain Rodrigo was carrying

his cargo to New York. The first granulated sugar ever processed by human hand. Unfortunately he didn't even get a hundred miles from the mouth of the delta, if the rumours I have heard are true."

"They are, I'm afraid," Harry replied. "We came across her not much more than a day's sailing from Fort Balize. Rodrigo's body we picked up closer to the delta."

McGillivray sat forward eagerly. "Please tell me what you found."

Harry hesitated for just a moment, still trying to fit the ship's destination and the way McGillivray referred to the cargo into what had happened with de Carondelet. He was also slightly troubled by the reference to the man's daughter. He distinctly remembered the unoccupied look of the cabin, with the chest that contained the clothes of what appeared to be a young girl. The one with the older woman's clothes and vomit-stained sheets had certainly been used. Surely that denoted another passenger? There was Rodrigo's wife, but it couldn't be her. Sailing with her husband, she had her quarters in the main cabin.

"Captain Ludlow?"

He brought his attention back to McGillivray, who was clearly anxious to hear what he had to say. He explained how they'd found the ship and how whoever had approached and boarded had almost certainly been known to the Captain. That made the giant Indian stiffen slightly, but he didn't speak. Then, without mentioning open boxes of sugar, Harry went on to describe Rodrigo's cabin, set for dinner, and what he'd found in the accommodation below decks.

"Did they go down with the ship?"

"No. My servant brought them off before *Gauchos* sank."

McGillivray sounded resigned. "So they are in the hands of Governor de Carondelet."

"Actually," said James, "they are still on board."

"I have been told that de Carondelet left your ship in possession of a chest."

"That was a different one, sir."

A moment's silence followed. Both brothers were surprised that McGillivray evinced no interest in that other chest—not that either of them would have told him what it contained. Still, his lack of curiosity was odd.

"How was she sunk?"

"They sent someone down to the bilges to knock out the planking," Harry replied. "I don't think they did a very thorough job."

"And there was no sign of a struggle."

"There was spotted blood on the deck, plus a great pool by the bulwarks. But when I examined that I was sure it was animal blood. There was nothing below decks or in the Captain's quarters."

"Animal blood?"

"Pork has a very peculiar smell, even raw. I think the blood on the deck was from a slaughtered pig. The manger and the hencoop were empty. I can only think whoever took the *Gauchos* was short of stores, but lacked the means to transport them live."

"Something small, then?"

"Very likely," Harry replied.

McGillivray sat down suddenly, hands clasped before him. "I have ten thousand questions in my mind, Captain, most of which would probably make no sense to you."

"I've told everything I know, sir. And I must add that a great deal of what I have imparted is mere speculation."

"What will you do now?" asked James.

McGillivray's black eyes fixed on him for a moment, with a threatening look. Then he stiffened, as if seeking to control himself.

"All the evidence points to a kidnapping. That's the long and the short of it."

Harry's next question was posed tentatively.

"When you say 'kidnapping,' do you assume she—your daughter, I mean—will be held for ransom?"

"Of course, Captain. I am, through my own efforts and that of my father, seen as a very rich man."

"Whoever would do such a thing can only be either an enemy or, at sea, a pirate."

"That is so."

"What if I was to say that the *Gauchos* wasn't taken by a pirate?"

"How can you be so sure?"

"Because we met the fleet of galleys that had just cleared out Barataria Bay off Fort Balize. A man called Charpentier was on one of them, in a cage."

"He is a prominent member of the fraternity, but he's not the only one."

"Captain San Lucar de Barrameda said he chased all the others into the swamps."

"I would beware of placing too much credence in the claims of Spanish officers." McGillivray paused before proceeding, unaware of how his opinion had pleased Harry. "But I agree with you, it was unlikely to be a pirate."

"Why?"

There was another slight hesitation before McGillivray replied, which this time entirely robbed his answer of verisimilitude.

"Because everyone in New Orleans knows who I am, just as they know the identities of the Barataria Bay pirates. Charpentier could have been picked up in any one of a dozen taverns in the last month."

"Knowing who they are is one thing, sir."

McGillivray emitted a hearty laugh, which given his distress over his daughter was singular.

"Do you think any of our buccaneers spend all their time in Barataria Bay? No, gentlemen. And if you had been to that god-forsaken place you'd know why. They're no different to other men, they like their comfort, especially when fortune favours them with a good capture. You're as likely to find them drunk in the *tiendas* outside the northern wall as on their ships. Given coin to throw around they'll do so and it's not long before they run short."

"A description that fits nearly every sailor I've ever met," said Harry.

"And there's precious little honour amongst them. If they were holding anything of value . . ."

"Like a rich man's daughter," James added.

"Exactly! Then the first one to run out of money would have sent me a message"

"So who are your enemies?"

McGillivray's shoulder heaved in a gesture of ironic humour. "It would take a week to list them."

"Try, sir," said James, solicitously, "in case it sparks some hidden memory."

"The Kentuckians, who want more Creek land as well as trading concessions on the west bank of the Mississippi. The Georgian land speculators, the same. French trappers, the fraternity of *coureur de bois* who would like a monopoly of the trade in furs being exported through the colonial government—at present that is a position I hold. The French colonists of Louisiana. They resent the fact that I do business with the Spaniards and prop up what they see as a usurping power, the Dons themselves, who don't really trust the Creeks, and are sure we are just waiting to betray them to the Americans."

"Is there anyone left?" asked Harry.

"Oh, yes, Captain. My business competitors, or any villain that would seek to make a fortune by exploiting any perceived weakness in my defences."

"I take it you're known to be attached to her?"

McGillivray put his face in his hands. "I am."

"Then pray to whatever gods you worship, sir," said James.

"I do, daily." Suddenly he rubbed his face vigorously and looked at the two brothers. "Thank you, gentlemen. Allow me to apologize for the manner in which you were brought to this room. Please understand that I was anxious."

"Of course."

"I shall await a demand. No doubt it will arrive in time. The lack of specie in the area will make it difficult to meet, but I cannot gnaw on that problem until it arrives. After all, it is only three days since the taking of the *Gauchos*. All I ask is that you return her possessions to me. Who knows, she may have left a clue."

"Harry," said James, "you can't leave matters like this."

Harry looked at James, his face free of any expression. But as he turned back to the half-breed Indian, James was sure he saw the ghost of a smile.

"Mr McGillivray . . . I don't know if what I'm about to tell you will ease your mind or trouble you further."

The black eyes were on him now, as hard as agate. And Harry's voice, had a light, inappropriate quality for the purveyor of chilling news. "The day after the *Gauchos* sank, we found more than the body of Captain Rodrigo. The raft was towing half a dozen casks, which we assumed to have been used as a slow method of disposing of others."

James interrupted in a more solicitous tone. He described slowly what they'd found, then Harry took up the conversation again.

"There's no concrete evidence to suggest who the victims were."

"The method was certainly barbaric," said James.

"It does not bode well," added Harry gravely.

McGillivray seemed strangely untroubled by this, which made James continue: "It seems to me that you are operating on a false assumption, which is that the *Gauchos* was taken because your daughter was on board. It gives me no pleasure to disabuse you of this notion. When we boarded the vessel we found dozens of boxes, which we subsequently confirmed contained sugar, which was granulated by a new process invented here in New Orleans."

McGillivray interrupted swiftly, waving a huge arm dismissively. "I know of this. If you are attaching some importance to that in the matter of the loss of the ship, I must tell you it means nothing."

"They were all opened," said Harry, in a slightly pedantic way, "with the top layers of their contents removed."

McGillivray shrugged. "The value of those casks is long term, to both Louisiana and the sugar trade."

Harry nodded. "Carondelet implied much the same."

"So what is it that is designed to change my perception of why the ship was taken?"

"I won't bore you with what happened off Fort Balize, but we were obliged to come upriver to New Orleans, because of stating that one observation to Captain San Lucar de Barrameda. Here we met the Governor, and though he did not set out to tell us so, he managed to inform us that the *Gauchos* was carrying a large quantity . . ." Harry paused, long enough to draw his listener forward in his chair, "of gold and silver."

McGillivray shot to his feet.

"Bullion," Harry continued, "to the value of two hundred thousand Spanish dollars. I fear whoever took the ship was not in pursuit of any ransom, nor there to kidnap anyone's daughter. It is my supposition that they knew the gold and silver was on board. Not only did they remove it, but they also took everyone off the ship."

"Why?"

"I believe I have already said it can only be because either their vessel was known or they were themselves familiar enough to be recognized without causing fear."

"I don't mean that, Captain," McGillivray said with a touch of asperity. "Why would de Carondelet want to ship a fortune in bullion to New York?"

"That is a question we have been asking ourselves," Harry replied, nonchalantly, "ever since you mentioned it."

CHAPTER TWENTY

MCGILLIVRAY sat down again, leaning forward, his black eyes aimed at the brothers. Yet he wasn't looking at them so much as through them, as he tried to fit what they'd just told him into the mass of thoughts which must now have filled his head.

"I must tell you that having lost his original consignment," Harry continued, "he has taken possession of a chest full of treasure I was carrying and intends to use it as a replacement."

"Sorry," said McGillivray, who'd been so lost in his thoughts that he'd barely heard. But he forced himself to attend to what Harry said as he listed the events which had occurred since they'd berthed. The odd quick question helped him to avoid any misunderstanding, though the information he was receiving was clearly not doing anything for his confidence.

"You know more about matters in New Orleans than either of us, Mr McGillivray."

"If you're asking me to advise you, Captain Ludlow, then I'm not sure I can oblige."

"I rather thought you were seeking our assistance, sir."

McGillivray nodded sharply, though his eyes carried a different message.

"That is something we can hardly do in ignorance. How well do you know Barón de Carondelet?"

"We've met simply because it is necessary. He has a deep suspicion of both me and the six tribes of the Creek nation."

"Why?"

McGillivray smiled slowly. "My agreements regarding the fur trade monopoly and defending the west bank of the Mississippi were made with his predecessor, Governor Miro. So in part it's just the usual official attitude which maintains that nothing which happened before his tenure has any value. But just recently I went to New York, along with several other Creek chiefs, to negotiate with the American government over land-grabbing by their citizens. Speculators in the east sell land they don't own and when the people that have bought it turn up they find Indians occupying what they think is their property. That leads to conflict."

"I take it the good Barón didn't approve of your journey," said Harry.

"No. I tried to make sure that everything was open and above board."

"Did your mission succeed?" asked James, nonplussed as to why Harry shot him a hard look.

"I received guarantees from George Washington himself that they'd respect our territorial rights. I have to tell you that the President is as upright a man as you're ever likely to meet, and I feel that as long as he is in office, or has any influence over policy, we are safe. Unfortunately, de Carondelet will not accept that Washington is honest and well intentioned. He suspects that there may be some secret protocol in which we have undertaken to ally ourselves to the Americans in a way that will harm Spain."

"Is that why you don't wish to be seen here in the city?" demanded Harry.

"Yes. If my presence here is reported to the Governor he'll wonder what I'm up to. He likes me to stay north of Pointe Coupée, on Creek land. The idea that I might be dabbling in politics worries him."

"I suppose it's pointless to ask if he has a reason," Harry continued, smoothly. McGillivray looked at him keenly. "Do you dabble in politics?"

"It's impossible not to. I've already listed my enemies. But they're not against me, or the Creek nation, for any personal reasons. We live in an unstable part of the world, gentlemen, where many different bodies are competing for advantage. So many that the Governor of Louisiana has trouble keeping an eye on all of them. His recent activities have done little to ease his predicament. That money you mentioned, if I'm correct, has been gathered in by de Carondelet's agents over the past six months. It has led to the worst shortage of hard coin I've ever known. We're practically reduced to a barter economy throughout the territory."

"I've already said that if we are to aid you it would help us to know something of this, if you could spare the time to enlighten us."

It was now James's turn to look questioningly at Harry. There was nothing in his demeanour to suggest he cared two hoots for McGillivray's daughter. But he did care about the money they'd lost. The Indian couldn't help him with that, but if Harry was about to embark on a quest for de Carondelet's ingots then such a man could provide invaluable information. Was it that supposition, the feeling that he was indeed being used, that caused their abductor to adopt such a biting tone?

"I can enlighten you on this. As Englishmen, you picked the worst possible time to allow yourself to be locked up in a Spanish harbour."

"We weren't apprehended!" said James, offended. "Unless you are referring to the way we were brought to this room."

"Why do you say that?" asked Harry, in a more normal voice.

"You don't know about Spain and France?"

"What about them?"

"There's talk of an alliance."

"There's always talk of that," Harry replied.

"This time it's more than just conversation."

"How much more?"

"Enough to make me nervous about the frontier between America and Spain."

"Why should you be nervous?" asked James.

Harry cut right across McGillivray's chance to reply. "How much of this is mere rumour?"

"It's not rumour, Captain. Manuel de Godoy has been under

pressure from the French ever since he signed a treaty with them."

"That wasn't a treaty, it was a surrender," said James.

"Which tells you how much power he has to resist, Mr Ludlow. Spain and France are old allies."

"The Bourbon Kings were old allies. This is a different France."

"A difference that makes it even more dangerous to a weak monarch. Carlos has subjects who'd like to do to him what their neighbours did to Louis, only they'd want to guillotine his wife first. And some of the hidalgos, given half a chance, would love to hang de Godoy. French Jacobins are just the type to help them."

"How reliable is this?"

"It comes from the American Ambassador to Spain, Senator Thomas Pinckney."

"Have you any idea how close they are to agreement?"

"I have a precise idea," McGillivray replied. "The only thing that's stopped them up till now is a lack of the means to finance it. Louisiana isn't the only part of the world that's bereft of real money."

Harry thought for a moment, then suddenly, before responding, gritted his teeth in a silent curse. "The Plate fleet!"

McGillivray nodded. There was no need to explain, even to a lubber like James. The Spanish Plate fleet was the stuff of legend, the fantasists' dream of plenty. Millions in specie, the fruits of their South American mines, shipped every year, in convoy, from Mexico to Cadiz.

"De Carondelet will know this," James said.

"Which is why he's not worried about stealing valuables out of an English ship," added Harry thoughtfully. Again James noticed he was looking at McGillivray in an odd way. "Is this common knowledge?"

"No. Quite the opposite, though how long it will remain so I cannot say."

"And I dare say that anyone in possession of such information could use it to advantage."

The Indian didn't answer, but his hard look was enough to convince Harry that he'd hit a nerve.

"Mr McGillivray," Harry continued. "I find myself at a stand. I've heard conflicting reports of the nature of Spanish rule in Louisiana. Could you enlighten me as to how matters stand in the colony?"

To James that was an odd request, given what they'd just heard, and the silky tone Harry had used was out of character. But McGillivray seemed happy to oblige. He reprised all the threats that the Governor had spoken of, as well as telling the story of the slave revolt which San Lucar de Barrameda had so enjoyed recounting. That gentleman was dissected accurately by the Indian as typically Spanish in his inertia, as well as a pompous oaf. El Señor de Fajardo de Coburrabias, though identified as a pander, procurer, and dishonest tavern keeper, was nevertheless accorded both affection and respect, as well as being identified as the most active man in the colony.

"If de Barrameda attacked Barataria Bay, you'll probably find it was de Coburrabias's idea. He's a good soldier, and a fair administrator, with the morals of a rattlesnake. Both he and de Barrameda were here with Governor Miro, and being high-born Spaniards have nothing but contempt for what they see as an upstart nobleman from a family that originated in Wallonia."

The Governor was described as a man who couldn't make a decision. When called upon to act, he oscillated between a weak response and employing maximum strength. This wasn't necessarily due entirely to his nature, but more to the manifold difficulties he faced in running such a disparate and huge colony that ran all the way from the Gulf of Mexico to the Canadian border. His troops, poorly paid, were not only too few in number, they were totally unreliable. If they weren't the scrapings of Spanish gaols, they were Cuban and not to be trusted. All except the detachment of Royal Walloon Guards de Carondelet had brought from Spain as a sort of personal bodyguard.

"They are the ones who guard his residence. It was their

muskets that threatened your ship when you anchored. Carondelet keeps them under his personal control, which creates great friction between him and his senior officers."

"Surely they'd be better employed in the field," said Harry.

McGillivray laughed. "You sound just like de Coburrabias. The only time, up till now, they've left New Orleans is if there's been trouble with the Kentuckians. That happens less since Pinckney's Treaty. Though opening up the river has solved one problem and created a dozen more."

"What has it solved?"

"Festering resentment by the frontiersman, who are as bellicose a bunch of people as you're ever likely to meet. They even rebelled against their own government over a proposed whiskey tax. If there's one thing a Kaintuck hates, it's a tax."

Pollock had said much the same thing about the peoples of Kentucky and Tennessee.

"I heard they threatened to secede."

"They did, and that's not settled. There's a strong party in the Kentucky and Tennessee legislatures who think they'd be better off on their own."

"And the drawbacks?"

"What de Carondelet needs is stability. If you take the territory as a whole, most of the planters, even the French, are happy with Spanish rule. The last thing a slave owner wants is any talk of equality and the Dons have obliged them by harsh reprisals for insurrection. But that doesn't apply in New Orleans. The urban French aren't like those in the countryside. And even if he excludes any more French immigrants how do you stop Americans from settling here in such numbers that their mere presence makes matters worse? Of course there are certain people who've been here for years, some of whom are just as much trouble as the French. The Spanish don't trust them but they're tolerated. But with the number landing goods at the levee on rafts and riverboats, not all of whom go back, banning immigration is a law that's impossible to implement. And the incomers are more inclined to agitate for the United States to take over control of the delta in perpetuity."

James cut in. "Is that a prospect that tempts the sainted Washington?"

"That I couldn't say!" snapped McGillivray. "But I take leave to doubt it."

"Why?" asked Harry.

"Because he's got enough trouble with the land they already administer. The Federal government is only seven years old and since they've begun to raise taxes it isn't universally popular."

"That will make our dear King George happy," said James with a grin. "He's never quite got over losing America. They say it's what drove him mad."

"Well, the Union is no different. The imposition of Federal taxes, especially on whiskey, had the frontier in open revolt. After they put down the Whiskey Rebellion in '94 matters improved. But it's not settled, by a long chalk. Our dear friend the Barón would, of course, be delighted to see them secede."

"Why?"

"Because it would be weak in the face of the more numerous states to the east. That means it would require Spanish help to sustain itself."

"And where do you stand on this?"

"In between," he replied, acidly.

"Which is why de Carondelet suspects you of carrying on an illicit correspondence with the American government."

"Who says we are?"

"I think you have, Mr McGillivray."

"I don't recall doing so."

"Do you recall saying you have a daughter, sir?" asked Harry, with a smile.

"I don't see such a subject as one to be treated lightly," replied McGillivray.

"When we were with the Barón de Carondelet tonight, he asked me how I knew certain things without being told. For instance, I put forward the notion that the bullion he shipped on the *Gauchos* was a secret so well guarded that not even Captain Rodrigo knew he had it aboard."

"I can't see what you're driving at."

James opened his mouth to say the same thing, then thought better of it.

"I asked him about passengers, Mr McGillivray. He couldn't tell me anything about them, in fact he didn't know that at least one existed, which was singular considering the cargo. Yet you are asking me to believe that the daughter of a man he regards as potentially dangerous was on that ship."

McGillivray shrugged. "If he didn't know who the passengers were . . ."

"I wasn't thinking of his ignorance, sir. I was alluding to yours. If you have a daughter, then I dare say she would be of more value to you, and your tribe, than a dozen crocks of gold and silver ingots. Here we have a sixteen-year-old girl, from the senior clan in your tribe. I am assuming that power will pass through her bloodline, in the same way it did with your own mother. Yet you are asking us to believe that you put her, a sixteen-year-old, alone aboard a ship, without enquiring whether there were any other passengers, and if there were, their identity."

McGillivray didn't answer. He just stared hard at Harry for several seconds.

"And I would also assume that a man in such a sorry pass would not have time to spend enlightening two complete strangers as to the problems faced by the Governor of New Orleans. In short, Mr McGillivray, your hanging about here doesn't make sense. What would make sense is if you were to tell us what you're really after."

"I'm not sure that would be wise."

"Then let me help you," said Harry, coldly. "If you want a certain chest kept from the possession of the Spanish, it must be because there is something inside it that you do not wish them to see."

"You're a clever man, Captain Ludlow."

James cut in. "Please don't say that, Mr McGillivray. He's hard enough to share a cabin with already."

"Since the ship was bound for New York, I assume that your chest contains some form of compromising correspondence with the American government. Letters that the Barón de Carondelet would find hard to understand."

"That's the irony, Captain Ludlow. We're talking about Creek land. For Carondelet to suspect us of making trouble for him is absurd. Nothing suits our interests more than that the Spaniards should stay in the Louisiana Territory. They may be a nuisance with their priests forever at us to take the Catholic faith. But all they do is build missions, and those are only ever home to a few people. They don't threaten us like the frontier settlers."

"Do they threaten you so badly?" asked James.

"They do because they are numerous and getting more so. Because every one of them who has nothing believes that by moving west he can become rich. All he needs is land. Yet I can't ally the Creek nation, outright, with a Spain that is too weak to really defend the frontier. I must stay on good terms with the Americans, since they are the only people with the power to contain their own settlers. Does that answer you, Captain Ludlow?"

Harry nodded. "You feared the chest taken aboard today might be yours."

"I had to know."

"Then I can set your mind at rest, sir."

"You said something, earlier, about Carondelet taking some money of yours."

"I'm afraid that is true. Whatever reason he had for sending that cargo to New York still exists. But the treasure doesn't. It is our misfortune to be in possession of enough to replace it. He has the temerity to call it a loan when it was forcibly removed from my ship."

"He offered us a bill on the Spanish treasury as security," added James. "Clearly, after what you've told us regarding the possibility of war, that was just a bluff to avoid unnecessary trouble."

"Spain will be at war with Britain before you can present it."

Harry smiled grimly. "His next suggestion was even less attractive. He invited us to find his gold and silver for him, saying that if we did so we could keep it."

"Well, out of the two, Captain Ludlow, the first is deplorable and the second near impossible."

"That depends on where it is, Mr McGillivray. If it's still in the Territory, it will be hard for anyone to hide, especially if they're tempted to spend any. Merely being in possession of too much of that commodity, in a land devoid of specie, would raise suspicions."

"Are you asking me for something, Captain?"

"I am. I assume you maintain a presence here in New Orleans, one that you use to keep yourself informed of what is happening."

The other man didn't answer. But his eyes narrowed enough to tell Harry he was right. Not that it took a genius to deduce such a thing. If McGillivray couldn't come to the city himself he'd be a fool not to have channels of information. The silence lasted for several seconds as he weighed up the pros and cons of aiding the two brothers. Not that it was possible to see this internal debate on his face, which remained impassive. Finally he spoke, careful to avoid anything that smacked of surrender.

"The loading of the *Gauchos* was, according to my people, a semi-public event, attended by every dignitary that could be drummed up for the occasion, which is an irony given that the *Gauchos* then stayed tied up by the quay another whole day. Much is being made of this sugar granulation as though it will provide some panacea to the endemic ills of running Louisiana at a loss. Too much in my estimation. Once the process is public, every sugar planter who can, will copy it."

"We know that the *Navarro* left her berth at the same time as the *Gauchos*. That strikes me as curious. Captain San Lucar de Barrameda is not someone I'd be inclined to trust."

"He's angling for the post of Intendant," said McGillivray.

"At present de Carondelet holds that as well as the Governorship, which is very unusual. The Dons generally like to split the functions of their officials so that no one gets too ambitious. They give one man control of the law and another control of the money."

"The Intendant looks after the treasury?"

"That's right. And in most cases he won't release any money to the man who has the responsibility for everything else. De Carondelet could never have done what he has without control of both offices. I find it hard to believe he actually raised as much as you say. The last Intendant we had fought Governor Miro every step of the way. As a system of government, it leaves a lot to be desired."

"So anything that would embarrass the Governor, would also please de Barrameda."

"Not just him."

"What about the members of the *Cabildo?*"

"Functionaries. Small-time businessmen and magistrates. If, as you say, the gold and silver was stolen at sea, I can't imagine any of them having the courage to be a prime mover. It would be easy to find out where they've been the last few days, since they rarely leave New Orleans."

"What if they had connections to pirates?"

McGillivray shrugged. "Possible, but unlikely. I've already told you what they're like."

"What do you know about Captain Pasquale Fernandez?"

"You ask a lot of questions, Captain."

"Especially for a man who flatly refused to help de Carondelet," said James.

"Fernandez!" said Harry, emphatically.

"Cuban. Not very highly regarded. A bit lazy, I'm led to believe. Neither a good soldier nor an example as an officer. Had a bit of trouble with a ranker. Balize is not the kind of command that goes to a zealous officer."

"So he's disgruntled?"

"I've met him once, Ludlow. And from that brief acquaintance

I'd say it's hard to know. He's not a man to say much, which makes him either the dullard he appears or a deep fellow with hidden talents. I incline to the former."

"De Coburrabias?"

"He was in Havana collecting replacements," said James.

"So he was," Harry replied, with a smile. "But what if he had an accomplice?"

"What exactly is the population of New Orleans?" asked James, sarcastically.

"Could you find out if any other ships, apart from the *Navarro*, weighed within twenty-four hours of the *Gauchos*?"

"I can tell you that now because I had an interest. Apart from the other galley there were none. Three merchant ships were set to depart but they were delayed by a sudden customs search. Given what you say the *Gauchos* was carrying that makes more sense now than it did at the time."

"I wonder if with your contacts and some judicious questioning we might not trace de Carondelet's property."

McGillivray hesitated for a split second before responding. "That's a tall order, Captain Ludlow, since you don't have the faintest idea where to start looking."

Harry's face took on a grim expression. "That's true, sir. But I have no intention of sitting still and doing nothing."

"And what do you offer me in return?"

"Either the return of your chest, sir, or at the very least the correspondence it contains."

"When?"

"At the point that I'm satisfied that you have done everything in your power to help us."

"That's not very reassuring, Captain."

"Nevertheless, Mr McGillivray, it is a case of take it or leave it. I cannot guarantee that whatever cell Charpentier is occupying will not soon accommodate us as well. I would say your earnest and speedy endeavours would count as enlightened self-interest."

"I will need some time to make enquiries," he said, avoiding actual spoken capitulation. But the expression on his face showed that he was clearly unhappy.

"Mr McGillivray," said James, "if I may be allowed to put your mind at rest: my brother is devious in the extreme, but he is not dishonest and neither does he normally indulge in extortion. I would also add, if our situation was not so bad he would hand over your property without asking for anything in return."

"Thank you, James," said Harry, eyebrows raised.

CHAPTER TWENTY-ONE

"THAT WAS exceedingly astute of you, Harry," said James. They were out in the bustling streets again, having made an appointment to meet McGillivray at a time of his choosing. "Not that it was a bad idea. A fictitious endangered daughter is so much more telling than mere compromising correspondence. Having said that, one wonders at the nature of the man to concoct such a tale. Personally I put it down to the Scottish blood in his veins."

"I am grateful to you, James," said Harry, quickly, not wishing to get drawn onto the subject of Caledonians and their perceived faults. "I think that intervention of yours set his mind at rest."

In fact he believed it to be true. By insisting that Harry was honest, a claim no man could rightly put for himself, James had gone a long way to putting aside the Creek chieftain's concerns. Not that he had much choice. McGillivray didn't know Harry well enough to be aware that the mere idea of his passing information on to authority, knowledge that would endanger an innocent party, was risible. Having finally decided to cooperate with the Ludlows he'd relaxed a great deal, adding a wealth of information about the city and its inhabitants to the knowledge he'd already imparted. Responding to Harry's evident impatience he had hinted that something might be achieved by a visit to the swamp area north of the city wall. There numerous taverns satisfied the needs of those who lived in New Orleans, as well as those that visited the city. Without giving away his source, Harry asked about the Hôtel de la Porte d'Orléans, alluded to by de Coburrabias, only to be informed that the soldier owned it. The hotel was the biggest bawdy-house

in Spanish America, impossible to miss, since it stood in full
majesty, the only gas-lit building outside the north gate of the city
walls.

Harry stopped suddenly and looked hard at James. "Do you
think me devious?"

"I know you to be, brother. Here I am, if anything your closest confidant, without the faintest idea of your true intentions. All
I know is that you have coerced another man into helping us,
without having the faintest idea why."

Harry grinned, then started walking again. "I'm either going
to get that treasure back from de Carondelet, or recover his
ingots."

"I suspected as much. Does it occur to you that the Governor might be the thief?"

"Carondelet couldn't have stolen the money himself, James."

"Why not?"

"Remember he's both Governor and Intendant. If he was going
to rob the treasury all he had to do was pocket it and concoct a
tale to cover the loss. Instead he set up an elaborate method to
smuggle it out of the colony. He tried to keep the whole thing a
secret, certainly. But look at the number of people who knew. Now
why go to those lengths? It can only be because he wanted to
ensure that if anything went wrong he wouldn't bear sole responsibility."

"Please do carry on, brother," said James, when Harry paused.

"De Carondelet is not as clever as he'd like to think. Either
that or he truly expects us to find it, which I don't believe for a
second. He lets slip things that he should keep to himself. Remember he said that the money was for the security of Louisiana; that
its loss was nothing short of a disaster. But he didn't tell us the
destination, which really rendered such a statement meaningless.
But now we know that it was *en route* to New York, which alters
the case considerably. Why? Given his position, the secrecy, and
the method, it can only mean that the bullion was intended to
protect the colony from some threat."

"The source of which lay in New York?"

"The solution lay there, certainly. I doubt that the danger comes from somewhere so distant, unless it's from the government of the United States."

"McGillivray didn't think that likely?"

"Perhaps he's not right about everything, James. If the frontier states are causing trouble the one way to bind them to the Union is for the American government to take control of the delta."

"He's certainly right about one thing."

"Which is?"

"That the task we face is impossible. We don't know where to start looking."

"Nonsense, brother. We have at least one place we can look, right away."

"De Coburrabias's tavern?" Harry nodded. "And what if that produces nothing? We can't sit here for ever, taking the risk that war might break out at any moment."

"Right now we are trapped," Harry replied, "not only by Spanish guns, but by our own parole."

"Does it occur to you, Harry, that regardless of your own inclinations, you may be forced to leave that chest in de Carondelet's possession just to gain enough freedom to save our skins?"

Harry was suddenly angry and the note in his voice was bitter.

"It does. And should that happen I can assure you that I'll sit off Fort Balize and search every ship that exits the Mississippi, war or no war. If that first consignment was bound for New York then he intends to use the Frenchmen's money to replace it. When he does, we'll be waiting. I don't care how we get it back, James, but get it back we will."

James patted his brother on the shoulder.

"Of course, Harry. But it occurs to me that we have, for the first time this evening, actually referred to the true owners of the treasure. It's not really up to us to decide if we are willing to accept de Carondelet's terms. It's up to our passengers. Since they're planning to stay in Louisiana, they may be very willing to take up the offer we refused."

"I'd feel safer giving them back hard cash."

"But you will give them the option, I take it?"

There was a cunning look in Harry's eye when he nodded in reply, one that James had seen before. "Yes. But I am also determined to see if we can find anything out in the taverns of New Orleans. You'd be amazed at what you can glean from a drunken sailor."

"Why, if we are going to scour these taverns, are we heading back to the ship?"

"Well, firstly it's to talk to our passengers. But more importantly, if we're going tavern crawling I want to collect Pender. You don't think I'd venture into such places without him at my back, do you?"

Before he returned to the ship, Harry took the opportunity to have a close look at the defences. He particularly wanted to examine them in darkness since any attempt at escape would very likely be undertaken at night. The galleys, illuminated, were still in place. But from his position on top of the levee he noticed immediately that the gunners had been stood down, the first indication that the Spanish were dropping their guard. Not that they were really required while a watch was on duty in the great stone bastion: even in darkness there was no place to hide from the guards on the parapet. Standing at the base of the angled walls Harry was in clear view. Though he had little time to spare, he walked all the way down the elevated track to examine the approaches to the octagonal downriver fortress.

"This is the fellow that really counts, James. With luck we could either get out of range of the one we're berthed by or so entangle ourselves with the shipping surrounding us that accurate fire would be impossible." Harry shook his head slowly, as he examined the wide, slow-moving river. "But to get past this fellow in what would be clear water . . ."

Since the levee formed the defensive barrier on the riverside the entire exterior of the gatehouse bastion was observable. The gate itself was a heavy set of double wooden doors, guarded by two sentries who stood under constant observation from their counterparts on the fire-step. And the exterior was formidable. Though not actually designed by Vauban, it was a testimony to the ideas of the greatest designer of fortresses the world had ever known. Sloping heavy stone walls, interlocked so that they would deflect shot rather than try to absorb its impact; grass footing with the rest of the walls coated in a moss that made climbing impossible; a dip on the western side that would take any attacker down into an area criss-crossed by deadly fields of fire right in front of the canal which acted as a moat. These killing grounds extended so that men climbing ladders to assault the wooden palisades would never be out of the sights of several dozen muskets.

But they'd gone for decor too, as if in a desire to emphasize the majesty of their works—a simple embrasure of smooth stone was insufficient. Each one was decorated with the royal crest of Spain, and the gateway was crowned with several sets of armorial shields. The garrison on duty was wide awake, not yet bored by the need to keep watch in case *Bucephalas* should try to slip her moorings. The side of the levee practically abutted the bastion. Looking over to where the earth sloped into the muddy waters of the Mississippi, it was possible to detect the high-water mark which reflected the surging spring floods. Millions of gallons of melting snow turned the river into a dangerous torrent, and the delta itself into something approaching a lake. But what interested Harry was the idea that the river had yet to descend completely to its summertime level.

Here was a weakness that had been either overlooked or forced by the exigencies of the landscape. Swampy grounds made the building of high stone structures difficult, while the height of the levee was necessary to hold back the flood waters of the river. So, if the river was low enough, there was a point at which the guns of the fortress couldn't be properly brought to bear. The angle of fire left, close to the actual shore, a passage that could, at the right time, provide security for a ship's hull. It would do nothing to protect masts and rigging, but they were a far harder target to hit than solid wood.

Harry looked at the base of the fortress. Watched by a curious sentry, he squelched around by the bottom of the walls. Even with the river low it was swampy. In a land where people had to be buried under ballast so that their bodies didn't float to the surface the Spanish had built a fortress from a design suited to dry land. Perhaps, under any pressure from flooding, the walls of the whole perimeter could become unstable. He didn't envy the man who'd designed this defensive structure, given the various demands that must have been made upon his talents. Wood, like that used in the connecting palisades, was the best material in soft ground, being lighter than stone, but that risked fire. It also lacked the majesty of stone, an important consideration in a land where power was held as much by perception as by actual force.

Finally worried about what he was up to, the sentry shouted down. Harry just waved in reply, then made his way back to the top of the levee.

"Come along, James. I think we've seen enough."

He needed Pender at his back when he faced the Frenchmen for the second time. The number of decisions they were required to consider had multiplied and with that the degree of fractiousness. Should they go ashore at all, with or without their money? Was it possible for them to accept the proffered methods of repayment? Should Harry Ludlow still be held responsible for the loss? Was it best, with the possibility of war in the offing, to depart from the ship regardless? No more than half a dozen souls could be brought to subscribe to any theory, with the mood becoming uglier by the minute. He had to shout himself hoarse to get any attention at all.

"We have no way of knowing if the Governor is being truthful about repayment. Let us put that to the test. If he is I would recommend that you go ashore."

"As paupers."

"Meanwhile, we will see what we can do to recover some of the loss. I have no intention of sitting idly by and doing nothing. I fully intend, this very night, to seek information."

"It's a mite late, Harry."

"I don't care if it's near dawn, James. I'd do anything rather than stay aboard and listen to this."

The road that ran out through the northern wall of New Orleans was slightly elevated, and for good reason, since the whole area seemed to be part of another swamp. Before making his planned visit to the Hôtel de la Porte d'Orléans, Harry determined to look over the area, a prospect that produced a groan from James. Clearly de Coburrabias's property was the best establishment. It stood right by the roadside, a wooden structure of some permanence, the substantial windows well lit and inviting. The whole building was raised on poles above the muddy ground, which was true of a number of the taverns that lay by the main thoroughfare. But the further away they got from the road, the less salubrious became both the *tiendas* and the state of the ground. At several points they were up to their ankles in mud, and confronted with lean-to shacks that catered for nothing but Negroes. By the roadway the whores had shown some evidence of beauty in their features and their dress. Here there were nothing but skinny slatterns in threadbare garments, who, when they tried to smile, exposed few teeth in their grime-covered mouths. The level of suspicion they were exposed to also seemed to relate to the nature of their surroundings.

"What do you think, Pender?" asked Harry, trying to shake some of the glutinous mud off his boots.

"I don't see no point in these here gin bins, your honour. If anyone was carrying the kind of money you've been on about they'd be up on the road." He jerked a thumb towards a lean-to shack that was close to collapse, the wood so rotted that the faint candlelight from the interior glowed through a dozen holes. "Nowt but a beggar would come to a place like this."

"There are certainly enough places to choose from," said James, kicking one boot against a live oak tree.

"Too many," said Harry, looking back towards the roadway. "We could be here for days and not see inside them all."

"Well, my sentiments are those of Pender," James added bitterly. "We've already been pointed towards the very best place. Let's start there. If that proves to be a blank we can work our way down."

There was quite a crowd outside the Hôtel de la Porte d'Orléans, some carrying flagons of drink, others trying to negotiate terms with the numerous multi-hued whores who were plying their trade. Various articles, from bales of cloth to wads of tobacco, were on offer as payment. Two men, who by their speech and dress came from one of the riverboats, were shaping up to fight over the favours of one girl: she, indifferent to their dispute, was looking over their shoulders for another catch. Harry noticed that once agreement had been reached, the girls and their customers headed down the darkened side of the two-storey building, presumably to a staircase that took them to the first floor.

"Well, brother," said Harry, pointing to one particularly fine mulatto girl, "this seems to be your sort of place. Shall we go in?"

Pender eased a long-bladed knife in the sheath on his belt.

"After you, your honour."

CHAPTER TWENTY-TWO

THE WALL of warm smoky air hit them as they walked through the door, with the sound of music barely discernible above the numerous voices. A tall grey-haired black man, dressed in a striped silk coat and tight black breeches, came from behind a desk, his approach slow and measured. Harry could see his eyes ranging over these new arrivals, sorting them out with a professional eye. Pender had dropped back slightly, but the reaction he produced when he saw their exceedingly muddy boots owed nothing to heirarchy. Harry asked him for a table, in French, and was a touch put out when the man addressed them in flawless English.

"Welcome to the Hôtel de la Porte d'Orléans, gentlemen. Might I be allowed to send you someone to clean your footwear before you enter the public area?"

"Thank you," said James, having looked down at his feet for the first time. He'd been aware that his shoes were dirty, but not the extent. "I'm afraid we got rather lost."

"So easy to do, sir, on such a well-illuminated road." James looked up to see the full white smile of the elderly Negro. The man was pointing to a long bench which stood off to one side. "If you care to take a seat, gentlemen, I will send a boy to attend to you."

Harry nodded absentmindedly. His attention was taken up with scanning the room. They could be in this one tavern for days given the warren-like nature of the place and the number of customers crammed inside its walls. The tables on the ground floor were arranged around an open space with a great gas flame in the centre, smack in the middle of a fountain. Several people, again a mixture of races, were dancing lively reels. Other small rooms seemed to serve different groups of serious drinkers. The balcony, apart from that section occupied by the musicians, was full also, with people of every colour in groups of various size, drinking, eating, and talking at the top of their voices. There was a separate section towards the back of the building, nearly as large as the main ballroom. Through the heavy smoke Harry could see a long crowded bar, full of oddly dressed men, noisily swigging drinks.

"I see our host caters for all tastes," said James, pointing in that direction. "He even provided a facility for the roughest portion of the populace."

Harry looked closer, noticing the mode of dress, and straining to hear he picked up the sound of what he took to be frontier English.

"I think they are the riverboat men, brother. And from what we've heard from both Pollock and McGillivray, separation would appear to be sound common sense."

Having given his instructions to another servant, the silk-clad Negro returned. "I must ask you, sirs, to deposit any weapons you may be carrying with me. If you lay them on the desk, I will label them with your name and return them to you when you depart."

Harry took off his sword and Pender surrendered both his club and the long-bladed knife. James, who'd only bought a stick, shook his head.

"Is that really all you carry, gentlemen? No knives tucked in boots, for instance?"

"None," Harry replied, allowing himself to be led, like the others, to the long bench that lined one wall.

"Then you are clearly strangers to the Crescent City. Now what name shall I place them under?"

"Ludlow." The old man's grey eyebrows shot up, which made Harry add a quick explanation. "We were invited to come here by El Señor de Fajardo de Coburrabias. He said we should ask for Mademoiselle Feraud, and present his personal compliments."

The old man who'd recovered his poise, stiffened at the name, like a soldier coming into the presence of an officer.

"Certainly, gentlemen. I will inform Mademoiselle Hyacinthe that you are here, Captain Ludlow."

"What a wonderful name," said Harry, as a small Negro boy began to work on their boots with a damp cloth. "Hyacinthe."

"Don't raise your hopes, brother. I've been in such places in Paris. They are, without exception, run by ladies of advanced years whose ugliness is only surpassed by their avarice. The 'Mademoiselle' is not a voluntary state."

Harry laughed. "It's not just in Paris, James. Such creatures are to be found in every port I ever visited."

"Did I detect a hint of recognition in that old man's face?"

"I think so," Harry replied. "He called me Captain. I take New Orleans to be as gossipy as every other anchorage. News has obviously got out about us, and our predicament. The question is, how much and how accurate."

"Would it be an idea if I was to get down among the rivermen, your honour? Who knows, with them being English-speakers I might pick up something."

"Good idea," said Harry, after a brief pause. "But don't get into any fights. They have a fearsome reputation."

Pender laughed. "You can say what you like about 'em, Capt'n, but they ain't no different to what you'd find in a Portsmouth tavern any day of the week."

He stood up, which produced a slight hint of panic in the shoeshine boy's face. He'd finished Harry and was halfway through James. Pender grinned at him and patted him on the shoulder.

"Don't you fret, nipper. I don't need no clean boots where I'm a'going."

It was doubtful whether the boy understood. But the tone of Pender's voice made him smile, white teeth that gleamed against his flawless, almost polished black skin. Harry saw a trace of a shadow cross Pender's face, and wondered if he was thinking of his own children, far away at the Ludlow family house in Kent.

His servant never mentioned how much he cared for them. But then he didn't have to say anything to men who'd seen the happiness he displayed when he received a letter from his eldest daughter. Both brothers followed his progress across the smoky room. Only when they looked back did they become aware of the lady standing before them. The major-domo who'd taken their weapons stood beside her. When they looked at him, which was several seconds later, he favoured them with a low bow.

"Captain Ludlow, may I present to you the head of this establishment, Mademoiselle Hyacinthe Feraud."

Neither Harry nor James gasped as they jumped to their feet. But if such a sound had burst from their breasts they would have been forced to admit it to be deserved. The lady that stood before them was an outstanding beauty, and what's more one who, judging by the smoothness of her skin, could not be more than twenty years of age. A half-caste, her features combined the best of the races that had contributed to her creation. That skin, smooth and glistening, was a dark coffee shade, but the nose and mouth were European. Her eyes, lively and large, were a deep, deep brown in colour, with the whites very obvious against the tone of her complexion. Dressed in a pink silk garment that showed the curves of her body, they were aware of the outlines of the willowy figure it contained. It was trimmed at throat and wrists by sparkling white lace, the *décolletage* cut low enough to reveal a handsome bosom. On her head she wore a matching pink and white scarf, piled high so that it added several inches to her perceived height, this decorated by silken ropes of pink, set with pearls. Even in the smoky atmosphere, the smell of her musky perfume wafted towards them.

"Captain Ludlow," she said, smiling. When Harry nodded she held out a hand and stepped forward. "Then you must be Monsieur James Ludlow."

"I am indeed, Mademoiselle," James replied, bending over the hand. *"Enchanté."*

"Cayetano came by on his way to Fort St Jean. He said that I should expect you, though not this very night. Were I to announce you to this assembly you would be the object of much attention."

"In what respect, Mademoiselle?" asked James, with an innocent air.

"Let us just say that when a ship receives such a welcome as yours, tongues begin to wag." An elegant hand was waved at the room behind. "Would you consent to take wine with me at my table?"

"Dear lady," said Harry, who hadn't once taken his eyes off her, "the whole Spanish Armada could not restrain us."

That made her laugh, which, being deep and throaty, only added to the stunning impression she was making on both her guests.

"Such gallantry," she replied.

"I was just about to make that observation myself," said James, wickedly. "My brother is more often noted for being forthright than gallant."

There was a sudden commotion down at the lower level of the bar, with raised voices and loud cursing. She glanced towards the noise, but neither Harry nor James, either through good manners or natural inclination, followed the look.

"I admire that," Mademoiselle Feraud replied, craning to see what was causing the fuss. "Though dalliance has its place. I shall ask Bernard here to show you to my table. I must see to one or two things before I join you."

"That was uncalled for, James," said Harry, as Bernard led them through the closely packed tables. Behind them the noise was increasing in volume. "I attempt a little flattery and you immediately set out to undermine me."

"I think you're being oversensitive, brother," James replied, his eye twinkling.

Harry grunted. He wasn't the jealous type, but he did consider James to be far more handsome than himself. His brother was slim and elegant while he, with years at sea to coarsen him, was of a much heavier build. Likewise, a sailor's rough life, combined with his combative nature, had led him into many a scrape and shaped his speech and manners. Not so James, a scion of the London salons, educated at school, at university, and in the drawing-rooms of his artistic patrons. The family likeness was there for all to see, but in James it had a classical dimension that Harry had forfeited years ago.

"Am I being sensitive?" Harry asked. "We have met two interesting people tonight. The first was informed that I am devious, and the second you tell I am forthright, which is a polite term for being downright rude."

"And which do you care about most?"

Harry sat down in the chair Bernard had pulled out for him, his face angry. "Does it matter?"

James sat too, and waited while another servant, who'd appeared behind Bernard, poured him a glass of wine.

"From the table of Monsieur Patrice Saraille."

"Where away?" asked Harry. The servant pointed to a fat man, round of face and pink, sitting at a table with two exquisitely dressed black women. The man raised his own glass to the Ludlows.

"He is the editor of the French-language newspaper, *Le Moniteur*," said Bernard.

"How does he know who we are?" asked James.

"Monsieur. Everyone who is anyone in New Orleans knows who you are."

Harry lifted his glass in response. He knew Bernard was not being entirely truthful. No one else in the crowded tavern was paying them any attention. Only the fat fellow who'd bought their drinks. Which implied that the major-domo was employed, no doubt for a fee, to keep the owner of the newspaper informed of any interesting arrivals.

"If we are going to compete for Hyacinthe's favour we'd better establish the rules now," said James.

Harry had to practically shout. The musicians had increased their volume to try and cover the noise emanating from the lower taproom.

"Who said anything about that!"

James laughed and shouted back. "I rather think you did, brother—if not in so many words, certainly by your face. But I must caution you. A woman like that tends to be spoken for. I doubt that El Señor de Coburrobias would take kindly to any attempt by either one of us to oust him."

"Just don't offer to do her portrait," Harry growled.

"My, my, brother, you are smitten."

Harry, facing the direction of the noise, saw Pender pushing his way through the throng. He waved to him to join them.

"What a bunch of rogues, an' no error," he said, as he sat down. Then he threw back his head and laughed. "I reckon your Mr Pollock had the right of it. I've never seen a set of men so willing to scrap as that lot down there. There's challenges flying about all over the place. For cockfights, dogfights, boat races, shooting contests, wrestling bouts, and fisticuffs. And drink! They got that heathen brew whiskey instead of a decent drop of rum."

"Perhaps that is the catalyst for their bellicosity," said James. "The Scots, who are famous for the short fuse, are wont to drink the stuff, and Johnson says that in their heathen tongue they claim it to be the very water of life."

Suddenly the band stopped playing, which left James sounding as though he too was shouting. Not that it was noticeable to an excessive degree, since the noise from the lower taproom seemed to be heading their way. The dancers, who'd been strutting in front of the table, suddenly scampered off the floor. It was easy to see why: a huge, scarred individual, with a flaming mass of red hair, was heading in their direction. His ruddy, vinous face was fixed in a fearsome scowl as he barrelled aside those who impeded him.

"Stand aside for King Kavanagh!" shouted a voice from behind him. "The best damned bareknuckle west of the Ohio."

"Damned right," growled the object of this veneration, ripping at his stained shirt to reveal an impressive hairy torso. "An' that's only cause I ain't been east of the Ohio."

"What have we here?" said James.

"A fight by the look of it," Pender answered. Then he shot to his feet as Hyacinthe Feraud appeared. Harry and James did likewise.

"Forgive me, Messieurs. Two of the riverboat Captains are set to fight. This will lead to much betting on the result. It will also mean that this table will become a dangerous place to sit. Might I invite you to retire to the balcony?"

"Who is the other contestant?"

"As usual, Thankful Tucker."

"As a name, that is even more colourful than Hyacinthe," said James.

She laughed. "He is a colourful man. And this has become a nightly occurrence since they opened the river to the Kaintucks. A while ago I decided that instead of them wrecking the salon I provide for them they should come onto the floor and fight properly. In that way, at least, they entertain my customers."

"Who supervises them?"

"Bernard." She gestured to the floor, and sure enough, there was the old elegant Negro, jacket off and sleeves rolled up, with a bell in one hand and a vicious-looking club in the other.

"Why the club?" asked Harry, who'd attended many a bare-knuckle contest in his time.

"The rules are rather lax but they are not allowed to kill each other, Captain. That would only cause more trouble. So Bernard, if they don't stop when he rings, gives them a little tap on the head."

"Do they have a prize of any kind?"

"They fight for what they own, Monsieur. Their boats."

There was a sudden round of clapping as the other competitor appeared. He was a big man too, scarred and tough, though not as large as his opponent. His black hair was cut so short as to make him appear near bald. Kavanagh was a good three inches taller and a lot broader, but that didn't seem to frighten him at all. He held up his hands and silence fell.

"Well, ladies and gentlemen. I've been waiting to do this for years. Over yonder is the unsightly countenance of King Kavanagh, who reckons he can scrap."

Suddenly he spat into the gas flame in a most derisory way. That produced a hiss from the fire and a simian growl from his opponent. Many of the audience clapped.

"He certainly has a way with the crowd," said James.

Hyacinthe smiled in a way that spoke volumes. "He has that, Monsieur. And not only crowds."

"It's a good way to unbalance your opponent, I think," said Harry, a remark which earned him a dazzling smile of agreement from Hyacinthe.

"And he's been traipsing round the frontier," Tucker continued, "telling all and sundry that he's the best, while taking care to make sure that he and I have never been in the same place, at the same time."

"Damn it, I'm here now, Tucker," Kavanagh shouted, a great spray of spittle emerging from his mouth, "and I hope you're thankful!"

Too far away to be affected, Tucker still pretended he'd been hit, slowly dragging a finger across one eye. This killed any humour in Kavanagh's pun on his nickname. The crowd laughed uproariously as two servants arrived to remove the table. Harry and James stood up and prepared to follow their hostess.

"I think I'll stay down here for a better view, your honour," said Pender.

Harry smiled, then stepped smartly in front of James so that it was him who was following Hyacinthe Feraud up the narrow, steep staircase. He could see her hips swaying beneath the pink silk dress, almost pick out each muscle as it moved. And he was in the wake of her perfume, which, acting on the warmth of her body, was so close to his nose that he had to turn away. By the time they reached the balcony rail the two contestants were in the middle of the floor. Tucker had a whiskey jug in his hand, and he was offering it to Kavanagh.

"Now I won't get the chance to tell you after I've licked you, Kavanagh, that there ain't no hard feelings. So I will drink with you now."

"Like hell, Tucker."

"Now that ain't the act of a gentleman, Kavanagh," said Tucker, spinning round to appeal to the crowd. Someone started a slow clap, shouting the word "drink." Taken up quickly by those watching it soon became a cry that shook the rafters. Harry could see that people were crowding in from the streets. Clearly the news of the fight had got around and customers were pouring in from other taverns, noisily ordering drinks and shoving money at the overworked servitors.

"This appears to be good for business," shouted Harry.

Hyacinthe, leaning on the balustrade, nodded happily. Harry leant beside her, letting his hand brush the silky skin of her bare arm. The effect was a sudden, tingling sensation that ran right through him. But what pleased him was the feeling that it had affected her too, since she turned and smiled in a slightly surprised, but very inviting way.

"Stand by to board," said James, in his ear. Then he gasped slightly as Harry's elbow dug into his ribs.

The cry of "drink" was repeated until Kavanagh relented. He took the jug off Tucker, crooked it over his arm, and took a great swig. Harry could see his throat working to take in the liquid. Having drunk whiskey in the past he knew it to be a fiery spirit indeed, and the frontier variety was said to be rougher than the Scottish brew that his brother-in-law, Lord Drumdryan, had pressed him to taste. That made Kavanagh's feat as impressive as it was stupid, since a gut full of alcohol would do nothing for his ability to fight. Tucker then took the jug and crooked it in the same fashion. But Harry saw that while he held it at his lips for quite a while, his throat didn't move.

Then Tucker passed the jug to a spectator. Immediately it was removed from his hand he swung round and hit Kavanagh in the stomach. A rush of air left the taller man's mouth. He bent slightly but recovered, hauling his head up to glare defiantly at Tucker. That's when his opponent spat the whiskey, which he'd secreted in his mouth, right into Kavanagh's eyes. Blinded, the best bare-knuckle west of the Ohio was easy meat. Tucker hit him time and again, at his leisure, driving him back across the small dance floor. Each punch was carefully timed for maximum effect, producing spouts of blood from Kavanagh's mouth and nose. Every blow to the belly would fold him in half, just as every uppercut sent his head flying upright. Tucker was relentless, inflicting cuts above his eyes with short telling jabs that turned the crowd delirious with joy. They cheered Tucker on as he slowly reduced his bigger oppo-nent to a hulk. If Kavanagh's eyes had cleared he'd taken too much punishment to regain the initiative. Finally, after Tucker boxed his ears a half dozen times, the big man dropped to his knees. As Bernard rang the bell, Tucker stepped forward and gave him an uppercut to the jaw that sent him flying. Harry was sure, even above the noise of the spectators, that he heard the bone go.

Harry touched Hyacinthe's arm again, feeling once more that delicious thrill. It was as if his blood was trying to ooze out of his body.

"I see that as you indicated the rules are rather lax."

She turned to face him. He could see her breasts heaving with the excitement of having watched one man destroy another. At one and the same time, that sight elated and upset him. Somehow she had diminished herself in his mind. Had Tucker won fairly he would have seen the attraction as a understandable response. But he hadn't. Even if there were no rules, he had cheated.

"To win, Captain Ludlow. That is the one and only rule."

CHAPTER TWENTY-THREE

IT WAS AMAZING how quickly the Hôtel de la Porte d'Orléans was back to normal. Inside two minutes it was as though no fight had taken place. Kavanagh had been carried out still dripping blood, the tables had been replaced, the band had struck up a tune, and the dancers returned to the floor. Hyacinthe led them back to her reconstituted table. Wine appeared in a flash, with their hostess proposing a toast to Thankful Tucker. Harry only hesitated for a moment, putting aside any idea of questioning the victory. He reminded himself of why he'd come in the first place, which had nothing to doing with bareknuckle fighting or beautiful Creoles.

"I was told that you entertain the men from Barataria Bay as well as those from the riverboats."

The dark eyes flashed, showing just a hint of the temperament that lurked beneath Hyacinthe's civilized veneer. "The one thing I never ask a man who comes in here is how he makes his way in the world, Captain."

"What would you say if I told you that one of your customers might hold a clue to the whereabouts of two hundred thousand Spanish dollars?"

The eyebrows flicked slightly, and she smiled, before putting her hand on his. "Then I would want you to identify him, Captain. There is a card room upstairs in which he would be most welcome."

Harry felt the squeeze that was meant to convey that she knew, as well as he did, where de Carondelet's ingots had gone.

"Unfortunately, the money doesn't belong to him."

"Money is treated in the same way as my clients. Where it comes from is of no account."

Harry was about to ask how someone who worked for a senior member of the Spanish administration could say that, but he did not get the chance.

"What money?"

Harry spun round to find Thankful Tucker, now fully dressed, standing right behind him. For reasons he didn't quite understand, that made him stand up abruptly. Close too, Harry could see the scars on his face that marked him out as a fighter. His hands, always a good indicator of a bruiser, were big and knobbled, showing red at the knuckles where he used them to pound Kavanagh. But his clothes were well cut and his linen clean, in sharp contrast to most of his fellow boatmen, who wore buckskins. In fact, despite the red-spotted bandanna at his neck there was just a touch of the dandy about the man. Hyacinthe Feraud made a swift introduction and, much to Harry's chagrin, invited Tucker to join them.

"Are you the poor souls that are sitting under Spanish guns?" asked Tucker.

"We are," Harry replied.

"Well, you're better off than poor Charpentier. He's probably stretched out on the rack by now. If they do the same to you the Governor will make you give back his gold, eh!"

James, seeing Harry frown, cut in. "That was quite a neat display, sir. But I'm curious. Could you have beaten Kavanagh without subterfuge?"

Tucker grinned, declined to take wine, and asked Bernard to fetch some whiskey. "I reckon so, Mr Ludlow, otherwise I would never have fought him. But without that little trick with the raw spirit I don't suppose I'd be sitting here now talking to you in such an easy manner."

"No," said Hyacinthe. "You would be upstairs again, occupying one of the beds for a week."

"With a brute like Kavanagh, a week would scarce be enough," he replied. Then he put his huge hand over Hyacinthe's. "But it would be worth it just to have these pretty little things bathe my bruises, one more time."

"So you have acquired a boat," said Harry abruptly, as Hyacinthe Feraud gave Tucker a dazzling smile.

"I have. Though it's a damned keelboat and of little use to me. If Kavanagh's got any money, or goods to trade, I'll let him buy it back. Otherwise it will be broken up for the wood and go towards the building of some local worthy's house."

"So this isn't the first time you've won such a bout?" asked James.

"My word, no. I've been fighting people for all manner of things, including their boats, ever since I first took to the river, and that wasn't yesterday. Fighting all the way from Pittsburgh to the Gulf."

"Have you ever lost your own boat, Captain Tucker?" asked Harry.

"Captain!" Tucker threw back his head and laughed. "I've been called a lot of things, friend, but it's an age since anyone addressed me as Captain."

"I dare say Kavanagh, when his jaw has healed, will have the odd unflattering epithet to add to the list."

Tucker stopped laughing and looked at Harry hard. "The only thing I ever lost a boat to was the river. Even if I've been on it for years it's damned unpredictable. No man has yet come close to matching the Mississippi, sir, and nor do I expect them to."

"It is bound to happen one day."

Tucker's eyes had narrowed, and the glass he was about to drink from stopped just short of his lips. "Do you have anyone in mind to take the crown, Ludlow?"

"Captain Ludlow and his brother are strangers here," said Hyacinthe quickly. "They don't know you, Thankful, or have knowledge of your reputation."

Tucker grunted and emptied his glass. Hyacinthe turned the

conversation round by leaning across the table to address Harry, which forced him to exchange the glare he had been giving Tucker, for a smile to match her own.

"We were talking about a lot of money. Two hundred thousand dollars. Some say it's all the coin in Louisiana."

"Let us by all means remember why we are here," said James.

Tucker whistled and rolled his eyes towards his hostess.

"Now that is real scratch. Enough to buy a plantation house fit for a princess like you. I can just see you, Hyacinthe, in an open coach, driving up the avenue of live oaks to the house. We will paint it yellow, so that it stands out from the surrounding trees. Would you care for white horses, or black?"

"Rumours are flying about the town, Captain Ludlow," said Hyacinthe, "that the money was stolen by you. That is why you are under the great guns."

"It wasn't, I'm afraid."

"Do you expect to be believed?" asked Tucker.

Harry replied sharply. "Yes, sir, I do. Especially since not even Governor de Carondelet thinks us the culprits."

Hyacinthe cut in, to provide information which had doubtless come to her through the rumour mill, this to reprise the view that he and James were the guilty parties. These rumours were now common currency, while the truth was still locked in the breasts of one of those they'd dined with that very evening. Certainly Hyacinthe's employer hadn't included what had transpired in his explanation about their potential visit. And Harry didn't feel inclined to tell them that his superior had just robbed them of even more money, quite convinced that if such a thing became widely known it would do nothing to help him get it back. But he did tell them about the dinner and some of what had taken place. Finished speaking, he was unsure as to whether he'd convinced her of their innocence, since she had listened to him with a knowing smile. Tucker, on the other hand, thought the whole thing a huge joke.

"Why, damn me, Ludlow, if old *Cochon du lait* has gone and

lost that much it'll make his eyes pop right out of his skull. No wonder he asked you to help him get it back."

"Perhaps if we explain precisely what happened," said James, addressing their hostess, "you will be able to point us in a direction that might help us recover it."

"Why in hell's name should you want to recover Spanish money?" demanded Tucker. "Has *Cochon du lait* offered you a reward?"

Harry ignored that question, and, for what seemed like the tenth time, albeit with some careful filleting, he related the events that surrounded the sinking of the *Gauchos*. Following that he went on to mention de Barrameda's raid on Barataria Bay, plus the opinion, unattributed, that it might not have been the success he claimed.

"Pirates wouldn't have tried to sink her," said Tucker, emphatically, long before he'd actually finished.

"How can you be so sure?" asked James.

"Because a ship is worth money round here, even if only for the wood. And the one thing that would puff their pride would be a real sailing ship with guns. Charpentier is a handsome fellow, I'll grant you, with a wicked wit to go with his looks. But he's an exception. Those scum that hang out in Barataria Bay ain't no Morgans or Kidds. In the main they're verminous cowards who use shallow-draft boats to attack the coastal trade and never, if they can avoid it, go far out to sea. Which is just as well given the leaky tubs they use. If this *Gauchos* was, as you say, a caravel, soundly built and in good order, he could have outrun them under topsails."

Harry was clearly reluctant to engage Tucker in conversation, but he seemed so knowledgeable that he had no choice.

"Are they easily recognizable?"

"They certainly are. You can tell them by the way their ribs stick out. Half the time they can't afford the price of loaf of bread, nor a drink. The idea of such a crew in sight of that kind of scratch makes me laugh. The sight of one of those ingots would have led to murder right there and then, with each one killing the other."

"I meant their boats," said Harry, tersely.

"I wouldn't know then, 'cause I never go beyond New Orleans. But if I was to sail out through the delta, I reckon it would take me no more'n a day to get a sketch drawing of every one of them. And I know that half a day south of Fort Balize they'd cease to be a worry."

"Mademoiselle Feraud." Hyacinthe looked up, then extended her hand as the plump figure of Monsieur Saraille bent over it. "Might I be permitted to join you?"

She hesitated for less than a second, her face fixed in an insincere smile. "Of course, if these gentlemen have no objection."

"I have a confession to make, Mademoiselle. It is a terrible thing to say to such a beautiful creature, but it is them I have come to see."

"I suspected as much," she replied, not apparently in the least put out.

"But then, only one such as you would have such fascinating guests."

"I don't suppose you'd favour me with a dance, Hyacinthe?" said Tucker.

"No, I would not," she said with a most affecting pout. "You dance like a jungle ape."

Tucker laughed. "I can't deny that I get carried away."

"Perhaps you have other matters to attend to," said Saraille.

Hyacinthe stood up immediately. "You may have my guests for ten minutes, no more. Come, Tucker, and I will try, once more, to instruct you in the proper way to control your feet."

"Yes, ma'am," the riverboatman cried, jumping up.

"One fiendish whoop, Tucker, I warn you, and I will have Bernard throw you out into the street."

They moved onto the floor and were swallowed up by the crowd. Saraille watched them depart before he turned to face the brothers. His round pink face held a beaming, insincere smile. But he only had James's attention. Harry was still looking at the point where the dancers had disappeared.

"Well, Messieurs, I was sorry to hear that you have had to make good the "pig's" losses from your own funds. The invitation to find his own must seem like an insult."

That got Harry's attention, though he answered carefully. "You know about that?"

"It is my business to know, Captain Ludlow. How can I tell the good people of New Orleans what new lies the Spanish are concocting unless I keep my ear to the ground?"

"I'm curious as to how you found out," said James.

"And I fear you must remain so, Monsieur. To tell you of my sources would be to risk them being exposed. But no one else in this room is aware of these developments."

"Did you know that gold and silver was being shipped out on the *Gauchos?*" said Harry, softly. The pale blue eyes didn't even flicker, but Harry had the feeling that he'd struck home. "Because if you did, then it multiplies the number of people who might have stolen it."

"The addition of one is hardly a multiplication."

"That would depend on who else was told, either by you or your source."

Saraille shrugged. "I haven't even said that I knew."

"We were discussing pirates just before you arrived."

That made him laugh. His large frame shook heartily. "Not pirates. You would be deluding yourself if you thought it was them. I grant you they like to be mythologized into heroes and bandits. But at heart they are petty criminals."

"Do you know who it was?"

"Let us say I know whom I would suspect."

Harry locked eyes with him. "And why do you think that the good Barón was shipping all that money to Charleston?"

That made him sit forward eagerly. "You're sure that was the destination?"

"No," Harry replied, sitting back and smiling. "In fact I know it wasn't the destination."

"Monsieur Saraille," said James, "it is, no doubt, part of your profession to pretend you have more knowledge than you truly possess."

The editor of the *Moniteur* wasn't offended. "I confess that is true. Just as I confess that I am willing to pay to find the real destination of that ship."

"We don't want money," said Harry.

"That does surprise me. I have been informed that the chest de Carondelet removed from your ship today contained a great deal of that commodity. And I have not noticed him giving it back."

"A little bit of truth, right now, will go much further than money."

"You are not seriously searching for his ingots, are you?"

"As of this moment, yes. But we're seeing de Carondelet tomorrow, and I hope that any further enquiries will be unnecessary."

"Who would you suspect?" asked James.

"A Spaniard. It has to involve one of the men who knew de Carondelet was shipping out the bullion on that particular ship."

"That could be a lot of Spaniards."

"You had dinner tonight with a group of people who only ever congregate in church. De Carondelet usually keeps them apart. That must mean that they would be the ones to know. Unless it was the ship's Captain."

"Rodrigo didn't know."

Saraille's thin eyebrows went up a fraction. "That is interesting. Are you sure?"

"Yes," Harry replied emphatically. "But did you?"

Saraille shook his head. "I had no idea until the news came from Fort Balize what those casks really contained. The first consignment of granulated sugar, yes, which made the loading of the ship an event. The truth came like a thunderbolt. That naturally raised all sorts of questions, why he'd nearly bankrupted the colony to raise it, but more importantly, why he was sending it and to whom. It is a very odd thing for de Carondelet to have done."

"I take it that, given information you will use it to embarrass him."

"Of course. The *Moniteur* is the organ of French feeling in the colony. Our greatest wish is that the Spaniards cede the territory back to France."

"So far, you haven't given us very much," said James. "Telling us to look at our fellow diners is small beer. Certainly not enough to warrant any reciprocation from us."

"I agree," said Saraille, then smiled when he saw that his response had surprised James. "But then I will have saved you a fruitless search for any other culprits."

He paused for a moment, then looked up suddenly. "Tucker and Hyacinthe are on their way back. I know you don't know me well enough to trust me, but I will be in your debt if you tell me what I want to know."

"Is it a debt you will repay?" asked Harry.

"Yes," gasped Saraille, slightly desperate.

Harry glanced at James, who nodded.

"New York, Monsieur Saraille."

The thank you was more of a breath than a word. He was getting to his feet as it was emitted, his pink jowls wreathed in a smile.

"Mademoiselle," he cried, "how can I repay you!"

"With a pair of new feet," she cried. "Tucker has quite destroyed the old ones."

"Have we done the right thing, Harry?" whispered James.

Harry replied in an equally low voice. "I don't know, brother. But that information locked in our heads had no use at all."

"Well, what do you think of Saraille?" asked Hyacinthe, sitting down. Tucker made to follow but she shot him such a glare that he retreated, laughing.

"Hard to say on such a short acquaintance," James replied.

"You disappoint me, Monsieur. I thought that you would be the type to spot a slug when you see one. I spend my life dodging his fat frame and oily compliments. And he's not to be trusted. I hope you didn't tell him anything of a confidential nature."

Both brothers shook their heads slowly. Hyacinthe threw back her head and let out a loud peal of laughter. "You look like two schoolboys who've been caught outside a young girl's bedroom."

Harry laughed first, but was soon followed by James. By the time Bernard brought another bottle of wine to the table all three were helpless.

"Oh, how funny," Hyacinthe said, pounding her chest to stop herself. "And all this makes my decision so much harder."

"What decision?" asked Harry.

"Why, I have instructions to entertain you from Cayetano." She looked at them both with an intensity that made her more beautiful than ever. "But how can I decide between two such handsome creatures?"

"What about El Señor de Coburrabias himself?"

"He has other outlets for his passions."

"That's good news," said Harry.

"For me, also," added James.

"But what am I to do?"

Harry's next words, preceded by a pleading look aimed at his brother, were emitted with a quite evident strain.

"Neither my brother nor I can accept your most generous offer, Mademoiselle Feraud."

She touched him again, producing once more the sensation that ran all the way to his toes. "You are not of the same persuasion as the gentlemen in the corner?"

Harry turned, along with his brother, taking in the noisy group. Their hair was dressed with elaborate care, and each gesture made in their excited conversation had an exaggerated air. He smiled at what was clearly a joke.

"We have a crew aboard the ship who require an assurance that their lives are not in danger."

"A task I am happy to perform," said James, standing up. "You stay, Harry, and I will go back to the ship."

"But . . ."

"No buts," James cried. "And let me say that, flattering as you have been to me, Mademoiselle, I think you do prefer the forthright to the gallant."

"You have a sharp eye, Monsieur Ludlow."

"Which is a source of pride to me. Let me say that surrendering the field does not come easily. You are a remarkably beautiful woman."

"Thank you."

"James," said Harry, his voice slightly hoarse.

"Not another word, brother. I shall leave Pender with you."

"My servant," said Harry, with a trace of guilt brought on by having completely forgotten about him. He turned to see if he was in view.

"He is down in the taproom," said Hyacinthe, "swapping tall tales with some boatman. Monsieur Ludlow, Bernard will arrange for two of my most imposing footmen to escort you back through the town. I wouldn't want anything to happen to so gallant a gentleman."

Harry awoke, wondering why he was in a soft feather bed rather than his own cot. But not for more than a split second. Hyacinthe Feraud's body was pressed against his, one willowy leg entwined as if seeking security. The silky skin was pleasantly hot and the natural odour of her body strong in his nostrils. She was still asleep, and all the more beautiful in repose. He felt the wonderful lassitude that comes from being utterly relaxed and images of the previous night's passion floated through his mind. Harry, like all sailors, was no stranger to the bawdy-house. But this was, and had been, different. Hyacinthe, unless she was a wonderful, consummate actress, had wanted him for himself, had felt that same tingling frisson the moment their bodies had come into contact. The fact that she was an experienced woman had added a wonderful dimension to their lovemaking.

Harry felt the slight ache in his groin brought on by erotic recollection. For some reason an expression of James's, used humorously to describe tumescence, came into his mind. "A girding in the loins" was a sort of private joke between two adult, experienced men, an expression at once so silly, and accurate, that it perfectly described the absurdity that often attended upon the condition. He felt his chest begin to heave, and fought to suppress the movement. That only made matters worse, and his shoulders shook. Hyacinthe, with her head crooked in the join between his arm and his body, was mildly disturbed. She groaned slightly and moved her thigh, seeking to get even closer to him. Since that was locked into his groin it did nothing to suppress his feeling of desire. It was so simple to turn upon his side, so pleasant to press his body against hers. She didn't open her eyes but smiled as she rolled onto her back. Her jet black hair, long and glistening, spread across the pillow and her tongue slid out to wet her lips as Harry's head dropped to her neck. The smell was overpoweringly sensual, mixed odours of human sweat, perfume, and sex all wafted up on the heat of her slim, graceful body. He felt again the slight shock at the sheer silky texture of her coffee-coloured skin. His hand was between her thighs, and as he touched her she moaned slightly. Impatiently her hand slid down and pulled him urgently forwards. Their lovemaking had none of the hungry immediacy of the previous night. It was slow, fluent, and quite profoundly better.

CHAPTER TWENTY-FOUR

WHEN HARRY woke up for the second time, not even the presence of a beautiful body could keep his mind off his troubles. Fortunately Hyacinthe had rolled away and was now curled up on the opposite side of the bed. Since berthing the day before, events had been driven by their own momentum, which gave him little time to think. He'd been forced to react as matters went from bad to worse. The idea that he could find de Carondelet's property here in a strange city was, in the cold light of day, absurd. Little hope had been added by his encounters with either McGillivray or Saraille. The seeming indifference of the Governor to the idea of upsetting Britain was now explained by the state of his own country's relations with Spain. If McGillivray knew that matters were close to a solution, then de Carondelet was privy to even more information. War was imminent. The Plate fleet usually sailed in spring, but of course the actual time varied as much as the route. And this one would be attended by more caution than most. Manuel de Godoy would know that once war was declared he'd have little chance of seeing another delivery of bullion from the New World.

Really the solution was simple: sling his French passengers ashore, tell de Carondelet the money was theirs, and let the two sort it out amongst themselves. Then he could weigh and get out of harm's reach. But time was not pressing. The Plate fleet might be at sea, but it never made the journey home without stopping off at some other colonial centre such as Havana or Port au Spain. If they'd already set off into the Atlantic, their southerly course, designed to bring them close to home right off Cadiz harbour, tended to take them into the prevailing winds. Even if they arrived early, and war was declared immediately, it could be November before the garrison in New Orleans was made aware of the fact. Besides, the first thing de Carondelet would ask his new immigrants was how they came by such an amount of money. That, plus a reluctance to play the scrub, would keep him here.

Lifting his head he saw the painting that dominated the wall, so large that the bottom was lost behind the bedhead. Even upside-down he could take pleasure in the beauty captured on canvas. Then he looked across the great feather bed. Hyacinthe was curled up, covers thrown off, with every bump on her arched spine visible, the crown of each vertebra glistening in the faint gleam of sunlight coming through the slatted shutters. He followed them down to the swell of her partly hidden buttocks. Using his foot to push the coverlet further down he exposed the whole of her slim body. One leg was straight, the other bent, showing the pale pink skin on the sole of her foot. As he rolled over towards her, and put his hand under her arm to cup her breast, he did wonder if there might be another good reason for eschewing haste.

"I nearly had a mutiny on my hands," said James. "The fact that you weren't aboard was bad enough, but it didn't take our friends long to work out that your absence was in pursuit of pleasure, rather than their welfare. I'm afraid that notion had quite incensed them."

"Damn their mood. Have they made any decisions?"

"Not yet."

"What about our own crew?"

"Funnily enough, less fractious now than even yesterday. As I suspected it was the presence of that chest full of coin that really worked upon their prejudices. They still bait the Frenchmen, but it's larded with humour, not bile."

Pender called through the open cabin door. "There's a boat putting off from the shore, your honour, with that droopy Captain from Fort Balize aboard."

"Alone?"

"No, he's got four of his soldiers with him, and that cock sparrow that was here yesterday, who's aide to the Governor."

Harry made his way on deck and watched as the boat pulled towards *Bucephalas*. Behind them he could see a detachment of de Carondelet's Walloon Guards lining up on the wooden jetty. Fernandez wore his usual bovine expression, but a day in New Orleans had allowed him to renew not only his dress uniform, but his everyday wear. His moustaches has also been trimmed so that they drooped less than before. But even barbered and in new clothes, he still aspired to smartness rather than achieving it. Being the senior officer, he came aboard first, but was then left to stand uselessly on the deck until de Chigny, who could communicate with Harry, came to join him.

"I have instructions for you from the Governor. You are to warp your ship into the quayside right ahead."

"Why?" demanded Harry.

"So that the *Navarro* can retire to her berth and the other galleys go about their duties. Captain San Lucar de Barrameda does not wish to keep his crews on alert indefinitely. A guard will be placed at both ends of the cables, two men fore and aft. There will also be a guard on the quay under the command of Captain Fernandez so that no one may approach the bollards, or ropes, that hold your ship secure."

"Anything else!" said Harry, looking at the fortress that would stand right above the berthed ship. Again, the smoke from the furnace drifted lazily into the warm, morning air.

"Yes," de Chigny replied. "The Governor has requested that you, along with your brother, come ashore, and bring with you the keys to your armoury, which will be secured with an extra padlock before we leave, this to be witnessed by either Captain Fernandez or me."

"And if I fail to do so?"

"Then we will be obliged to place a substantial guard on them also. And in that case, I must tell you that the Governor would not be content to allow your crew to stay on the ship. A camp ashore would have to be constructed to contain them."

"And feed them," said Harry.

De Chigny nodded. "He is sure that they will be happier consuming the food they are accustomed to than making do with anything we could provide."

"All this sounds like an act of war."

"It is an act of wisdom. The Barón de Carondelet has decided to put both you and your men under protective custody. And to remove from you the temptation to act unwisely."

"For how long?"

"That he didn't tell me."

Harry was terribly tempted to mention the Plate fleet. But that would give away the fact that he knew more than he should.

"Does he have any instructions regarding my French passengers?"

"I believe he has told you that they are free to go ashore, Captain, and to travel anywhere in the Territory."

"They may decline to oblige."

"Then that is your concern, not that of the Governor."

The murmuring behind mystified him until he realized that James was translating the exchange for the benefit of at least one or two of the crew. Judging by the unnatural stillness of those on deck the news of their fate was travelling fast. But their situation hadn't changed. To attempt anything without the aid of surprise bordered on madness. And even then it could prove suicidal. But, in time, as their guards grew lax, something could be attempted. And he had one idea, a long shot, which might just make escape possible. But now the whole garrison was on alert. Any resistance and de Carondelet would remove them from the ship. He needed the crew aboard, that was certain, so anything that threatened that had to be avoided.

"Pender, get a cable over the side and man a boat to haul it ashore."

He looked keenly at de Chigny to see if he understood, but the lieutenant's face was blank. Likewise Fernandez.

"Tell the men not to worry, when you get the chance. We need time, that's all."

"Aye, aye, Capt'n."

The deck suddenly came alive as Pender shouted out his instructions. If any of Harry's men were wont to disobey, Pender's willingness to comply should assuage their fears.

"James, take Captain Fernandez below, fetch the key to the armoury from my cabin, show him it is locked, let him put on his own padlock, and then fetch both keys back on deck."

He turned back to face de Chigny.

"I require your permission to address my French passengers. You must understand that coming ashore here will require a degree of courage, even from men who have already shifted their domicile more than once. I want to speak to them alone, so that I may reassure them that I am still responsible for their welfare, and that should they need assistance they can count on my help."

"I'm not sure that I am permitted to oblige," said the Spaniard.

Harry looked at him hard. "This is a demand, Lieutenant de Chigny, which if it remains unmet will ensure that I refuse to cooperate at all. If you choose to stand beside me while I speak they will not believe a word I say. You may, if you wish, explain to the Barón de Carondelet yourself why he has the task of housing and feeding my crew."

The Spaniard still hesitated.

"Pender, belay!" Harry yelled.

Every member of his crew froze, with a discipline that cheered him even in such a dire situation. De Chigny looked at them for a moment. Then with as much grace as he could muster, conceded.

"Carry on, Captain Ludlow."

"If you stay on the ship, you will do yourselves no good. You may even suffer if war does break out."

"Will we be better off ashore?" asked Lampin.

"I can't say."

"Why did you tell them the chest was yours in the first place?" demanded Brissot.

"If we tell him he'll give it back," another voice cried.

"You may do that if you wish. But I doubt it's a good idea to tell de Carondelet that the treasure chest is yours, not ours."

"You think he will steal it from us also?"

"He will most certainly want to know how you came by it. He looks at me and sees a successful privateer, a man who can show him letters of marque signed by my sovereign. What does he see when he looks at you, a group of itinerant Frenchmen?"

Harry hesitated, not wishing to add the word uneducated. But that was true. Even with the likes of Lampin and Couvruer, who were definitely a cut above their fellows, none of the group who stood before him were gentlemen, at least not in the sense that a Spaniard would understand. Thinking like that made him uncomfortable, since being a sailor he was well aware of the loose nature of such an appellation, that it had more to do with birth than any innate disposition. Given their money, some of these men would naturally elevate themselves. Others could have ten times the amount and stay uncouth wretches for the rest of their lives. But at this moment they looked like what they were, a group of tradesmen and artisans who'd only come out to the Caribbean because they'd failed to make a living at home.

"I cannot think of an explanation that will satisfy him. If he finds out, or even suspects, that your wealth stems from what can only be called piracy, then I can't see him ever relinquishing it."

"What are we to live on?" asked Lampin.

"I have money to give you. Not a sum that will match what is missing, I grant you, but there is at present very little specie in Louisiana, so it will command a high value."

For a moment, Harry toyed with the idea of telling them everything. About McGillivray and the destination of the gold and silver, of Saraille's conviction that the man who stole de Carondelet's ingots was Spanish. Even of his half-thought-out plan to make an escape. But most of all the fact that, once war was declared, any connection to an English privateer would be fatal. That all he was doing was buying time. Yet experience told him that they were not a group who acted rationally, but a set of competitors who with more information would only end up more divided. And there was the thought that nothing he imparted would remain secure. Once ashore, someone could talk, if only from the fond belief that by helping the Spanish they'd get their money back. Added to that was his own natural inclination to keep things to himself. One or two of them growled uneasily.

"If I could force him to return it I would. But my hands are tied. And I have to look to the needs of my ship and crew."

"And if we refuse?" asked Couvruer.

"It would make me very unhappy to insist."

Harry felt uneasy the moment they were shown into the Governor's quarters. His bulging blue eyes held a look of barely controlled anger. He took the keys of the armoury from de Chigny with a grunt and threw them onto the desk. As they clattered off the other side onto the floor he picked up a printed broadsheet and waved it at the brothers.

"How did the editor of the *Moniteur* get information that the *Gauchos* was sailing to New York?"

"New York?" said Harry, feigning surprise. "Was Captain Rodrigo bound there?"

"Are you telling me that you don't know?"

"I am. His charts, which I handed to Captain San Lucar de Barrameda with the ship's manifest, showed him on course for the Florida Keys. I had assumed his destination to be Spain."

De Carondelet seemed unaware of the contradiction which existed between his words and his manner. His opening remarks had sounded like a confirmation that the information was true. And now he seemed to be attempting, by sheer bluster, to withdraw from it. Harry was left with the thought that the Governor

considered himself clever and others fools, which was a dangerous premiss. "If this information did not come from you, where
did it come from, Captain? You were seen in Saraille's company
last night, so don't deny it."

"I wasn't aware that you were having us watched," said Harry.

"I was not. But I was told."

He began to dart about the room in his agitation, his heels
digging hard into the bare wooden floorboards.

"Saraille?" said James, raising a finger to Harry. "Was not
that the fat fellow with the pink face who bought us a drink?"

"I think you're right, brother."

"An unsavoury creature," James continued, clearly enjoying
himself, "with such an unbecoming opinion of the administration.
I would not wish to repeat publicly the things he said about you,
Barón. It does not surprise me in the least that he follows such a
low occupation."

"Low is the word," snapped de Carondelet. "His newspaper
is nothing but an organ for misinformation."

"Then he has succeeded admirably, sir, in being the purveyor
of this evident falsehood. I am sure the merest hint of a refuta-
tion will lay him even lower."

"It is not that simple!" de Carondelet shouted.

"It would help us to know what makes such information so
significant," said James.

That stopped him in his tracks, since to answer would be to
confirm that Saraille had printed the truth. "It is mischievous,
designed to undermine both me and Spanish rule. The whole city
now knows what was stolen out of that ship."

"With respect, Barón," James continued in a silky voice, "that
still does not explain why you're so agitated. Everyone also knows
that newspapers print any nonsense that will tempt people to buy."

"It makes me sound like a thief," he cried, trying to cover his
tracks. Then he thrust the paper at James. "Can't you see that?"

After a brief perusal, James replied, "I must admit, I cannot,
sir."

"Shipping bullion to the capital city of America."

"Nowhere here does he say that you are a thief."

"Of course not! But it is implied."

James's response was like a knife entering soft butter. Harry had to turn away from both the Governor and his aide for a moment lest they see him laughing.

"Then let us hope he doesn't hear a word about the chest you took out of *Bucephalas* yesterday, Barón. That I fear will do your already dented reputation no good at all."

De Carondelet stopped as though he walked right into a wall. He turned slowly to look at James, whose face bore a completely bland expression. Harry saw him puff himself up to a yell, so cut in.

"Now that we have seen to your honour, sir, perhaps you will explain why you have virtually clapped the crew of our ship in chains."

"I assume Lieutenant de Chigny has told you, Captain. It is to prevent you from doing anything foolish."

"The only foolish thing we have done up till now is to be open with you. Had we sailed into New Orleans keeping the fate of the *Gauchos* to ourselves, we would still be in possession of our property."

"Do not lecture me, Captain Ludlow. You are a mere private individual who has the good fortune to own a ship. I am a high official of the Spanish government with duties and responsibilities that you cannot even guess at. And here in this colony I am the law. If I see fit to take over the property of any subject of King Carlos, then I am within my rights to do so. Dissatisfied, he may appeal to Madrid for justice."

"I am a subject of King George."

De Carondelet slammed his fist on his desk. "Who does not rule here."

Harry reached into his coat and produced a piece of parchment. When he spoke, he adopted a formal tone which the other man recognized right away.

"I have here a written demand for the return of my property."

"Which I accept," de Carondelet replied with a smile. "With the sad acknowledgement that my duty to my King does not permit me to comply."

"Then do I have your active assistance in the matter of finding your property? I wish to be allowed to talk to certain people, not least the members of your *Cabildo* and the prisoner Charpentier."

"I have my own watchmen to carry out enquiries, and I must insist that should you uncover any information you must pass it on to them. On your own, you will cause more trouble than you will solve."

"With your permission we will return to the ship."

"No!"

"What?"

"I require that both you and your brother stay ashore, Captain. Leaderless, your men will cause us no trouble. Without your crew, you will be similarly constrained."

"I cannot agree," said Harry, coldly.

"Then I must tell you that any hope you have of restitution is forfeit. You will also find that the accommodation I shall force you to occupy is extremely uncomfortable. Believe me, in a city like ours a dungeon has special attributes. Agree, and you can choose your own place of residence. I expect you to accept, and when you do I will demand a parole that neither you nor your brother will go near your ship without an officer of my garrison in attendance. Failure to keep to your word will also endanger our agreement, and lead to your immediate arrest."

He nodded to de Chigny, who opened the door to the chamber. Four Walloon Guards marched in, muskets at the present, and bayonets fixed.

"Which is it to be, Captain?"

"Are we allowed servants?" said Harry wearily.

"Of course. Do you wish me to recommend lodgings?"

"No," Harry replied. "I think I know where we will take up residence."

"Well, brother," said James, softly, "it's an ill wind."

Harry didn't even consider that Hyacinthe might refuse to take them in until they were actually outside the Hôtel de la Porte d'Orléans, and his sudden display of nerves provided James with both amusement and concern. He knew his brother well now, the gaps in their relationship when he was a boy repaired by all the time they'd spent together at sea. Harry was impulsive in most things he did, not least in the way he sailed and fought his ship. But that paled beside his personal relationships, since the snap decisions he was prone to take seemed to be based on less sure knowledge than he displayed at sea. Oliver Pollock was a classic example. James had found the man amusing enough. But half the reason he repaired so often to Madame de Leon's bawdy-house in St Croix was that he was less smitten than Harry, whose regard for the American bordered on infatuation.

There were manifest reasons for this, not least the common one that such things afflicted all sailors. Away on voyages that could last a year, denied normal social intercourse, they were, as a breed, inclined to sharper emotional shifts than their lubberly brethren, and the very nature of their trade, where death from any number of dangers could occur within seconds, made them impatient fatalists. So when they came across a person or a place that excited them, their whole being was thrown into ensuring a successful outcome to whatever they desired. That such an attitude usually produced the exact opposite of what they intended was well known; a subject for cartoonists, dramatists, low comedians, and pamphleteers, all of whom took delight in pointing up the failings of the sailor fresh home from the sea: and nowhere was that more in evidence than in a tar's relations with the opposite sex.

Yet once they were ensconced in the hotel, James was forced to examine his feelings just to check that he wasn't indulging in unnecessary cynicism. Not only did Hyacinthe welcome them with open arms, having banished him to the attic she set Harry up in a room right next door to her own; and watching them together over the following days, the depth of their regard was so obvious that even an exercise in wit that alluded to their passion seemed churlish. For once, James realized, his brother had matched himself with someone equally high spirited. Hyacinthe Feraud, who'd never had any difficulty in attracting the opposite sex, seemed as enamoured with Harry as he clearly was with her. They were drawn to each other in a way that practically excluded everyone else, arriving at the kind of intimacy shown by long-standing lovers almost immediately and exuding happiness in the process.

For all that, there was caution born in James that had as much to do with his own past as any protective strain he felt for his brother. The residual suspicion existed that Hyacinthe Feraud, who had ample experience despite her youth, was playing with Harry's emotions, and that the whole thing would end in tears. To ask Harry to examine that possibility would only earn him an angry rebuke, but Hyacinthe was another matter. Since she was such a beautiful creature, and amusing company, it was a pleasure to engage her attention, and James was well aware, even if his brother was not, that time alone would reveal the true depth of her feelings.

CHAPTER TWENTY-FIVE

FOR HARRY, the next few days were a mixture of bliss and frustration. Saraille, even with his sources of information, could provide him with little help—happy to discuss the various members of the Spanish administration, his general bile towards them as a group robbed much of what he said of real value—and the Hôtel de la Porte d'Orléans provided three opinions for every two people he questioned. The loss of de Carondelet's secret cargo was the main topic of conversation in the city, which obscured the truth rather than revealing it. If de Carondelet was indeed investigating he showed little sign, his routine seemingly unchanged from before his loss. Walking around the building which housed him, his administration, and his prisoners, or standing in the square in front, Harry could see no way of penetrating the well-guarded entrances to recover the treasure without serious loss. Looking at his ship, and observing the infinitesimal fall in the river level, was even more galling, reducing him to a quiet fury as his impotence was underlined.

Hyacinthe provided the bliss. If there had been any rivals before he came on the scene, they'd been routed. Tucker, on the two occasions he'd been encountered, was so drunk his insults carried neither force nor clarity. The time was spent either in her apartments or down in the tavern, watching her go about her business with an efficiency which was remarkable in one so young. She spoke of those whom Harry had a right to suspect of intercepting the *Gauchos,* but that was mostly gossip, or useless details of their sexual preferences. One thing was certain: for all their upright Catholic attitudes, they were not averse to the charms of

Hyacinthe's girls. Not surprisingly, when success had attended his endeavours Charpentier had been a customer. She confirmed Harry's initial impression of a man who was rogueish, but he was also said to be ineffectual, more interested in spending money than acquiring it, and she made it clear that the pirate was not the type of man to attract her. None of the Barataria Bay fraternity was available to be questioned, which lent credibility to San Lucar de Barrameda's assertion that he'd cleaned out their base and dispersed them in the swamps.

So the couple ate, drank, and danced together. They made love often, beneath her portrait hanging above the bed. And when they talked it was Harry who opened up, telling Hyacinthe things that he rarely discussed with anyone: of the disappointment he knew he'd been to his father; and of the duel with a superior officer that in its aftermath and his refusal to apologize had ruined his naval career. He also told her of his homes in Kent and London and the nature of life in England. She was entranced by tales of Europe, asked questions about dress, manners, and morals, the answers to which alternately amused, amazed, and horrified her. Born into poverty, with her beauty her only asset, she had been in some senses rescued by her predecessor, trained by her to take over the hotel. She liked and admired de Coburrabias, as much for his acumen as for the lack of hypocrisy that was his abiding trait. And, it seemed, she loved Harry Ludlow, rushing to be with him as soon as chance allowed.

The idyll could never entirely shut out his difficulties. And with a servant like Pender, he had an instrument with which he could circumvent some of Carondelet's restrictions.

"Fernandez has set himself up in your cabin, and the ship is crawling with the buggers half the time."

"Did the Frenchmen finally go ashore?" asked Harry.

"They did, and I managed to sneak two sea-chests full of powder ashore with 'em."

"Good."

"Couldn't have done it without that Lampin cove. He's all right, he is, and sends his thanks for the money you advanced.

Him and Couvruer have taken charge of them as though they're personal stores. If they can keep their mates' noses out from them we should be safe. They've found a place, two floors of a house, in a street called the Calle des Ursulines, hard by a convent. Belongs to the nuns it seems, and them being homeless Papists they've taken pity on them."

"What about the crew?"

"Well, it's hard for 'em, Capt'n. Dreaver told me they can see the town if they climb to the cap, and can hear music an' all sorts after dark. I had a look around and there's an old royal warehouse right by the river that's used for public dances. Not fussy either about who they let in. Word has it the slaves go there as well as the free, and the owner told me he's already had his collar tugged for it. Fined and the like, 'cause old Carondelet don't like it. Says it gives the blacks ideas. Not so, says Santiago. Decent cove, to my mind. *Bucephalas* is moored right on the other side of that there bank, so our lads'll be able to watch the comings and goings."

Pender was reaching into the deep inside pockets of his coat, leaving Harry to wonder how his servant, with not a word of Spanish or French, had not only found all this out but had also got on friendly terms with the owner of the dancehall. But that was typical of him. He had a way with people that made them warm to him: he could engender trust in even the most cynical breast—but more important than that he could pick locks. Harry's smile turned to a grin as two pistols appeared, with Pender producing them like a fairground trickster.

"They ain't as good as your own, Capt'n. But they'll do for close-quarter work. I'll get Mr James a pair tomorrow." He looked around the room. "Where is he?"

"He's on the roof with Hyacinthe," said Harry, pursing his lips. "She is sitting for a portrait. As if there weren't enough of the damn things around as it is. I told him there was one in the bedroom but he replied that since he was unlikely to benefit from seeing it he'd do his own."

"He don't waste much time, do he, your honour?"

That wasn't something Harry wanted to think about. "Do you think they'll notice the armoury's been opened?"

"No. The lads say they never do nothing but check the extra lock they put on, and that is still on the hasp. I've set one of the chippy's mates to making a wooden copy that can be swapped if we need to gain a bit of time. The rest are carving out dummy cut-lasses so that if they do look inside they won't notice what's missing."

"That's an interesting piece of news regarding the public dancing. Perhaps I can persuade de Carondelet that keeping them on the ship is a recipe for trouble. He might agree to let them ashore in quotas. We'd have to make our break sometime after dark and a party already ashore would be a great bonus."

"Perhaps some of them should kick up a fuss on their own account."

The door burst open and Hyacinthe careered in, followed by James. Both were laughing, with that open, happy air of people totally at ease in each other's company. Harry felt a pang of jealousy that evaporated immediately she threw herself into his lap.

"It is too, too hot, Harry, even under a parasol."

"If you could be brought to sit still, Hyacinthe, then you'd be cooler. Honestly, brother, I've never known such a fidget."

"How can you wear that coat, Pender?" she asked. Then her eyes strayed to the table. She leant forward and picked up a pistol between two fingers.

"Have to have it to carry these, Miss H.," said Pender quietly. "Otherwise they'd be seen."

She frowned and Harry uttered a silent curse. In the time they'd been at the hotel, Hyacinthe had not once posed an awkward question, content to avoid any knowledge of what they might be up to. Yet she must know Harry to be a man who would never allow someone like de Carondelet to dictate to him. That active personality was a great part of his attraction. But her attitude seemed to be that if she knew nothing she could say nothing. The pistol on the table, which should have been kept out of sight, breached the hope that she would not be put in a compromising situation.

Cayetano had a call on her loyalty, but fortunately the connection seemed to be very tenuous. Hyacinthe had explained that as the highest-ranking army officer in the colony his association with a bawdy-house had to be kept as discreet as his own sexual dalliances. In fact, he owned several establishments in the town, operating them at arm's length and was only really concerned that no trouble should emanate from his properties, only profits. It said something about the city of New Orleans that he could be a zealous and competent officer in the Spanish army as well as a brothel keeper.

"Put it out of sight, Pender," said Harry, as Hyacinthe gave him a sad look. Then, because she hated to be unhappy, her face brightened. "I shall get Bernard to fetch us some iced lemonade."

"Such luxury," said Harry, looking at the bright summer sunshine outside the window.

"That is what first brought me here," she said, now looking wistful. "The first time I ever set eyes on the hotel. I was only a child, and I saw the unloading of great blocks of ice on the levee. I'd never seen it, nor even heard of such a thing. It had come all the way from the mountains of the north and was covered in bales of straw. One of the boatmen let me touch it, then asked me if I'd like to try some. It was so cold, so beautiful."

"I could take you to places where it stretches for a thousand miles," said Harry.

"Will you take me, Harry?"

"Of course I will," he replied. Gazing at Hyacinthe, he didn't see the look that was exchanged between Pender and James. Neither did she, but that didn't stop the look of anger. She got out of Harry's lap, and went to look out of the long windows.

"Then the filthy pig with the ice, he told me what he wanted in return and I said *non*. I followed the cart all the way through the streets and ended up here, where I learned that most men are no different . . ."

She turned and looked hard at Harry Ludlow, walked briskly across the room, and pulled the bell to summon Bernard. Harry wanted to say something, but the words could not be uttered with James and Pender present. The door opened with a speed that surprised them all and Bernard entered and gave him a note. Hyacinthe ordered the drinks while Harry tore at the plain seal. The writing was odd, all capitals and deliberately crabbed to disguise its origin.

I REQUIRE MORE NEWS OF MY DAUGHTER. IN RETURN I HAVE SOME INFORMATION THAT WILL BE OF GREAT INTEREST TO YOU. IT MAY EVEN HELP TO RESTORE YOUR FORTUNES. SAME PLACE, ANY TIME. TODAY OR TOMORROW.

It could only be McGillivray. Harry cursed himself as he crumpled the note and threw it towards the empty fireplace, realizing that he'd forgotten all about the Creek chieftain's correspondence. Aware that it was in the sea-chest Pender had taken off the *Gauchos,* he'd anticipated, without really giving it much thought, handing the whole thing over unopened. It was no concern of his what those letters contained. Besides, when he'd gone back aboard after their meeting he'd been distracted by the need to deal with the Frenchmen, and, of course, having spent the night with Hyacinthe, he'd not returned. The following morning, contracted to meet with de Carondelet, he'd had no idea that he wouldn't be allowed back on board. So McGillivray's chest lay where it had done since it had been brought off the ship, in his side cabin. He was about to say something to Pender when he realized that not only was Hyacinthe present, so was Bernard. He stood up and walked out, indicating that his servant should follow. They waited on the landing until Bernard passed them, giving them an odd look before descending the stairs.

"Pender, what are the chances of getting into my side cabin, unseen?" he whispered.

"Slim, your honour," Pender replied. "Captain Fernandez has set up home in the main cabin. If I'm allowed in there at all, it's only with him beside me. That's why I couldn't get your own pistols out of the desk drawer. He examines everything I take out."

"You know those sea-chests that you took out of the *Gauchos?*" Pender nodded. "One of them contains something I need very badly."

"Well, you're whistling for a wind, Capt'n, without you can get Fernandez out of the way."

"The casements are on the same side as the jetty."

"Only five feet high and ten yards from two sentries sittin' on a bollard. Now they're lazy sods an' no error, but they're not blind nor deaf."

"I have to find a way," Harry insisted.

"What is it we're after?"

"Letters."

"An' they're in that chest?" Harry nodded, as Pender continued. "Where?"

The blank look made Pender frown impatiently. "Are they just in the chest, or hidden away?"

"I don't know."

Harry was suddenly distracted by the sound of Hyacinthe's laughter. He heard James's voice too, producing another witticism that would amuse her. Pender tugged his sleeve hard to regain his attention. "Then, your honour, we need to find out."

"What's the point, if we can't get to them?"

"There's always a way, like for instance your notion of the lads getting shirty because they can't get ashore to join in the dancing. Only thing is the timin', which is a bit hard to fix. If I could get in there I don't know whether I'd have five seconds or five minutes."

"How long do you need?"

"If'n I'm sure of where I'm looking, seconds, even if it ain't locked. But if I have to search." Pender shrugged eloquently. "Which would it be?"

Harry conjured up a picture of McGillivray. He didn't strike him as a man who would panic, but if he had information to impart, the mere idea that his secrets weren't yet safe might induce caution. If he heard that the chest had been left unlocked within ten feet of a Spanish army officer, he could easily refuse to trade.

"I don't think I can ask for an exact location."

"Then I need time."

"Would a fight on deck fetch Fernandez out of my cabin for five minutes?" asked Harry.

"Depends on whether he likes to watch a scrap. Anyway, it's worth a try."

"There has to be another, surer way."

Hyacinthe laughed again, a pealing delightful sound. Pender turned his head towards it. "There is!"

"What is it?"

"He's a man, ain't he?"

Following Pender's look, and the sound, it wasn't difficult to deduce his meaning. "I can't involve her!"

"You don't have to, your honour. Just ask her to look over the ship. Since she's soft on you, the idea would likely please her. All she has to do is get the sod out onto the deck for a while and I can do the business."

"I don't like it. First, involving her. What happens if anything goes wrong?"

"Then I'm for the high jump," said Pender, sharply.

Harry winced, realizing that in his concern for Hyacinthe he'd forgotten the risks his servant was proposing to take.

"Sorry. I'm just not sure that she can distract Fernandez for any length of time."

It was Pender's turn to grin. "Why not, Capt'n? She's managed to do it to you!"

CHAPTER TWENTY-SIX

HYACINTHE, taking an early dinner, listened as Harry delivered his strong and continuous hints. Her lack of interest, or indeed of any response, forced him into ever more desperate enthusiasm, as he described *Bucephalas* in terms that made the ship sound like a work of art to rival a sculpture by Michelangelo. Finally, having sat with a bland expression on her face, she burst out angrily.

"I am not an idiot. Would it not be better, Harry, to tell me the truth."

"Truth?" he replied lamely.

"Yes. You want me to go to your ship for a reason. I saw that gun today. I know you have a plan to escape. Why should I help you to do that?"

"You wouldn't want to see me trapped here for ever, would you?"

She lifted his hand gently off the table and placed it on her left breast. "Here, yes, Harry. In New Orleans, no."

"I'm sorry."

"What for? That you have tried to lie to me, or that one day, perhaps soon, you will leave without saying goodbye?"

"I wouldn't do that," he insisted.

She smiled. "You are a man, Harry. That is exactly what you will do. Now tell me why you truly want me to visit your ship so I can make up my mind."

"I won't leave without saying goodbye, Hyacinthe. Indeed, I might not want to go without you at all."

"Then you are a fool," she snapped. "You are going back to England, yes? What will you do when you land there and meet all those grand, rich people you know? Will you say to them,

'Meet Hyacinthe Feraud. She was a whore in New Orleans but she is a lady now'?"

"You are not a whore."

"No, Harry, I am the keeper of a brothel."

"True. But it's a very fine brothel."

She threw back her head and laughed, leaving Harry to wonder, for the hundredth time in three days, how someone of such beauty and wit could be so self-deprecating.

"You must understand, Hyacinthe, that if I have any grand friends I don't give a toss for what they think. If you don't believe me, ask James."

"Tut, tut, Harry. He is the last person to ask."

"What do you mean?"

"I like your brother. He is amusing, droll, and he uses his brushes like a divine saint. Already he has shown me the way he is painting me."

"He hasn't shown me."

"While he dabs, we talk, and certain things I get to know. Perhaps he has more of the sense than you. He likes me. But here, in the Hôtel de la Porte d'Orléans, he would not care to see me even aboard your ship. And he would have a horror to imagine me on your arm, walking around in London."

"You're wrong, Hyacinthe. James is an artist, and I might add rather unconventional. He's not like that, at all."

She shook her head slowly, then abruptly changed the subject. "Tell me why you want me to visit the ship."

Hyacinthe showed her intelligence right away, pointing out to Harry that for her to go aboard *Bucephalas* alone wouldn't work: being well known in New Orleans, only a fool would believe she was interested in a ship. Cayetano couldn't fail to know who was sharing her bed, since he'd more or less ordered it, so her idea was to involve him, let him ask to have a look at her new lover's floating home, taking her along. Harry wasn't convinced that de Coburrabias was the romantic soul that Hyacinthe described, and was extremely doubtful, but she was sure that loving all things military he'd oblige. A note was sent off immediately and the soldier, still less than a morning's ride away at Fort St Jean, agreed with alacrity—that he should be invited, while the senior naval officer was not, amused him. This provided a double bonus, because with El Señor Cayetano de Fajardo de Coburrabias on deck there was no way that Fernandez could stay in his cabin. Indeed he had to be on deck when his superior arrived, with a guard of honour lined up to greet him.

Pender, apparently on the ship by coincidence, insisted on organizing the men to pipe the Spanish commander aboard. He then suggested, by much slow talking and arm waving, that Fernandez could hardly carry off such a visit without providing refreshments; that only he, as Harry's servant, knew where the best was to be found in the way of delicacies and plate. Thus he found himself alone in the cabin for a good half-hour, with more than enough time to search McGillivray's chest. He found the letters, in a pouch, in a secret compartment in the bottom, under the silk lining. He also managed to stuff two cutlasses, wrapped in canvas, into the leather case that contained the portraits they'd found aboard the *Gauchos*. He lowered it out of the casement while the Spaniards, officers and men, were occupied. Then he left the ship without anyone saying a word.

"It took ten minutes, your honour," he said, when he returned. "And if you hadn't said they were there for certain, I might not have found 'em at all."

"What did Hyacinthe think of the ship?" asked Harry, swiping at an imaginary enemy with one of the swords.

"I didn't enquire, Capt'n, but she seemed happy enough."

"Did the crew take to her?"

"Course they did, like they would to any good-looking woman in her finery."

"That's not what I meant," Harry replied. He picked up and fingered the beaded pouch of letters that Pender had placed on the table.

"Let's just say, Capt'n, that the idea of a woman aboard when they're at sea only gets their superstitions twitching."

Pender made no attempt to keep the slight note of disapproval hidden, and Harry looked at him with some sadness. "You don't approve, do you?"

"It's not up to me to do one thing or the other, your honour. I like the lady, if'n that's what you want to know. But I also reckon that what's fine when the sun is shining don't always look so good when it clouds over."

"Harry," said Hyacinthe, bursting in. "I love your little ship. Cayetano tells me you have named it after the horse of Alexander. He gave me this for you."

She handed Harry a note, which he opened immediately. "De Coburrabias has invited me to go hunting, would you believe. Where is the Manchac Post?"

"On the border where the Americans are."

Harry laid the note on the table and held up the beaded package to show Hyacinthe. "We were successful."

"Oh, I know that." She took Pender's arm and squeezed it. "This rogue here, as he left the cabin, he give me a big thing with the eye."

Hyacinthe followed that with a huge wink. Harry laughed, and was pleased to see that his servant, still clutched by Hyacinthe, despite his reservations about her, was prepared to join in the hilarity. She spotted the rolled-up canvas that had been dragged out of the leather case when Harry had removed the sword.

"A couple of portraits we took off the *Gauchos*," Harry said, as his brother walked in. "I cannot comprehend what Pollock was talking about, James, when he said you'd do well in America. It seems to me that every living soul has been immortalized on canvas."

He threw him the other cutlass and presented himself. James did likewise. Watched by Pender, none of the men noticed that Hyacinthe had opened the inside portrait just enough to see the mantilla-covered head, and the pale wistful face underneath. They didn't observe the odd colour, almost grey, that tinged her face. Nor, because of the clash of metal, did they hear the small gasp. By the time Harry, sweeping James's cutlass aside, turned in triumph, the portrait was back on the table, but the effect had not entirely gone. He saw her face and walked over quickly.

"Are you all right, Hyacinthe?"

She gave him a wan smile. "Of course. A little sun perhaps."

"Do you wish to lie down?"

"Rogue," she said, forcing a smile as she dug him in the stomach. "I have work to do."

"I didn't mean that," he insisted.

Her eyes fixed on his with some intensity. "Did you mean what you said yesterday?"

"I said a lot of things yesterday," he replied guardedly.

"I know what I'm saying, Harry," she whispered, this so that James and Pender couldn't hear. "Will you take me away?"

Harry barely paused before he answered. "Yes. I will."

That produced another thin smile. "All you need is your money."

Harry bent forward to breathe in her ear. "This close to you, Hyacinthe, I'm not sure that need is so desperate."

"I had the luck, Harry. There are girls who came to the hotel at the same time as me who will end up like ragged skeletons shivering outside those leaky *tiendas* on the edge of the swamp."

Harry slid across the bed and ran his hand down her chest, just below her breasts, his fingers picking out each rib, wondering why Hyacinthe seemed depressed.

"I can feel your bones already."

He'd meant it as a joke, but her response, even if she knew that, was slightly querulous.

"Can you imagine how many men I have heard make such jokes?"

"Only too well, Hyacinthe, since you made no secret of it."

He, in turn tried to sound as though that didn't matter. But of course it did, even if he knew that it was ridiculous to come into someone's life and behave as though he had a commitment that preceded the first meeting. Everyone had a past, including himself, that was entirely their own affair, and judgements, moral or otherwise, were futile. She had been quite open about hers, without in any way labouring the point. The luck she spoke of he understood, since her rise to her present position had been seamless. Given her looks and intelligence it was entirely understandable, but he knew from his own experience the fickle nature of good fortune. Yet her background wasn't something he could ignore under this roof, with at least one of her previous lovers, Thankful Tucker, still hovering about.

"Do you trust me, Harry?"

The question, given the nature of his thoughts, caught him completely by surprise, and made his positive reply sound what it was, automatic.

"Some men I have known trusted me more than they did their own wives. They told me things that they should have kept to themselves. Sometimes I think I have heard confessions that they would not even have dared tell their priest."

"That doesn't surprise me," he replied, squeezing her flesh in his hands to add a degree of reassurance.

"You are not like that."

"What makes you say that?" he replied, his voice betraying the fact that he was slightly stung.

She laughed. "You are not the type to confess, Harry, I think. That would be a weakness. You like your secrets too much."

He lifted himself on to one elbow, and looked down into her eyes. "I can't think of anyone I've been more open with than you. Do you believe me?"

Hyacinthe put a hand behind his neck and pulled his face towards hers till his head was buried in the crook of her neck. She was thinking about honesty; of the note she'd picked up the day before, crumpled and forgotten, with that disguised writing and the effect of seeing that portrait. Harry had secrets he shared with Pender and James, from which she was excluded. But lovers lied to each other all the time. She, too, had been less than truthful with Harry: when she'd described how she'd come to be at the hotel, leaving out those things which were painful, it had been as much for her benefit as for his. How could she tell him about the degradation she'd been exposed to, as her virginity had been sold a dozen times to slobbering lechers so jaded in their appetites that any girl over the age of twelve was too old to arouse them? Of working the road outside, just as her successors did now, and the luck that had plucked her from that path and set her up here, as the madam of the place, free to choose her partners rather than obliged to accept anyone, drunk, or deformed, who offered enough money? Nor could she say how transient her situation was, that a flick of one man's fingers could see her back on the streets; nor how she longed for a security she'd never known.

The lie she told now came much more easily, since she wasn't obliged to look this enigmatic Englishman in the eye. He would not see the pain his lack of trust inflicted, nor detect the hope that she could somehow make that change.

"Yes, Harry. Of course I believe you."

CHAPTER TWENTY-SEVEN

HARRY NOTICED the escort well before he reached the junction of the Calle de Bourbon and the Calle San Luis. Two Indians were ahead, one behind, while another was on the opposite side of the street. They didn't look at the trio of Englishmen once. Instead they scanned the route to ensure their charges weren't being followed, even casting a wary eye over the almost endless scaffolding that surrounded those buildings still under construction. Harry, equally cautious, slowed his pace as he approached the black door that opened onto the corner. Able to see the building for the first time, he observed that it was unremarkable. The dun-coloured walls were flat and featureless, the street-level windows shuttered in wood, and decoration was confined to metalwork on the balcony that ran around the first floor. With the same magical air as they'd experienced before, the door opened as they approached. All three walked into the cool, dark hallway to find Alexander McGillivray standing at the end. He gestured to them to follow him, and made his way up the stairs. They entered an upstairs room, a comfortably appointed affair, cooled by a slight breeze coming through the open full-length windows.

"This man is your servant, yes?" he asked, indicating Pender.

"He is and he isn't," Harry replied, enigmatically.

"Then he should wait out here."

"No," said James.

"You trust him?"

"We both trust him," said Harry.

McGillivray looked Pender up and down. "Are you armed?"

"Do we need to be?" Pender replied.

"No!" McGillivray smiled, exposing again that even row of gleaming white teeth. Then he opened his black coat to reassure them.

Pender looked into the room, then, satisfied that it was empty, produced a club from inside his loose breeches. "Then you'll want to see this put somewhere we can all keep our eye on it."

"On the table will do fine," the Creek replied, before looking at Harry. "You have my letters."

"Pender!"

McGillivray's eyes followed the pouch as it was passed over. Harry held it up so that he could get a better look. The Creek held out his hand.

"I believe you have something for us."

"I have information."

"About de Carondelet's bullion?"

"You could say that," McGillivray replied.

"Please do not bait us," said James, with evident impatience. "Either you have something to tell us or you don't."

"When I have that pouch and I have checked that the seals on my letters have not been tampered with."

Harry threw it gently. McGillivray caught it with ease and immediately opened it up, tipping the letters onto the table beside Pender's club. He stood to the side of one of the windows and carefully examined each one.

"Thank you, Captain. If you'd care to sit down." Harry and James obliged. Pender stood behind them, as McGillivray began to pace the small area before the fireplace. "After we spoke the other night, I suddenly remembered something, a piece of information which I at the time thought had little significance."

"Which was?" asked Harry.

"I wasn't in New Orleans when what I'm about to describe took place, but it was within hours of the time at which the *Gauchos* was being loaded with those sugar casks. One of my informants told me that a party of Royal Walloon Guards had set out north, on horseback, with a train of a dozen pack-animals.

No one, it seems, was informed of their ultimate destination."

"Is that so very remarkable?" said Harry. "There are garrisons all the way up the river. And if I'm not mistaken, the whole territory is riddled with Spanish missions, all of which have small pockets of troops to guard them."

"It's remarkable in New Orleans, Captain, where knowing what is going on is a civic pastime. Something kept so secret has an odour about it, especially since the Dons rarely bother with subterfuge. Look at the display that surrounded the loading of Rodrigo's ship, a comprehensive charade seemingly designed to hide a greater truth. Also, I don't think you understand the lure of the waterways. Even going upstream to the main garrison at Manchac no one would use a horse if they could make the journey afloat. Why ride around Lake Pontchartrain or Maurepas when you can cross them from Fort St Jean? If you're going west or north-west you'd be bound to use the river system. Yet this party did just the opposite."

"Perhaps they weren't going very far."

"The party headed out north at first, as though they were making for Fort St Jean. That's a common occurrence and would excite no comment. But they turned west well short of the fort, crossed the Mississippi just west of the German Coast, clear of any settlements, and struck inland. We know they're not heading for the Manchac Post since they've already passed behind the Arcadian settlements further upriver, without any of the settlers being aware that they exist. Since they left New Orleans they've bypassed all habitation, including the missions. In fact, the local garrisons, all the way up to the border, know nothing of their presence."

McGillivray looked at them closely, his black eyes examining them to see if they'd caught his drift.

"Do you know why?"

"Obviously they didn't want questions asked about their ultimate destination. In fact they replenished their supplies, and paid for them, at a trading station run by a Choctaw half-breed called Leslie. Paid for food and livery that they could have requisitioned for nothing at any number of places. That can only mean one thing."

"That whatever they are about is something that requires secrecy."

"Which naturally leads to the question of what it is."

"He sent his gold and silver by ship," said James, well aware that everyone had already made the connection.

"Did he?"

"What makes you say that?"

"Who told you that it was on the ship?"

"De Carondelet," James replied. "And if we are talking of the kind of sum already mentioned, then he'd hardly send it with such a small escort."

"He might if he wanted to avoid being asked questions," McGillivray replied emphatically. "De Carondelet only has the Walloons at his disposal and he can't denude the city of the only troops he can personally rely on. If he wanted more men he'd have to ask de Coburrabias, and explain his intentions to the *Cabildo*. Hell-bent on secrecy, he might have taken the lesser of two evils. Since no one in his right mind would entrust such a sum to anything less than an army, none of his officials will ever guess what he's doing."

"But loading it onto the ship was confirmed by the others."

"Not confirmed, brother," said Harry. "You implied before, Mr McGillivray, that the Barón doesn't get on with his officers and has scant regard for his magistrates. Are you now implying that he has created this charade to mislead them?"

"It's possible."

"Is there any way of finding out?"

"Yes. Stop them and search their pack-animals."

"I meant here in New Orleans," said Harry tersely.

"Let's assume that what I suggest is true. Then the only people who would know for certain are de Carondelet and the officer he's put in charge of that party of mounted soldiers."

"Does that officer have a name?"

"He does. His name is Pascal de Guerin, and he's the commander of the Royal Walloon Guards. He's Spanish born, but his grandfather was an official in Charleroi when Spain ran the Low Countries."

"De Carondelet is from the Old Spanish Netherlands as well," said James.

"De Guerin, like his detachment, arrived with de Carondelet. So did de Chigny, another Walloon. You see what I'm driving at, don't you? He doesn't care for San Lucar de Barrameda nor is he the type of man to trust de Fajardo de Coburrabias. They, in turn, are hidalgos, and look down on him as a Flemish upstart who has no right to be Governor of a Spanish colony. He brings with him his own bodyguard plus an officer to command them, one who just happens to share his background. And to crown all this he may well be filching the King's money and salting it away in New York."

Harry shook his head. "No, he's not stealing it, otherwise he'd never have allowed them to know it was being loaded on board the *Gauchos*. And that also means that whoever it's destined for, and the purpose it's designed to serve, has official approval. My guess is it's some kind of payment for services rendered, or the promise of something to come. So the money is for person or persons unknown, in New York, who have the power to affect some political aim."

"The American government?" said McGillivray, his voice full of doubt.

"Stipends paid to foreign statesmen are not unknown," said James, with a touch of irony, it being a well-honed practice in most capitals for high government officials to accept money to advance a particular agenda. "I don't see that the Americans should be so very different."

"That's because you don't know them," said McGillivray. "And being a European cynic, I don't expect you will believe me when I say that the men who run the Federal government are not like that."

"You are right on both counts, sir," James replied.

"Who would de Carondelet want to bribe?"

"Anyone who will help him protect Louisiana."

Harry got up and walked to the window, taking a deep breath of the heavily scented air.

"I'd prefer it if you weren't seen, Captain."

Harry spun round to face the Indian. "Let us assume for a moment that you're right, that that caravan you told us about is carrying the bullion. Let's also, despite your protestations, say that it is destined as a payment for someone who can influence the activities, or at the very least divine the intentions, of the American government. What would that person, in relation to de Carondelet's problems, be trying to achieve?"

"A halt to westward expansion. Spain wants America to stay put on the east bank of the Mississippi?"

"Yet you've told us yourself that you consider it can't be stopped. So it's not that. What would de Carondelet, and the King of Spain, be prepared to pay two hundred thousand dollars for?"

"They like the idea that frontier states might secede. Kentucky and Tennessee, as separate entities, would be worth more than the sum you've mentioned."

"Both are, at present, states," Harry continued, "so they will have representatives in New York."

"Of course. Their senators and congressmen."

"Which appears to justify the concept of sending a bribe there. But while I admit my knowledge of American procedures to be scant, if the decision is made to secede from the Union it won't be taken in New York. It will be taken in . . ." Harry paused. "Do they have provincial centres?"

"Louisville and Nashville," McGillivray replied.

"Then that is where I would send the money."

James stood up as well. "This is all very interesting, Harry, but you're indulging in wild speculation."

"It ties in with what Pollock said."

"Oliver Pollock?" snapped McGillivray, suspicion evident in both his look and his tone.

"A passing acquaintance," said James, airily, as Harry nodded.

"We met him on the island of St Croix. Naturally we fell to talk-ing about the Americas and he told us what a fractious tribe you frontiersmen are."

"Why didn't you tell me this before?"

"Because we had no reason to," said Harry. "And at this moment I have no idea why the mere mention of his name causes you annoyance."

"It doesn't," the Creek replied, in what was clearly a lie. "I know him myself, that is all."

James turned his attention back to Harry. "This leaves us still speculating."

"There has to be a way to find out," Harry replied.

"Would Saraille know anything?"

"You know him too!" McGillivray cried.

"Perhaps," James snapped, "you could give us a list of people you disapprove of and we will avoid mentioning them."

"Is there anything more you can tell us about this?" demanded Harry, cutting off McGillivray before he put James in his place.

"No. I will ask, of course. If something comes to me, I will pass it on to you."

"Then we will bid you good day," said Harry, turning to open the door.

"One more thing," said James. "If this was such a secret I wonder at the identity of your informant."

"Europeans are so used to seeing Indians about, and so con-vinced of their stupidity, they rarely spare them a second glance."

Pender picked up his club, gave McGillivray a hard look, then followed the brothers out into the hallway. He said nothing till they were outside the black door.

"That took a lot longer than it should've done, your honour."

"What makes you say that?" asked Harry.

"Well, he could have told you, instead of leaving you to work things out for yourself."

James smiled at Pender. "You believe that he'd already guessed everything we subsequently deduced?"

"He's a close one, for sure. But I had my eye on him all the time you was talkin', and that's the way I see it."

"You don't like him."

"I'm not bothered one way or t'other," Pender replied. "Though I can't see how come if he's an Indian chief, a savage, he sounds just like Lord Drumdryan."

Harry didn't get a chance to stop James, who was onto the opportunity presented by the question in a flash.

"Because, Pender, like our brother-in-law, the Scots have no more control over their loins than they do over their avarice."

"Thank the Lord you're not like that, your honour," replied Pender, with devastating irony, leaving James and Harry wondering who he was referring to.

Saraille returned to his cupboard of an office in quite a sweat. His fat pink face was excited, though he tried, with his manner, to behave otherwise.

"Your information is correct. De Guerin left at night, a party of twelve soldiers, each with a spare mount and a pack-horse, carrying rations for ten days."

"Who told you this?" asked James.

"The quartermaster," Saraille replied, with an air of triumph. "I slipped him the gold that you gave me, which is something he's not seen for an age. If you want to know what is going on in an army, ask the men who issue their food and clothing. They are without exception open to a bribe."

Harry forced himself to sound uninterested. "Did he tell you what else they were carrying?"

"No. But he did tell me what they didn't take with them, and that is just as important." James opened his mouth to speak, but Saraille held up his hand. "No guns or ammunition, except standard rations. No stores of the kind that they would be carrying to an outlying garrison. And, unusually for soldiers, there was no gossip about their destination, or moans about the journey."

"That is very interesting, Monsieur."

"It will be even more interesting to see how de Carondelet reacts when I pose the question in the *Moniteur*. A mission so secret that I think he hasn't even told the officers of the army or navy, or the members of his *Cabildo*."

Harry leant forward. "I think you are right. But if I was to say to you, Monsieur Saraille, that should you hold fire I could bring you a much better tale, what would you say?"

"What kind of tale?"

"One that would so embarrass the Barón de Carondelet, and so incense his neighbours and his superiors, that the whole edifice of Spanish control in Louisiana could be threatened."

"Can you not tell me now?"

"No. But I can say it is well worth waiting for."

The pink jowls shook excitedly. "When would this be?"

"Of that I can't be certain," Harry replied, leaning back. "It could be a week, or a month."

"Will I be the first one to hear it?"

"Monsieur Saraille, you will be the only one to hear it. Everyone else will have to read it in the *Moniteur*."

"What a fine piece of legerdemain, Harry. You've got Saraille salivating for a story that you don't have. He's going to be very disappointed when he finds out that you've misled him."

"I think you're being overly pessimistic."

"Even after what Pender observed you believe that McGillivray is telling the truth?"

"Let's say that his supposition is the only one that fits all the facts."

"Facts! There are no facts, Harry. You have not established one single certainty on which to base a conclusion. If you wish to go dashing up the Mississippi and have a fight with a dozen Royal Walloon Guards on what is probably a wild-goose chase, don't clothe it in this cloak of false verisimilitude."

Harry smiled. "Is that all I'm doing, James, looking for a fight?"

"I believe so."

"So you will not even admit that I may have the right of it? That there might be two hundred thousand dollars in ingots strapped to those pack-horses?"

"May and might in the same breath, brother. Not a shred of certainty. I rest my case."

Harry was grinning now. "Let's go and see if we can get some, shall we?"

"And where will we do that?"

"In the Governor's quarters."

"You're going to ask de Carondelet?"

"I don't know, James. I might."

"How can you suggest to me, Barón, that I can restore my fortune by locating what you have lost if you will not answer any of the questions I ask you, nor allow me to question anyone?"

"I have not refused to do so, Captain Ludlow. But the enquiries you pose border on the offensive. And you lard them with direct insults."

"I merely asked if you trusted your officers and the magistrates. Let me remind you that the *Gauchos* was intercepted by someone who knew what she was carrying. That implies a betrayal of trust. If only those present knew the secret, then it must be one of them, unless of course . . ."

Harry's voice trailed off, as though a solution had suddenly presented itself. James was deliberately looking at de Carondelet's portrait, trying to avoid participation. But the sharp note in the Governor's voice made him turn round.

"Unless what?" demanded de Carondelet.

"Does it occur to you that the ingots may not have ever been loaded on the ship?"

De Carondelet turned away abruptly, hiding his face from both men. "Don't be absurd, I supervised it personally."

"You mean you actually put the gold and silver in the boxes, then loaded them on board?"

"No! The task was undertaken by my most trusted subordinate. He filled the boxes in full view of all the people you have mentioned. He then took them down to be loaded aboard the *Gauchos*. Since I accompanied the carts almost to the levee, there can be no doubt that he carried out his task to the letter."

"And who, sir, is this officer?"

"Captain de Guerin, of the Royal Walloon Guards."

"I haven't met him."

"He is not in the city at present," said the Governor, turning back to face the brothers.

"That is most unfortunate. When will he be back?"

"Why?"

"It would be helpful to have him confirm that the gold was safely stowed aboard."

"Are you implying that my word is not good enough?"

"I am saying that the only person who can say with absolute certainty that those boxes remained untouched before being put into the ship is Captain de Guerin."

"Then there can be no doubt. He is a most honourable officer, a man I have known since childhood."

"Even the most honourable creature can be tempted by a large sum of money, Excellency," said James.

De Carondelet didn't respond to the gibe, even though, judging by the way his eyes bulged, he understood what James meant.

"This is an officer I would trust with my life."

"That is an irrelevance, Barón," Harry snapped. "The question is, do you trust him to look after two hundred thousand dollars?"

"I do."

CHAPTER TWENTY-EIGHT

"IF HE MEANT the past tense, James, he'd have used it," Harry insisted. The three men, Pender slightly to the rear, were walking north, heading back to the Hôtel de la Port d'Orléans. "He most definitely used the present."

"This is like some kind of religious experience, brother, one of the Papist variety, where a stone Madonna sheds tears. Any enlightened person knows it to be trickery, but thousands are convinced."

"We'd have to go after them by boat," said Harry, who'd only been half listening. "Even riding hard we'd never catch them on horseback."

"We could steal the cutter," said Pender.

"It would be missed, and so would the hands that we took to man it. Which would mean trouble for the rest and a warm reception for us when we returned."

"I think, right or wrong, you're guaranteed that," said James.

"We'd be lucky to stay out of the galleys. The cutter is the wrong kind of vessel for the river anyway. It's too small for the numbers we require, and the wind isn't likely to favour us so we'd have to row. I can't see us leaping out of a boat in the right condition to take on an equal force of trained soldiers."

"I'm glad to observe, Harry, that you're not incurably romantic."

"James," Harry replied testily, "if you have nothing positive to add, please remain silent."

"You can't talk to me like that!"

The reply was just as firm. "I can and I do. You have done

your best to persuade me against this. Having failed I expect your support, not a constant carping that you suppose, quite erroneously, to be humorous."

"When I'm convinced you're right you shall have it. Until then please allow me to speak as I find."

James strode ahead, every firm step he took evidence of his anger. Harry, equally upset, didn't respond to the look he was getting from Pender.

"Are you saying we need one of the keelboats?"

"Do you approve of this, Pender?"

"You keep askin' that and I keep sayin', it's not up to me to one way nor the other, Capt'n."

"Nonsense."

"Then let's just say that I know you're set on the trip, which I'd rather make with you than stay behind. But I won't say that there ain't parts of the notion that don't worry me."

"Such as?"

"Well, it don't do much good to go upsetting folk when it can be avoided, especially them that's close. And if we can't use the men from our own crew, where's the muscle goin' to come from to overpower well-armed soldiers? But the real bit that gets me is this. Why should a man like this McGillivray, who seems pretty convinced himself that these soldiers are carrying a fortune, pass the chance to intercept them on to you? Especially when all he has to do, if I've got it right, is send one of his savages upriver and he can command an army."

"You think he wants me to steal it from the Spanish, so that he can take it off me?"

"Now that might just make sense." Pender lifted his hand to indicate James's retreating back. "As much sense as an apology, Capt'n."

Harry smiled. "Between the two of you it's hard to keep hold of the idea that I'm Captain of anything." He increased his pace, almost running to catch up with James, and came abreast of him just at the bottom of the steps that led up to the main floor of the hotel. "Put it down to frustration, brother. I never was one to remain inactive."

"I hadn't noticed that you'd done that, Harry," James replied, indicating the building before them. "Given what you've been up to these last few days I should have thought frustration was the least appropriate word you could use."

"What do you think of Hyacinthe, James? Really think?"

"She's young, beautiful, witty, and clever." Harry nodded happily. "She is also, though of tender years for the title, a madam who runs a bawdy-house. Which is fine here in New Orleans, but would be frowned upon elsewhere."

"Like Kent?" asked Harry, his smile evaporating.

"I doubt it would even pass in London, Harry." James patted him on the arm. "I have the feeling that you were hoping for a different opinion. But I cannot do that just to please you."

"No. I don't suppose you can."

"Harry, how many ports have you been in, how many women have you known?"

"It's not the same."

"No," James replied sadly. "I can see that. Just as I can see that being the kind of person you are, the idea of taking Hyacinthe back to England as a mistress while denying her the opportunity to be respectable is not likely to be one you could subscribe to."

"I had rather hoped you'd be less stiff."

"Because of my own past?"

Harry nodded. James had been involved with a married woman, and scandalized London by his open relationship with her. Never mind that her noble husband was a drunken rogue, a profligate gambler, and a disreputable rake. Society had its rules, even for noted artists, and James and Lady Farquhar had breached them. Being forced to give her up had reduced James Ludlow to a wreck. Being at sea with Harry had, with time and circumstances, restored his pride and self-esteem.

"Perhaps it is that very background," James continued, "that makes me urge caution."

"Just caution."

"Oh, yes, brother. If the emotion you feel is strong enough to withstand the level of disapproval you'll encounter, then do as you will. England is not the only place a man can live. Besides, in the years since my own débâcle, I've come to know you much better. I've learned that disapproval is not something you pay much heed to."

"Tucker sold the boat back to him this morning," said Hyacinthe. "He's not fond of keelboats. Besides he's been in New Orleans so long that his own crew have drifted away in ones and twos, so Kavanagh's boat wasn't much use to him. He would have done it sooner if the great oaf could have talked any sense. He was feeling guilty, after the way he won it."

"He didn't strike me as someone overburdened with much of that commodity," said Harry, all his suspicions regarding Tucker registered in his face.

Hyacinthe smiled. "Thankful Tucker is a better man than he appears at first. That's true of a lot of these Kaintucks, for all their rough ways."

"Of course," James replied, his face blank. "You know them so much better than we do."

"What are the chances of buying another one?" Harry asked, quickly.

"Poor," she replied. "They love their boats, ugly though they are. But, Harry, why do you want to buy one?"

Harry shrugged, well aware that James's eyes were on him and that by providing an answer that was an excuse he would also expose the fact that he didn't trust her. Yet he realized suddenly that it was true. He hadn't even told her that the money Carondelet had confiscated wasn't his. But there was no alternative. If he was going after the soldiers it had to be surrounded with the same level of secrecy as that employed by the Governor.

"I can't just sit around and do nothing. Here I am on the edge of a huge and fascinating continent which is begging to be explored. I've even got an invitation to go hunting. Besides, I still feel responsible for those Frenchmen we brought to New Orleans. We promised them so much in the way of land and opportunity. Perhaps, if I take them upriver with me, I can find them somewhere to settle."

"Frenchmen would be happier here in the city, I think," she replied. There was a look in her eye that made Harry uncomfortable, one that made him think she saw right through his attempt at dissimulation.

"Maybe," he said emphatically. "But they should be given the choice. How can I do that when I don't know what is available?"

The suspicious air disappeared suddenly and Hyacinthe gave him a charming smile. "You know, Harry, you are a lot like these Kaintuck men. They are cursed with feet that itch. You too cannot stay in one place too long."

"Odd then that Tucker is still here," said James.

The floor was as crowded with dancers, the taproom for the riverboatmen just as vociferously noisy as the first night they'd arrived. Hyacinthe moved around the tables dispensing charm and making arrangements for the better class of girls who occupied the upstairs rooms. Lots of her customers had their favourites, for which she'd produce a little book, to write down a name and time. Bernard had the job of collecting the goods from those whose credit did not extend to such transactions and he followed her round assiduously, extracting payment in advance. Given the shortage of coin, it was interesting to see what people used in its place. Whiskey was popular since it could be sold on; tobbaco, light in weight, for the same reason. Some preferred to sell goods like knives and musket balls. Few went further than a bale of cloth. Those with a line of credit tended to pledge a proportion of future crops, cotton, sugar, rice, and indigo, and Harry and James knew that since they'd been at the hotel Hyacinthe had acquired a number of horses, two mules, and one cart. Anyone, like them, with real coins to disburse was extremely popular as drinking companions, being people who extracted high value for their money.

"I wonder how much de Coburrabias makes out of his extraneous activities," said James idly.

"Enough," Harry replied, "considering he never comes near the place. Hyacinthe tells me has has opened a warehouse to stock his goods since the colony ran out of coins."

"And what about her, how does she get paid?"

"No idea."

"Do you think she will tell her employer, when you fail to turn up, of your intended trip?"

"What trip? I've no means of making it. I was down on the shoreline all day, getting absolutely nowhere, even with real money. All the rafts, which are useless anyway, are broken up as soon as they arrive. The only thing I could have had for the asking was a fist fight."

"That seems like an attempt to evade an answer, Harry."

"All right! I don't know."

"What if she does say something to him? He of course knows nothing of de Carondelet's alleged subterfuge. So, in passing, tucked away in a despatch, he mentions to the Barón that having accepted his invitation to hunt upriver, you have failed to show up. I wonder what happens to *Bucephalas* then."

Harry opened his mouth to reply, but Thankful Tucker had approached their table unseen. "Why, if it isn't Mr Cuckoo and his brother."

"I'm sorry?" said Harry.

"You don't like the nickname, Ludlow." Tucker replied. His face was red and his breath heavy with the odour of whiskey. "Was a time I was sat at that table. Was a time that Thankful Tucker wasn't slung out into the street when the lights were dimmed."

"Thankful!"

The riverboat Captain turned to face Hyacinthe, swaying slightly. He leant towards her and waved a hand drunkenly.

"Why there you are, the sweetest flower in the delta."

"Then don't breathe on me so. I'll wilt."

"I was just telling your cuckoo Englishman that possession of that seat he's occupying tends to be temporary." He turned to leer at Harry. "And with the seat goes all the other little things that are so pleasant to taste."

"You're drunk, Tucker," said Harry.

"Only a whippersnapper would call this drunk. But then maybe you can't hold your liquor."

"Don't answer him, Harry," said James.

"That right, Ludlow. Best if you don't say nothing."

"Are you trying to pick a fight with me?" asked Harry.

Half his attention was on Hyacinthe, the only person with the power to prevent the inevitable. Her eyes seemed excited and her breathing was heavy for someone not actually exerting herself.

"Pick a fight with you," called Tucker, his voice loud enough to be heard at all the surrounding tables. Then he shook his head slowly. "You, with your high and mighty English ways, might think I have no dignity. But I have a care only to raise my hands to a man who can stand toe to toe."

As Harry came slowly to his feet the noise in the tavern died away. His proximity forced Tucker to move slightly backwards. Then he shoved out his left foot and, raising his hands, adopted a pugilist's defensive stance.

"If you can look down without falling down, Tucker, I think you'll observe a toe."

"I know what I'm fighting for, Ludlow. How about you?"

"I believe I'm happy to take you on for the same stake as Kavanagh."

"My boat?"

Harry nodded. Tucker smiled slowly, then pulled himself up, his whole manner changing as the air of drunkenness dropped away. His speech changed at the same time, becoming much more clear and precise. "I won't ask what you'd want with a Mississippi galley, Ludlow, but the stake suits me."

James stood too. "I think, Harry, that you've just had a mouthful of whiskey blown in your face."

"Kentucky rules," said Tucker.

"What are they?" asked James.

"Anything goes," the American replied.

The musicians stopped playing abruptly. The only noise to be heard, as both men removed jackets and shirts, was the scraping of wood on wood as chairs and tables were hastily dragged out of harm's way. Bernard appeared on cue, in shirtsleeves, the club that stood as sole referee swinging lazily in his hand. Out of the corner of his eye Harry saw James following Hyacinthe up to the balcony. Was she aware that for Tucker she was the prize in this encounter? That in turn forced Harry to examine his own feelings. If, as he'd implied to James, he was in love with her, he'd not give her up just because he'd lost. Therefore, did what was about to happen make sense? And what of her emotions? If she'd accepted the outcome of his defeat, what did that say about the depth of regard for him?

Such thoughts had to be banished, as Tucker, stripped to the waist, turned to face him. Harry was momentarily puzzled by the glistening state of his torso, then he realized that the Kaintuck, in a fashion that was clearly habitual, had engaged in a little more subterfuge. He'd set out to goad Harry, determined to engineer a fight, something James had spotted as quickly as his brother. As a precaution, he started by greasing his body in advance of his approach. This would mean that any blow Harry landed which wasn't square on to a fistful of flesh would slide harmlessly to one side, with a subsequent diminution of effect. It was an old pugilist's trick.

They edged towards each other, an act which brought the first cry of encouragement from the watching crowd. This was soon followed by others till it seemed as though no voice was still as numerous bets were placed on the outcome. Both had their fists up in a protective manner, left hand slightly ahead of the right, elbows held in tight to protect the vulnerable solar plexus, while the knuckles stood guard over that other fragile area, the chin.

Harry looked into Tucker's brown eyes, seeking that flicker of the lids which presaged action, all the time edging closer to his opponent. Tucker, likewise, was staring at him, gaze steady, every muscle on his shining body taut and knotted, ready to carry him forward or spring him back out of danger. Suddenly Harry let out a great yell and flung himself forward, arms outstretched. Tucker, alarmed as much by the sound as the act, tried unsuccessfully to leap backwards. In facing what looked like a boxer he'd obviously not expected this kind of assault. Even so, Harry only just caught him. He dug his fingernails into Tucker's shoulder so that the greased flesh wouldn't slip away, and using every ounce of his strength pulled his adversary close. Tucker had opened his hands to push Harry off, but these had been brushed aside. Seeing Harry was determined to get even closer, he opened his mouth and jabbed his head forward to bite his nose.

The head butt that Tucker received lost some of its force because of his swift reaction, but in jerking his head back to avoid damage he allowed Harry to get both arms round his waist and pull him into a bear hug. The teeth that Harry Ludlow sank into the lobe of Tucker's ear were not designed to do more than distract him, even if the act did produce first blood. Those watching could have been forgiven for wondering what the Englishman was about, as he ground his body against that of the keelboat Captain in an almost sexual manner. Harry leapt back just as quickly as he'd jumped in, taking himself well away from his opponent, his hands now rubbing into his body the grease that had transferred itself to him.

"Just thought I'd even matters up a little, Tucker, while I had the chance. Now we're both slippery customers."

Tucker smiled. "And I thought you English fought upright and bareknuckle, with fair play paramount."

"You should try serving on a man-of-war, Tucker. You'd soon find out that your Kentucky rules have a long pedigree."

Tucker skipped forward on his toes, left foot always to the fore, his stance more akin to that of a fencer than a boxer. As the crowd yelled encouragement his left fist shot out, aimed at Harry's unguarded chin. It missed as the head was jerked sideways, but the right followed up, landing a heavy blow to the side of the ducking head. Harry recoiled a fraction, but this was more to achieve a proper balance than because he was hurt. Safe on one foot, his boot took Tucker right beneath the knee on his leading foot. That caused the Kaintuck to drop forward slightly, his lack of balance making the blow he aimed at Harry's chest ineffectual. The one he received in reply was anything but, a crunching fist crashing into the top of his jawbone that spun his head sideways. Tucker was no fool. He knew that the Englishman would follow up, so he used the force of the punch to spin on his back foot. Harry's left hand missed his chin by a whisker, an act which ruined his own stability, carrying him forward. Tucker spun right round, his leg rising higher and higher, till his toecap landed square in Harry's kidney. Some of the agony was dissipated by the fact that he was already moving in the right direction. But not all of it, and Harry staggered, his face screwed up in pain.

Tucker was after him, raining blows on his body as he sought to turn. In the small arena there was little space to back away from the assault, and the screams of the crowd were loud in Harry's ears as the Kaintuck, having him on the defensive, grabbed hold of his hair. Harry immediately ducked as low as he could, legs spread wide, trying to occupy a space that not only took the force out of Tucker's remaining fist, but protected any vulnerable areas, while at the same time denying him the opportunity to either kick or knee him in the groin. He swung his head back and forth, only to have it jerked savagely by his opponent, giving, by his uncoordinated actions, the appearance of a fighter in dire straits. Tucker was attempting to pull his head up so that he could hit him, Harry equally determined, despite the pain, to deny it. Of the two men the latter had a clearer idea of what he was trying to achieve.

Harry Ludlow had been here before and knew exactly what he was about. Each time he swung his own head, Tucker had to change his balance to tug at it, trying to bring it back within range of his flailing fist, growling all the while in frustration at his inability to land a proper punch. This required a constant change of pressure on his feet, and it laid him open to Harry's counter-attack. Pulled viciously to one side, Harry dropped one knee, swinging the other leg in a wide arc. The floor, polished for dancing, was exceedingly slippery. The Kaintuck's legs, taken low and hard, flew up in the air. He had to let go of Harry's hair in a vain attempt to try and save himself. His body crashed to the ground with a resounding thud, the air escaping from his lungs in a clearly audible gasp. Harry's heel did nothing for his ability to breathe, since he ground it unceremoniously into the Kaintuck's guts. But Tucker used that against his opponent, grabbing the offending foot and twisting it till Harry lost his balance and crashed to the floor beside him.

What followed completely lacked science as each man sought to wound the other before they could get to their feet. It started with kicks and jabs, feeble by previous standards, inflicted from a lying position, proceeded to even gentler, almost childlike blows as they struggled to their knees. Both simultaneously made a grab at each other, and the resulting clutch took both men back to the floor. First one man was on top, then the other. Bared teeth sought ears and noses as thumbs were used to try and gouge out an opponent's eye. Knees and feet flashed out trying to land a telling blow in the groin, to little practical effect. With the grease on their bodies, hot and slippery, now spread to every part of their anatomy, purchase of any kind was near impossible. What looked like a fierce fight to the uninitiated was nothing of the sort. Harry and Tucker could go on like this for hours and get nowhere.

Both men seemed to realize this simultaneously, as they pushed apart enough to gain their feet. Now they were breathing heavily, and sweating profusely from their exertions in the heat of the overcrowded tavern. But they were also wary. Upright again, they crouched low, fists at the ready, circling each other like two wild animals, eyes alert for the first sign of a guard dropped. The fists, jabbing forward, at first were exploratory, designed not to hurt but to discomfit, aimed to draw an opponent into leaving a gap for something more dangerous. There was a musical quality to the tempo of these movements as they increased, like a man beating the wooden block on an ancient galley to increase speed. Tucker got through Harry's guard first, landing a painful blow that cut him just above the eye. But the response was immediate and just as effective, as Harry's fist sank into Tucker's exposed torso. That set the pattern for what followed, as the crowd were treated to a display of bareknuckle boxing of the most relentless kind. The sound, of two men toe to toe, raining blows on each other, was like that of a razor strop being used by some mad barber.

The crowd could see that neither the Englishman nor the American was prepared to yield an inch of floor. They'd been through the preliminaries, realized that each knew his way in a fight, and were aware that to win or lose was a now a matter of sheer courage. No subtlety was to be employed, just raw ability. They screamed encouragement, mostly for Tucker, since he was a local hero who'd won them much money in the past. But there were those who'd been supporters who knew that no matter how hard-cased or devious a fighter was, one day he'd meet his match. And given that the odds were greatly in his favour, they could safely take some of their previous winnings and wager it against him.

Each man seemed to sink a fraction lower as the minutes went by. Both sets of upper arms were now bright red from the numerous blows that they'd taken. Tucker was cut above both eyes, while Harry, though suffering on only one side, had a deeper gash to contend with, one which flowed with such a copious stream of blood that it threatened to blind him. As it was, it covered almost the whole of his face. Their breathing was now decidedly laboured and the skin on their fists raw from the constant contact with flesh that, being a thin layer over bone, often failed to yield. Every time one man struck a bone, the sound changed, bringing forth an increase in the noise. Yet neither man could prevail. Bernard stood,

his club useless, as they slugged it out, only the marginal dip of
the knees above the pool of blood, spittle and sweat, that stained
the floor between them evidence that they were achieving anything.

Then the tempo altered, this time slowing infinitesimally as
the wind needed to sustain such a relentless assault began to fail.
Had it been uneven, that man who'd lost his puff first must con-
cede the fight. But it wasn't. It was as though their abilities were
so evenly matched that they sank together. The punches lacked
their previous force, being dragged, as they were, from a rapidly
dwindling store of energy. Few now landed on the face or chin,
being confined instead to the lower body or the less protective
arms. Suddenly they collapsed onto each other, their blows now
swung round the back to try and damage the kidneys or the neck.
Harry put both his fists on Tucker's shoulder and pushed himself
away, staggering slightly as the gap opened and his support disappeared.

They stood swaying for a moment, trying to recover some
strength, before closing again, an act which merely rekindled their
embrace. Then it was Tucker's turn to try the same manoeuvre.
This time they stayed apart, flailing at each other with arms that
seemed to be full of lead. Neither man could hold his balance
properly, so they staggered first together, then apart, time after
time. Tucker, aiming a haymaker that had no chance of connecting, got his arm hooked around Harry's neck, and lacking the
energy to lift it clear he pulled his opponent down. This gave him
little advantage since his own knees collapsed, leaving both to try
and fight each other from a recumbent position. First one then the
other, finding the effort to stay upright too great, sank back onto
the support of their lower legs and feet. This took them out of
range so that the fists, with what force they could muster, failed
to make any proper contact.

Pender stepped forward at the same time as Bernard. The
Negro servant had handed his club to a spectator. He put his hands
under Tucker's arms and pulled him slightly back. Pender did the
same with Harry, leaning over to whisper in his ear that there was

no point in continuing. With his usual stubbornness, Harry shook his head, sending spots of blood flying in all directions. He tried to use Pender's stability as a lever to regain his feet. Tucker, gazing at him through bloody and swollen eyes, seeing the move, sought to emulate his opponent. Bernard looked at Pender, who nodded hard, and both men found themselves being dragged backwards, without the strength left, after their fight, to resist.

"Well," said James, standing upright. "That was a pleasure to watch."

Hyacinthe, still leaning on the balcony rail, her eyes alight, failed to detect the irony in his tone.

"Oh, yes! Wonderful."

It was with a slight sense of distaste that James saw a shudder of deep pleasure run through her lithe body.

CHAPTER TWENTY-NINE

HARRY KNEW that he was in a strange room. He felt as though he was in possession of someone else's face, and that was without recourse to any available mirror. The difference seemed to be even more exaggerated inside his mouth, the swelling in his gums leaving little room for his tongue to move around. When it did move, like every muscle in his body, it engendered pain in varying degrees. Licking his lips was an act stranger than any other, since they bore no relation in size and shape to those of recent memory. For all the misery such acts produced, they did not induce despair. Harry Ludlow, man and boy, had been in too many fights. He knew just how temporary such feelings would be. In two or three days he'd be left with a multitude of bruises and the odd wisp of cotton, but little evidence of actual discomfort. In a week, little would remain to show that he had been on the receiving end of a blow.

He'd been stitched and bathed, the gentle hands of Hyacinthe Feraud causing him alternately to wince and groan. Then he'd slept, fitfully, with Pender in attendance. Now, lying as still as he could, letting each ache take its turn to register, looking at the slits of light patterning the ceiling, he saw his actions of the preceding night for what they were: real stupidity. The whole farrago about a boat now seemed like an excuse to cover his jealousy. He'd allowed Thankful Tucker to get under his skin because James disapproved of his liaison with Hyacinthe. He'd fought the man to prove the depth of his regard, an act he would have scoffed at if undertaken by another. The bit about the keelboat had been a momentary inspiration to cover his foolishness.

Eyes fixed on the ceiling he heard the door open. He waited, expecting Pender, who since first light had been in and out every twenty minutes. But no servant appeared to lean over and blot out the strips of light. The voice of Thankful Tucker, altered to a mumble by his own swellings, surprised him.

"What, in the name of Jesus, Joseph, and Mary, do you want with a Mississippi galley?"

Harry raised himself onto his elbows, sending several agonizing stabs through his upper body. Tucker was half in shadow by the door, so he couldn't see his face, but the changed note in the voice assured him that Pender was telling the truth. The Kaintuck had suffered as much damage as he. He smiled, ignoring the cracks in his lips that seemed to open as soon as he stretched the skin.

"It's the best way to get upriver, I think."

Tucker shuffled halfway across the room and fell back into a chair. Harry, who could see him more clearly now, was sure he heard a stifled gasp. "Damned right, Ludlow, though that don't go no way to explaining why you want to go there."

"Curiosity."

"Horseshit!"

"Being offensive comes very easily to you, Tucker."

"Only an Englishman of your stripe would think so," Tucker replied, calmly, while he eased his position. "In Kentucky that particular answer accounts for about half the total wordage."

"What an entertaining set you must be."

"So what is the true answer?"

"Does there have to be another?"

"Sure does."

"I have a group of Frenchmen I'd like to see settled."

"I heard about them. Artisans and the like. They're holed up with the Ursulines." Harry nodded slowly. "New Orleans is about the best place for the likes of them."

"They don't agree. They might have begun life in various trades but most have spent the last few years on plantations. They think that given some virgin land they can enjoy greater prosperity."

The mixture of truth and lies tripped off his tongue very easily, but his mind was racing, slotting into place his real need of a boat, as well as the very pressing reason for it.

"I'm curious myself, Tucker. Why are you asking?"

"Maybe, after our little bout, I've come to respect you, Ludlow. Happens that I'm feeling a mite guilty about the way I set things up last night. So I'm asking if you want a boat."

"Are you conceding defeat?"

The friendly tone evaporated immediately. "No, sir. I am not."

"Then what are you offering?"

"You could rent mine for a token sum. If'n it would help, at all."

Harry examined that for the truth, concluding very easily that it was in fact dishonesty. Tucker resented his proximity to Hyacinthe. Harry Ludlow rowing up the Mississippi would be out of New Orleans, leaving the field clear for his visitor. It was as simple as that.

"I'm not sure I know how to handle one," he replied cautiously.

"Don't see why you need to bother, Ludlow. That's my job."

"You're proposing to come with me?"

Tucker's slow and painful nod, added to what appeared to be an earnest look in his eye, made Harry feel very much like a scrub.

"Only trouble is, I ain't got no crew."

Harry fell backwards on the bed, suddenly remembering that to all intents and purposes, neither did he. Hot and sticky, the draught that swept across him as the door flew open was welcome. Less appealing was the sudden increase in light as Hyacinthe flung open the shutters. She walked across the room and looked down at him, reaching out a hand to gently stroke the stitches over his eye.

"You are such a fool, Harry. Both of you are fools." Her hands drifted close to his swollen lips. "I've a good mind to kiss you, very hard, then get into bed with you and insist you make love to me."

"Please," he croaked, in a voice that was only half-joking.

Tucker added a grainy cough to remind them both that he was in the room. That made Harry sit up, his determination to have a proper look at his late opponent in full daylight overbearing any increase in pain. Tucker was there somewhere, under enough bumps and swellings to make him look like a grotesque. The small flash of triumph disappeared quickly as he realized that he must look very much the same.

"Tucker has suggested I rent his boat."

"That is very good of him," said Hyacinthe flatly. "I told you he was not the ogre you imagined."

"I think it was James who expressed that," Harry replied. He'd only spoken to cover himself: he was assessing Hyacinthe's calm reaction to the news of Tucker's offer. There'd been a change in her behaviour in the last 48 hours, subtle but detectable, almost as though she'd dropped her previous reserve and decided to be more committed to his cause. That someone prepared to fight him last night could be so generous was singular, even if he was guilty, but it didn't take a genius to see where pressure might come from. Had Hyacinthe told him that he needed to do something to make amends? In a sense, it didn't matter; such an avenue opened up several possibilities. He waited till she left the room to fetch some water with which to rebathe his wounds before he broached the subject.

"How many men do you need to crew your galley?" he asked.

"Half a dozen coming downriver on a spate. Twenty at least to man the oars if you're going up against a real current. Right now, with the river falling, half that would do."

"What would you make in a day?"

"Twenty to thirty leagues, if you can clear the eddies and avoid whirlpools and driftwood."

"Do you have to tie up for the night?"

"People need to sleep, Ludlow."

"What if you have enough people?"

"Night-time is dangerous. There are sandbars and islands, not to mention whole tree trunks from the logging that goes on upriver."

"Logs apart, surely the danger is greater coming downriver than going the other way. Even if you run aground the flow favours you."

Tucker thought for a moment. "That's true, Ludlow. But if you've ever been on the Mississippi you'd know what a cruel river she can be. I've been up and down that old muddy mistress since I was a boy, and I still wouldn't claim to be too familiar. And should you meet one of them damn logs at the wrong time, you'll find a nice big hole in your hull that's beyond repair."

"All I'm asking," Harry mumbled, "is this. Is it possible to make more than the speed you've just mentioned?"

"It is. You might just get a bit of help from a wind. But mostly it's sheer muscle. The men who man the oars will suffer."

"They might be willing to."

Hyacinthe came back into the room, a bowl of steaming water in her hands. As she started to dab at his face, he reflected that his unease was misplaced, that her regard for him was obvious in the way she fetched the water herself instead of asking a servant to carry out the task.

"If Pender's not asleep, I'd like a word," he said. The attempt to smile died as the pain in his face registered.

"You'll need de Carondelet's permission," said James, quietly, "which might just make him suspect what you're up to."

"Why should he, brother? He has no idea what we know."

"I shall avoid the temptation to point out to you how little that is."

Harry glanced over James's shoulder, to where Hyacinthe sat at a desk, totalling her accounts. He indicated that they should go up onto the roof, out of earshot, to continue their discussion. She waited till they'd left before closing her ledger and walking out onto the balcony outside her windows. Harry and James couldn't see her, but she could hear them, as Harry restated his conviction that de Guerin and his twelve Walloon Guards were carrying the gold and silver.

"Killing Rodrigo doesn't make sense if the bullion was in the hold," said Harry. "With the rendezvous arranged, whoever came aboard was an accomplice. But if he felt betrayed because there were no ingots, and suspected the Rodrigo had cheated him, that would explain such a bloodthirsty response."

"You think he was tortured to extract information."

"I do," Harry replied, sadly. "And I rather fear it was something he didn't have."

"And the rest, including the women, were murdered to keep them silent."

"If they were killed. Half a dozen barrels and no bodies."

"You said the sharks . . ."

"That is a guess. I'm troubled by the way the food was removed."

"This is a new tack you're on."

"Not really, brother. It is, like all of this, speculation. And if I might be allowed to indulge in a touch more, what would you do if you discovered that two hundred thousand dollars you knew to exist wasn't where you expected it to be?"

"I'd want to find out where it had gone," said James, "and having done so I'd then need a way to get my hands on it."

"What if you can't ask?"

"Because you're supposed to know?"

"Exactly!" said Harry. "You can't even hint that those ingots are missing, because if you do, you reveal the knowledge that it wasn't aboard the *Gauchos*."

"That would be very frustrating."

"But you do know this: that thanks to our opportune arrival, the Governor has the means to make good his apparent loss."

"I think you've moved from speculation to certainty, Harry, something you're prone to. You've entirely failed to explain why Carondelet, who knows that his property is safe, has gone to all the trouble of stealing what he thinks is ours."

"Security," said Harry, emphatically. "Our thief doesn't know if he's been tricked or robbed. What he does know is that the Barón has the money to try again. If he's close enough he will know who it is intended for. The pressures that caused de Carondelet to nearly bankrupt the colony have not evaporated, therefore at some point he should ship out our Frenchman's money. What the thief doesn't know is that it's already on its way."

"And if what McGillivray thinks is correct, the longer de Carondelet waits, the safer he is, because the thief will have his eye on the specie he took from us?"

"Yes."

"You and the Governor should be friends, Harry, not enemies. He's nearly as devious as you."

"This time I will accept that as a compliment."

"So perhaps, when he is sure that his money has arrived, he'll return that chest to our ship and let us depart."

"Do you really believe that?"

"No, Harry, I don't. Which brings us neatly to the problem of what we're going to do about it."

"Time is our ally, that and the hurricane season. The Plate fleet couldn't sail until that is well and truly over. Look how we were caught out. And even with the best will in the world, since it must call at either Havana or Port-au-Spain it cannot make Cadiz before August. Given the ways of the Spanish navy, I'd bet on September. A fast packet needs a month to get back to New Orleans. That means October, which, according to Tucker, just happens to be the month when the river tends to be at its lowest. So I reckon to have three clear months to go after de Guerin and get back again. In the meantime, I expect that those guarding the crew will become so used to their presence that they'll relax."

"Do you still need to get men ashore?"

"Yes. I'll ask de Carondelet at the same time as I request permission to take up Don de Coburrabias's invitation."

"No!" said James forcefully. "If you post two requests he's bound to deny you one, just to prove he's in control. You ask for the hunting and leave the other business to me."

Harry raised a stiff arm to pat James on the back. "It's good to have you on my side."

"You'll need me, brother," said James harshly. "You entirely lack the charm necessary to persuade our Frenchmen that their best interests will be served by going upriver with you."

Harry groaned as he dropped his arm, partly through pain, but more through anticipation. If they said no he was sunk.

De Chigny arrived after they'd gone, first to look over Tucker's boat and give him money to buy stores. Then they would proceed to the Calle des Ursulines to try and persuade the Frenchman to crew it. In his hand, the lieutenant carried Harry's written permission to go hunting. Hyacinthe took it on his behalf, promising to deliver it when Harry returned.

"You are dusty and hot, Señor," she said, walking towards the stairway. "I will order you something to cool you down."

"Thank you," he replied, forced to follow by her assumption that he would accept.

She led him up to the salon, and sat him on a chaise-longue, joining him once she'd rung the bell. They chatted amiably till the lemonade arrived, sipped it after it was served, and she stood to refill his glass. She sat down again, her position much closer than hitherto, so close that her knee made contact with his. De Chigny, being pale-complexioned, could not disguise the blush that coloured his face.

"My lieutenant," she said, dropping her voice a complete octave. "That is not where I normally expect a man's blood to go when he touches me."

Her fingertips stroked the seam of his breeches, which made him colour even more. "You are so elegant, you Walloon Guards, especially the officers. I admire Captain de Guerin too. He is such a handsome fellow at a ceremony like the King's birthday. I have had the honour of entertaining him more than once."

"Mademoiselle," he croaked.

"He is, I believe, up north?" she asked, leaning slightly closer.

His reply was near breathless. "All I know, Mademoiselle Feraud, is that he is on some private business for the Governor."

"Ah yes! The Barón's little charade with the gold and silver." De Chigny's eyes nearly popped out of his head. Hyacinthe put a finger to her lips. "Sshh! I am the soul of discretion. It would not do to let the Governor know that his confidants are prone to gossip, or that they visit such places as the Hôtel de la Porte d'Orléans during the day."

She stood up and waved an arm to encompass the whole room. "If the good Barón ever found out some of the things that I have heard within these walls . . . But it would never do for him to suspect, would it, Lieutenant? I might be put to the rack."

His expression had changed. There was just a trace of guilt or fear in the eyes, which pleased Hyacinthe, since it indicated that he'd understood her perfectly.

"Does your duty permit you any leisure?"

"Some," he replied, his voice suddenly more military. "But the Barón gives me many tasks to perform."

"Then he must trust you, Lieutenant. I would not take it amiss if you were to call on me, when your duty allows."

He got to his feet, clearly suffering a degree of physical discomfort, which required, to effect a disguise, the use of his tricorne hat. She smiled sweetly as she rang the bell to summon Bernard. "I do so love a man in breeches."

If he'd blushed before it was as nothing to what happened then. His face had gone the colour of beetroot. He positively dashed out of the room, mumbling apologies, as soon as the servant opened the door.

With de Chigny gone she went to her ledger and extracted the note Harry had received two days before. Smoothing out the creases, she penned a quick letter, copying the style of the block capitals rather than employing her normal handwriting. She sealed it with wax and took it downstairs.

"Take this to Calle des Ursulines, Bernard. Give it to Captain

Ludlow. You are to say that it came by an Indian messenger who would not name the sender. That I thought it best to take it on his behalf and send it on to him, unopened."

That note saved Harry from an embarrassing rebuff, at a time when the Frenchmen looked set to refuse his invitation to join in the expedition north. Spoken out loud, it had sounded like an absurdity to him, especially with James's eyebrows flickering at every anomaly in his explanation, a reaction noted by even the most eager of his listeners. In a situation when he needed to appear certain of his aims he was just a touch hesitant. So when Bernard gave it to him, and as he read it, the buzz of conversation was wholly negative.

"From McGillivray," he said, passing the square of paper to James. His brother read it quickly as Harry thanked the messenger and Pender ushered him out of the room.

"Well, Harry," he said. "The case seems altered."

It wasn't plain sailing. There were those like Brissot who so distrusted him that no amount of letters would convince him of the truth. But slowly he and the others were overborne till their protestation lost force, since it now looked like a choice between poverty in New Orleans and security elsewhere. They conceded unhappily, and with no grace whatsoever. But the important objective had been achieved. Harry Ludlow had an objective, a boat, and a crew.

Lampin was put in charge of getting them aboard, moving in small groups so as to avoid unwelcome attention. The nuns of the Ursuline order would have to be told, but Harry wished them to know as little as possible. The chests full of gunpowder were to be left as evidence of their intention to return. Harry gave them money so that they could make a donation to the convent funds that would ensure that the Mother Superior remembered them fondly, then went off with Pender to find a pair of horses.

"Is there no other way, your honour?" Pender asked.

"No," Harry replied. "We can't go in the same boat as the

Frenchmen. That would be bound to attract notice, and I want to give the impression I'm in no hurry."

"Well, you know what I think of horses."

"It won't be for long. As soon as possible we'll leave the road and make for a rendezvous upriver."

Pender's groan was suppressed, but it was audible.

"He is not in comfort, your Pender," said Hyacinthe, looking at James. "And neither are you."

They were standing in the window, looking up the road that led to Fort St Jean. Harry, who'd already turned to wave, sat easily in his saddle. Pender kept his face rigidly forward, trying to avoid slipping sideways every time his horse changed gait.

"I've never known a man who so loved danger," James replied, without looking at her. Mentally he was cursing his inability to speak freely. He wanted to say that he thought Harry slightly mad, that everything about this trip had a convenience attached to it that left a rank smell. But he couldn't, because the fiction that Harry had told Hyacinthe needed to be maintained. So what he said made him feel and look inadequate. "And I fear the consequences if he encounters any."

But Hyacinthe was looking at him, well aware that he was on the horns of a dilemma, and in some way enjoying the fact. It was almost as though she and James stood as equals in Harry's estimation, each only trusted with a portion of the truth, each convinced that his journey was a mistake, since the solution to everything lay here in New Orleans, not in the wilderness to the north. And since she herself was playing a similar game it was easy to avoid any resentment. Gaining trust from James was important, since he had the power to sway his brother. This trip provided time for that, time to prove to both men that she was worthy of more than mere appearances would indicate, that Harry's promise, fulfilled, was not something he'd live to regret either making or keeping. She stroked the back of his hand gently.

"You have a painting to finish."

CHAPTER THIRTY

"THERE'S ONE or two who are less than happy," said Tucker, cradling the long rifle in his arms. "Might have jumped overboard if I hadn't mentioned alligators. Who's that big ape with the beard?"

Harry followed Tucker's pointed finger, only to be greeted by a furious glare. "Name's Brissot. He's not much given to trusting people."

"I don't care if'n he don't trust me, but with the looks I've been getting I thought I was going to have to fight him. And after what you and I had just been through I didn't expect to win."

Harry examined Tucker's face. The swellings, like his own, had started to recede, but his face was a mass of scratches and bruises, the latter darker than they'd been the day before, and as he moved, Harry could see that he too was careful to ease his discomfort. The two of them must present an interesting sight. Tucker had changed into loose buckskin garments, dark brown with beadwork edging the collar and cuffs. There was a round fur hat hanging on a hook by the door of the deckhouse, and a powder horn with elaborate carvings. His clothes were made from the same material as the cover he used to keep his rifle dry, so that for all his frontier dress Harry could still imagine him a man careful of his appearance. They'd been formally introduced to the weapon, Practical John, a long rifle nearly five feet in length. Tales abounded of the accuracy of the weapon and the skill of the frontiersmen in their use, and it was clear, when Harry hinted that he would welcome a chance to fire it, that Tucker regarded it in the same way as legend dictated. "Why, I'd no more let a man fondle Practical John than I would let him near my mother."

They were at anchor, just offshore, in a wide expanse of the river that turned due east, which was actually to the south of New Orleans. The land on either side was flat and featureless, dotted with plantations and fertile in the way of all deltas, and judging by the high levees, just as prone to flooding. He and Pender had cut across from the road to Fort St Jean, riding as hard as Pender's ineptitude would allow, aware that time was an enemy in more senses than one. The amount they could spend away from New Orleans was limited, but more pressing was the fact that every day increased the distance de Guerin and his party of Walloon Guards could put between themselves and de Carondelet. Tucker had come this far on a north wind using the single square sail, but the wind had swung round into the west and it was now useless. It was time to row.

"Let's prepare to get under way."

"Can't do that without a dram, Ludlow," said Tucker, reaching for a ladle that poked out of a covered tub. "And I suggest the same for your Frenchies, before they're put to the oars."

Harry looked around the small boat, wondering if he should address the men and remind them of the task ahead. It was fairly broad, with two narrow walkways for poling on either side of the deckhouse. More of a low hutch, this sat amidships, leaving a foredeck that matched the size of the afterdeck on which they stood. A great sweep lay at rest beside them, long enough to contest the sudden variations that were to be found in the faster-flowing parts of the river. Beneath the walks lay the rowing stations, ten a side, which opened onto the cargo hold. Really there was no place on the boat that could be considered out of earshot.

Tucker's French was far from perfect, but he'd quickly understand any references to gold or silver, and this was one of the problems Harry'd yet to resolve. Once Tucker found out what it was they were after, could he be trusted, not least to stay quiet? Harry's knowledge of frontiersmen was limited, but from what he'd seen and heard they had a trait, other than fighting and drinking, that marked them out: their desire to boast. Given that Tucker was a member of that breed, and a man who couldn't move without a dram, they'd have to avoid not only Spaniards but Kaintucks and Creoles, otherwise the whole territory would hear about de Guerin's caravan.

"Pender, ask Lampin and Couvruer to join me in the deck-house. We need to sort out crews and reliefs."

"What about Brissot?" Pender replied, indicating that the bearded giant was still giving them malevolent stares.

"Ignore him!" snapped Harry.

The trip upriver started reasonably well and proceeded so as they pushed through the broad flowing waters around the German Coast. Not accustomed to rowing in such numbers, and also out of sight of each other, it took time for the Frenchmen to get a proper rhythm, which led to much yawing as one side applied more pressure on the oars than the other. Tucker, handing over control of the great sweep to Harry, resorted to the oldest method of control in the world, banging a piece of wood on the foredeck. Lampin and Couvruer took on the task of interpreting his instructions, each being responsible for one side. Surprisingly, given their situation and problems, the majority of those engaged showed a welcome sense of humour, with many a shout of derision aimed in the direction of anyone whose grip slipped. In all the time Harry had known these men he'd never heard them laugh. That they were doing so now did much to lighten his own mood. It didn't survive actual contact; they might be happy to share a joke with each other, but not with him, and that applied especially to those who distrusted him the most.

Within a couple of hours, with each side relieved and all the oarsmen worked in, they were making steady progress. Tucker, who knew the river well, steered from side to side, so that the current was kept to a minimum by the kind of lee shore provided by the knuckle of every bend. On either side of the dark brown mass of the river imposing plantation houses caught his eye, each surrounded by blooming orange trees, in some cases but a stone's throw away from them, and it was curious to observe that while the orange fruit at the top of the trees was ripe, that in the middle was not, while at the very base of the leafy cascade the buds were no more than blossom. They passed fields full of toiling Negro slaves, sweating profusely in the hot humid atmosphere.

Within 24 hours the weather began to change quite dramatically, the sunshine and still, warm air replaced on the horizon by dark, forbidding clouds. The distant rumbling thunder warned of the approaching storm well before it arrived. There was an uncomfortable ten minutes for those on deck while they roasted in their oilskins. When the rain arrived it seemed to be nearly as hot as the air. The deluge that engulfed them, full of flashing lightning, was enough to remind Harry how close they were to the Tropics. They rowed on through the morning at a steady pace, the discomfort of water dripping through the planking adding to the misery of an hour at the oars.

"Best have the crew off watch take over," cried Tucker, who'd hitherto been fairly silent. "We need them fresh. Them that comes off the oars should be standing by with poles."

Harry looked forward as Tucker pointed. Even at this distance he could see that the bend they were approaching was tighter than those they'd already steered through.

"We're coming up to Judas Point."

"Named for treachery, no doubt?" shouted Harry.

"Damned right," Tucker replied, opening his mouth to let the rainfall fill it. "You'll need to take a position by the hatch where you can relay my orders to the oars. Pender, I'd be thankful if you'd fetch me a ladle of that whiskey then come and assist me on the sweep."

Harry moved forward to the rear of the deckhouse, looking down the cramped companionway. He could hear the rhythmic grunts of the rowers as they hauled on the leather-covered grips. Sheltered from the noise of the storm, he issued his orders and watched as the men changed over. Those that came on deck to take up poling positions had nothing to protect them from the elements, but if this bothered them, it didn't show. They were happy to ease their aching limbs. Even Brissot had stopped glaring at everyone.

"Best warn them, Ludlow, that if we hit a bad eddy I'll ask them to ship. And advise them they're not dangerous. They don't suck you under like they can at sea, they just dance you round a trifle then spit you out."

Harry ducked his head back under cover to relay this information to his charges. One or two of them grinned at him, at which point he realized that he was smiling too, addressing them in the same tone he adopted with his own crew. But the majority still greeted him with a look of distrust which forced him to alter his expression. Tucker's shout brought him out into the rain again.

"There she goes!"

Harry felt the ship begin to spin, the head coming round despite Tucker's and Pender's efforts on the sweep. "There's a pile of driftwood off to starboard, Ludlow. See if those men can get their poles onto the wood and keep us clear."

The boat was now athwart the river, head due north. But it was also being forced to the southern bank by the force of the whirlpool. A huge mass of logs and tree trunks lay there, so entangled that they were locked together, the force of the river's current holding the whole edifice in place.

"Ship!" Tucker yelled.

The rowers responded just in time, lifting the oars clear of the wooden island. Those on deck shoved out their poles and locked them into any gap which presented itself, struggling hard to keep the galley in clear water. Their efforts were only partially successful. The gap was closing. Without knowing what kind of danger this represented, it was obvious that contact would considerably slow their progress. Tucker shot past Harry, leaping over the side of the boat onto a log that looked near six feet in circumference. Harry held his breath, waiting for the wooden mass to part and swallow him up. It didn't happen. They were crushed so firmly in place that it was as safe as an earthen shore. Tucker waited till the boat was close enough then leant out and begun to push it, trying to edge it past the most prominent projections. Feeling useless, Harry made his way to the bulwark and, heart in mouth, jumped down to join him. He was immediately assailed by a stream of instructions.

"Two poles on that Douglas fir, another on the live oak just behind it. You come by me and push like hell."

Tucker's face was bright red with exertion, as he pushed against the side of the galley. Suddenly a gush of blood erupted from his already swollen nose, immediately washed off by the teeming rain. It didn't interfere with his pushing, but it produced a stream of invective that told Harry it was a curse he had suffered from before.

"Clear water coming, Ludlow. Get yourself back aboard."

Harry didn't wait to check if Tucker was right. The idea of staying where he was terrified him, his mind full of the image of himself slipping underneath the logs, unable to find a way to the surface. He'd heard it from people who knew about the dangers of logging, knew it was possible, and could hardly believe that it hadn't happened already. The low freeboard made the jump relatively simple, but the wet wood, being slippery, nearly proved his undoing. Harry's foot didn't quite reach the top of the rail and his hands began to lose their grip. Someone grabbed the collar of his oilskin coat and he was lifted bodily inboard. Raising his eyes he saw the rain-soaked black beard and dark hair that framed Brissot's unfriendly eyes.

"Your hand, Ludlow!"

Harry was up and leaning over the side in an instant. Tucker was walking along the logs, utterly unconcerned by any risk of slippage. Just as he reached the point where the galley made clear water, he leapt nimbly for the side. Harry's hand was no more than a gesture to help him inboard.

"Damned nose of mine," Tucker said, pulling off his dripping fur hat and shaking it. "Happens every time. Only thing to cure it is a dram of whiskey."

"I think I'll join you," said Harry, grinning.

"Let the whirlpool take us round, Pender," called Tucker, ladle in hand. Then he gave it to Harry. "Just hold her steady as she is."

Harry, who'd thrown the contents of the large spoon down his throat, gasped and staggered forward slightly, his eyes wide with surprise.

"That's a fine brew you just consumed, friend. The best that Kentucky can offer, an' not watered down for milksops."

"Thank you," Harry gasped. He leant back, opened his mouth, and let it fill with rain.

Tucker drank his down without discomfort, smacked his lips, them went to join Pender on the sweep. The boat shuddered as a piece of driftwood rammed into the side. Looking overboard, Harry saw an astonishing amount floating by, including whole trees with their branches intact, rolling over and over in the turbulent water.

"Must have been some twisters upriver," said Tucker. "There's a mite more'n usual."

A steady stream of thuds came from just on the waterline, the noise of each one a clear indication of just how big a piece of drifting debris had rammed them. Tucker sent two men with poles to the bows to try and fend some of them off. Harry was examining the slow-moving whirlpool, visible even in a river lashed by huge drops of rain. Judging by the run of the water it was a half-mile in circumference. He'd never seen anything to equal such a phenomenon in his life. Tucker, steering by himself now, made for a point near the centre, and used the force of the current to bring the galley's head round.

"Stand by on the oars, Ludlow, if you please. When I give the shout tell them to haul like heroes. And I'd be thankful, after that, for your help on the sweep."

The storm increased in tempo, great flashes of lightning searing across the black sky. The river itself, with the pounding deluge, was made to seem like something live. Harry watched Tucker's lips, not sure in such a squall if he would hear him speak. It was faint when it came, but clear. He called down below and was gratified by the way the Frenchmen set to. Then he ran back to the stern. Close to Tucker, straining on the sweep to keep the head steady, he could hear the caressing tone in the man's voice.

"Come on, my beauty. Take us out of here. That's it, that's it." The pressure on the sweep eased as he gave a great shout. "That's it! We're clear."

"Thank the Lord," said Harry, smiling. Pender was grinning too. That disappeared when Tucker responded.

"Next one's a mile off and twice the size."

"I've been stuck in those for more'n two days before now, Ludlow. Going round and round in circles set to make a man dizzy. We were real lucky. The rain deadened the spin a touch, I reckon."

The bad weather which persisted for two whole days had passed over, and the night sky was a carpet of bright stars. Smoke was pouring out of the chimney amidships, as one of their scratch crew prepared a meal using the stores Harry had sent aboard and some fish they'd caught over the side. Tucker was steering still, having set them to proceed at a quarter of their best pace. This eased the strain on the oarsmen and lessened the risk of serious damage from driftwood. He tried hard to stay in mid-channel. Every time they failed, and slid towards the shore, the whole boat was attacked by swarms of mosquitoes.

"Is that the worst we have to face?" Harry asked, wondering if there could be a section of the river as tough to get through as the one they'd just managed.

"No," he replied, grinning. "The worst you have to face is when a log holes you so bad you're sinking just at the spot that the alligators like to gather."

"I dare say you walk on them with the same equanimity that you showed on that log."

"Equanimity. That's a mighty fine word, Ludlow."

"It's certainly a better one than horseshit."

"That's no error," said Pender.

Harry grinned at him, before addressing Tucker. "Have we made good time?"

"Better than I expected when that storm broke."

A burst of laughter came from the hutch.

"The Frenchmen have performed well," said Harry. "Fighting the Mississippi has done them the power of good."

"Now that we're past some of these little local obstacles, I was wondering if'n you were going to tell me what it is we're chasing in such an all-fired hurry?"

"Of course. There a party of twelve Royal Walloon Guards heading north on horseback. We're after them."

"Why?"

"They have something I want," Harry replied.

"I'll grant you don't know me well, Ludlow. I'll also own to the fact that our meeting each other could've been smoother . . ."

"But?" asked Harry, as he paused.

"You're going to have to trust me."

"Just being here means I do."

"No. Let me tell you about the Manchac Post. Used to be called Fort Bute and it stands right where the Iberville River joins the Mississippi. Built by the English after the Peace of Paris to command the only other route out of the interior that didn't mean going through the delta. Goes right down the Amité River through Ponchartrain to a set of narrows that lead out into Lake Borgne."

Tucker paused for a moment to let that information sink in. Harry was visualizing a chart. He knew that Lake Borgne was a deep salt-water bay that led out into the numerous islands that filled the Chandeleur Sound, islands that provided a wealth of routes out into the Gulf of Mexico.

"There's an expression you would hear if you sat drinking in any riverside tavern often enough. It's 'doing a little Manchac', and it means smuggling. Now the Dons don't like that too much and so they stop quite a few boats that pass Manchac going upriver or down."

"I thought we were going to try and pass it at night?"

"We are. But since that's also the time that smugglers like to do the dirty the Dons are pretty wide awake."

"You mean we might not make it."

"Yes. But it also means I might have to tell a lie. That's not something that bothers me none, but I prefer to do it when I know what the truth is. Kinda makes it easier, you know, especially since I'm carrying no cargo."

"All right," said Harry. "We're after those Walloons because I think they're carrying two hundred thousand dollars in gold and silver."

Harry considered Tucker a hard man to shut up, but that statement kept him quiet for a good minute.

"I'll save you trying to work it out for yourself," he said, and explained, in detail, what he'd learned and what he hoped to achieve. "Do you know McGillivray?"

"I know of him," Tucker replied.

"Is what you hear good or bad?"

"Depends who's talking. For some folks the only good Indian is one that has gone to join the spirits. To others he's a mite heroic. Rumour has it that George Washington, who hates to touch another, shook his hand."

"That not really what I was asking."

"You want to know if he's truthful?

"I do!" Harry replied emphatically. "Pender here thinks that he knows more than he's saying."

Tucker looked at Harry's servant questioningly.

"I reckoned, from the very first meeting, that he knew that this de Guerin has the bullion, that it was less than the guesswork he wanted us to think. That's been made more so by the way he timed that note to the Captain."

"Pender wonders if once we have it he might try to take it off us."

"He damn sure can't do it himself," said Tucker. "A party of

Indians strong enough to do what you intend, in the wrong place, would cause a whole neckful of hackles to rise. Folks would be calling for troops to protect them. Some people can't see a Redskin and his squaw without imaginin' a massacre."

"So, what do you think?"

"When it comes to that kind of money, normal guessing won't get you very far. And Indians ain't like white folks. They work by their own code, not ours. But from what I know of McGillivray, he's rich, he's straight, and he aims to keep the peace."

Lampin came out of the hutch bearing three bowls on a plank of wood. The smell reached them before the food, onions, garlic, and wine.

"This is what fishermen eat at home," he said, laying the three steaming bowls before them. "We call it *caudière.*"

Harry dipped his spoon into the pinkish creamy stew. Lumps of fish came up to the surface. As he raised it to his lips he blew on it as a precaution, smelling the herbs and the tangy odour of cooked wine. It was delicious, filling and nourishing.

"If we can have a time to fish each day, and the milk stays fresh, the pot will stay as full as the whiskey butt."

Tucker had already sampled his, and when he spoke, a thin stream of the sauce trickled down his chin. "Not if I have my way."

The following days, with better weather prevailing, saw little repetition of the events of the first 24 hours. The levee, which ran all the way to the Pointe Coupée on both banks, acted as a sort of elevated roadway connecting the various riverside settlements. Every time Tucker got close enough to the side he was engaged in a shouted conversation with anyone who was passing, with many a mutual acquaintance mentioned. News of a local nature was readily forthcoming, a list of births, deaths, and marriages appended. He in turn imparted news from New Orleans and the wider world, plus the reassurance, often required, that the Dons were sticking to the terms of the recently signed treaty with the United States.

"Why if they live in Spanish territory, are they so concerned about that?" asked Harry, having heard the question put for the tenth time.

"The alternatives," Tucker replied, "like the possibility of a war. This area is just starting to recover from a failure of the indigo crop. Most have switched to cotton or sugar, which finds its market elsewhere. Trouble on the river spells ruin. And the further north we go, the more anxious people get."

Tucker hove to south of Bayou Manchac well before dusk, and bade the Frenchmen replenish their pot, then once they'd eaten return to their oars. "Tell them to go easy, Ludlow," he said. "The Dons have guard boats out on the river, though they tend to look upriver rather than south to catch folks."

"If you think we won't make it, pull for shore."

"Why?"

"I have an invitation to go hunting with de Coburrabias."

"You don't say," replied Tucker with a grin.

"I'd rather not use it."

"For two hundred thousand Spanish dollars I can see why."

"The sky looks set to come to our aid," said Harry.

Tucker looked at the increasing cloud cover, which would go a long way to covering the moon. "If it thickens we'll be safe, just as long as we don't bump into anything."

CHAPTER THIRTY-ONE

TUCKER handed the sweep over to Harry then went forward to set the rowing pace. Fine adjustments were needed to find the right combination that produced progress with the minimum of noise.

"We could muffle the oars," called Harry.

Tucker shook his head. Pender, right beside him, understood why. "Reckon he'd find that just too hard to explain away, your honour, that is, if we do get brought to. Then even your invite wouldn't make them happy."

The gloom, once the sun had gone, increased rapidly, and within half an hour complete darkness fell. Lights had begun to appear, pinpoints from candles in dwellings whose upper storeys looked over the levee. Tucker climbed onto the top of the deckhouse, which allowed him a better view. If it grew too dark those lights, and the silhouette of the embankment, were going to have to keep the boat on course. In the glim Harry saw his hand go up, and following it picked out the glow of a greater concentration of light on the horizon, which increased, turning to an orange arc, as they approached the Manchac Post. Coming round a long sweeping bend that had the river running west to east allowed them to see the actual source as, right ahead, the mass of torches lining the battlements came into view. Tucker, climbing down, steered them towards the northern shore.

"We'd be better off on a clear night," he said.

Harry could see he was right. The cloud cover had increased, but it had also lowered, so that the lights from the elevated fortress bounced off it, extending the effect over the width of the river.

"Trouble is, the fort is right on a sharp turn. They have a

picket on the opposite shore, with sharp eyes looking for fools trying to slip by. It's a favourite trick of the smugglers to get down-river first, then come up all innocent before slipping into the Bayou Manchac."

"What do you suggest?"

Tucker rubbed his chin and cheek, fingering the last of the swellings from his fight with Harry.

"The only question is this. Do they have enough light to see that this is my boat, and that by its draught, it's empty?"

"It would be very inconvenient if we were stopped, Tucker. The crew would require some explanation, but they might pass. But Pender and I would have to land, then fashion some method of escaping from de Coburrabias. That would take up valuable time. But I can't judge the risk, only you can do that."

"Then it's all hands to the oars, the middle of the channel at full pitch, and if they dip their flag to haul us to, we ignore them." Tucker laughed. "One Mississippi galley looks much like another, and lifting a finger to the Dons is mighty tempting."

"I agree."

"How are you at singing, Ludlow?"

"Not good," replied Pender.

"A ladle of whiskey all round, Pender," said Tucker. "Two, even. Every man to sing as loud as he can without giving up on the rowing. They think we Kentucky men are heathens who do lit-tle else but get blind drunk. Let's prove to them that they are right."

The flag at the mainstaff, which stood at the centre of the pal-isaded fort, jerked up and down several times before they fired a cannon. Being a signal gun it was not designed to do any dam-age, but it was soon followed by something more substantial, and a fountain of water sprang from the muddy waters of the orange-tinged river. Harry was belting out a tuneless rendition of "Britons Strike Home" while the Frenchmen left on deck waved their poles and sang, surprisingly, the Revolutionary *"Cà Ira."* Tucker was staggering about on top of the deckhouse, looking at any moment as if he might tip into the water, as he conducted the singing going on beneath him.

The single gun was followed by a salvo which pitched a hundred yards ahead, right in their projected path, a warning that should they enter that stretch of water they'd have to row through a second deadly discharge. The Dons would have every nuance of range worked out to the foot, firing from a fixed platform into an area in which they could practise at will.

"You there," cried Tucker to the men with poles, who included Lampin and Couvruer, "get to the side and show them your arse!"

Translating that took several seconds, and occasioned a few shaking heads. But Tucker repeated his instructions more forcefully, physically demonstrating his intentions. The men laid aside their poles and lined the side of the boat. At a single command from Tucker they loosened their breeches. He did likewise, spinning round and whooping out an unintelligible insult. As he dropped them he bent right over, an action which was copied by the Frenchmen. Harry wondered what the officer on shore, who would have a glass on the galley for certain, would make of this row of pale white moons.

"Better than carronades, I reckon," said Pender, heaving with laughter. Harry, as affected by whiskey as his servant, nevertheless waited to agree. He didn't even smile till they'd passed through the patch of water still disturbed by that first salvo. By the time they were clear of further danger he'd joined in wholeheartedly with the humour that now pervaded the entire deck.

"If only Drake had known that's all it took to frighten a Spaniard! By God, we'd own Madrid."

The following day saw them meandering through the bends of a relatively untroubled river. Flat country had been replaced by deep forest. At one bend they came across an area of woodland that looked like some angry giant had attacked it. Trees were uprooted whole, many lying along the shoreline. The tornado had ripped a path a mile wide through the forest, flattening everything in its path, including the levee, as it followed its twisted course. Teams of Negroes were working to repair the dykes, singing low mournful dirges as they toiled indifferently at a task that would have to be completed before the autumn rains. Coming round the arc of the river bend brought them to the place where the twister had crossed the wide watercourse, to continue on its destructive path. It was here that Tucker showed his skill with the rifle.

"Any feller can shoot a squirrel, Ludlow. The trick is to scare the livin' daylights out of it while leaving it whole." He pointed at a set of trees full of the creatures, and took careful aim with his weapon. "Come on now, Practical, you just bark at that there critter so he jumps ten feet."

The gun went off with a loud roar, a streak of flame gushing out of the barrel. Harry had a glass on the squirrel. He saw it do just as Tucker demanded. At a hundred yards on a less than perfect platform, the riverboatman removed a strip of bark from right under the animal's belly. By any standards, it was a tremendous shot.

"Can you do it again?"

"Later. We're getting close to a couple of settlements."

Baton Rouge, a small town of about a hundred houses, was, like the Manchac Post, passed during the night, this time in silence. The following day saw them approaching the middle channel of the twin islands that lay below Pointe Coupée. Tucker explained that the outer channels were safer, indeed sluggish in comparison to the one he'd chosen, but the settlements there were large enough to contain either Spaniards, or, working for them, officials of French or American origin, any one of whom had the right to call them to question. With no idea of what news had preceded them upriver, it was safer to assume the worst, even if it did entail greater effort.

The channel was like a tidal race, with the river forced to increase its velocity by the narrowness of the bottleneck. Water moving at that pace precluded sandbanks, but there were rocks, with boiling foam around their base to warn of their presence. They, of course, were easy to avoid. But it took all of Tucker's river knowledge to spot the flow of brown water over submerged obstacles, and all of the strength of everyone aboard, above and below decks, to avoid them. Those put to poling had a busy time, being commanded to work one side of the boat then the other. When they finally cleared the narrows, the oarsmen collapsed where they sat. Everyone on deck, including Harry, Pender, and Tucker, fell back against the low bulwarks, stretching to ease their aching limbs.

In continuing fine weather their progress was good. Occasional whirlpools or excessive drifting debris would slow them. But compared to men on horses, needing constant stops for remounts, rest, and feeding, they were racing along. They opened the mouth of the Red River after fifteen days, a watercourse that tinged the brown Mississippi with its rouge sediment. Harry, by this time, was on the lookout for some sign of a message from McGillivray. The first major Indian trading stop, around the settlement called Concordia, lay between Natchez and the Red River. De Guerin had, according to the Creek chieftain, crossed in that direction three weeks before. It was a natural place for the Walloons to secure fresh horses and since they must by now be beyond Fort Rosalie, the last Spanish outpost, there was every chance that they'd cross the river into the Mississippi Territory. The guess that they would head away from the river was just that. If they didn't, he could get ahead of them easily in Tucker's galley. But at some stage, pursuing people tied to the land, he knew that he too would need to engage in mounted pursuit.

It was three more days before contact was made, time which dragged heavily. It was easy for Harry, in moments of introspection, to see what he was doing as a waste of time, a mere indulgence by a man who found it hard to sit still. The Frenchmen wavered from optimism to pessimism on an hourly basis, their mood swings easily calibrated by the way they looked at, or spoke, to Harry, at its worst manifesting itself as a low, continuous grumble of indistinct complaints. Pender was his usual rocklike self at such times, even though he didn't trust McGillivray at all. Tucker, who rose day by day in Harry's estimation, was inclined to agree.

"You've got to see things from where he's lookin', Ludlow," he said, waving his arms towards the east bank of the river. "That was all tribal land twenty years ago. Still is, I suppose, except it's awash with Americans and filling up by the year as more an' more settlers arrive. The thing he cares about most is hanging on to what the Creek nation have left."

Being from Kentucky himself, Tucker knew everything there was to tell about frontier politics, as well as the reasons behind such things as the Whiskey Rebellion and the continuing threats of secession.

"It all comes down to money, or the lack of it, since there's practically none west of the Cumberland Gap. In a land where rye is the staple it's also the currency. It has to be transported west by horse, and sells for around forty cents a bushel. Now that makes profits hard to come by. The same animal that can carry four bushels of rye can carry two eight-gallon kegs of whiskey, and that will sell at fifty cents a gallon. Trouble is, the Federals wanted to slap an excise on it, which to frontiersmen, quite a few of whom supported King George twenty years ago, is not to be borne. When the revenue men arrived, they were roughly handled, and I know of one who was tarred and feathered."

"So what's the solution?" asked Harry. "All governments need money."

"More prosperity. That's why Pinckney's Treaty was so vital. If the frontier prospers they won't mind paying a little. This boat of mine carries bushels by the hundred, and before de Carondelet stripped out Louisiana, I could get paid in hard money. Twenty-five years' navigation and rights of deposit aren't enough, but it'll do to start. It might provide enough time to wean the folks upriver onto another means of earning a crust. Anyway, as long as they can use the river to get their produce out, and sell it at a proper rate, then it's a fair bet they'll stay loyal."

"And McGillivray?"

"Will be happy to see the Spanish stay in control of the lower Mississippi. That means no more settlers to him."

"And this gold and silver?"

"That's larded with all manner of possibilities, some of which won't even have occurred to either you or Pender."

Pender hesitated for just a second. But his curiosity got the better of him. "For instance?"

Tucker seemed distracted, looking over Pender's shoulder as though what he was saying mattered little.

"You take that bullion, which those Walloons won't give up without a fight. McGillivray takes it back off you and returns it to de Carondelet with you and your Frenchmen in chains. Suddenly the Governor, who doesn't really trust him, changes his tune, and all is sunny and sweet in the Creek nation."

"Is that all?"

"Nope. You say you reckon it's going to New York as a bribe. What if the Creeks decide to take it off you to use it for the same purpose?"

"McGillivray claims to be a rich man. Surely he could do that anyway?"

"Certainly he's rich, Ludlow, but not in specie. The Spaniards pay him in kind and any money he does get goes to buying trade goods from American agents. He has land and trading concessions that are worth a fortune. But unless he realizes those assets he has little actual money to distribute. So that precious metal could come in very handy. It would buy them just as much influence as it would de Carondelet."

"It would harm his case while anyone who knew of its provenance was still alive. That would mean not only disposing of us, but of the Spaniards as well."

"Kinda chills the blood," said Tucker.

He pulled himself to his feet and pointed to the canoe heading out from the bank of the river, its prow aimed right amidships. Harry and Pender stood up as well. Those Frenchmen not row-

ing lined the side, watching silently as the Indians manoeuvred the
flimsy craft with practised ease. It was alongside within minutes.
Harry leant over the side, meaning to speak. But he was obliged
to take an oilskin pouch from one outstretched hand, with the
canoe turning away as soon as it was delivered.

"Does that have a superscription on it?" asked Tucker.

Harry opened the pouch, took out a letter, and held it out, so
that the Kentuckian could see his name written in large capital
letters on the cover.

"How in hell's name did they know this was the right boat?"

"I don't think we've been out of their sight since we set out,"
said Pender, his eyes still fixed on the retreating canoe.

Harry broke the seal and opened the letter.

"De Guerin crossed the Mississippi north of Natchez two days
ago. McGillivray thinks he's headed for something called the
Natchez Trace."

"Used to be the old Chickasaw–Choctaw Trail," said Tucker,
responding to Harry's look. "Runs from Natchez all the way
through Colbert's Ferry to the Cumberland River."

"It's a road?"

"Of sorts," Tucker replied.

Harry looked at the letter again, reading silently for several
seconds. "McGillivray advises that we head for a place called the
Bayou Pierre. We will be met by another messenger, who will confirm de Guerin's route and provide us with horses."

"Horses?" said Tucker. "He's sure going to a lot of trouble.
You say you did him a favour, Ludlow. Just how big was it?"

Harry waved the letter. "I can't believe it was big enough to
justify all this."

"Do we proceed?"

"Yes. But we must put our minds to finding a way to ensure
that should we find that money, McGillivray can't find us."

Tucker walked back to take hold of the sweep. Grinning, he
slapped Pender on the shoulder as he did so.

"He likes a tall order, your Captain."

• • •

Now was the time for maximum speed. The river, given the continuing good weather, had slowed somewhat in the time that they'd
been on it, which lessened the effect of its obstacles, and past the
Loftus Heights and Fort Rosalie they were clear of Spanish territory, so no precautions were required to avoid officialdom. The
following days settled into the steady routine that was reminiscent
of life aboard *Bucephalas* at sea: the orderly changing of watches,
of meals prepared and consumed, of sleep taken and men brought
awake to their duty, all proceeding at the proper pace. The crew
had been apprised of what McGillivray had said, which raised
their confidence and earned Harry the odd unbidden smile.
Natchez was passed within two days, as they continued to reel off
the miles.

The contrast, as Tucker steered the galley into the Bayou
Pierre, was marked. From an open river they'd now entered a
dank, stagnant piece of water surrounded by tall willows and
poplars. There were few sounds; the croaking of numerous frogs,
with the occasional bull-like roar of an alligator echoing eerily off
the wall of moss-strewn forest. The air was still and oppressive,
full of flying insects, with mosquitoes attacking everyone on deck
in droves. He advanced about a quarter of a mile. A hail from the
shore caused him to head for a convenient willow which grew
right in the middle of the river, to which he attached a cable. Immediately a canoe set out from the shore, in the bows a man in
European clothes.

"Judge Peter Bryan Bruin," he called, coming aboard. Harry
thought he detected a trace of an Irish accent. The face was florid
and square, the smile wide. "I have a plantation just to the south
of here. Alexander McGillivray asked me to give this to you."

"Is the title Judge an honorific?" asked Tucker.

"No, sir, it is not. I am employed to administer the law in this
part of the Mississippi Territory."

He passed Harry another unsigned letter, written in the same

disordered capital letters, then indicated to Tucker that he should
proceed further into the swamp. The atmosphere became, if anything, even more oppressive the further they travelled. Bruin
chatted aimiably about the area and its commercial prospects. If
the deep suspicion harboured by the three men beside him was
evident, he ignored it.

"Might sell up and move to Natchez," he concluded, as the
canopy of trees thinned overhead. "Being a judge don't leave me
much time to run the land."

They emerged into a clearing, which had a levee of medium
height, and contained a few ramshackle houses, a tavern, and a
cotton gin.

"You're to disembark. The horses are corralled on a piece of
high ground about a quarter of a mile from here. They will take
you to wherever it is you're planning to go."

Bruin looked from one to the other, as if hoping that they
would explain what was clearly a mystery. But no one obliged so
he bade them good day and, now that the gangplank was out,
went ashore.

"Does that letter say anything about your Walloons?" asked
Tucker, as soon as he was out of earshot.

"Still on the Natchez Trace." He passed the letter to the American. "McGillivray has drawn us a map."

"If he wrote this, Ludlow, and gave it to that judge, then he's
not in New Orleans."

"He can't be," added Pender.

"So where is he?" demanded Tucker.

"Ahead of us, I should think, shadowing our quarry."

Tucker looked at the black waters of the bayou. "This whole
thing stinks so much it makes the swamp smell like perfume."

Harry twitched his nose, which was full of the corrupt odours
of rotting vegetation. "The scent of betrayal, I think."

"He's even got the local law on his side. But you still won't
turn back."

Harry shook his head slowly. "McGillivray is counting on us outnumbering the Spaniards. But he can't believe for a moment that we mean to murder them."

"If he was plannin' to do that hisself," observed Pender, "he wouldn't need us here."

"That's right," Harry replied, before turning back to speak to Tucker. "So your theory must be correct. He daren't let anyone see him, especially the Spaniards, in case they, as survivors, spread word of his involvement. If any of what you suppose is true regarding his handing us over to the Spanish, he has to take us on his own land, otherwise de Carondelet will smell a rat."

"And have you thought on long enough to foil his plan?"

Harry indicated the knot of Frenchmen, who were watching the trio closely. "It was really never possible for these men, having recovered their money, to return to New Orleans. So what is there for them to the north?"

"Millions of square miles of America," Tucker replied.

"And a lot of settlements that a generation ago were French."

Tucker was quick to see what Harry was driving at. "All of them on the river."

"That's right."

"And you have a ship stuck in New Orleans."

"Yes."

"You think de Carondelet will let you go?"

Harry shrugged. "I will plead that my liberty is more important than money and take his draft on the Spanish treasury, so his reasons for detaining me will disappear."

"Good luck, Ludlow," Tucker said with heavy irony. "Don't bother to tell me what you intend to try. But I will say that whatever it is doesn't have a prayer if de Guerin gets back there before you."

"It would be helpful if he too were to continue north. Even a few days' head start would make all the difference."

"So, let me get this aright. You want me to take these men further up the Mississippi . . ."

Harry nodded. "As long as they are out of Spanish territory they should be safe."

"And at the same time you want me to make sure that the Walloons you intend to rob are kept from telling what's happened."

"I don't have the means to pay you, Tucker. But if we are successful, our crew most certainly do. And I think, under such circumstances, you could name your price."

Tucker thought for a moment, his head dropped to his chest. When he looked up his eyes were twinkling with amusement. He picked up his long rifle, encased in its buckskin sheath. "Seems to me, if some of that bullion is coming my way, that Practical John and I ought to be there to see it returned to its rightful owners."

Harry held out his hand. "I'll be glad to have you both along."

Leaving the boat, even though they'd been forewarned, rattled the French. It was as though the hull provided a security that they were loath to surrender, and the surrounding countryside, dense and unfamiliar, reinforced it. Brissot started the argument, but it was rapidly taken up by some of the others; and though it was never actually stated, it was certainly implied that if Harry wanted to get rid of them then this was a perfect place to do so. He took no part in the discussion, leaving Lampin and Couvruer to sort it out, aware that if they'd come this far, they wouldn't turn back, and prepared to accept that they were only moaning to let him know he wasn't, yet, entirely trusted.

CHAPTER THIRTY-TWO

FINDING the Natchez Trace was a job for a man who could read a compass. The dense forest provided ample trails, all wide enough to accommodate the party of horsemen in single file, but the lack of sunlight added to their winding nature made certainty of direction difficult. Tucker, a riverboatman, having no need for such a device, had never used one. Harry'd lived with the constant presence of that instrument since he was a shaver, and using it to steer by was second nature. Initially they'd had to manoeuvre their way through low swamp or marshland. But within a couple of miles the ground began to rise, to become firm and dry. Near the river, and the rich alluvial soil provided by the Mississippi, lay substantial plantations, but the uplands, being less fertile, were sparsely populated. The houses, log cabins in the main, seemed rough and ready compared to the dwellings they'd left behind. Harry did his best to avoid coming in sight of these homesteads. A party of forty horsemen would not go unremarked, and their sudden appearance would cause a fear that could send ripples of alarm around the countryside.

McGillivray's instructions took them slightly south, to join the Trace at the nearest point to the Bayou Pierre. Though not a road in the proper sense, it was wide enough, and straight enough, to allow them to increase speed, and being a major route to the northern states it was dotted with the occasional post-house. Mean-looking affairs in the main, with avaricious owners, they all had two vital functions: the corrals contained remounts, while the ostlers who ran them knew of everyone who'd passed ahead of them. De Guerin, no doubt feeling safe in the Mississippi Territory, made little attempt to conceal himself en route. Not that he gave anything away—to avoid excessive curiosity he stopped only to exchange horses which were weak or lame—but enough had been left behind to satisfy Harry that, with frequent remounts of his own, he was still overhauling the Spaniards.

Not all the Frenchmen were happy on horseback, which slowed them somewhat, but none was as bad as Pender, who disliked the beasts with a passion born of total discomfort mixed with genuine fear. Harry had never seen him faced down by any man, nor step backwards when presented with the prospect of action. Indeed he was always to the fore, generally the first to board, and to be found at the heart of any mêlée which ensued. Dogs and children responded to him with affection, but to see him choosing a horse was to observe clear evidence that no human being lacked an Achilles' heel. Great care was taken to find the quietest animal, but lacking true knowledge of the equine temperament, he had an uncanny knack of picking out the one beast that was docile only as long as no one was on its back, and that was compounded by a lack of any skill once mounted.

"Give me a leakin' barky any day," he moaned. He'd slipped sideways as they were fording a river, sliding out of the saddle into the deep mud created by those who'd preceded him, and this on an animal that he'd only been up on for half an hour.

"Let me choose the next beast, for God's sake," Harry snapped.

"Never in life, Capt'n. I trusted Thankful Tucker to sort out this bastard for me, an' I ain't gone a single mile without falling off."

A sudden burst of translation came from the bank above their heads, where the rest of the party were lined up waiting. That was followed by laughter. Looking up, Harry could see Tucker beaming at Pender, a man made happy by a jest that had paid the proper dividend.

"Damn you, Tucker, we've no time for this," Harry shouted.

But his voice lacked any passion, indeed he'd only made the

remark to avoid openly joining in the laughter. They were close to de Guerin, very close, a fact that had emerged at the last post-house. The Spaniard had been forced to exchange two lame horses, with the ostler adding that most of the rest of the mounts, barring the pack-animals, looked under-nourished and blown. If he was pushing hard, that meant he was either late for a rendezvous or so close to it that the state of his horses mattered little. Harry dismounted to help Pender back aboard, checked his girth, and adjusted his stirrups, all this accompanied by an injunction to use his damned knees.

"Next stop I'm going to take a mule," Pender growled.

"Ludlow," said Tucker. Harry spun round. Whatever humour had been in the American's voice was gone now. "I think you might have a messenger coming."

Harry grabbed his horse's reins, as well as Pender's, pulling both up the steep embankment. He saw the lone figure riding towards them through the avenue created by the encroaching forest. He was sure, just as Tucker had been, that he was an Indian. The long feathers that protruded above his head were one indication, but more telling was the way the man rode his horse, as though he and the beast were one, which could only mean that he was bareback. As he came closer, and the canopy of trees thinned to allow some sunlight, Harry could see his copper-coloured skin, and by the time he reined in his horse, several yards away, Harry was aware of the slightly slanting black eyes, set in an unsmiling face. Reaching into his coat, the Indian produced yet another letter. But he was determined that the recipient should come and get it, clearly not even prepared to dismount to effect its delivery.

"He's camped near a place called Doak's Stand, which is less than a mile ahead." Tucker shook his head, indicating that the name meant nothing to him. Harry waved the letter. "This says he's settling in, including digging a latrine."

Tucker dismounted. "So he's not stopped for the night."

Harry showed the American the second page, which had a

rough drawing of what he assumed to be the area ahead. It showed the Natchez Trace clearly, running through a valley. There was a small copse off to the western side, behind which de Guerin had set his camp, and judging by the indicated elevation, that gave him a view of the road with a modicum of concealment to protect him from anyone not actually seeking him out. "Which explains the horses," he said.

"But why change the lame animals?"

"Perhaps he wants to ensure a swift retreat."

"According to that ostler he's got plenty of pack-horses."

Harry gave the American a wolfish smile. "They won't be going back with him, obviously."

"You to come with me," said the Indian, pointing to Harry. Still mounted, he looked even more unfriendly than he had when he'd arrived. "You only."

"Pender," Harry said quietly. "Follow on foot."

His servant slid gratefully to the ground, then bent over to rub his aching thighs. "Aye, aye, Capt'n."

"Tucker," Harry continued, his eyes still on the stony-faced Indian, "any danger and I will fire off one of my pistols. If you hear it, put the river between you and us then prepare to defend the crossing."

"Will do," he replied. "If all else fails how do I get the Frenchies to run?"

"Just shout *sauve qui peut*."

The Indian spun his mount and trotted off up the trail. Harry mounted and went after him. Pender, moving off to the side to get some cover, followed easily. The Indian left the trail after about a quarter of a mile, heading into the forest. Soon they were working their way uphill through the trees, following a well-worn animal path covered in pine needles that deadened the sound of their hoofs. Twenty minutes brought them near to the edge of the treeline, where his guide finally dismounted. Harry did likewise. To say that the Indian smiled when he looked back down the trail would be an exaggeration. But his lips did part, which lessened the near permanent scowl. His eyes swung to Harry and the head moved in what was clearly a gesture of disbelief. They stood for several minutes before Harry heard Pender. To his sailor's mind, he was making little noise. To this Indian, who'd picked up the sound of his progress a lot sooner, Pender must sound like a charging bull.

"Stop him," the man commanded.

"No," Harry replied, with a look just as hard as the one he was getting.

They stood for a moment, staring at each other. Then the Indian shrugged and turned round. Crouching down, he edged forward to a point where a round of deep undergrowth fringed the copse. Harry waited till Pender was in sight, held up a restraining hand, then slid forward himself. De Guerin's camp lay below them behind the line of trees, shown on the map, that overlooked the road. His men were employed putting up tents or gathering wood. The horses, well spaced out in their lines, grazed contentedly, cropping the thick grass that covered the slope. The Indian indicated a newly dug trench that lay off to one side of the horse-lines, right by the opposite line of trees. This was part of the same wood which, arching towards the top of the slope, continued down the other side of the pasture.

The Indian pointed to the trees behind the latrine, made the two-fingered sign for "walking man," this followed by a grip on his nose. That was followed by a hand round his ear and four fingers to denote a horse. Then he covered his eyes and swept his hand through an imaginary sky. He was proposing that their line of approach should be from the trees opposite, coming in behind the latrines so that the horses, even if the wind blew towards the camp, wouldn't pick up their scent. Likewise, the noise of the animals would deaden any hint of their movements, and beasts accustomed to humans would not react overmuch once they were in amongst them. All of which should take place in darkness, when the moon had crossed the sky. In other words, just before dawn.

Harry repeated every gesture till his guide was sure he understood. Then the Indian stood up, went back to his horse, mounted, and without so much as a backward glance, rode away.

"Do you have a knife, Pender?" Harry asked, his eyes on the retreating back.

"Aye, aye, Capt'n."

"Good. Mark the trees as we make our way back to the road. We've got to come back this way. And when we get to the river bank, fill up a saddlebag with some of that mud."

Moving over thirty armed men through the woods was a great deal more difficult than his own previous journey. Unused to humans, the forest creatures had shown no evidence of fear, but such a large group couldn't maintain silence—they'd scare off even a bear. Harry changed the direction of their approach to avoid alerting the Spaniards, who couldn't fail to see the startled wildlife, mainly birds, if they came too close to the edge of the forest. He led them in a wide circle, till they were facing downhill, then walked them into their final positions in twos, having first streaked their faces with mud. Pender and Tucker were first, with an injunction to keep an eye on their quarry.

"You can use the telescope from here, because the sun is now behind us. It will be near dark by the time I've got everyone in place. Locate the sentries and time the changes."

"I reckon de Guerin must be in that tent," said Tucker, pointing to the largest piece of canvas, a square structure that sat in the centre of the neat row that lay behind the trees.

"Along with the bags they took off the pack-horses," added Pender.

"They've stacked their weapons, regulation fashion," Tucker added. "I'm surprised he hasn't taken more precautions."

"He doesn't know we're here, does he? And if he has made his rendezvous, the people he's expecting are coming in from the north."

"I'm afire to find out who it is."

Harry shook his head at Tucker. "With luck, we'll never know. We'll be gone before they arrive."

Harry paid them several visits during the remaining two hours, to gather information with which he could direct the rest of the men. They were correct about de Guerin's occupancy of the large tent, and he'd set his guards in the trees to watch the road. Really the Spaniard had too few men to mount a complete picket, so what he'd done wasn't as stupid as it first appeared. It was dark by the time Harry finally joined, with only a faint glim of the low moon breaking through the canopy of trees. He too had muddied his face. He'd also removed his coat and smeared his shirt-front, so that from the rear it showed white. Below them the large fires created great pools of light around the tents, the white of which reflected it over an even wider area. The Spaniard's men sat round talking quietly, occasionally pushing food on a bayonet into the flames.

"We've got a good six hours," Harry whispered, "before we move in. I've told everyone to get some rest, one at a time. You two do the same."

"And you?" Tucker asked.

"Don't worry, Tucker. I'll sleep as well. But you go first."

He woke the American, and with Pender still slumbering, he took a chance to deflect him from joining in the coming action.

"I intend that no one should be harmed, which means that come daylight they are going to be able to see our faces."

"And if they spot me in New Orleans one day?" The sentence didn't need to be completed.

"It would be best if you stayed here."

Tucker rubbed his rifle. "Then Practical John and I'd miss all the fun, Ludlow. You say that you intend no bloodshed, but those men down there are soldiers, some of the best the Spanish army has got. Even if you surprise them there's going to be a fight."

"Which you want to be part of?"

"Come to that, you have to go back to New Orleans. And though I'm willin' to take on your Frenchies, I don't see that having a load of Walloon Guards on board is goin' to keep my face a mystery."

Harry nodded agreement, remaining silent while he sought a solution.

"We will have horses, they won't. Nor will they be left with the means to buy any. All they'll have is food and their boots. We'll take them far enough south to make sure that they don't meet whoever is coming from the north, then abandon them."

"So let me take part. I promise I'll be out of sight by sun-up."

"Your turn to watch," Harry replied, moving back into the undergrowth. "Don't use the telescope. The light from the fires will reflect in it."

"Aye, aye, Capt'n," said Tucker, turning away.

He didn't see, or hear, Harry shake Pender awake. His servant's eyes opened immediately. They exchanged a glance, Pender nodded and raised himself on one elbow. Liking Thankful Tucker and trusting him, in the presence of so much money, were two different things. Harry knew very well what gold did to men. That wasn't evidence of piety. It had a similar effect on him.

Men moved silently out of the trees as soon as they saw the white of Harry's shirt. With the moon now low in the sky behind him it was like a beacon. Every one of them had been assigned a tent, with instructions to use no knives unless threatened, and to employ their firearms as clubs. Harry was carrying a twisted lump of wood, his pistols stuck into his belt. Only Tucker and those assigned to subdue the sentries had muskets. The distance between the latrine and the horse-lines, around a hundred yards, was critical. Harry had told them to avoid too much stealth, but it was impossible not to crouch down and attempt to move forward silently. He found it so himself, and the combined approach of thirty men in the same mode spooked some of the more nervous beasts. The remaining glow from the fires was insufficient for humans, but a horse has good night vision, as well as acute hearing. He dashed forward, followed by those closest to him, and grabbed at the halter of one of the more nervous beasts. Those who knew horses pulled their heads down, then covered their nostrils with their hands. Pender, not by any means the sole offender, did the opposite, which allowed the animal he was trying to quieten to rear instead. It whinnied loudly, something which was bound to bring the sentries to investigate, suspecting the presence of something like a puma or a bear. But they wouldn't have to get too close to realize that their mounts were spooked by humans.

The cry that came from his throat had every horse in the lines dragging at their halters. As he rushed through, heading for de Guerin's tent, he saw one animal kick out wildly. Its hoof caught one of the Frenchmen right in the back, just below the neck. It sent him flying. The man rolled several times then lay still. He was the only silent man in the clearing. Every attacker was yelling as they charged forward, their cries echoed by the panicky screams of men suddenly awakened and unready for combat. A flash of orange light shot out from the downhill trees and Harry felt the air move as the ball whipped past his head. A grunt from behind indicated that the man who'd fired had found flesh, but there was no time to stop and investigate.

They were good soldiers. Not one forgot his duty by trying to mount an individual defence. Each trooper, once he'd retrieved his weapon, fell back towards the main tent in an attempt to form a line. The man Harry assumed to be de Guerin was out, sword in hand, shouting clear orders, his demeanour the very antithesis of panic. The two sentries had moved sideways to give themselves a clear chance to fire, and two more flashes lit the night sky. Half a minute's grace would have allowed the Spaniards to succeed, and the attackers might have run headlong into a frisson of bayonets. But with the slope in their favour, Harry and his men didn't grant them the time. With Pender on one side and Tucker on the other, he crashed into the still disorganized Walloons, clubbing everyone who stood in his path. Muskets were fired from behind

him to subdue the sentries, and these, passing close to the packed
ranks, increased their disorder.

Pushing two men aside, Harry nearly ran full tilt onto the officer's sword, now held out before him in regulation fashion. He
swung the club wildly and pushed the blade aside. Carried foward
by his own momentum he crashed into de Guerin, which took
both men through the flap and into the tent. A small table, bearing an inkwell and some papers, crumpled like matchwood as they
fell on top of it. Aware that the Spaniard still had his sword, Harry
threw himself to his left, so that he could pin the hand that held
it. De Guerin, with his other hand free, used it to good effect,
fetching Harry a telling blow on the ear, which sent a flash of
bright light through the back of his eyes.

The sword was the problem. If he could get that free Harry
was in real trouble. He knew he'd been lucky to nullify it first
time. But this man beneath him, an officer in King Carlos's best
regiment, had to be a competent swordsman. No club, however
well employed, could keep such a weapon in such hands at bay.
So he pressed down hard, letting the Spaniard hit him repeatedly,
as he sought to free one of his pistols from his belt. That spun
him slightly, and made him aware of the silhouette framed in the
doorway.

"For God's sake, Tucker," he yelled, "do something!"

The American shot forward, but not by his own volition. Pender came through the flap behind him, his head swinging to take
in what was going on. His pistol came down on de Guerin's swinging arm just as the man tried to clout Harry for the fourth time.
The butt caught him below the elbow, making him recoil, and that
gave Harry enough time to ease his own position. With one hand
holding the sword arm, his fist shot out, catching his opponent
right under his exposed chin. There was a moment's stiffness before
the Spaniard went limp. Harry got up onto his hands and knees.

"Why didn't you interfere?" he demanded.

"Looked like fair goes to me, Ludlow," Tucker replied. "Don't
do to interfere unless someone might die."

The vibration, faint at first, came through Harry's hands. Tucker, whose hearing was probably more acute than any of the others present, suddenly hissed: *"Horses."*

"I can feel them," Harry replied. He jumped to his feet and shot outside. The soldiers were on the ground, those unwounded sitting with their hands behind their back. Others, obviously wounded, lay where they'd fallen.

"Tucker, get these men tied up, even the wounded ones."

"Hell's teeth and damnation," said Tucker, looking north.

Harry grabbed a musket of one of the men standing over the prisoners and headed for the line of trees, yelling for those still armed to follow him. Tucker's knife was out of its sheath before he'd finished his expletive, slashing at the ropes which held the tents upright. Those Harry'd left behind, because they were wounded, bemused, or slow-witted, caught the lengths of hemp as he tossed them. Tucker grabbed the nearest prisoner and began to lash his hands. Seeing what was required, the rest followed suit.

The first hint of daylight tinged the sky just above the hill opposite as Harry and his party reached the other side of the narrow copse. The approaching horses could be heard plainly now, their hoofbeats a steady tattoo that grew louder as they approached. Harry fired the musket, knowing that the riders were out of range, but the act had the desired effect of slowing them down. The noise of hoofs died away completely, which gave him time not only to reload but also to organize a ragged defence which corresponded to the line of the trees.

"Pender! Back to that tent and see if the bullion's in there."

"And if it is?"

"Don't let it out of your sight. Send Tucker himself to tell me."

The note of a singing bird, raised to greet the coming dawn, surprised Harry, but it convinced him that his musket shot had succeeded beyond his expectations. Whoever those horsemen were they'd remained still, which had allowed at least one creature to assume that no danger existed. The floor of the valley was still in darkness, the contrast of the increasing light in the sky making it impossible to see anything clearly. Several minutes went by before Tucker arrived, rifle in hand. He slapped Harry on the shoulder, his face wreathed in smiles.

"A fortune, Ludlow, all in nice thin gold and silver bars."

Harry nodded to indicate he should look down the valley.

"McGillivray?"

"The horses are shod," Harry replied. "You can tell by the noise they make. I profess a limited knowledge of the noble savage, but I do know they don't use farriers."

"He's a half-breed, Ludlow. And there's no guarantee that his party have to be Indians."

"My guess is we are about to come face to face with whoever de Guerin came to meet."

They knelt in silence as the light increased, finally touching the valley floor. The sky above the opposite hill was now blue, growing brighter and changing to gold as the sun rose. Birds sang in numbers now, calling to each other from their branches, before swooping from the trees in search of food. The glistening rim appeared growing quickly into full daylight.

"Look!" said Tucker.

"I see them," Harry replied.

The group of horsemen emerged from the point at which the trees re-enclosed the road. They were armed, their muskets held towards the sky in an unthreatening way. Facing east, Harry had to use his hand to shade his eyes. The sun flashed off the odd brass button as they jigged along. Apart from the man in the forefront, all seemed to wear similar dress; dark blue coats with red facings. The party stayed on the road, moving at walking pace, until they were abreast of the trees. Then, at a shouted command, they swung round in an orderly line. Only the odd man out, in a green frock coat, rode forward. His hands were both on the reins, and he appeared to carry no weapon.

"Are they soldiers?" asked Tucker, indicating the party on the road.

"They are," replied Harry, standing upright.

"You going to talk to him?"

"That's what he wants, I think."

Tucker raised his rifle, taking careful aim on the approaching rider, as Harry walked out through the undergrowth. The horsemen stopped as he moved forward down the hill. When Harry was within 25 feet he removed his hat. Harry gasped as he saw the ruddy face.

"Well, Harry Ludlow," said Oliver Pollock. "I never thought to find you so far from the sea."

CHAPTER THIRTY-THREE

"**BRIGADIER** General James Wilkinson, of Kentucky," said Pollock, his face grim. "That's who the money's destined for. I believe I mentioned his name in St Croix. He's a hero of the Revolutionary War, one of the most handsome men in the country, a spellbinding orator, and a fine soldier. He has just taken over Detroit from the British and is being put forward as the next inspector general of the Federal Army."

"Quite a character."

"That's his version, Harry. He also happens to be an endemic schemer who plotted against Washington, has taken part in fraudulent land speculation, and is a very good friend to the Spanish."

"And you?"

Pollock smiled. "I'm here to make sure that for all the gifts that the good God has bestowed on him, good and bad, he never receives this one."

"So you intended to steal, as well."

"Steal is a strong word, Harry. And since I'm acting on behalf of the American government, hardly appropriate. My instructions are to ensure he doesn't take possession of it, preferably by sending it back whence it came."

"Why?"

"There are those who feel that such a man should not be accepting payments from Spain. One of them is close enough to the general to have inside knowledge of his attachment to the interests of King Carlos."

"You are saying he's a traitor?" asked Harry.

"Not by his lights. In his own mind he's a patriot. Only problem is, he's more loyal to the Kentucky legislature than he is to
Congress, and Kentucky plays second fiddle to his love of money.
I believe we've spoken before about the difficulties the Federal government faces with the frontier states. Someone like Wilkinson
thrives in such an unstable atmosphere."

"Could I ask you to dismount, Oliver?"

"Not with those muskets poking out of the trees."

"One of them is a rifle, longer than normal, and in the hands
of a riverboat captain from Kentucky. I've seen him bark a squirrel at a hundred paces."

Pollock shrugged and put a finger to the middle of his head.
"So at this range, I'm a dead man."

"If you stand down your men, I will do likewise."

"You still haven't explained why you are here, Harry."

"That's precisely what I want to do. But it's not simple enough
to be done in one or two sentences."

"You sailed into New Orleans carrying all that money?"

The interruption was unwelcome, since he'd barely begun his
story, which made his response rather terse. "Slightly more, I
think."

Pollock shook his head in disbelief, unaware that he'd only
heard half of Harry's tale. "Forty Frenchmen was bad enough.
Why didn't you tell me about this?"

"I'm like you, Oliver, not much given to discussing my business in too free a manner."

Pollock acknowledged, with a grimace, the way his own
words had returned to haunt him. Harry went on to explain the
rest, alluding forcefully to the offer he'd had from the Governor
of New Orleans, that if he found the original consignment, he
could keep it.

"Not that it's really mine, of course. It belongs to the Frenchmen and should be handed over to them."

"That's a tall order, Harry."

"Your instructions are to stop Wilkinson getting his bribe."

"That's true. But if that amount of money goes missing on American soil, how am I going to explain it?"

"You only know it really exists because I've told you."

Pollock jerked his head to indicate the men behind him. They too had dismounted, though they'd kept their weapons at the ready.

"You will observe that I'm not alone."

Harry looked at the line of dismounted soldiers and frowned. "I want to put forward a guess, Oliver, which I'd be grateful if you'd truthfully confirm."

Pollock had followed his gaze, which caused him to grin, when he turned back to face him. "Now I recall what I like about you, Harry. You think like me."

"So they don't know?"

"They are aware that we are to intercept a party of Spanish soldiers who have illegally crossed into the Mississippi Territory. Wilkinson's bribe was never mentioned."

"What would you do if the money did fall into your hands?"

"I wouldn't keep it, Harry."

"Would your government?"

"I doubt it," Pollock replied, his voice turning sour. "They'd probably return it to de Carondelet as a warning to desist from meddling in American affairs."

"Not a policy that meets with your approval?"

"No!" he snapped.

"Much as it grieves me to say so, I'm prepared to lead these Frenchmen in a fight to keep it. And you lack the numbers to mount an effective attack."

"Let's walk, Harry. My mind works better when I walk."

Pollock set off, cutting a path through the long grass parallel to the line of trees, hands behind his back and his head pressed down on his chest. After about forty paces he turned and retraced his steps. Harry walked alongside him, saying nothing. This, he knew, was a time for silence. Pollock had to examine all the alternative courses of action, subjecting each possibility to rigorous examination.

"Tell me, Harry, you've been to New Orleans. What do you think of it?"

"What I think has little value. It's what people like you think that counts."

Pollock stopped and raised his head to look at the sky. "You were right when we had dinner aboard your ship. Do you recall it, the way you referred to the idea of having France back on our borders?"

"Yes. And I rather imagine that, unlike your previous response, you're now going to agree with me."

"I'm not alone in thinking it a bad thing. In fact, I dislike having any European nation on our doorstep, Spain included, since that drags us into the mire of their competing politics. The treaty we've signed with Spain regarding the Mississippi delta looks like a good thing to most Americans. To me it was just the opposite."

"You'd prefer a war?"

"I'd prefer to see New Orleans and the delta as our own property rather than be granted favours because it belongs to someone else. What we're doing only serves to make what was an untenable, unattractive colony, which might have fallen to us by default, a rich prize that someone more powerful might covet."

"France."

"I spent an age touring the Caribbean when I heard that de Carondelet was gathering gold and silver, trying to ensure that no new lines of credit would be made available to the Spanish."

"St Croix."

"Børsenen's are one of the leading neutral bankers close to the Gulf. I wanted to dissuade them, should they be tempted, from either lending the Spanish money or investing in New Orleans."

"Was this a private venture, Oliver?"

Pollock grinned again. "Let us just say that it wasn't entirely sponsored by every member of the government. There are some

who agree with me, and others who don't. But I had enough lever-
age to say to Børsenen that if he did business with the Spanish,
then any notion of similar opportunities in the United States would
be severely compromised."

"So where does this leave us?"

"Can I countenance all that money going back to New
Orleans?"

Harry stopped suddenly so that Pollock wouldn't see him
react. The American paused, then continued pacing.

"Regardless of what others think, if it does, it will just resur-
face in another form, and quite possibly be put to its original use.
I've been racking my brain for a way to avoid that without finding a solution. And now I find, thanks to you, de Carondelet
doesn't need it."

The last words were delivered with some venom. Pollock had
fallen silent again, leaving Harry to ruminate himself. He didn't
think his friend was being entirely truthful, but was at a loss to
know, if there was a lie in his statement, which one it was.
McGillivray's words about George Washington being a man tired
of war came to mind, that and his absolute certainty of the American President's upright moral character. For all the Creek
chieftain's possible duplicity, when he'd uttered those words he'd
spoken with real conviction.

Obviously Pollock belonged to a group that would dearly love
to invoke a conflict with Spain over Louisiana. How much of that
was genuine patriotism and how much it was dictated by personal
gain was irrelevant. It was merely a fact. But it was not a view
that found universal favour in New York, with someone like Washington at the head of a government dedicated to peace and
consolidation, a man surrounded by others of like persuasion, who
would find such an act anathema, given that it could only be
brought to pass by subterfuge and double dealing.

Pollock couldn't appropriate the money for himself. To hand
it over to people who'd return it to de Carondelet, whether they

were American politicians or intinerant French settlers, was an unpalatable option. Nor could it be passed on to Wilkinson. All of which, added together, suited him perfectly. It had been Harry's intention to keep quiet about his decision to keep going north, but now being open about it seemed more effective. Typically, he made it sound as though the thought had just occurred to him.

"Where would they settle?" Pollock demanded.

"I'm sure I could accept your advice on that," Harry replied. He waited with baited breath, aware that if Pollock accepted that duty, he'd also accepted the notion of the retention of Wilkinson's bribe.

"It would have to be outside Kentucky or Tennessee," Pollock growled. "That kind of sum would be just as dangerous on the frontier as it would be in the delta."

"I must have a suggestion to put to them."

"There are several old French settlements west of the Illinois River, in the region of the Great Lakes. They can be reached by water if they can find themselves a boat."

"That would suit them," Harry replied, without elaborating.

"And they can't go wandering around the country with that amount of money," said Pollock. "They'd need somewhere to deposit their funds."

"They would accept your advice on that as well, I'm sure."

"I will recommend them to the Morris family of Philadelphia. Robert and Gouverneur Morris are friends of mine."

Harry grinned. It looked like agreement, but behind the smile he was thinking about those two names. Robert Morris had been the leading banker to the Continental Congress during the Revolutionary years, and quite a power in the land. What was his attitude to the Mississippi question?

"What about the money they had originally?" Pollock snapped, breaking his train of thought.

They started pacing again while Harry filled in the details of how de Carondelet had come to sequester the treasure. This inevitably led to an explanation of how they'd found the deserted ship and what was aboard, which engendered a raised eyebrow, especially at Harry's description of the open sugar boxes. Then the mention of San Lucar de Barrameda brought forth a curse, one that was extended to de Carondelet and his entire *Cabildo,* as well as the officers of the Spanish garrison.

"De Fajardo de Coburrabias is a clever rogue," he said, when the soldier's name emerged.

Harry continued his tale, refering to de Carondelet's offer of redress. "Worthless in my opinion. McGillivray thinks—"

"What has McGillivray got to do with this?" Pollock demanded.

The explanation didn't raise Harry in Pollock's eyes, which was clear from the grinding of his teeth. "You've been used, man, can't you see that? As soon as you and Pender recross the frontier, he'll steal it off you."

"Except that now, Oliver, we won't have it."

Pollock threw back his head and laughed. "I'd like to see his face, Harry. I hope it gives the bastard a stroke."

"Do I detect the fact that you don't like him?"

"He came to New York a couple of years back, and did more harm than any other man has a right to."

Which translated meant that McGillivray had only reinforced the American government's reluctance to do anything underhand, or even overt, regarding Louisiana.

"He told me he and George Washington esteemed each other."

Pollock gave a heartfelt sigh. "One thing that we learned from being subjects of King George, Harry, is that no man, however elevated, is infallible."

"Anyway, all this is academic," Harry continued. "The only way I had of getting that chest back from de Carondelet, according to him, was to reunite him with his bullion. He convenietly forgot to mention that it wasn't even on the *Gauchos.* I suppose if I'd found the murderer that would have—might have—made his position more uncomfortable, but I'm still not sure it would have induced him to make redress."

"Murderer?"

"We found, tied to a raft in the Gulf, the body of one Juan Baptiste Rodrigo."

"Rodrigo?"

"The Captain of the *Gauchos*."

"Captain? The man's no ship's Captain. He's a smuggler. What was he doing out in the Gulf in a merchant ship?"

"Presumably," Harry replied tersely, "he'd been engaged to transport what he thought was boxes of sugar."

"John the Baptist Rodrigo is a man I first met in the cells of Moro Castle in Havana. I was put there, like him, by Galvez, one of de Carondelet's predecessors. My crime was to meddle too overtly in local politics, his to steal too much from the treasury by his smuggling. Are you telling me that the *Cochon du lait* actually engaged someone like him to transport his gold and silver?"

"No, Oliver, I said he'd been engaged to carry casks of sugar." He went on to describe what he'd found on board, including the cabin and the table set for dinner. "De Carondelet confirmed to me my original supposition that Rodrigo knew nothing of the real cargo."

"And you believed him?"

"I had no reason not to," Harry replied, with an anger that had a lot to do with the sudden realization of his own possible gullibility. "And none of this matters a damn. He's not going to part with that chest no matter what I do. What is more vital is that I get my ship out of New Orleans. Right now it's berthed under one of the New Orleans forts, with a furnace full of shot ready to sink me if I try to move."

"Harry, it's worse than you think. The French and Spanish are on the verge of signing a pact that will bring the Dons into an alliance against Britain."

"I know that, Oliver. McGillivray told me. But he also said

that the Dons would wait until the Plate fleet had reached Cadiz. That can't happen until September at the earliest, so I have a little time left to act. That coincides, as you will know better than I, with slack water on the Mississippi. When the river is low, I can't see how the fortress guns can depress enough to threaten me, and given that the guards will have grown lazy I have a good chance of getting clean away without much damage."

He stopped, wondering why Pollock was looking at him so hard, biting his lip with evident discomfort.

"You don't think it will work?"

"I mentioned the Morris brothers earlier."

"The bankers?"

"Yes, though they are politicians as well." Pollock hesitated for a fraction of a second before proceeding, as though he needed to gather his thoughts. "As you will guess, such men have sources of information that transcend those of government. They have to in order to protect their investments."

"Go on," said Harry, with a sinking feeling in the pit of his stomach.

"I saw them recently."

"Please be frank, Oliver. It was Robert Morris that informed you of this rendezvous."

"I won't affirm or deny that, Harry. What I will say is that Morris knows that I have a home in New Orleans and that matters pertaining to Spain are of interest to me."

"And?"

"It's no secret in London that the French are determined to get the Spaniards into the war on their side. It is also common knowledge that the only thing Manuel de Godoy is awaiting is the money contained in the Plate galleons. So the Admiralty despatched a squadron of four frigates to intercept them."

"With, or without, war being declared?"

"Without. Their orders were to take them regardless, and stop that money reaching the Spanish treasury."

"If they succeed they'll be rich. The annual cargo from South America is worth four or five million guineas."

"So you don't need to be told how hard they will try."

"The ocean is big, Oliver."

"The Spanish are sailing in peacetime, Harry. They will have received a hint, if they haven't been actually told, of the importance of their mission, so they will have sought to make their landfall quickly. And their destination is as well known to you as it is to those four Captains."

"You make it sound as though they've already been taken."

"If I do, it is only because I suspect it to be true. Just as I suspect that such news will spread rapidly. Every ship sailing west will hear of it. And so will de Carondelet as soon as one touches at New Orleans. I believe that your room for manoeuvre has been shortened by a month to six weeks."

"Can you detain the Spaniards we captured?"

"What?"

"Oliver, I have to get back to New Orleans, even if you have implied that I might be too late. What I don't need is the possibility that the men we have overpowered will get there ahead of me."

"They're foreign soldiers on American soil." Pollock slapped a fist onto his palm. "Damn."

"What's the matter?"

"Wilkinson. He's two days behind us, three at the most. We had news that he'd crossed the Muscle Shoals at Colbert's Ferry a week ago."

"Can you avoid him?"

"No. I didn't get here without being seen at every post-house on the way. My only claim to innocence is in not seeking to hide. I had half a hope that my presence would embarrass him so much that he'd decline to come on, but the man has the hide of an elephant. It makes little difference. Once he reaches here and finds that something has gone wrong he'll likely set the whole area alight searching for his bribe. The only thing I can do is continue south.

But I have to return through the Frontier States at some time. Remember I'm not alone. At the first place where I find the law, I'll be obliged to hand them over. How long do you think it will be before Wilkinson finds that out?"

"I need a week, Oliver."

"I can't guarantee it."

"But you will try."

Pollock nodded.

CHAPTER THIRTY-FOUR

POLLOCK marched south, the remaining Spaniards on foot between their American escorts, all informed that they'd been rescued from certain death at the hands of renegade Frenchmen. It wouldn't hold forever, but it was enough to keep them in check. And they would be able to honestly confirm, to an enquiring authority, that Pollock and his men had been too few to engage in a battle with the men who'd attacked them. With luck he could escort them so far south that the question of their freedom would become academic. Up by the latrine the Frenchmen were burying two of their own number, and four Spaniards. The dead all being Papists, Harry left whatever burial service was required to those overseeing their interment.

"Even if you have foxed this Wilkinson fellow," said Tucker, "that still leaves McGillivray. And he must be close."

"He might even have an eye on us this very minute," added Pender, scanning the surrounding hills. "I don't suppose that sour-pussed Indian that led us here in the first place is too far off."

Harry was now pacing very much in the same manner as that adopted earlier by Pollock, head down and brow furrowed. Tucker, leaning on his rifle, continued.

"Even if you could avoid him, and de Carondelet is no wiser about those frigates, you have to get your ship out of New Orleans before news gets back of what happened here. I can't see McGillivray keeping his trap shut, especially when he finds out you've cheated him out of his neat little triumph."

"How do you think de Guerin intended to get home?" asked Harry, stopping suddenly. "Not on horseback, surely. Even if he did change those two lame animals, he could hardly relish the idea of another six weeks in the saddle."

"Boat would be best," said Tucker.

"From where?"

Tucker shrugged.

Harry looked towards the tent, now partially collapsed because of the way Tucker had cut the guy-ropes. "Did he have any maps amongst his possessions?"

"I'll have a look," said Pender, diving under the canvas. He emerged after a few moments carrying a flat leather case. Harry took it off him and flipped it open. The first page showed his route from New Orleans to the first stop for remounts, with each successive page showing a different section of his long journey north. Impatiently, Harry flipped it over so that he was looking at the very last map. He held it out to show the two other men. *Doak's Stand* was written in large letters, with the spot on which they stood marked in faint ink. They examined the line of march, also faintly drawn, heading due east. This culminated at a twisting blue line that was clearly a watercourse, the total, a distance of some sixty miles as the crow flies.

"The Yazoo River," said Tucker. "Runs into the Mississippi just north of Walnut Hills."

"Navigable?" asked Harry.

"It is on the lower reaches. Near an eighth of a mile wide in parts."

"There has to be a boat there waiting for them, Captain," said Pender. "This map don't show no settlement an' they wouldn't just go there on the off chance."

"Arranged by Wilkinson, no doubt."

"Which means that once he gets there, he might not head south."

Harry looked at the sloping clearing, at the horses grazing quietly in their neat lines. To hide the evidence of an encampment was impossible. There were the scorch marks where the Spaniards had lit their fires, the indentations made by their tents, palpable evidence of numerous creatures grazing, and most telling of all, that freshly dug latrine, now being turned into newly dug graves. With his own animals, de Guerin's mounts, and the pack-horses the Spanish had used, he had two beasts for every man in his party; he remembered the bullion, whose weight had to be distributed over at least a dozen animals, but that still left him spare horses, an advantage that was unlikely to be held by either of his pursuers.

McGillivray, who'd controlled matters up till now, wouldn't know where they were going. Expecting Harry to head back south on horseback, he'd be temporarily out-manoeuvred by his change of direction. Against that he would probably manage to keep them under observation. Wilkinson, if he arrived and saw the evidence, might guess his destination, but he too might assume that they'd gone south on horseback. So he must surprise one and out-run both. Once they got to the river the horses were superfluous, and even if the Indian kept himself abreast of their progress he wouldn't worry as long as they headed downriver. After all, he knew exactly where Tucker was berthed.

"Pender, I think I'm going to have to tie you onto your horse."

They pushed the animals without much regard for their well-being for the first ten miles, before slowing to a canter. Harry was no cavalryman, but he knew that no horse could cover the entire distance without rest and fodder. Nor would the men, who'd slept little the previous night, be much use if they had no rest. He found a clearing close to a steep hill, and set the animals to graze and Tucker to hunt for food. The Frenchmen, and Pender, were bidden to rest. Equally tired, he climbed to the top of the hill and found a spot that gave him a view of the route they'd followed on what must be an old Indian trail. The wisps of smoke from the three fires differed only in their density, the closest one, no more than two miles away, being the thickest. The idea that McGillivray knew exactly where he was didn't bother him much, but if Wilkinson picked up his tracks it was another matter. Not that he could do anything about it, and the fires were proof that the Creek chieftain wasn't close. If he was, he wouldn't need them. Two hours later, after a quick meal from the Spaniards' stores, they were on the trail again, with Pender groaning continuously at the discomfort.

Harry stopped them as night began to fall, leaving them just enough light to tether the horses, set a rough picket, and find a place to rest their heads. Pender, having had the gift of some sleep during the day, was given Harry's timepiece and charge of the first watch, with orders to wake Tucker at midnight. He had Harry up before dawn, and by full daylight they were again on their way. By Harry's reckoning they'd covered over half the distance on the first day. The second was harder, since he ruled out any notion of stopping. They rode up one hill and down the next, each following heavily forested rise visible from that which preceded it, but late in the afternoon the land began to slope steadily downwards towards the river, and Harry called a halt so that he and Tucker could go forward and investigate. They found what they were looking for easily enough, tied to a makeshift jetty by a long stretch of sandy beach, with trees running to within twenty feet of the water's edge.

The boat, with what appeared to be three guards aboard, was not designed to transport much cargo. It was a long, narrow keelboat, sleek and manoeuvrable, perfectly suited to a swift journey downriver. It was also a touch too small for the number he needed to load aboard. Tucker knew the limitations better than he.

"Being low in the water's all right as long as you don't hit anything, and the old river is sparse now, so that means the channels ain't as deep as we would like. And overloaded makes it harder to work if we get into any danger."

"Which we must put against trying to ride to safety."

"That, as they say, is not a contest."

"We'll have to take those guards with us part of the way, or they'll talk."

"No point," Tucker replied. "Any man with a brain will guess we'd be goin' downriver. Best tie them loose and leave them here."

"Then let's work out a way to overpower them."

"This is a job for a Kentuckian," said Tucker, grinning. "I'd be thankful for the use of your pistols."

"Wouldn't it be better to come with you?"

Tucker looked at Harry's clothes—dark blue coat, breeches, and boots. They'd suffered somewhat from his recent adventures, still streaked with dried grey mud—his shirt particularly—but they were unmistakably the accoutrements of a man who lived in a city, and they contrasted sharply with Tucker's loose buckskin garments.

"The sight of you will have them reaching for weapons. But finding a frontiersman here might just make them pause."

Harry gave him the pistols, already loaded and primed, which the American stuck in his belt. Tucker pulled out his chewing tobacco and took a bite, before cradling his rifle in his arms. Then he moved forward, adopting an arrogant swagger as he emerged from the trees. The sight brought the three men to their feet, and Harry edged slightly closer, ready to rush forward if his companion's ruse showed any signs of failing. Tucker stopped, staring at them as though he had all the time in the world. And when he spoke, his tone was a lazy drawl, almost a mockery of the frontier bumpkin.

"Why, that's a mighty fine boat you got there, boys. Bit like one of 'em dogs bred to coursing. Not much use in the freight line, I reckon."

"Who are you?" asked the man in the middle, a thick-set fellow who by his posture was the leader. He'd picked up a buckskin cover very like Tucker's own, then slipped out a long rifle. The two other men had clubs.

"Name's Boone," Tucker replied.

"Boone!"

Tucker moved forward to the side of the boat, leant his long rifle on the side, then bent to examine the planking, running his fingers along the wood. "Close relation to Daniel, son, tho' I'm a mite upset at the way he's sullied the family name."

"Sullied?" There was no offence in the question, just surprise.

Tucker was now leaning on the side of the boat, his head just above the gunwale, and the bulk of his body out of sight. The leader had lowered his rifle, more interested in the conversation than security.

"Reckon you might see him as a hero, what with all that folks writ about him. But Cousin Daniel has a mouth, son, which he opens and shuts a mite too readily. Not something my family takes kindly to. Reckon I'll have to whup him one of these days and see if'n I can keep him quiet."

The armed man turned to grin at his two companions. Harry's pistols came up over the gunwales at exactly the same point, one aimed at his back, the other waving towards his two companions. They saw the guns before he did, but the startled look on their faces alerted him and he began to spin round.

"Don't be a fool, son," said Tucker. "Cousin Daniel ain't the best shot in the family."

The rifle stayed down as Harry rushed forward. He grabbed Tucker's own weapon, flipped off the cover, and levelled it at the deck, praying that they couldn't see it wasn't loaded. Tucker, though he had to do it out of the corner of his eye, glared angrily.

"Two choices, boys," he said, in the same slow drawl. "Drop your weapons or we drop you."

The thuds, as the clubs hit the deck, were simultaneous. The rifle took a little longer. Slowly they raised their hands.

"You will oblige me by unhanding my rifle, friend."

It was a moment before Harry realized that Tucker was growling at him. He laid Practical John down gently.

"I thank you. Now, you boys, down on the jetty, nice and slow."

"Who is Daniel Boone?" asked Harry, as the trio complied.

"You don't know?" said Tucker, obviously amazed. Harry shook his head. "My, what a sheltered life you've led."

◆ ◆ ◆

The horses, content to graze as soon as they were freed, had to be chased away from the river bank, with Harry fretting at the loss of time, his predicament watched stoically by the three men lashed on long ropes to the nearby trees. Pender had measured the lengths, cutting them just short of the point where one could reach the other, then tied complex knots, thus ensuring that it would be some time before they would free themselves. The keelboat, having been pushed away from the shallows by the jetty, was crammed full, low in the water, with just enough room for the men to work the sweep. Tucker had insisted on the poles being used, even if there was limited room to work them, arguing that at the very least they could be used to slow the boat down if he thought they were at risk. The vessel, released, and already in deep water, swung out into the current and immediately gathered speed.

"This would be one to try in the spring, Ludlow," Tucker called. Harry, on the other side of the sweep, just grinned and took a firmer grip. "And as soon as we're out of sight, I should take possession of the long rifle that feller had. Seems to be a pretty fine weapon."

"Why wait till we're out of sight?"

"No need to hurt the man's feelings, Ludlow. I had a word with him before we unhooked. He was near to tears when I said we was takin' it with us. It's called Able Mabel, but now that it's yours, feel free to give the damn thing a new name."

"We used to name our cannons on men-of-war."

"That's all very well and proper," Tucker replied, with a grin. "But who ever heard of taking a cannon to bed with you?"

Where the Yazoo was wide and straight, the journey was pleasant, but getting round the numerous shallow bends was a struggle that required strength, determination, and foresight. Worse awaited them if they encountered any narrows, usually caused by some mid-channel island, with the pace of the river, to which the keelboat was wholly subject, taking control. It was very different from coming upriver in a galley, where the muscles were needed to row: now everything depended on keeping control of the sweep. The poles helped to slow them in deep water, but as soon as any rocks appeared, Tucker had to haul them inboard and let the current do its worst, for fear that one of them would snag and cause the boat to broach. Trees, growing unchecked from the river bank, formed a tangled arch over the route, with branches hanging down into the water thick enough to kill. Those steering could only duck and weave, and hope that reactions that were instinctive would keep them from harm.

After each constricted passage of river, it was essential to stop, let others take the sweep, and rest aching arms. But progress, even in a sluggish current, was swift, and they ate up the miles until darkness fell. After a short night's sleep they were back on their way at first light. Settlements began to appear on the lower reaches of the river, places where the tall canes had been cut back or burnt to provide land on which to build. It was impossible to avoid bringing attention to their passage. Riverside folks always had time to stare at a boat, and one so clearly overloaded could not expect to pass by without exciting comment.

Once they'd cleared the Yazoo, Tucker took the galley well out into the centre of the main channel of the Mississippi, which followed a very erratic route at this point, turning to the north-east before swinging round in a long arc to a southerly course at Walnut Hills. On the second bend stood a fort, once Nogales under the Spanish, now the American Post of Fort M'Henry. If they were noticed from the ramparts they were not called upon to stop and they proceeded downriver with Tucker calling off the various locations: Palmyra, Point Pleasant. They passed the mouth of the Big Black River, a deep confluence only forty yards wide that acting on the current caused a sudden and unnerving increase in their speed.

"We're coming to the Grand Gulf next," shouted Tucker. "So if you've a mind to pray, I'd be thankful for your efforts."

The river, he explained, narrowed at Trent's Point to a mere quarter of a mile, while at the same time turning sharply south-west. This acute angle and sudden compression formed two great eddies, one on either side, just below the narrows, which ran for about half a mile.

"Don't be fooled by that sluggish water on either side, Ludlow. This is one of the deadliest stretches of the river. We have to stay plumb in the middle. If we get sucked in with the crowd we've got aboard we'll very likely capsize."

Harry was looking hard at a pair of portholes close to the stern. His aching shoulders spurred on his tired brain and he had Pender run ropes from the sweep through the gaps so that the men on the deck could take some of the strain of holding the weight.

"Nice idea, Ludlow," said Tucker. "Just as long as they don't hold on when they should let go."

The speed increased alarmingly, the water rushing down the side now creaming as it swished by. The river dead ahead seemed designed by a godlike hand, with the two swirling eddies marked out by the flat, benign nature of the water. Their avenue was like a foaming arrow down the middle, so constrained that the boat seemed to fill it. The ropes Harry had rigged creaked and strained, the noise of that and the rushing water made the orders Tucker gave hard to hear. At one point the bows swung right towards the larboard bank. Tucker cursed, his voice rising above the river noise, calling for a supreme effort by those steering to bring it back onto its course. The keelboat began to tip to one side, the deck canting enough to dislodge some of the passengers. Men were yelling in panic when the pressure suddenly eased, the boat came level abruptly, and the men on the sweep fell to one side. When Harry stood up, he could see that the eddies were behind them and the pace of the keelboat had slowed. He turned to look at Tucker, who was smiling.

"Next stop, Bayou Pierre," he crooned. "And to my mind, that's cause for celebration. I'd be thankful if someone would fetch me a dram."

Tucker's galley was still where he'd left her, nestled against Judge

Bruin's levee. They transferred men, stores, and bullion rapidly, soaked with sweat in the humid, sticky atmosphere of the swamp. Tucker went ashore to buy a pirogue for Harry and Pender, that being the only vessel that the two of them could manage by themselves on the river.

"No Indian in his right mind would go far in a bark canoe on the Mississippi," he explained, "and they're none too fond of the night."

Harry looked at the boat, a hollowed-out tree trunk, in which Pender was loading their possessions, with something less than enthusiasm.

"So this represents the fastest way to get to New Orleans. If McGillivray is not ahead of you now he will never be, as long as you manage this properly."

"A bit o' advice wouldn't go amiss," said Pender.

"Well, it's a lot like a horse, Pender," Tucker replied, grinning when Harry's servant groaned. "A mite contrary. You've got to recall it's heavier than a planked boat, and long, so if you're going to turn a Mississippi bend you must start early, especially if'n you're in any kind of fast water. But you'll find that in normal currents the paddles, once you get used to them, are better on the river than proper oars. As long as you work together you can turn on a small coin. When you stop for the night choose a midstream island. Don't bed down on the ground in case of alligators, pay out a piece of rope and sleep in the bottom of the canoe."

"How long?" asked Harry.

"I've done Natchez to New Orleans in a week, and that's in a keelboat. You can shave two whole days off that, I reckon."

There was little time for farewells. Tucker was taking the Frenchmen north, in a boat that Wilkinson wouldn't recognize, should he be on the river. McGillivray, they suspected, would come to the Bayou Pierre, which could take him several days. Harry and Pender took time to shake each man's hand, warmed by the affection that they showed. Brissot had tears in his eyes, which caused Pender to observe that he was "a contrary bugger an' no error."

Harry was closer to Lampin and Couvruer, the two who had done the most to ease relations between the groups. Lampin, who in some ways had assumed the leadership of the entire party, pressed a package of de Carondelet's ingots into Harry's hand, overcoming any objections that he might have by alluding to the danger the crew of the *Bucephalas* faced. He opened it to discover four thin bars, two gold, two silver, each bearing the royal crest of Spain, twinned with that of New Orleans.

"Good luck in America," Harry said, his hands on both of Lampin's shoulders.

The bright blue eyes flicked to the sparkling ingots, which had been passed to Pender. "If we can keep possession of the rest of that, then we should never have a care."

"Look after Tucker," said Harry softly. "I think he is sacrificing his livelihood to help you."

Lampin nodded and spoke softly. *"Certainement."*

The American was by the side of the boat, prepared to help them down into the pirogue, his final contact a handshake of the bone-crushing variety.

"Now just you make sure, friend, that the next time I'm in New Orleans Hyacinthe Feraud is there, and you ain't, otherwise we might have to take off on that dance floor where we left off."

Not sure if he was joking, Harry kept his face blank. Tucker grinned suddenly. "Apart from that, Harry Ludlow, I'm right thankful I met you."

"Likewise," said Harry, with genuine feeling.

Tucker had fired Wilkinson's keelboat before they'd paddled out of sight. Through the thick humid air they heard him order the Frenchmen to the oars and the galley followed them down the bayou to the Mississippi. For all that Harry needed speed, he waited, holding the pirogue steady till Tucker exited into the main current. The boat swung north, its oars dipping steadily into the dark brown waters of the river. On the air, Pender and Harry heard the first bars of a song, a rhythm that would keep the beat of the oars steady.

CHAPTER THIRTY-FIVE

WITH JUST the two of them in the pirogue, on a stretch of river that was wide and slow, the urgency which had been a feature of their lives for the last weeks fell away. There was a speed that could be decently achieved and that was that. Harry had a sailor's ability to avoid fretting over things he could do nothing about. Time and tide had their own momentum, which no amount of gnawing and gnashing would alter. Not that his mind was a blank: the Mississippi required a lot of attention, especially from their low elevation, since hazards which they could not see ahead would come upon them quickly; he was mulling over his plan to get *Bucephalas* and the crew out of danger. Then there was Hyacinthe Feraud, the thoughts engendered by her image making him somewhat uncomfortable. Added to that was the need to cover himself against any hint of duplicity, especially with such a suspicious character as de Carondelet. If his reason for being out of New Orleans was a stated desire to hunt with El Señor Cayetano de Fajardo de Coburrabias, the logic demanded that even if it delayed him, he'd be wise to fulfil such an obligation, if only to furnish himself with evidence of a visit.

But most of all he was racking his brain for a way to detach de Carondelet from that chest full of treasure. Now that the Frenchmen had the Governor's bullion, what he'd robbed them of was fair game. The safety of the ship and his crew was paramount, but if a way could be found to safeguard them, effect an escape, and steal the money, then Harry would be an exceedingly happy man. Since leaving Deal the previous year he'd not enjoyed much in the way of success as a privateer. Not a single member of his crew—who shared in the proceeds—had alluded to this, aware that circumstances had deflected their Captain from pursuing his chosen occupation. But he didn't relish the thought of sailing for home with empty coffers. Certainly, with war against Spain imminent, he could soon take prizes in the Gulf of Mexico, which would be a clear hunting ground for any privateer already in the area, but the problem was then a place to sell what he captured that didn't involve long voyages for the prize crews. His options in the Caribbean, the closest landfalls, were limited, and added to that, the goods he could expect to trade, cotton, sugar, and indigo, would be more profitable if sold in Europe.

Thinking that turned his mind back to the *Gauchos* and those boxes of sugar; to Rodrigo and the raft. If, as Pollock said, the man was a smuggler, then he'd probably risked his neck many times. But he hardly deserved the fate he was granted, and that probably for being honest. Harry had been in a lot of ports in his time, but thinking about New Orleans and the Louisiana Territory he could recall few places where people so rarely told the truth. San Lucar de Barrameda had falsified a report that had led, indirectly, to their internment and the loss of the treasure. De Carondelet had lied to Harry more by omission and despite what it had cost it was hard to feel too personally aggrieved. After all, he hadn't even been honest with his own subordinates and officials. Idly, as he paddled along, he and Pender discussed these matters, the taking of the *Gauchos,* and the various potential culprits.

"What about Fernandez?" said Harry. "Capable of violence, remember. He was closest to the point at which the ship was intercepted, had a cutter, which would have been perfect, though I will own he didn't look the type to walk past a square meal."

"But you just said that very few people knew the stuff was supposed to be on the ship. Fernandez was stuck in Balize when it was loaded, and he can hardly be rated as popular with the nobs."

"I've revised my previous assertion that Rodrigo didn't know."

"Why?"

"He wasn't supposed to know. But just think about the cabin. Do you remember it? I'd assumed that the owner of McGillivray's chest was a passenger. I now know that was not the case. So there weren't enough people aboard to justify the number of places set."

"What about the master?"

"You don't know the Spanish, Pender. They're not much given to sitting down with those they consider their inferiors."

"So whoever came alongside was invited to eat."

"Was expected, Pender. It was a rendezvous and a happy one. It was only when the first box was opened that things changed."

"Rodrigo had a mate who reckoned he'd been dunned."

"It makes sense. One of the people de Carondelet had witness the loading of the ingots into the sugar casks tipped the nod to Rodrigo, made the rendezvous, then killed him because he thought he'd been cheated by the only person who could have accomplished it. He couldn't know, because it was an even better kept secret, that it was never loaded aboard. Neither did Rodrigo, so protesting his innocence must have sounded very hollow indeed."

"Poor bastard," said Pender, sitting up suddenly. "Current's gettin' up, Capt'n."

Harry sat forward too, his paddle dipping into the water with greater force as both men worked to keep the pirogue on a true and safe course. They hadn't quite mastered the techniques and once the hollowed-out tree had yawed it was the very devil to get back on course. On top of that Harry lacked Tucker's knowledge of the river, so they were not always best placed in the stream to avoid trouble, and furious paddling was required to get them out of whirlpools and eddies that they should never have got into in the first place, hazards that were thankfully lessened by the low water-level.

"I'm not one to be untouched by men dying," said Pender, as they exited in calmer waters. "But what difference does it make to you who killed Rodrigo?"

"None," Harry replied. "But it would give me enormous pleasure to find out, if only to give de Carondelet a bilious attack."

"If'n he went to all that trouble, would he care? He must've suspected that his bribe was at risk."

"He would if it was printed in the French newspaper. He hates Saraille with a passion."

"Well, if'n I were you, I'd leave Fernandez out of it. I've met him more times than you an' I reckon he's not that way inclined. Mind, that would be more through bein' lazy than anything else."

But Harry wasn't listening, instead mentally ticking off all the possible culprits. The three members of the *Cabildo,* de Lovio, de Pontalba, and de Aquivar, didn't impress him as having either the brain or the brawn to contemplate such an act, being no more than functionaries elected to carry out de Carondelet's wishes. De Chigny, the Governor's aide, was in the city the whole time, while de Guerin was heading north with the true cargo before the *Gauchos* was set adrift. McGillivray had been genuinely surprised and would never have shipped anything in the *Gauchos* if he'd had knowledge of the bullion. De Fajardo de Coburrabias had come in on the transports. That left either someone completely unknown or Harry's favourite candidate, San Lucar de Barrameda. He had the means, was in the vicinity, and had lied about the *Bucephalas,* an act which made complete sense if he was trying to cover his own tracks. Against that he had several ships with him, as well as his own crew. Perhaps he'd left the *Navarro* and taken to something smaller. But was he devious enough to create the elaborate illusion that Harry had come across, on a ship that someone had apparently tried to sink? San Lucar de Barrameda might not be much of a sailor, but even he would know how to go about sending the *Gauchos* to the bottom without leaving a trace of her presence. And that, if he was intent on covering his tracks, was a far better method than his lame attempt to blame the innocent Ludlows.

"How're you doing, Capt'n?" asked Pender.

"I just realized why I care, Pender. Much as I'd like to beard de Carondelet, sinking that pompous oaf de Barrameda would be much more satisfying. Trouble is, for all I think he's a fool, I cannot bring myself to believe he's that stupid."

"You've lost me."

"Anyone with an ounce of knowledge about ships could have sunk the *Gauchos*. Why leave it floating about in mid-ocean?"

"That puts old Fernandez back in the pit, I suppose."

"Yes, Pender, I'm afraid it does."

Two days saw them approaching the Manchac Post with Harry still undecided as to the best course of action: to stop and visit de Coburrabias, using an excuse to make a swift departure, or to try to skip past the guard boats and get back to New Orleans as fast as possible. In the event the decision was taken out of his hands. As they entered the bend to the north of the post a flag was hoisted atop the ramparts. There was nothing ahead or behind him, so that Harry couldn't advance any excuse for a failure to stop, and to ensure his compliance, a guard boat was patrolling the river, with armed soldiers aboard.

"What are we going to do about them ingots?" asked Pender, as they began to steer for the shore. The boat swung in a wide arc to cover their stern and an officer advanced onto the jetty, waiting to greet them as they landed.

"Throw them in the bottom of the boat with Able Mabel and cover them with some canvas." Harry leant forward and picked up his coat, reaching inside for El Señor de Coburrabias's invitation. Once he'd found it he held it up. "Let's hope that this protects us from a search."

"An' if it don't?"

"Pitch it over the side. Because if they find it they'll probably hang us like that poor fellow."

Pender looked round to see what his Captain was pointing at. The desiccated body of a Negro swung from a gibbet at the end of the jetty, with the remaining flesh on the head barely enough to disguise the coming skeleton. Close too, the smell of putrefraction was overpowering. It didn't seem to bother the Spanish soldier, who stood patiently while Harry tied the pirogue to the jetty. He climbed onto the planking, jacket in one hand and safe conduct in the other, to be faced by an officer whose sole interest seemed to be in the stained nature of Harry's linen.

"My compliments to your commanding officer, Monsieur," his visitor said in French, proferring the letter. The officer took it without bothering to acknowledge if he'd understood, and began to read it with a supercilious look on his face. That changed when he saw the contents, which were written in Spanish. He came to attention immediately and favoured Harry with a bow.

"Señor."

"My servant will stay here with the boat," said Harry, pointing down to Pender, still in the boat. That wasn't questioned, being to a Spanish mind only right and proper. "I trust that El Señor de Coburrabias is here."

"I regret to inform you, Señor, that he left for New Orleans some ten days ago and has not returned."

"Ah!" said Harry, hardly able to believe his luck. "So no hunting."

"I regret to say no."

"Then I'd best return to New Orleans." Harry hesitated a fraction. "I'm afraid I do not know your name."

"Lieutenant Oliverta."

"I will mention to El Señor de Coburrabias that we have met."

"But the *Comandante* would never forgive me if I let you go without offering refreshments." He turned to indicate the fort behind him.

Harry was in a quandary. Time was pressing, yet to decline the offer would look like bad manners. He had the young man's name, and had a reasonably close view of the fortifications, which would suffice to establish that he had visited the post. But how much more telling it would be to have been inside. He could, with embellishments, make it sound as if he'd tarried at Manchac for quite some time. De Coburrabias had been gone for ten days, so he could easily imply that he spent a week here.

"Then it would be unforgivable to refuse."

The whole structure was made of wood, even the quarters of the *Comandante* and his officers, the only stone building a handsome Roman church, yet they'd made their surroundings as elegant as they could, bringing good furniture and plate from New Orleans. Oliverta led him into a long chamber with a large polished table in the centre. The wall behind was dominated by a large crucifix and at the eastern end hung a decent-sized portrait of King Carlos, while the western wall held a slightly smaller one of de Coburrabias. Servants appeared at the sound of the bell and were despatched to fetch wine and fruit.

"You came from the north?" said Oliverta, a quizzical expression on his face.

"I got lost on horseback, Señor," replied Harry quickly, walking towards de Coburrabias's portrait. "Having found myself north of the post I knew the one certain way to my destination to be the river."

"Surely you could not have been lost for long, Señor. Did you not ask at the missions?"

Harry pretended not to hear. "He cuts a handsome figure, your *Comandante*."

Oliverta smiled, since Harry was right, and got no further with his enquiries as his guest forcefully discussed the picture. His remarks flattered the youngster's superior, but then so had the artist. The features were accurate, but the brush had caught the combination of arrogance and humour that was the core of his subject's personality. He was in the full regimental dress of a hidalgo officer, the steel breastplate on his chest half hidden by a dark red cloak. The helmet of a Spanish soldier nestled under his arm, nearly touching a glittering, jewel-encrusted decoration, shaped like a bursting star. The background was one of the gatehouses of New Orleans, with an avenue at his back leading down to the levee and the faint trace of masts and rigging that topped its height. Harry ranged over the whole landscape talking through the arrival of the refreshments. Running out of things to say, he pointed to the small white dog which sat against the bastion wall, looking forlorn.

"A pet?"

"Not that I'm aware of, Señor."

Harry spun round and headed for the other end of the room, to examine and discuss the painting of the lieutenant's King. Here was a less imposing creature altogether. Hard as he'd tried, the artist, probably executing a copy, had failed to disguise this mad monarch's shifty look, or brush out the pose of a man expecting a blow. But Harry couldn't say that, of course, so he fell back on everything James had told him, discussing the way that the two different artists had used their brushes. This involved him in a great deal of bluff and bluster, plus a parade from one end of the room to the other, and the topping up of his glass each time he passed the decanter. He dredged everything James had ever told him from his memory. The majority of it was totally irrelevant, but he was sure that this youngster knew even less about art than he did, and it served to keep the conversation off the route by which he'd come there.

"I wonder, Lieutenant Oliverta," he said finally, looking down at his mud-streaked shirt, that being followed by a scrape of the chin, "if I could ask you for some clean linen and the use of a razor. I'm afraid mine was mislaid by that fool I have for a servant."

"Of course, Señor. I will lend you one of my own shirts. My manservant will shave you. Please follow me."

Harry was led into a suite of private rooms, small but adequate, with Oliverta shouting as they passed down the narrow corridor. A servant appeared, then immediately rushed off for water. Oliverta produced a shirt from a deep drawer and gave it to him.

"If you take the chair before the mirror."

"Most kind."

Oliverta bowed and left the room, giving Harry a chance to sigh with relief. Half an hour later, shaved and in a clean shirt, he re-asserted his dominance of the renewed conversation, hardly pausing for breath as he gabbled on, happy to observe that his host's eyes were showing signs of glazing over.

"Rude of me, I know, Lieutenant, but since Don Cayetano isn't here, I wonder if you'd take it amiss if I set out to return to New Orleans?"

"No!" said Oliverta, jumping to his feet just a shade too quickly.

He was out of the post and back on the river within ten minutes, almost hustled off the jetty by a man who'd identified him as a bore.

"It's perfect, Pender," said Harry, gaily, as they steered the pirogue back out into the channel. "I can even pretend to be put out that having accepted his invitation I arrived to find him absent."

"I don't care what excuses you use, your honour, he'll still wonder why you took your time in gettin' there."

"Let him," Harry replied, chucking his servant some fruit he'd lifted from the table. "All I have to do is put you up on a horse, let you trot, and the reasons for the delay will be self-evident."

Harry landed the pirogue upriver after dark, in the residential area outside the city walls, then used the palisade to guide him to his destination. As they made their way through the now dried-out earth outside the northern wall his eyes were searching for the gaslit beacons that would identify the Hôtel de la Porte d'Orléans. He was close before he realized that, unlike the other taverns, they were unlit, that the whole building, apart from a few candles, was in darkness.

"Somethin's a bit rum here, your honour."

"You're right," Harry replied softly.

He stopped behind a tree, examining the hotel which lay across

the dirt-track road. The lights from the nearby buildings illuminated the front, but that only served to underline how quiet it
was. There were no girls plying their trade, nor customers arguing for their services. The double front doors were shut tight and
any noise they heard came from other establishments.

"Call it instinct, Pender, but something tells me that a knock
at the front door would be a bad idea."

"I make you right, your honour. Do you want me to get round
the back an' have a look?"

"Let's both go."

The forlorn look of the place was underlined by the view from
side and rear. The veranda was silent, the long set of windows
that led out into the garden shuttered, with only a faint glimmer
coming from Hyacinthe's private apartments above.

"Happen they've been shut down, Capt'n."

"No happen about it," Harry said. They walked gingerly up
the stairs which led from the garden and Harry tried one of the
windows. It was locked and he stepped back as he heard the jin-
gle of Pender's picks.

"No noise," said Harry, unnecessarily.

"There's a latch as well as a lock," Pender replied, pulling out
his thin-bladed knife. He inserted it between the two doors and
raised it slowly, a grin splitting his face as he felt the resistance of
the latch. Gently he eased it up and opened the door, moving it
faster at the least hint of a creak to minimize the noise. The thick
drapes were only half drawn, and once through them they were
plunged into near total darkness. Pender put his hand on Harry's
chest for a moment, until their eyes became adjusted to the small
amount of available light, then inched his way across the room to
the foot of the main staircase.

"Walk up near the wall, your honour," he whispered. "They
creak less there."

Harry nodded and went ahead of him, feeling rather foolish.
The sudden thought struck him that de Carondelet had shut the
place down for some misdemeanour, that he'd open a door and

find Hyacinthe and his brother calmly playing cards. Yet by the top of the stairs he was wondering if danger threatened. The silence was all pervasive, too overwhelming to be a recipe for a happy outcome. They stopped outside the door to Hyacinthe's private apartments. The door was very slightly ajar and Harry pushed it wider. The silhouette at the untidy desk perplexed him for a moment, then the figure turned slightly and he recognized James. That brought an immediate feeling of relief. At least he was safe. But what was his brother doing sitting at Hyacinthe's desk, going through what looked like her papers?

"James?"

He spun round, his face fearful. "Harry, you're back."

There was no joy in either the voice or the manner. "Where's Hyacinthe, and why in God's name is the place shut up and dark?"

James stood up as Harry closed the gap between them. "Don Cayetano shut it down."

"Why?"

He took Harry's arm and led him to the door that connected the salon to Hyacinthe's bedroom. He tightened his grip on his brother's arm as they passed through the open door. The coffin lay on two trestles in the middle of the room, a set of candelabra at either end. Both men walked forward slowly.

"I'm sorry, Harry," said James, "so desperately sorry."

Harry Ludlow fell to his knees before the body of Hyacinthe Feraud.

CHAPTER THIRTY-SIX

"SHE WAS left to be found, Harry," said James. Her body had been discovered on the edge of the road, right by a swamp. But he didn't go on to say how easy it was to feed a body to the alligators in this part of the world, which made murder, and the disguising of the deed, very easy.

"She was last seen alive in the Calle Borgana, and it was assumed she was making her way back to the Porte d'Orléans. No real attempt was made to avoid her discovery. It's as though the torture was meant as some kind of warning."

Again James was dissimulating for Harry's benefit. Clearly Hyacinthe had been killed in one place, then left in another. Harry sat, his head bowed over his knees, eyes closed and hands clasped. He said little since he had seen Hyacinthe's mutilated body, except to emit groans of despair. James had left him alone for a while, with a huge glass of brandy, and talked quietly to Pender, but time was short, with the funeral due to take place at eight. His brother had to decide what he was going to do. He thanked the Lord that Harry hadn't seen her before the embalmer had made good some of the ravages on her face and body, hadn't been present when one of de Carondelet's watchmen had examined her and made a cavalier remark about her death being that which commonly fell to whores. James had been tempted to strike him. Harry would have killed him on the spot.

"The tongue," croaked Harry.

"Yes."

"Just like Rodrigo."

James patted him on the shoulder, then drew his hand away as Harry sat up suddenly. His face was drawn and grey.

"Pender asked me on the way downriver why I cared about what happened on the *Gauchos*. I didn't really. I made some flippant answer about skewering San Lucar de Barrameda. But I care about this, James."

"Of course."

"But what am I to do about it?"

"This is hardly the time."

"We have no time, James. We must get *Bucephalas* out of here as soon as we can."

"Pender told me."

"Did you get the men off the ship?"

"Yes. Ten at a time to begin with, but the Dons have ceased to count."

Harry made a gesture, as if to say ten was enough. His waving hand disturbed the papers on her desk.

"Why were you going through these?"

"Something Bernard said. She went to see the pirate Charpentier in his cell, claiming that he was an ex-lover. Hard to believe that after all this time they plan to garrotte him in a day or two. Anyway, it was hard to refuse such a request."

James paused, sighed slightly, then continued. "Bernard said that she briefly entertained de Chigny the day we went to the house near the Calle des Ursulines. There were other trips into the city, unexplained ones, made on foot. She wore a veil on several occasions. I was trying to find out where she went."

"And did you?"

"No. But I found something else."

James stood up and went to the desk. He came back with the first note Harry had received from McGillivray. Harry looked at the crabbed capital letters, deliberately used to obscure the correspondent.

"Bernard told me that the note he delivered didn't come from

McGillivray. It came from Hyacinthe. She must have used this one to copy out the lettering. There's no good time to say this, Harry. She instructed him to lie to us."

Harry's body shook violently. His hands clasped together hard as he tried to control himself.

"What time did you say the burial would take place?"

"Eight o'clock."

Harry stood up and walked towards the bedroom door. "I can't go, James. I don't want anyone to know I'm back. I only have a limited time and there's a great deal to do. So leave me alone for ten minutes while I say my private goodbyes."

He shut the door firmly as James turned to exchange a worried look with Pender.

"Do you think he'll forgive me, Pender?"

"Yes, your honour. But I don't know that he'll forgive himself."

Harry and Pender slipped out of the house, in darkness, before the servants rose, and took up a position from which they could watch the funeral cortège depart. De Coburrabias arrived, with a small military escort including a drummer, ready to lead the procession. James took up a position by his side. Harry saw Saraille, the newspaperman, hovering about, very much in the manner he had adopted when Hyacinthe was alive. The camaraderie of the people who shared the district was shown by the number who emerged from the other taverns, even the mean-looking shacks that stood furthest from the road. The catafalque was a highly decorated flat-bed cart drawn by hand, onto which the servants of the Hôtel de la Porte d'Orléans loaded the heavy coffin. They were followed out of the building by the girls Hyacinthe had employed, all brightly dressed, which would have accorded with her wishes. Both groups then took up station behind, the drum began its funereal beat, and the chief mourners led the procession toward the city gate. There they would loop through the

streets, before exiting to the south-west and the consecrated burial ground. Harry waited till the last faint beat of the drum faded
before moving out and heading towards the rear of the hotel.
Pender opened the window again and both men entered the silent,
empty building.

The ground was dry enough to dig a proper grave. De Coburrabias spoke a few words after the priest had finished, describing
his regard for Hyacinthe and his sorrow at her death. Then he
lifted up some shingle and threw it into the grave. Bernard was
next, followed by a line of servants and girls from the hotel. James
stood for a while after they had gone, watching as the gravedig-
gers loaded the heavy rocks on to the top of the lid, weights that
would keep the coffin in place if the water table rose. When they'd
finished, and just before he departed, he threw in a single flower
for Harry.

He was gathering a few personal possessions that Pender hadn't
already packed, wondering whether he should take some memento
of Hyacinthe. He glanced at the portrait at the top of the bed. It
was too large for his cabin, but there would be a place for it at
Cheyne Court, his house in Kent, or even in the drawing-room in
London.

"Take that picture out of its frame, Pender. I will want to take
it with us when we leave."

As Harry turned away, to go back to the desk, his servant
climbed onto the bed and lifted the frame clear. The bottom section, where it had been hidden by the bedhead, was covered in
dust, which flew up in the air. Using the coverlet to wipe it clean,
he had to suppress a sneeze as he laid the portrait face down on
the floor. His knife sliced at the canvas, as close as possible to the
point where it joined the wooden frame. Once free he rolled it up.
Looking around he saw the leather case that contained the other
pictures, the ones from the *Gauchos*. Quickly he unbuckled it

and slipped Hyacinthe's portrait inside. He knew his Captain wouldn't want the others, but this was too painful a moment to ask him what he should do about them. When he went back into the salon, Harry was at the desk writing a note.

"Do you remember where McGillivray's house is located?"

"I reckon I do."

"I want you to deliver this note."

"You think he's back, then?"

"If he's not, Pender, he won't be far behind."

"D'you mind if I ask what you're sayin' to him?"

"No. I'm thanking him for his assistance." Pender produced a small grunt, half humorous, half disapproving. "I've also pointed out to him my need to stay out of de Carondelet's clutches. Details of what happened on my journey north would be as damaging to him as they are to me."

"In other words, steer clear."

"Precisely."

Harry had to admire the way that Saraille controlled his excitement. The story of his trip upriver, and what he thought had happened in his absence, would set the whole of New Orleans on its ears. But the editor scribbled the details as though Harry was describing a christening. He asked several questions to check the details, each slight change notated. Finally he looked up.

"This is an extraordinary tale, almost unbelievable. You realize, Captain Ludlow, that you're saying that someone close to de Carondelet is a murderer, who has killed both at sea, and here in the city."

Harry nodded. "And a thief, Monsieur Saraille, albeit a failed one."

"I'm not sure I can print either without ending up in a cell."

"But if you had proof you could."

The editor shook his fat pink jowls. "How to find it?"

Harry put as much conviction into his voice as he could, hoping that Saraille wouldn't detect his uncertainty. "I intend to find it, and when I do it will be yours to use as you see fit. Can you get in to see Charpentier?"

"Why?"

"Hyacinthe Feraud went to see him while I was away, saying that they had been lovers. She had to have another reason."

"Other than the one she gave?"

That produced a grim smile. "She made no secret of her past, Monsieur. Made no attempt to disguise her attachment to Thankful Tucker, or anyone else. The excuse she gave when she went to visit Charpentier was a lie. What makes me curious is why."

"De Carondelet might not agree. He and I don't often see eye to eye."

"The one thing he fears is trouble on the streets. Tell him that a statement from Charpentier might avoid that. The last words of a Frenchman condemned to die."

Saraille sat, his hands under his knees for a full minute, his bland face betraying nothing. "I can't blackmail him, not with what you told me regarding the gold and silver. To do so would only see my presses smashed and me in gaol. My only hope is that if he refuses I could threaten to write Charpentier's last testament myself, and hint that it could be so inflammatory he'd have another riot on his hands."

"It's good of you to do this for me."

The pale blue eyes fixed on him, and Harry thought he saw just a trace of pain.

"It's not for you, Monsieur. They call people like Hyacinthe Feraud free people of colour. To me, she was merely a French Creole, and that is a far better title."

"I understand," Harry replied. Then he remembered that, as well as being enamoured of Hyacinthe, the newspaperman had, locally, many sources of information.

"Hyacinthe behaved very oddly these last weeks. Bernard said that she made several trips to the city alone. Do you think it possible to trace her movements?"

"Possible, but difficult. You have no idea what she was doing?"

"None that exceed speculation."

"That is better than nothing, Monsieur. To a man in my profession it is usually where one starts."

"Find out what she asked Charpentier and perhaps we'll know."

Pender, wearing a huge straw hat to keep off the searing late August sun, pushed the handcart along the jetty towards *Bucephalas*. He was carrying Harry's instructions as well as the family luggage. The picket by the downriver bollard, all that remained of the original guards, were busy playing cards under an awning. They didn't even look at him, and the hard glare he gave the men on deck stopped them from giving him too overt a greeting. He picked up the case containing the portraits, along with James Ludlow's easel and paints, without any sign of haste. Coming aboard he noted that he was going down the gangplank, instead of up, clear evidence of how much the river had dropped in their absence. It was like a furnace on the deck, the levee seeming to create an enclosed area where the heat was trapped. Dreaver, alerted by one of the crew, sauntered up the companionway and approached Pender, his manner and carriage almost a caricature of innocence. Harry's servant dropped the things he was carrying behind a gun carriage.

"What's the state of play in the cabin?"

"Where's the bloody Captain, Pious?"

"Safe and sound, mate, and getting ready to shift out of here."

"Thank Christ."

"So tell me what's been goin' on."

"We've been going stark crazy, that's what's happenin'. What with the heat and hardly a word for weeks, except the odd note from Mr Ludlow. Then there's rumours growing by the day that war is in the offing, all topped off by the Captain's lady bein' done in."

Pender was sympathetic, but this wasn't the time to show it. His voice, when he replied, had gravel in it. "Then it's time to stop gabbling and put our minds to what matters. Tell me about the way you're guarded."

Dreaver looked as though he was about to put Pender in his place, but clearly thought better of it.

"There's always a sentry on that gun platform above the gate-house, but you can't see him unless you go right to the starboard rail. Not that he pays much heed to us any more, he can't really see much since the river went down. He's more interested in keeping an eye out for officers. The lot on the jetty rely on him. He tips them the wink when there's someone important about, otherwise they could be asleep for all the heed they pay to guarding us."

"So I noticed, mate. They didn't even spare me a look." Pender called softly to two men to fetch the rest of the luggage then turned back to Dreaver. "How do you go for gettin' off the ship?"

"Come and go as we please now. That's what's kept us sane, though a few of the men have taken to the bottle and women in a way that the Captain won't like."

"And the cabin?"

"Fernandez sleeps there. He's out most of the day—don't ask me what he's up to, 'cause I don't know, but he's usually had a drink or two on his return. You can hear the bastard snorin' from the heads."

"Right. I'll have to speak to the lads, but I want you to get hold of anything cloth on the boat that's red, white, and blue, Captain's orders. Take it to the sailmaker and I'll tell him what to do with it."

"When are we goin'?"

"Soon, mate, very soon."

CHAPTER THIRTY-SEVEN

PENDER went below in the dark interior of the ship and was immediately surrounded by an eager crew, dying to know what, if anything, was happening. He stood by an open scuttle to take advantage of what little breeze prevailed, and put a man at the bottom of each companionway so that he could explain Harry Ludlow's orders without being disturbed.

"You got them guards the way you want 'em. But that won't stay so if you start doin' anything different. You've got to carry on in a like manner or they might sniff somethin' is up. The Captain ain't told no one he's back, and is walking around in a hat like mine which is big enough to keep sun and pryin' eyes off his face. But you'll notice how low the water is, which is what he's been waitin' for. Now, one at a time, I need you to report."

It was only the leading hands who did so, with the rest nodding as they confirmed the way they'd carried out Pender's previous instructions. Dreaver had kept the stores topped up, excepting wood and water, all paid for by James Ludlow. Every day they loosened the sails, still on the yards, their excuse being to air them, so that men aloft would excite no interest. At sundown they took them in to keep them free from the evening dew or sudden nighttime showers. With the guards growing lax, they'd raised extra sail, insisting this was necessary to avoid mildew in the locker. The need to keep a perfect deck had stood as sufficient reason continually to move the guns, thus ensuring that all the breechings operated properly. Rust wasn't a serious problem on a fresh-water river, but all the shot had been shifted and kept chipped and round.

Blocks were greased in rotation and every rope that needed tar had its full measure.

The gunner had kept everything up to the mark, wads ready and pouches filled, with a dumb show on the gun-deck so that the hands could keep their gun-laying skills honed by constant practice. The rafts he'd made to carry powder barrels were stacked ready for use, though he had balked at drilling a hole in perfectly good casks of dry powder to make them effective.

"Do it now," said Pender. "And refill the turpentine bottles."

He had a quick word with Dreaver, who got the praise he deserved, then he made his way to where the cook was minding his coppers.

"It's been hard, Pious," said Willerby, "what with the lads not knowin' what was goin' on. They're full of grub and drink, but I wouldn't say they was right up to scratch. This heat's sapped their backbone."

"Bread and biscuit?" said Pender.

"Now that is to the mark, just like the rum."

"Right, then. I can tell the Captain we're ready for the off. There's just the sailmaker."

"I heard about the red, white, and blue. That bastard Dreaver swiped two of my clean aprons. What they for?"

"You'll see, old mate."

"They asked me to take charge of their property and ship it upriver. If it is convenient, my servant will come and collect the two chests in the next few hours."

The Mother Superior gave Harry the kind of benign smile that was part of the clerical armoury. Her aged skin was translucent, evidence of a sparse, indoor existence, with brown patches on the backs of her hands, but her eyes were still youthful.

"You may come when you like, Monsieur."

"You will not be closed if it's after dark?"

"Our cathedral, the Church of St Louis the Martyr, was dam-

aged in the last fire. Until it is fully repaired we have added responsibility for the bishop's flock here in New Orleans. Day or night
there is always someone awake. I will tell the doorkeepers to admit
you to the storerooms."

"Thank you," said Harry, reaching for his money. "If I may
be permitted to make a personal request of you . . . I myself am
not of your faith, but I had a high regard for someone who was.
Hyacinthe Feraud."

The eyes first registered surprise, then dropped discreetly.

"I've been informed that burial above ground in a specially
constructed sarcophagus avoids certain risks."

"That is so, Monsieur. If the river rises and floods the surrounding countryside, the coffins float to the surface. The stones
we use to weight them down do not always suffice."

"I wouldn't want that to happen to her. Would your order
take responsibility for her remains and see them re-interred above
ground?"

"If you leave us the means to do so."

"The nature of my business keeps me moving. I would also
want her grave to be attended on a regular basis."

"And prayers, Monsieur. She must have prayers for her soul."

"Of course." The lump in his throat was so big he couldn't
continue for a moment. He held out a very heavy purse, full of
gold coins. "I would be grateful for your advice on what is
required."

"Above the cost of the sarcophagus, nothing is required, my
son. The lady you mentioned was kind to us when still alive and
has more than earned a call upon our good offices."

"I knew her to be a Catholic, but I never suspected piety."

"Hyacinthe Feraud was not pious, Monsieur. I had reason to
chide her often for not attending mass as regularly as she should.
My remonstrances bore fruit these last few weeks. Perhaps she
had a premonition of her terrible fate and wished to make her
peace with God. She was here on the night before she was killed,
to take the sacrament and say confession. For all the life she led

it is pleasing to know that she died, as near as is possible, in a state of grace."

"Confession!" said Harry. "Who took it?"

"The priest who attends to our needs." She must have spotted the look in his eye and guessed at his next question. "You will be aware that such things are sacrosanct."

"Of course," he replied, slightly crestfallen. "You said she came to mass more frequently. How many times?"

"Three or four."

"Would it be breaching a confidence to ask when?"

"No. She certainly came on the last three Fridays. That is a day of high attendance." The Mother Superior put her fingertips together and closed her eyes. "Indeed, a constancy on Fridays can lead to ultimate salvation."

"And when she attended mass, she would, like all the ladies, wear a veil."

"Of course."

Harry recalled the first night they'd met, and Saraille's comment about the dinner he'd just attended with de Carondelet and his officers and magistrates, delivered across a crushed pillow. "They hate each other. The only time you'd find them together would be in church."

"Does the Barón de Carondelet worship here?"

"With the cathedral under repair, everyone does."

"His officers?"

"All the leading citizens of the town, French and Spanish."

Harry stood up, leaving the purse on the table. "I will leave you this. If you do not need all of it for Hyacinthe, please use the rest for the poor."

"May God go with you."

Harry walked out into the street, to find James waiting for him.

"Did you ask Bernard which days Hyacinthe went out in her veil?"

"Fridays."

Harry nodded and moved off. James waited to make sure no one was following him before setting off after him.

"Noticing someone in church is like seeing a person eat," said Saraille, quite upset at the way Harry had berated him for not mentioning it. "Even Hyacinthe. So commonplace that it does not justify a remark."

"But she didn't go to church regularly?"

"Nor, I'm afraid, do I."

"But you were there last Friday?"

"Yes. I said so, didn't I?"

"Did Hyacinthe talk to you?"

Saraille's eyes dropped, making it unnecessary to answer the question. Harry wondered if he knew how much she'd disliked him, or the steps she took to avoid him.

"She was busy elsewhere."

"Who with?"

"Everyone. That particular mass is a very social occasion, a place to gossip."

"Think."

Saraille needed to pause. For his own self-esteem he couldn't give the impression that if he had taken his eyes off her it wasn't for long. Nor could he bring himself to say, too overtly, that she hadn't spoken to him.

"The officers, de Chigny, de Coburrabias, even San Lucar de Barrameda. She had a few words with the magistrate de Lovio."

"Anyone else?"

"A couple of ship's Captains."

"Which ones?"

"You wouldn't know them," Saraille snapped. Then he obviously had a thought, since he snapped his fingers. "You might, though. They were the masters of the troop transports that you ran into off Balize."

"Are they still here?"

"They've been to Havana and come back again, more than

once. It's their regular route. Normally they carry cargo, not men."

"Anyone else?"

"I saw her help that Cuban, Fernandez."

"Help him?"

"He was drunk, which was a bad idea with de Carondelet around. The Governor was doing his greetings at the main entrance. Hyacinthe took him out through the transept."

"Thank you. Now what about Charpentier?"

"I was given twenty minutes with the poor fellow. He is very cast down, and cannot understand the reason why they want to garrotte him. He had hoped for freedom. It is all the doing of San Lucar de Barrameda, who wants to use his execution as an example. De Carondelet is, I think, less bloodthirsty."

"When?"

"Tomorrow morning," Saraille replied sadly.

"Did you ask him about Hyacinthe's visit?"

"It was difficult. They had a guard with us all the time. It seems she asked him about the way he was captured."

"San Lucar de Barrameda?"

"No. He was taken by some men from the *Navarro*, but not the Captain. Once he'd got inside the bay the pirates scattered, using the bayous too narrow for the galleys to follow. De Barrameda ordered his men to pursue them in boats, taking one himself. He didn't come back aboard till the next day. When he returned he ordered that Charpentier be suspended in a cage on the deck."

"Tell me, Monsieur Saraille, how do the local French population feel about this man's execution?"

"Angry, Captain Ludlow. Very angry. Had it happened right after his capture, then perhaps it would have been seen as a just reward, but not now, nearly two months later. Charpentier might be a rogue. He is most certainly a thief. But he has never used violence, indeed he has the reputation of always being polite to his victims. Myth, of course, partly of his own creation, which is that of a gentleman who only robs rich Spaniards. But that is what is going to see him garrotted. It is to lay that myth that he is to die, not for his crimes."

The soft tap at the door made Saraille jump and his face went grey as it creaked open.

"All set, Capt'n," said Pender, as he slipped through the narrow gap. "The chests are on the cart."

"Good," Harry replied. He turned back to Saraille as Pender took station behind him. "It seems to me, Monsieur, that if the people are angry they should let de Carondelet know."

The editor's jowls shook as he responded in the negative. "He has extra troops on the streets, Monsieur. And his watchmen. He's expecting trouble."

"I am no more keen to disappoint him than your Creole settlers. What if I were to take care of some of those troops, so that the good citizens of New Orleans could express themselves?"

Saraille knew from experience just how expressing themselves would be manifested. "A mob has its own logic, Captain Ludlow. It is not always easy to manufacture a riot."

"Come along, sir. If anyone knows the people who can whip up the populace, you do."

"They would need an excuse. Charpentier, much though he is seen as one of us, might not be enough."

"What if you were to tell them the story I told you? How would they feel if they knew that in the Spanish administration there was a murderer and a thief who might never be brought to justice, while one of their number faced death just as an example?"

"I could only print that story if I was absolutely sure of his name."

"Print the rest, Saraille, leave just the name out. Show it to those who can whip up a mob."

"The name, Monsieur."

Knowing he was lying made Harry uncomfortable, but not enough to stop him. "Tell them you will have it by morning, before Charpentier is due to be garrotted."

"That might not be enough to convince them that anything I say is true."

Harry turned to Pender and spoke quietly. His servant reached inside the bag he was carrying over his shoulder and handed him one of the ingots which he'd received from Lampin. Harry laid it on the desk. The candlelight glinted on the twin crests of Spain and New Orleans.

"Then show them this, Monsieur, and bid them use it, with what wisdom they can muster, for your cause."

Outside, once they'd joined James, Pender couldn't resist asking the obvious question.

"I wish you joy, your honour," he said, "but how in hell's name are you going to name the man who's done murder?"

The voice that replied held all the despair that Harry felt.

"I can't. I knew long before I ever talked to Saraille that the task is impossible. I don't have time unless I'm prepared to sacrifice everyone aboard *Bucephalas*."

CHAPTER THIRTY-EIGHT

DARKNESS fell quickly at this latitude. By the time the light had completely faded twenty of Harry's men, moving in ones and twos, were off the *Bucephalas*. Some carried turpentine-filled bottles, slow-match, and flints, others coiled lengths of hemp, wrapped round their bodies and covered with their shirts. Pender had unlocked the armoury and the real weapons had been replaced by the wooden replicas they'd been working on for weeks. Nothing larger than a knife or a marlinspike could be taken ashore, but cutlasses and muskets for the whole crew were concealed all over the ship. Pender was there, standing by the two chests full of gunpowder he fetched from the Ursulines. He ordered them to leave the items they'd sneaked off the ship beside the chests which he'd hidden at the back of Santiago Coquet's dancehall. The warehouse was already full of mixed groups, black, white, and coloured, drinking and dancing to the tuneful sound of three well-played, sharply strung fiddles.

Finding the rendezvous in a city so evenly quartered was simple, and on the crowded Calle Real their presence, standing in a group, raised no comment. Not so the Creole speaker that Saraille had found. A natural demagogue in the Danton mould, he stood at the street corner haranguing the crowd. Ignored initially, he soon attracted the less reputable members of the local fraternity. Mostly inebriated without being too drunk to stand, they were loud, argumentative, and gratifyingly inclined to sing.

"I think they'll do," said Harry. "The trick now is to get them to the square in front of the Governor's house without de Carondelet's watchmen interfering."

James, sent up the Calle Real to keep watch, came running through the gathering crowd. "Ten soldiers and a sergeant," he called. "With two of the watchmen in the lead."

"Walloon Guards?"

"No. Cubans, I think."

Harry turned to his men. "Four of you to stay here with my brother. James, if any soldiers come from the waterfront try and hold them up. If they're too numerous at least start a fight amongst yourselves." He counted off a dozen sailors. "You come with me, the rest join Pender."

As they made their way along the street it was nearly empty: those inclined to enjoy trouble had gravitated towards the loud speakers along the Calle Real. The other citizens, with a sure nose for an impending riot, had cleared the street.

"Two groups," said Harry. "Take one side of the road each."

The soldiers, with the watchmen a few paces ahead, were marching with fixed bayonets towards a potential trouble spot, occupying the centre of the Calle. At a command from Harry his men stopped, adopting poses of half-interested curiosity as they came abreast. The sudden attack when he whistled, delivered from two sides by men who knew their business, took the armed party completely by surprise. They were given no time to swing their muskets before the crew was in amongst them, clubbing with marlinspikes at heads that carried no more protection than a tricorne hat. The Cubans had faced crowds before, but never any as determined as this, and all the frustration of men who'd been cooped up for weeks was evident in the fury of the attack. The soldiers went down before them, dropping their weapons in an attempt to avoid the raining blows. Harry's men had been told that inflicting real wounds was not required. Their Captain wanted them to run, to spread the word that whatever had happened in New Orleans in the past, this was different. The watchmen led the way, with the now disarmed Cubans at their heels.

"Pick up the weapons and any pieces of uniform and put on your cockades!" Harry yelled as the Cubans scattered. That was mostly hats, but one, in his panic, had torn off his coat. Harry formed the men up into a column of two, as groups of curious onlookers seemed to emerge from the surrounding woodwork. Then, having attached a Revolutionary cockade to a Spanish hat, he skewered it on the tip of a bayonet, raised it high, and retraced his steps up the road.

"Charpentier, Charpentier! *Allez en enfer, Cochon du lait!*"

Harry turned and repeated the shout, waving his arms to encourage his men to do likewise. What emerged was certainly not a clear invitation for the Governor to go to hell, but it was loud, confused, and sounded French enough to make those gathered before the Creole agitator part to let them through to the centre. A loud murmur and much pointing greeted the tricolour cockades, a reminder to the French of the storming of the Bastille. As his men handed out more cockades to the crowd, Harry presented the speaker, who had stood on a barrel, with the musket and hat. *"Vive la France!"* he shouted, before slipping backwards into the mass of bodies. The noise had risen around him, so that he had to yell to be heard. But that he did, jabbing at the sky with the bayoneted musket, and exhorting his listeners to action.

"I hope you're aware of what you're about, Harry!" shouted James in his ear. He'd emerged from the back of the crowd, followed in dribs and drabs by the men he'd led. "This is bound to end in bloodshed."

James recoiled when Harry turned to face him. He'd seen the glint of battle in his brother's eye before, though nothing like the mad look that was present now. But the voice, for all that it was harsh and indifferent, wasn't loud.

"Time to get them moving, I think. Get the men up ahead with those muskets and send to tell Pender to act as a rearguard."

He plunged back into the mêlée, shouting in French. James heard the word *Bastille*, first from one throat and then from a dozen, as the crowd were whipped up into a frenzy of quasi-Revolutionary fervour. The speaker, who seized the cockaded hat, was now calling for the head of King Carlos. He jumped off his barrel and pushed his way through the crowd. A tricolour flag appeared from nowhere and was raised on a pole. News had spread through the town and groups of men were running towards them, torches aloft, eager to join in the mayhem, perhaps from conviction, more likely for sheer mischief. James had to jostle hard to get to the front. There he saw Harry, well ahead, with his armed men fanned out like the advanced guard of an invading army. Before him the street was empty, but in the distance bugles blew to sound the alarm. Suddenly Harry stopped and fell to one knee. A small party of white-coated soldiers was advancing up the street at a run. His voice carried just enough to be heard.

"Fire when I give the command. Aim either at their feet or above their heads."

"We can bring 'em down, Capt'n," shouted one of the crew.

"No! If we kill anyone they'll only turn their guns on the civilians. Let's see if we can drive them off without bloodshed."

There was a pause, before the word *Fire!* was drowned out by the simultaneous discharge of half a dozen muskets, which in the confined space between the houses made enough noise for fifty. The crowd stopped momentarily, nonplussed at this development. But when they gazed down the Calle Real, through the drifting smoke from the guns, they could see the white coats of the hated Walloon Guards as they retreated back towards the Governor's house in some disorder. Harry's hope, that gunfire in the streets, where prior to this they'd only faced sticks and stones, would unnerve even the best troops, had paid off. Nothing could have raised the spirits of the mob more, and with a yell they started to run after them, yelling and screaming insults, laughing and whooping like madmen. Harry, knowing his work was done, led his men up a side-street, letting the rioters rush by. James had to draw back into a doorway to avoid being mown down. Through the dust kicked up by hundreds of feet he saw Pender and his men bringing up the rear at a steady, disciplined pace. Once they came abreast James fell in with them, Harry doing likewise as they reached the side-street he'd used to get out of the crowd's path.

Harry stayed well to the rear as they approached the square before de Carondelet's residence. The platform on which Charpentier was to be garrotted stood right in the centre, before the windows of the Governor's quarters. The gas-lights over the doorway illuminated the white coats of the Walloon Guards. There was no disorder now. More numerous, they were standing, bayonets at the ready, to bar the passage of these malcontents. De Chigny stood before them, sword at the ready. The crowd pressed forward only far enough to hurl insults. Harry grabbed a torch and pushed his way to a point near the front. Tossed high, it arced over the heads of those before him and landed right on the execution platform. That brought forth a roar from several hundred throats and a whole stream of torches followed suit. The wooden structure, as dry as tinder, was soon fully ablaze, the flickering flames adding an infernal light to the faces of the mob.

More and more people were arriving in the confined space before de Carondelet's temporary residence. But of greater import to the men of the *Bucephalas* was the way that troops from the outlying forts, north and south, were being fetched in to beef up the defences. That didn't mean their original posts had been deserted, but they had lost part of their strength, and what was left would be concentrating on a threat from the town rather than the river. Against that, everyone on duty would be alert, and the one group that would still be at their posts, or close to them, would be the artillerymen in those stone bastions.

Santiago Coquet's dancehall was too far away from the riot to be affected, the noise of music and merriment drowning out anything from outside. They'd know, of course, since that kind of news travelled faster than fire, but few, if any, had left. The old royal warehouse backed right on to the levee, and was thus a perfect spot for Pender and his party to make their preparations. James was sent to the rim of the embankment to make sure that the guard on the jetty below hadn't been increased, while the rest spliced the short pieces of rope together to make decent lengths. Others were drilling holes with their knives and slipping slow-match into the two chests full of powder. All the time Harry was talking to Pender, issuing quiet instructions.

"For God's sake, Pender, don't let anything happen to you. I've lost enough in New Orleans."

"More than any man should," his servant replied.

"As soon as we get under way we'll lower the cutter."

Pender's reply was quite brusque. "You've said that twice already, Capt'n. If you don't get goin' them soldiers will chase off the Frenchies then start looking for someone else to get at. An' since I'm the party ashore I don't fancy that one little bit."

"Just take care," Harry replied softly. Then he turned, signalled to the four men he was taking back to the ship, and climbed up to join his brother on the rim of the levee. The first thing he felt was the easterly breeze on his face, which cooled the sweat caused by his exertions; it wasn't strong by any means, but it might be enough to extract *Bucephalas* from the anchorage. His eyes were automatically drawn to the *Navarro* and her two consorts, tied up opposite the open space of the parade ground. Presumably the alarms in the city meant that they too would be more alert than usual. If he could get close to them before they could get under way, that wouldn't aid them much. Stationary like that, he'd blow them out of the water. With luck he'd damage the lead ship before he even got close. What a pity that San Lucar de Barrameda would probably be ashore.

"The guards are fewer, but wide awake," said James, pointing down to the jetty. Harry could see that only two of the original four were still in place. They were standing by the bollard, one facing up, the other down, muskets at the ready.

"What about the one on the firestep?"

"If he's there at all, I think he's likely to be more interested in what's going on in the town."

"Well, it's time to pretend we're drunk."

Harry started singing quietly, gesturing to the others to join in. It started badly, disjointed, in an embarrassed way. But cajoled by their Captain, the shanty he'd begun to sing took on some of the sound of drunken revelry. It was not the kind of thing James could manage, so Harry advised him to stagger silently, while keeping an eye on the firestep above their heads. The guards showed no alarm at their approach. This had been a nightly occurrence since de Carondelet had given permission to go ashore. Indeed they looked at the approaching party with keen anticipation. These *ingleses,* when drunk, could be quarrelsome or generous. The former was easily attended to by a gentle swing of the musket. But the latter meant they shared their drink, and to a group of men whose pay didn't extend to much luxury the thought of a free share of their bottle made their attitude rather benign.

The crack as Harry hit the first one was followed by the dull thud of his companion collapsing under the attentions of a marlinspike. Two of Harry's men immediately went to work, dragging the coats off the pair. An anxious minute followed, in which the singing kept going by the rest had a strained quality. If the other sentry crossed from the landward side of the bastion he'd see them for certain and raise the alarm and that would make the planned escape difficult, if not impossible. Harry required a fair amount of unobserved time before he could cast off.

The men on board were wound up to a fever pitch, not knowing whether the planned escape was about to go ahead. Harry went round them all, greeting them and admonishing them to calm down and do their tasks with the minimum of noise. The topmen climbed the shrouds like ghosts, their bare feet making no sound on the horses as they edged out onto the yards. The cutter was gently tipped to one side, the water used to keep its seams tight allowed to run down into the bilges. The carpenter's rafts, with the barrels of powder attached, were lowered into the water, each with a length of slow-match cut to a calculated point. This had been decided by the gunner, who'd floated a piece of debris downriver and watched its progress till it passed the hull of the nearest galley.

Those left on deck loosed the guns, running them back in silence, then levering the port battery up to maximum elevation.

The loading drill was carried out in the same silence, with the gunner and his mates tripping barefoot over the wooden deck with wads and charges. A party was put to fetching up the small arms they would need to repel any attempt to board, cutlasses, pistols, and muskets, and James went below to set up the cockpit as a temporary hospital.

The cabin smelt of Fernandez, a mixture of sweat, garlic, and cheap cigars, and it was untidy in a way that Harry would never have allowed. Dreaver came in, carrying the things Pender had fetched aboard that morning, including the portrait case. Harry ignored that and his sea-chest, grabbing instead at the untidy package lashed to James's easel containing the long frontier rifle. Slipping it out he began to load it quickly, ramming home the ball viciously.

"Put this where I can get it, Dreaver, somewhere close to the wheel."

"Aye, aye, Captain. Everything is just about in place."

"Right. Signal to the men ashore to cast off."

"They should lower the cable into the water, or the splash might be heard."

"Well said," replied Harry. "Send someone down with a line to help them."

Dreaver ran out. Harry was about to follow when he saw the case lying there. Action had allowed him to block out the pain of his loss: it came flooding back now. He knew he had no time to spare for such an indulgence but he couldn't resist opening the buckle and extracting the paintings. He threw the two that they'd taken out of the *Gauchos* onto the foot-lockers and gingerly began to unroll the one that had come from Hyacinthe's bedroom. It was a bad idea. The sight of her enigmatic smile, which seemed to be there only for him, depressed him utterly. That was cast aside too, but more gently, before he walked out of the cabin door and up onto the quarterdeck.

"Damn my eyes," said Dreaver, leaning over the side. "There's that sod Fernandez."

"Belay," called Harry to the men lifting clear the cable, in what could only be described as a shouted whisper. Then he ducked beneath the bulwarks. One sight of the ship's Captain on his own deck and even a dolt like Fernandez would guess that something was amiss. Harry tapped the knife that was stuck in Dreaver's belt. "Get down that damned gangplank. Those two dressed as sentries will never fool him. If you can't get him aboard without making a noise chuck him in the river."

Dreaver was only halfway to the jetty when Fernandez's shout rent the air. One of the men so badly disguised as a sentry ran forward and took a wild swing. He hit him, but not hard enough to knock him down, and instead of trying to run, Fernandez, still yelling, made for the gangplank, as if by his own efforts he could stop what was taking place. If he'd been unsteady on his feet before he took a blow he was doubly so now. The idea of pretending he was drunk was not an option. In darkness, with the tops full of waiting men, Harry dismissed the thought that he could engage in bluff.

"Cast off that damned cable," he shouted, "and the one at the stern, and get back aboard."

The thick rope was off the bollard in a flash, dropping into the river with a huge splash. Those on deck left the guns and ran to their stations as the orders rang out. The shore party pounded along the jetty, since by casting off the bow the ship's head would edge away from the shore, while the wind would push her forward, putting a strain on the stern cable. Harry, by the taffrail, couldn't see the firestep on the bastion but he heard the first ragged volley of musket shots aimed at the topmen, and the cry as one was hit. Looking aloft he saw, silhouetted against the starry night sky, the struggling feet of the wounded sailor, who'd obviously had the wit to grab hold of something.

"Get a line round that man."

Dreaver's voice floated up from below. "Stern cable's too tight, Capt'n. She won't budge."

"Axes," Harry yelled. "And you on shore, get back aboard."

Three men appeared beside him, the first axe flashing at the thick rope before he stopped running. Harry grabbed his rifle and moved to the opposite side of the ship.

"Gunner, get a man over the side and fire those barrels. Cast them off as soon as they're ready."

Jumping onto the bulwark by the mizzen shrouds he looped one arm through them so he could balance and fire the weapons. The embrasures of the bastion, and the firestep, were easily visible, their shapes black against the light from the torches behind. He hoped and prayed that in the summer heat the Spaniards had not kept their furnaces alight. The rumble of a gun carriage on stone mingled with the steady beat of the axes, and the gunners above ran out their cannon. At the same time several heads appeared, muskets poking forward, each with a topman in its sights. Harry fired off the rifle, aiming for the very top edge of the thick wall. With the shipping moving very slightly the ball didn't hit anything, probably going right over their heads. But the crack alarmed them enough to cause a swift withdrawal.

The trio who'd been on the jetty leapt onto the deck. Fernandez was bundled unceremoniously back, collapsing in a heap, the men too busy casting off the ropes that held the gangplank to pay him any attention. They succeeded in loosening them just as the distance opened between the ship and the shore, and it dropped into the river. Harry hauled his yards round, and put his wheel down hard in an attempt to keep *Bucephalas* close inshore, away from the point at which the great forty-two-pounders could take aim on his hull. At the same time he had men with capstan bars ready to pole him off if he started to scrape the shore. Ahead de Barrameda's galleys were coming to life, with men on the deck pointing to *Bucephalas*, while others, more efficient, were rousing out those men needed to get under way.

The first forty-two-pounder ball whooshed through the rigging and hit the river right by his larboard main chains, sending up a great fount of water. If he'd needed to be told how dangerous it was to haul away from the shore, that one shot would have underlined it. If one of those balls wounded a mast he would be in serious difficulties. He kept his head pointed straight towards the still berthed galleys, his heart sinking slightly to see that the one closest already had some of its oars in place. His plan was unravelling fast: he'd hoped to get under way before the land-based gunners noticed anything—once close to de Barrameda's ships, with one already damaged and drifting, those fortress cannon would risk hitting his own and probably cease firing. He'd then intended to sail past the unprotected sterns of the galleys, taking them and rendering them useless before they could mount an effective defence. But that wasn't going to happen. At least one, perhaps all three, were going to be mobile, with the advantage of manoeuvrability in the confined waters. The wind wasn't strong enough to allow a square-rigged ship to nullify that, and nothing had yet happened to the downriver bastion that Pender was supposed to attack.

He saw the gap open up between the jetty and the nearest galley, as the oars dipped in reverse to take it away from the shore. The Captain of the next ship was busy hauling his stern round so that he could bring the cannon in his bows to bear on *Bucephalas*. It was a shrewd move, designed to trap Harry Ludlow between at least two arcs of fire whatever he did. The four barrels released by the gunner were drifting away from the shoreline, and might well be too far away from their intended target to do any harm.

"Man the bow chasers and the larboard guns. And carronades. If you don't take out that moving galley first time, we might as well strike."

Another ball whooshed over their heads, cutting through several ropes on the way, fortunately none of them vital. A block swung down, and with no netting rigged it caught one of Harry's gunners right on the shoulder, breaking bone. He fell to the ground just as a great explosion rent the air. The sky downriver was lit up by a great flash, as the second of Pender's charges, laid against the gatehouse door, went off, triggered by the explosion of the first.

"Gunners stand by," Harry shouted, as the din subsided. "To larboard, fire as you bear."

CHAPTER THIRTY-NINE

THE GALLEY still tied to the jetty opened fire, guns aimed high to damage the rigging. Harry's bow chasers, which went off simultaneously, were directed at the hull. A galley had to be light in its construction, to make it easy to row, while its interior strength was lessened by the need for the oarsmen to work and move. The weak spots would be at bows and stern, where the planking joined the timbers connected to the kelson. Spring those, and there was little in the way of cross-bracing along the length of the ship to keep them in place. Both vessels had the smallest of targets to aim at. Not so the larboard galley, now out in deeper water. He had nearly the whole length of *Bucephalas* in his sights, and with a swift dip of the oars on either side he could alter the angle of his fire to bring it to bear on exactly the point at which his cannon would do the most harm. Harry couldn't ignore the galley ahead, but he knew the other one to be the most dangerous, since he was moving so slowly that adjustments to range and direction were child's play, and any attempt by him to swing round to reduce his profile would bring his bows out into the firing pattern of the forty-two-pounders in the fortress.

The first of the gunner's floating barrels went off. It was too far from anything solid to do more than drench a few sailors, but it had the unforeseen effect of concentrating minds downriver on it instead of *Bucephalas*. Harry saw the gunners who should have continued reloading hanging over the prow, gesticulating, trying to draw their commander's attention to the spluttering trace of burning slow-match which was easily visible in the darkness, then his mind was dragged back to the danger he was in as the other galley, out in deeper water and having steadied itself, let fly with both guns. The whistling sound of bar-shot had him craning his neck—two lengths of metal fixed by a chain was lethal in the rigging.

The short range worked in Harry's favour, since the chain had little time to spread itself, but it was still effective, one set slicing the slings for the main-yard, the other cutting through the forestay at the foremast. Taut rope burst asunder, the lower end whistling across the foredeck. That it failed to decapitate anyone was a miracle. The very end whiplashed, then cracked against one of the twelve-pounder guns, demonstrating its force by shifting more than a ton of metal sideways. Apart from that one weapon all his cannon were trained forward and ready to engage the galley to larboard. Harry gave the command and the first nine-pounder fired, its discharge the signal for the next gun in line. The broadside rolled down the side of the ship, the discipline so perfect it was hard to credit that his men had been idle for months. The carronades sang a louder tune, a deep rumbling roar very different from the nine-pounders' sharp crack, and without a sea swell the firing platform was as good as *terra firma*. Given the age and experience of his gun captains, honed over many months of constant practice, it wasn't surprising that they found the target.

Not that they looked themselves. As soon as each weapon was fired, recoiling back inboard, the crew stepped forward to reload. Sponges were inserted before the gun was stationary, cleaning out the dirty cartridge fragments. With the gun brought up short by its breechings, other crew-members stepped forward with the cartridge and the wad, rammed them down the barrel with venom. Then came the ball, and as that was rammed down the barrel, the gun captain pricked the cartridge by ramming a thin wire through the touch-hole, then, from the horn he wore round his neck, he sprinkled in a drop of powder. The whole crew, except him, was on the ropes, ready to pull the weapon back up into its firing position. Crowbars and handspikes were used to trim the aim, stuck under the carriage and trapped on the deck, levering the heavy wood and metal. Squinting along the barrel, the Captain called out his orders, held up his hand when satisfied, then pressed a length of burning slow-match to the powder around the touch-hole. A fizz lasting less than a second was followed by a great orange flash as the ball was blasted from the barrel, hurtling to bring death and destruction to its target. The whole exercise was completed in just under a minute.

A carronade ball, nearly four times the size of the nine-pounders', had raked one side of the galley, splintering oars, the pieces flung as deadly shards in all directions. Over the flat river water Harry heard the screams from below as men were struck by the wood of the great sweeps that suddenly jumped in their hands. The decorated prow went completely, the ball carrying on to wreak havoc on the quarterdeck. Another struck just below the bulwark, slewing the galley round just as the two cannon in the bows fired. They completely missed *Bucephalas*. Great chunks of the earth from the levee flew upwards, and the balls, ricocheting, leapt up into the air, carrying on towards the buildings at the rear.

No sooner had Harry's rear gun fired than the first followed, in the kind of assault that made the Royal Navy such a feared opponent. The Spaniards, if they'd seen action at all, would never have experienced anything like it, a maelstrom of shot and flying wood that, with the accompanying noise, made even strong men cower for safety. There was no respite; given only a single target, there was no point at which one or more guns were not raking the enemy deck. Concentration, on such occasions, tended to be replaced by self-preservation and panic.

Bucephalas shuddered as the ship downriver, having managed to get her guns reloaded, let fly at point-blank range. The second of the gunner's floating barrels went up at the same time, right by the bow, blowing apart the man trying to pole it clear. As the waterspout fell back to give a clear view, Harry saw that the galley had split in two, right down her whole length, and the strakes of the planking gaped open like a dragon's jaws. Water poured into the bilges, taking the vessel down by the head. Men were jumping for the quay as the weight of the guns, running forward, added to the list. They would not drown, since the depth under the keel was not even enough to wet the base of the masts, but it was heartening to see that one of Harry's enemies was now out of the battle. The larboard galley was now coming abreast of him and that reversed the previous advantage. Not only was the Captain faced with a rate of fire he couldn't match, but aimed right at his bows were the entire massed guns of a far more formidable ship. He tried to get clear by pulling back, but that only added to his woes as the imbalance in his rowing strength, caused by the ball from the carronade, swung him broadside on.

Never was the discipline of Harry's crew more evident. There was no hint of excitement, or of firing off the guns in a hurry. He watched each gun layer bending, taking his time, aware that the target thus set couldn't fire anything but muskets in reply. Harry went forward to supervise, his hand raised. From the first gun to the last he called for each shot, watching as most of the side of the galley disappeared before he'd reached halfway. To put a pair of carronade balls into such a target was murderous, a fact apparent to the Spaniards, who were either trying to get below or jump over the blind side. Neither course proved safe as the solid iron smashed into their ship. The impact was so great the galley nearly rolled over, her mast dipping perilously close to the water. Anyone on that side would have been driven under. But the men below probably fared worse, as the metal ripped through the planking. With nothing much to impede their progress, the balls smashed through to the larboard planking of the ship, so that it was holed on both sides.

The men of the *Navarro*, still tied to the jetty, stern out to the quay, suddenly realized what was coming their way. The shock would be total, since Harry surmised that with their two consorts in action they'd probably not expected to engage. Unfortunately, as Harry's eyes swept the crowded deck, there was no sign of San Lucar de Barrameda. He slept ashore, but his officers were there, trying to stem the tide of their men rushing for the bows and a chance of safety. Not even the stern chaser gunners had stayed at their posts. In order to pass the ship ahead Harry had to leave the safety of the shore for the area covered by the fortress guns. Much as he wanted to sink the *Navarro* she was more important as a shield for *Bucephalas* once he had slipped across her stern. He manned the guns as though the worst fears of those who'd deserted their posts were about to be realized. On an almost deserted deck, the officers had lined up, with a few youngsters working frantically, if haphazardly, to load one of the stern cannon.

The first forty-two-pounder fired as soon as Harry put the helm down and showed the long beak of his bowsprit. He knew that he had to face more: these were artillerymen, soldiers who did nothing else but train to discharge these guns. The angle of aim was such that only two could be brought to bear. That was small comfort in a situation where only one, placed in a delicate spot, was enough to sink him. The ball missed, churning up the water ahead, but the man who aimed the second cannon had better luck. He tried for the stern of the ship, just below the waterline. A true hit would have taken away Harry's rudder, something which would have rendered escape impossible—unable to manoeuvre Harry'd never get away from the shore. It missed that vital target, but it struck the hull with such force that the whole ship vibrated. The sound of wrenching, tearing wood came from below as the ball passed down towards the bilges, its path marked by the way *Bucephalas* shuddered each time metal made contact with wood, and she slewed sideways before coming to rest.

"Dreaver!" Harry shouted. "My compliments to the carpenter and would he find how much damage we've sustained below. You might ask him to look at the after cabins if he has time."

Mentally he was counting off the seconds as the great guns reloaded. He needed to know how good they were, since that would tell him how many salvoes he'd have to face. Too many and he'd never get clear without terminal damage, but if he suffered, perhaps, only two more, then providing the Spaniards didn't get lucky, he might make it. While these thoughts ran through his mind *Bucephalas* began to cross the *Navarro*'s stern. For all the peril of his own situation, he had to admire the stoicism of the men who'd stayed aboard the galley. They were looking down the loaded muzzles of a row of cannon that spelt certain death. But not one of them so much as ducked his head. If Harry had been wearing a hat, he would have lifted it in their honour.

The youngsters had managed to haul the stern chaser up into its firing position. One slip of a lad, probably a servant, who couldn't be more than ten years old, put the slow-match to the touch-hole. The cannon roared out and shot back, sending the makeshift crew flying in all directions, and the ball whistled harmlessly overhead, passing under the fore course to land in the river. His gun captains were looking at him, awaiting the order to reply. Harry shook his head. He hadn't come across much in the way of honour in New Orleans, but he was seeing it now. He could not bring himself to give the order that would result in these brave souls paying the ultimate price.

His reverie was rudely broken by the next forty-two-pounder ball, which whistled past his ears and hit the trunnions on one of the larboard guns. The effect was startling as the nine-pounder was smashed against the bulwark with such force it went straight through. The breechings left behind, pulled by the weight of the gun, ripped out a ten-foot section of wood and carried that down into the muddy waters. But not all the debris followed. Pieces of the gun carriage, lumps of heavy wood, studded with bolts, spread in all directions, taking out the entire gun crew. Men were thrown in a wide circle, every one suffering multiple telling blows from more than one flying object. One wheel cut the swabber near in two, carrying the parts over the side into the river. The gun captain took a great chunk of timber low in the groin, and that lifted him from his side of the deck to the other. He was dead before he landed. Smashed bodies lay all around, too stunned to scream, some separated from legs and arms. The gun crews on both sides were yelling wildly, slapping their bodies in panic, till they realized that the blood and gore that covered them from head to foot belonged to others. The next ball landed a few seconds later, still aimed at the stern, but the gunlayer had not done enough to increase his range and the ball hit the river at an acute angle. By the time it reached the ship's hull it had lost all of its force. With luck, with his bowsprit well past the *Navarro*, he'd only have to face one more salvo, and that would expose the gunners in the fortress to the risk of hitting their own vessel.

A sharp crack in his ear, and the sudden gouge that appeared in the deck behind him just as he gave orders to see to the casualties made him look up. A party of Walloon Guards had taken up a position at the top of the levee, their muskets prodding forward to play on his deck. Harry called to the forward gunners, who, jamming their bars under the gun barrels, removed the quoins that controlled the elevation. Reaching the soldier on the rim was impossible. But Harry hoped he'd be able, at least, to give them some kind of fright.

"Remove the top of that levee, as near as you can, then reload with grape. Larboard gunners take up your muskets and keep the heads of those buggers down. All guns to fire on my command."

The broadside, as each gun went off together, heeled the ship over, so great was its force, which added marginally to the height. Great clods shot skywards, completely covering the soldiers, the weight of the earth dropping on their heads, forcing them downwards. Musket balls were sent into their midst, increasing the havoc rather than inflicting wounds. Looking ahead Harry caught his first sight of the downriver bastion, flames sprouting from the top. Perhaps Pender had set fire to the interior, either deliberately or by the use of his charges. It made no difference. With that level of conflagration, no one could work the guns. They'd be lucky to flood the magazine. Perhaps the whole edifice would go up in the air. The orange glow lit up a pair of ships berthed just offshore. Harry recognized the two merchantmen that Don Cayetano had used as transports, the ones he'd first spied off Fort Balize.

A glance back established that the *Navarro* was shielding him from the other great guns, though that wouldn't last if he continued downriver: the artillery would soon be able to fire over the deck of the galley at a target still well within range. Another salvo of musket fire swept across the deck, striking two of his men, then he saw the Walloons move along the jetty to take up a fresh firing position ahead of him. Harry rushed forward, calling for a line to be dropped from the maintopsail yard. Slung in a block it would provide the purchase he needed. Half a dozen men were sent to take the other end while he lashed the dropped line around the muzzle of the nearest nine-pounder.

"Haul away," he cried, arm raised. As the muzzle of the gun came above the level of the bulwark he shouted again, this time to belay. "Now run the gun up as normal."

The gun crew didn't ask why, nor did they need to when they realized what their Captain was about. "Some gammoning under the muzzle, then stand clear."

A shout lowered the nine-pounder onto the padding that had been placed along the bulwark. Harry grabbed the slow-match from the gun captain, squinted along the barrel at the row of white coats, and touched the hole. He then leapt for his life, pushing the curious gun crew back as he went. No one could know how the cannon would react when it fired. In fact, it shot upright. It nearly tipped off its carriage to flip back onto the deck, but after hovering for a second with its muzzle to the sky, it dropped forward with a crash. The grapeshot it had contained swept the top of the levee, just as the Walloon Guards, who'd considered themselves safe from anything but an occasional musket, shaped up for another salvo. The small metal balls scythed through the ranks like the Grim Reaper. Hardly one of their number was unaffected as they spun and fell, emitting a sort of collective scream that was loud enough to drown out all the other sounds of battle.

"*Navarro* getting under way, Captain!" shouted Dreaver.

That surprised Harry, who ran for the taffrail. The Spanish

officers, realizing that their ship was protecting *Bucephalas*, had poled the bows clear and were using the current to get themselves out into the channel. They represented no threat in themselves, but without the bulk of the ship he'd be exposed much sooner than he'd anticipated to the only weapons that could hinder his escape. He ran back to the wheel, shouting for men to get aloft and set more sail. Others were commanded to man the braces and see if by trimming the yards they could coax an extra ounce of speed out of their ship. Their Captain put the helm down, taking *Bucephalas* out into deeper water, his bowsprit aimed for the stern of the nearest merchantman, which produced an immediate increase in speed. He realized that the Mississippi current, stronger away from the shore, was working in his favour. For the first time in an age he had a chance to look around. What he saw was a scene of destruction, made more ethereal by the fire downriver. The first galley he'd attacked was wallowing, close to foundering, as she was carried downstream; the one destroyed by the gunner's barrel was also in view, now that the *Navarro* had pulled away from the jetty. The stern was high in the air, probably being held there by the cable attached to the quay.

For a short while it was silent, until a ragged volley of gun-fire from below the burning bastion reminded him of the need to provide for the men ashore.

"Dreaver, get the cutter over the side and tally off a party to go and rescue Pender. They're to make for the watergate that runs under the drawbridge. But tell them to look close to the levee first, just in case our men are trapped upriver."

The flash came first, an orange and red flame fifty yards long, then the thunderous boom. Finally the ball hit the larboard side a glancing blow that dented the planking but didn't pierce it. The ball carried on to bounce on the water three times before it sank out of sight. By that time the second gun had fired. They'd used too much powder or elevation, since it screeched across the deck all the way from stern to figurehead, the blast of air from its passing knocking men flat. How it missed the masts Harry didn't stop to consider. He began counting immediately, ticking off the seconds till the next salvo.

He barely noticed the cutter going over the side, a party of men already aboard, nor the commotion on the deck of the merchant ship. Like him, those aboard *Bucephalas* who had nothing to do stood and watched as though fate had robbed them of the power to move. Both cannon fired together, and in the split second between the flash and the arrival of the ball Harry mouthed a prayer. He held the wheel steady, cutting across the merchantman's stern, his very skin crawling in anticipation of the moment when he could put up his helm and slip to safety behind her high sides. One ball passed over to land in the river, sending up a great fount of water, the second took the top off the mizzen-mast just above the cap, slicing through the great tree trunk as if it was matchwood. The force of the ball lifted it out and up, causing it to tear at the restraining rigging. The quarterdeck was deluged with pulleys and blocks, all torn from their positions aloft. Only a miracle saved those on that part of the deck from serious injury, and many suffered minor wounds from chains and debris landing on their cowering frames. Then the mast fell over the side, in its travel causing even more damage, and *Bucephalas* yawed away from the safety of the larger ship.

"Get some lines onto that ship and haul us in close," he shouted.

Suddenly the merchantman's side was lined with shouting, gesticulating men, who tried to catch and return the grappling irons that were being cast from the privateer. Muskets already loaded, it took only a second to clear them. One iron caught the high bulwark, and Harry's men hauled on it till the ships nearly touched.

"We should be safe now, lads," he shouted.

The crash of metal striking wood drowned out his command to look to the wounded. The merchantman shuddered and rocked as she crashed into *Bucephalas*. Another salvo followed, at exactly the same range. Great chunks of wood from the far bulwarks shot up in the air, some of the deadly shards scything across Harry's deck. No one knew what that did to the crew on the merchantman, but it caught three of Harry's men still on the ropes, trying to secure *Bucephalas*. There was nothing worse on a ship's deck than shards of flying wood—the uneven edges, some razor sharp and as pointed as a stiletto, caused the deadliest of wounds as they ripped into soft flesh. Blood spurted everywhere as the men fell, writhing in agony. Harry led the rest of the crew forward at a rush, to get these unfortunates off the deck before the next salvo. There was too little time, but the gunners must have altered their weight of powder, since the next salvo landed in the water upriver.

No care could be shown to the wounded. They were dragged to the companionways and hauled down below, with Harry ordering their rescuers to stay with them. He and Dreaver dived for the bulwarks, just as the next pair of cannon balls, blasted off with a proper charge, hit the merchantman. The mizzen-mast was smashed at the base. Fortunately, when it toppled, it fell on the upriver side, clear of Harry's ship. But it was a warning. Whoever commanded that battery was so determined to sink Harry Ludlow that he was prepared to destroy the ship shielding him, plank by plank. Another salvo produced no flying splinters or wounded rigging. But it hit the caravel amidships, and from the little that Harry could judge, close to the waterline. Panic reigned aboard the Spanish vessel, as the small crew rushed from one place to the next trying to escape this unforeseen attack.

"Get a party together," Harry yelled to Dreaver, pointing towards the companionway. "We're going aboard that ship to cut her anchor cable. And I need a line to lash the wheel so that we can control her drift."

"What are you going to do with the crew?" asked Dreaver.

"I'll turf them onto our deck. At least they'll be marginally safer here."

Two more balls smashed into the merchantman's unprotected side, sending a shock wave through her entire frame. Harry knew he had to be quick. If he stayed here she would sink, leaving him with nothing but clear water between himself and those cannon. He had to get out of range, and that could only be achieved by drifting on the current. A call to Dreaver brought his men on deck. Rushing forward he led them up the shrouds, and once high enough he leapt for the deck. As soon as he landed he had to throw himself flat as another salvo hit the vessel. He felt the deck planking lift below his hands, a measure of the force with which those guns, properly ranged, could batter their target. More men followed, carrying axes, some going forward while he rushed for the wheel. The man cowering behind it was dressed well enough to be the Captain, made more likely by the ship's log he clasped to his bosom. But his hat was gone and his wig was askew.

As Harry approached he caught sight of the man's eyes, wild with fear. His injunction to get out of harm's way fell on deaf ears, and the need to lash the wheel took precedence. The ship shuddered again, her timbers groaning at the strain of the shock. The splinter came from nowhere, missing Harry by a hair's breadth, and hit the Captain, crouched behind the wheel, in the shoulder. He fell back, still clutching his log, the first cries of pain emerging from his lips. Harry turned to yell for assistance, aware that the slight feeling of movement beneath his feet meant that the ship was drifting freely. Two of his men, who'd been busy helping the original crew over the side, rushed to join him.

"He's bleeding badly, probably too much to be moved. But if we don't get him off this deck I think he'll die anyway."

Screaming with pain, the wounded man passed out as soon as they lifted him. The log dropped from his hands to the deck and Harry picked it up before rushing to the side to call down to his own deck. The gangplank, slung amidships when they'd escaped, was raised to make a platform, which at least made the passage to the deck much smoother. Harry jumped down, followed by the rest of his crew, just as the sixth salvo hit the caravel.

"Have men standing by with axes. If she looks as though she's going down, cut us clear." He threw the log at the foot of the binnacle then turned to the two men carrying the wounded sailor. "Get him below to my brother."

Ten more salvoes hit the ship, shattering the planking on the far side with enough force to inflict serious damage. And she was lower in the water, the distance between the two bulwarks sinking by the minute. Harry had climbed up the mainmast to observe the fall of shot, glad that the guns seemed to lack the elevation to overshoot the target and hit him. He also had his eye firmly fixed on the merchant ship's deck, looking for the tell-tale signs that she was about to break up. The crack of timbers below decks was soon almost a constant, and finally he gave orders to man the braces. With the sails still set, *Bucephalas*, cut free, turned easily, taking the wind on her quarter, and sailed out of range of the guns a few moments before the ship that had kept them safe broke in two and sank.

CHAPTER FORTY

AS SOON as he was sure he was safe from attack, Harry anchored and sent three lanterns aloft as a signal to Pender. He also rigged blue lights in case the Spaniards tried to come for him in small boats. Then he waited, gnawing at the thought that perhaps he'd sent his servant on an impossible mission. Aware that his pacing of the deck was attracting too much attention from the crew he ordered the barge and launch over the side then went below to see James, who was still in the now crowded sick bay. He spoke to those of his men that had the power of speech, thanking them, uttering reassuring words and the odd apology for having got the crew into this predicament in the first place, while trying simultaneously to avoid looking at the silent bodies and covered faces of the dead. James, his apron and forearms covered in blood, poured Harry a much-needed tot of brandy as he explained how things lay.

"I don't think we're in any danger of attack. Certainly not without warning. After all, we sank two of their ships already. My only worry is that we've stung their pride very hard indeed, and that tends to make Spaniards dangerous."

"Well, here's one who will be no danger to anyone," James replied, pointing to the wounded man that Harry had brought off the sunken ship.

"Did he come round, at all?"

"No, thank God. I'm ham-fisted in the medical line, brother. I rather think my ministrations might have done for him. As it is, like one or two of our own, if he doesn't get a surgeon I fear he'll expire. It's a bad wound."

"So we still don't know who he is."

"Someone told me he was the Captain."

"He was certainly dressed like one," Harry replied.

James picked up the well-cut satin coat, now ripped and blood-stained. He began to search the pockets, as well as examining the lining, looking for a clue to his identity. Harry looked around the cramped cockpit. He had three dead men in view, seven wounded, two of whom were not expected to see the dawn, as well as one poor soul who'd already gone over the side. Dreaver lifted the canvas screen, his already foxy face made more pinched by the sight and smell of so much blood.

"No sign of Pender yet, your honour. An' the boats are crewed and in the water."

"Right!"

"There's nothing here, Harry," said James, holding up the coat.

Harry was already halfway to the canvas screen when he replied.

"I think he was carrying his ship's log when I found him. I brought it on board and slung it down by the binnacle. If he is the Captain his name will be in there."

The fire in the bastion that Pender had attacked was now no more than a red glow against the arc of light that covered the city, but it served as a point for which the two boats, in line ahead, could aim, that being the route by which they expected him and his party to join. Those very embers were evidence that his task had been completed. And his orders for escape, regardless of success or failure, had been the same. Make for the bridge over the watergate, where a boat would be waiting to take them off. But Harry was worried he might have left launching the cutter too long. He'd always considered himself a lucky man but since coming to New Orleans, especially in the last few days, he was no longer certain. Try as he might, he could not keep visions of Pender dead or mutilated out of his mind. His heart felt like a lump of lead, so acute was his depression, and his eyes were closed tight.

The sudden fusillade brought them open, and, standing up, he followed the outstretched fingers of the crew, who'd ceased to row and were pointing towards the shore. That, they told him, seemed to be a mass of muzzle flashes. He was looking in the right area when it happened again, as if a battle took place. Harry observed that those nearest the city were not only more numerous, but were ranks of disciplined muskets. Those that fired in reply seemed ragged, and had the shorter flashes that denoted handguns. Even with such scanty evidence it looked like an uneven contest, and that put Harry in an agonizing position. He waited for the next fusillade, trying to count the number of guns. It was impossible, but it didn't remove the feeling that whoever was fighting to get away from the city was heavily outnumbered. Even if it was his men, of which he had no sure knowledge, could he justify putting his small party ashore, without the certainty that their number would affect the outcome? He couldn't bear the thought of leaving Pender in the lurch, but at the same time he had the safety of the ship, and the entire crew, to consider.

"Back to *Bucephalas!*" he yelled. The crew didn't react right away, quite a few giving him looks that indicated a desire to argue. It was hardly surprising that the loyalty which he'd taken for granted had considerably waned. He'd led these men into a trap in New Orleans, seemed to desert them first for his pleasure then for the pursuit of strangers' gold, and lost several of their peers trying to escape from something that should have, and could have, been avoided. But right as they might be to temper their trust, he had to command them, or nothing could be achieved. His next words were shouted so loud they were probably heard on shore. *"Row, damn you!"*

The barge spun so quickly that Harry was thrown into the thwarts. He didn't mind that, merely raising his head to check that the launch was in his wake. Then he sat upright.

"Row, lads, as if your life depended on it. We have shipmates to rescue."

The whole attitude in the boat changed, as men smiled and bent their backs. It hurt him to think that he'd sunk so low in their estimation that they could actually consider that he was planning to desert their mates. The grunts, as they hauled hard on the oars, took on a rhythm of their own. Harry was shouting orders long before he was certain he would be heard. The movement on his deck, as men who'd been set to undertake repairs dropped their tasks, was gratifying. By the time he came aboard the anchor had been catted and fished, and men were aloft to set the sails. Those who came aboard with him didn't stop to talk, but went straight to their stations. Within a minute everyone aboard knew what had happened. None as yet could figure out what their Captain intended to do about it, though his command to leave all the boats in the water indicated that they were planning some kind of cutting-out expedition.

"Dreaver, fire off those blue lights as soon as we get under way. I want Pender, at least, to know we are coming. As soon as they're fired, rig a second set."

"What do you think happened, Harry?" asked James.

"If that is Pender and his party they've been forced to retreat up the road by a superior force. Somehow, we've got to get them off."

"Mr James!" cried Willerby, who'd popped his head on deck. "One of the lads has started bleeding again, real bad."

"I'm on my way," James replied, with a deep sigh.

They had to haul the yards near fore and aft to get them to take the wind, and with the current against them progress was painfully slow. Dreaver fired the blue lights, which added a ghostly tinge to everything; ship, sails and the anxious faces of the crew. The lookouts with the sharpest eyes were sent aloft, with Harry pacing down below, knowing that to look towards the shore was pointless. The first cry from the masthead had him running up the shrouds at a pace he'd not matched since his days as a midshipman. And when he joined the lookout in the crosstrees it seemed to no avail.

"You'll see them in a minute or two, Capt'n, if'n you just follow the set of my finger."

Harry stared hard into what seemed like total blackness, with not even the starlit sky providing anything to see by. Suddenly a ripple of tiny lights flashed to larboard.

"I've got them," he cried. "That's the same as we saw in the barge. But damn it, where's the return fire?"

"Would we see that, Capt'n? They might well be firing away from us."

"I saw them earlier."

"But you was abreast of 'em, I hear. Stands to reason, if one party is lettin' off with their guns, they must have somethin' to aim at."

"What's that?" asked Harry, as a pinpoint of red light began to glow. It grew rapidly in intensity.

"Fire of some kind," said the lookout.

The first sparks flew up, visible even from this distance. Harry hoped and prayed it was some kind of signal.

"Keep your eye on it. If you think there's anything I should see, shout."

"Aye, aye, Capt'n."

Harry slid down the backstay to the deck and went to take charge of the wheel. From there he issued a string of orders regarding the trim of the sails. More general instructions followed.

"Guns both side loaded with grapeshot and run out, if you please, and men tallied off to take to the boats at a moment's notice. Lay out weapons for them as well. And put a man in the chains with a lead."

The fire, blazing merrily, was now visible from the deck. There'd been no rain in the delta for weeks and everything was tinder-dry, so it was hardly surprising that whatever it was had gone up so quickly. Harry steered well north of that, then spun round to take both wind and current. Handing over the wheel he took a telescope to the rail and leant over, his entire being concentrated on the area surrounding that patch of flickering red light.

James had come back on deck and was standing behind him.

"We lost another man, Harry. I'm sorry."

Harry looked round just long enough to reassure him that the sad news had registered, then renewed his gazing. "Got them. Their white coats will be the death of the bastards."

"Got who?"

"Walloon Guards!" Harry cried. He pointed over the rail just as the fire suddenly flared up. A huge spiral of sparks rose towards the night sky. "There, can you see them?"

The light was just sufficient to pick out the silhouettes of a mass of men against the red of the flames.

"They are behind that embankment. No one downriver can see them, but we can."

Harry put the helm over to take the ship further inshore. The only sound to be heard, as they ghosted along, was the cry of the leadsman as he reeled off the soundings, each cast evidence of the decreasing amount of water under the keel. They could see now that some kind of building, perhaps a barn, was on fire, its gaunt frame a black skeleton in the mass of flames. On deck, every gun captain was bent over his piece, squinting through the open gunports for a sight of a target.

"Blue lights," said Harry softly. "We'd best be sure."

The rockets shot into the sky and burst open, to hang there and illuminate the scene below. The combination of the fire and the rockets created a more balanced light, one in which the disciplined ranks of Walloon Guards stood out as clear as day. They should have run, but they delayed too long. By the time they'd begun to break ranks, it was too late.

"Fire!" yelled Harry. A split second later the flames of the cannon spewed out. There was nothing like this cannonade in the normal military experience, save a massed attack on a well-defended fortress. The small metal balls scythed through the serried ranks. These men suffered tenfold what their fellow soldiers had endured on the levee. They started to run before the second salvo, but the Captains had spread their aim and the result was just as devastating. Harry called for men to man the sails and they came about practically in their own length, but there was nothing much to aim at any more. Those who could run had gone; those who could stagger, a target too pitiful to shoot at. The number of bodies that lay still testified to a carnage that no body of troops, whatever their discipline and regimental pride, could support.

"Boats," cried Harry, heading for the side.

They found de Chigny walking amongst the remains of his command. His own wounds were slight, a ball having grazed his head. But the blow to his pride was massive. It was his orders that had kept their formation intact, his lack of experience that had presented Harry with such a juicy target. When his captor suggested he come aboard *Bucephalas* to have his head dressed he consented with a resigned air, the status of possible hostage obviously preferable to the idea of facing his superiors after such a defeat.

"I thought you'd forgotten all about me," said Pender, wincing as James applied alcohol to one of his several surface wounds. "We got to the watergate all right, but there was no boat. Then that army came out after us and we had no choice but to show them our heels."

"How could I possibly forget you?" said Harry, with a slight twinge of guilt.

Stretching painfully, Pender pulled the bag he was carrying over his head. "Why not, you forgot this? I reckoned that if'n you could go off without the Frenchies' presents, you could just as easy go off without me."

Harry looked into the bag, which contained the remaining ingots he'd been gifted by Lampin. "Now you know why I was so keen to rescue you."

Pender gave Harry one of those smiles that never failed to cheer him up. It seemed to light up his whole face. "Then I'm right glad I hung onto it," he said with a bitter tone that wasn't matched by his expression.

There was a degree of mutual embarrassment created by this exchange, one that Pender solved by pointing to the wounded Spaniard. "Who's this?"

"We don't know," Harry replied.

"Yes, we do," said James, reaching behind him for the ship's log that he'd found on deck. "Name's Quinterras. If there's any doubt he is the Captain we can always get de Chigny to identify him."

Harry took the book off James and having fingered the embossed lettering on the cover started to idly flick through it.

"I wouldn't bet on his identifying his own mother at the moment. He's in our cabin staring at the bulkhead."

"Sitting moping, is he?" said James. "Hardly a very soldierly way to behave."

It didn't need Pender's look to make him wish he'd bitten his tongue. Harry had been the same not 36 hours before. And his brother's feelings were clearly hurt. His lips were tight and his face drawn. Without saying a word, he spun on his heel and left the cockpit.

"Damn," said James, with feeling.

Harry walked into his cabin with the logbook still open. De Chigny was no longer staring at the bulkhead. Instead, much to Harry's annoyance, he was sitting on the foot-lockers perusing Hyacinthe's portrait. The look he got had him throwing it aside and picking up another, as if to demonstrate that he was interested in art, not the female form. Before he could unroll it, Harry thrust the log at him.

"Lieutenant, would you be so kind as to translate this for me?"

He followed Harry's finger. "June 4th, latitude 25' 38" N."

"The figures are unimportant," said Harry, testily, without explaining that they would merely confuse him, since a Spanish vessel would not use Greenwich as a meridian.

De Chigny continued sheepishly. "Rendezvoused with El Señor de Fajardo de Coburrabias off the Dry Tortugas as arranged.

Raised anchor immediately he came aboard and set course for
N.O. Winds NNE light but favourable."

"And this one, if you please?" said Harry pointing to an
inscription further down the page.

"June 6th, latitude . . ." He paused as Harry growled, then
continued, "Winds strengthened; still favourable. Extremely heavy
swell. Many troops sea-sick. El Señor convinced he heard gunfire.
No one else confirmed. Changed course due west to investigate.
Boxed area as commanded for several hours. No sighting or further incidents, resumed northerly course for N. O."

"Thank you, Lieutenant," said Harry, falling back into a chair.

James came in, prepared to apologize, but de Chigny's being
present made that impossible. The youngster, at a loss to know
what to do, unrolled the picture he'd grabbed so hastily. With that
facility of the young to recover from all misfortune, he found himself able to laugh. Harry lifted his eyes and glared at him, noticing
that the picture he held was the one with the sober-looking lady
in the mantilla, the one they'd originally found in the leather case.
James walked over and took it out of his hand, examining it closely.

"What is so funny about that?"

"You would not know the lady, Señor. But that air of piety
and chastity is really quite droll. It's just the sort of thing that El
Señor de Fajardo de Coburrabias would do."

"What connection has this lady with him?"

"Mademoiselle Chrétien ran the Hôtel de la Porte d'Orléans
when it first opened. Of course, she has risen since then."

"Risen?"

"She has been the Comandante's mistress for years. He asked
the Barón for permission to marry her. Quite rightly, that was
refused. Then he petitioned Madrid, only to receive the same reply.
Rumour has it that she had not entirely forsaken her old occupation."

"Harry . . ." said James.

"I know, brother," he said sadly. "Would you leave us alone
for a moment, Lieutenant?"

CHAPTER FORTY-ONE

HARRY sent a boat in at first light under a flag of truce. The contents were quite terse. He intended to make his way downriver the following day, quite prepared to destroy, on his passage, the meagre fortifications that lined the route. De Carondelet would know that with only one galley immediately available he was in no position to stop *Bucephalas,* just as he would know that the fortifications at Fort St Mary and Plaquemines were too weak to hold out against him. Not even Fort Balize could withstand a determined assault. The threat was not stated, but it was implied that Harry would sit across the mouth of the delta and destroy or turn back every ship that tried to exit, something he could do with impunity until a warship of greater strength could be found to dislodge him. He had prisoners aboard that he'd rather leave in New Orleans, but failing any agreement with the Governor he would keep them aboard. All of this could be avoided by the return of his chest full of treasure, plus the services of a surgeon. Such matters, he knew, required discussion and he was prepared to receive aboard the Barón's envoy. Past disputes debarred San Lucar de Barrameda. His position disallowed the Governor. Harry therefore suggested that El Señor de Fajardo de Coburrabias had the seniority and the experience to satisfy both parties. Provided the Barón was prepared to stand down the gunners on the remaining riverside bastion, he was prepared to come upriver and berth off New Orleans.

Harry tore at the seal, eager to read the reply. James was watching him closely, well aware that his brother was close to cracking

THE PRIVATEERSMAN MYSTERIES

the thin veneer of indifference he'd adopted. He'd only agreed to the invitation to Don Cayetano on the condition that he be present throughout the talks.

"Yes," cried Harry triumphantly. "He's coming."

"You still have a chance to withdraw, Harry."

"I must know, James. If I don't find out this way, I doubt I'll be able to leave." His voice rang out across the deck. "All hands to make sail."

The wreckage of the galley still hung from the jetty, but a party of men was aboard trying to salvage what they could. The *Navarro* was tied up alongside, the Bourbon flag flickering at the masthead. Harry had the same good eyes aloft watching the forty-two-pounder guns. They took at least ten men to operate and the lookout had instructions that if he observed more than four, he was to call out. He saw the party approach the *Navarro* and go aboard, de Coburrabias very prominent both in his clothing and bearing.

"Pender," said Harry, quietly. "Man-of-war fashion when he comes aboard."

"Aye, aye, Capt'n."

The *Navarro* cast off, oars dipping into the river to propel it out into the anchorage. She made quick progress, as though those on board wanted to impress the Captain of the ship that could so easily have destroyed them. Being a galley it could come right alongside with little difficulty, so de Coburrabias was not required to transfer to another boat. They shipped the oars with commendable precision and drifted into the fenders that Harry had put over the side. The gangplank was pushed out to form a bridge, and to the sound of pipes, the senior soldier of the Louisiana Territory, followed by the surgeon, was welcomed aboard. Harry had his fists balled so tight his nails were digging into his palms, but he forced himself to smile, and to bow. Then, having handed the doctor over to Dreaver, led the way to his cabin, which had been laid out for the conference. On his desk lay a chart of the Gulf of

Mexico, and under that were stacked the three paintings. Formal greetings were exchanged, as protocol demanded, then at last they could get down to business, taking their places at the round dining table. He knew James was watching him, afraid that he'd suddenly strike the soldier, so he smiled to reassure him. Oddly enough it was genuine. He felt utterly calm, as if he'd drifted out of his body and was watching his actions from afar.

"I am instructed to inform you that the Barón de Carondelet cannot agree to your proposals."

"What, Don Cayetano, not any of them?"

"Naturally he would like his prisoners back, especially Lieutenant de Chigny. And he is perfectly prepared to allow you to depart the Mississippi unmolested."

"That is decent of him. Will he be sending me the money he stole?"

"The Barón would not accept that his actions be described as theft."

"Very well, Don Cayetano. You may tell His Excellency that I am prepared to depart without my money on only one condition."

"Which is?"

"That he hands over to me the man who murdered Juan Baptiste Rodrigo and Hyacinthe Feraud."

The soldier didn't even flick an eyebrow. "That seems a strange request. It is made doubly so by the fact that the Barón does not know who the person is, or indeed if it is only one."

"No, Don Cayetano. I don't suppose he does." Harry stood up quickly. "May I show you something?"

"If it has a bearing on our discussions, yes."

"It does, I do assure you."

Harry walked over to his desk, waited for de Coburrabias to join him, then stabbed a finger at the chart.

"To make a landfall at Havana you have to go south to latitude 23°, to the top of the Yucatan Channel, then allow the Gulf Stream to push you up to the Florida Straits. You must do nearly twice the distance to cover the same ground. And coming back that same tide is against you."

"I fail to see—"

Harry cut right across him. "But if you only go as far as the Dry Tortugas, you're still in the Gulf of Mexico. James, could we have the logbook?"

Harry took it off his brother and opened it at the marked page.

"As you can see, sir, you're quite prominently mentioned."

"It is the price of my rank."

"Not being a sailor, perhaps it would be helpful if I explain to you, before I send word to the Governor, what this means. You have adopted an air of Olympian detachment in the matter of the loss of the *Gauchos,* quite simply because you claim to have been in Havana. Yet this log shows that you were not."

"A forgery."

"The trouble with the story you told is this: once it is questioned it tends to unravel."

Harry lifted the chart to show the first of the paintings. It was well controlled, but he was sure he saw de Coburrabias jerk. "For instance, you are known to be attached to this lady, indeed you have gone to all the trouble of petitioning Madrid to be allowed to marry her. Where is she now, I wonder?"

"This is all very interesting, but the purpose of my visit is—"

Harry interrupted him rudely. "The purpose of your visit, Don Cayetano, is to ensure that my money stays in Louisiana. Here it is much easier to steal. But I am in a position to trade with you. I will tell you the whereabouts of an equal sum, and one that is easier to transport."

The gold ingot landed on the table with a thud, identifying marks uppermost. For all his rigid self-control, the soldier's eyes nearly popped out of his head.

"Where did you get this?"

"Perhaps we found it on the *Gauchos.*"

"No!"

"That is something you can only know if you were aboard the ship. But really what happened on the *Gauchos* is no concern of mine. That chest full of money is." De Coburrabias was looking at James. Harry could almost see his mind working, getting ready to propose a hostage. "My brother sails away with me, as do my crew."

His fingers reached out, to touch the gold, and Harry saw in his eyes that look he'd seen so often, the strange fascination that this metal exercised on men's minds.

"I am at liberty to discuss every matter you raised."

"Including our money."

He gave a curt nod. "Yes."

"Splendid. As the Barón de Carondelet's senior military adviser you will be able to tell him just how much havoc we can cause. And since he knows that war is imminent, he will be aware that the normal neutral rights are something I can contravene at will."

"Who told you war is imminent?"

"Captain Pascal de Guerin, whose body, at this moment, lies buried just north of the Manchac Post. He told me, though not willingly, that all de Godoy is waiting for is some money. I must say I know exactly how he feels."

"You killed de Guerin!"

"In rather the same manner you dealt with Rodrigo. Only I was more successful than you, Don Cayetano." It was Harry's turn to finger the ingot. "I got something for my trouble."

"De Guerin had the gold?"

"Yes. I must say General Wilkinson will be so disappointed. Not least to know that a Spanish officer, albeit reluctantly, betrayed him. But then if he's truly friendly with Spain, he, in turn, will betray America for nothing. That is, unless you would like to pass it on to him."

"I would like a glass of wine."

"Certainly, James, would you mind?"

Silence reigned while it was poured, Harry taking a glass as well. De Coburrabias drained the first one straight off and held his hand out for a refill. And all the time his brain was racing, trying to find the flaw in what Harry had said. His real problem was that none existed. Harry left him to stew for a bit before continuing.

"De Carondelet, as you are aware, is not a trusting soul. And he certainly reposed no faith in you or de Barrameda. So he pretended to put the gold on the *Gauchos* when, in fact, he sent it north with Captain de Guerin. Rodrigo was telling you the truth. You tortured him for nothing. But, of course, once you'd killed him you had to dispose of the rest of the crew. A good idea to put him on the raft like that, so that everyone would suspect pirates. What a pity for the first time in his life de Barrameda did something properly. And there were suddenly no pirates around to blame. More wine?"

The contents of his glass disappeared again, and were replaced.

"She wouldn't have sunk if we hadn't towed her. But we moved the plug that you placed to keep her afloat. What was the plan, Don Cayetano? After all, you diverted those two transports to look for her. Was it the notion that once the ship was brought in, de Carondelet would have to tell you the gold wasn't on it? Or was it a desire to find out if you'd been cheated?"

"What I'm trying to work out, Captain Ludlow, is how you found all this out."

Harry kept his face rigid, and tried to swallow some wine to cover his feeling of triumph.

"Well, the unfortunate de Guerin was a rich source. You must remember that I am as ruthless as you."

"Is that likely to threaten me?"

"Possibly. But I would really rather get out of here with my own money. To get to the north of the Manchac Post again . . ."

"Again?"

"If you were to ask Captain Oliverta which way I came when I tried to visit you, he will tell you I came downriver. As I was explaining, the easiest way is to do, how do you say it, a 'Little Manchac'. By the way, that's a fine portrait you have on the wall

opposite your King, though I didn't much take to the miserable
cur cowering in the background."

"Where is de Guerin buried?"

Harry held up his hand. "All in good time, Don Cayetano.
First we must discuss my gold and silver, before we discuss yours."

"I was asked my opinion on the cost of ignoring you."

"This would be after you were asked if you could stop me."

"Yes." He smiled, for the first time since coming aboard. "It
will not surprise you to know that El Señor San Lucar de Barrameda offered to bring you to the Barón in chains."

"I'm tempted to let him try. But I'm more interested in your
opinion."

"I told that Wallonian idiot the truth, that if he wanted you
stopped he'd better get a couple of frigates here quickly."

"Yet you advised him not to pay us back."

"I said to await the outcome of our preliminary meeting."

"Good. I take it you will now advise him to trade."

"How do I know you aren't lying?"

"You don't, Don Cayetano. I told you I was ruthless, didn't
I? Do you really think that I would let you stand between me and
my money? Given that I know all about your recent exploits, as
I think you will admit, down to the last detail, it seems unlikely."

"And what if I tell de Carondelet about de Guerin?"

"That is no problem to me. I am protected by his parole and
a flag of truce. But I wonder, might he not just ask you why I was
so forthcoming?"

"I will need to take this with me."

"Feel free to do so. After all, it will soon be yours."

"Time to go back, I think."

"Tell me, will you stay in Louisiana?"

"Yes."

"Now that Mademoiselle Chrétien is dead."

"Rodrigo, of all people. She cuckolded me with that slug."

"Women!" said Harry with a shake of the head. "Though I
had to admit to being rather fond of Hyacinthe Feraud."

De Coburrabias looked hard at James. "She would have betrayed you, Ludlow. Perhaps, in her foolishness, she did already."

"Then it's as well she is dead, though I'm curious as to why."

"She asked questions that were inappropriate."

"People are usually killed for answers, not questions."

"One leads to the other. Best to remove the means of doing both."

Harry nearly cracked then, the way de Coburrabias was so cold-bloodedly discussing the way he mutilated Hyacinthe. But his longer-term aims won out. As they watched him depart, Harry turned to James to thank him.

"What did he mean when he said Hyacinthe had probably betrayed me?"

"I think he meant mischief, brother. He didn't say what questions she asked."

"You sound as if you know, James."

"De Chigny recognized Mademoiselle Chrétien, did he not? That portrait was in her quarters at the Hôtel de la Porte d'Orléans all the time you were away. Hyacinthe would recognize it just as quickly, and know that if that portrait was on the ship, so was the lady herself. The natural person to ask about that would be Don Cayetano. I doubt she was equipped to understand the ruthlessness, never mind the devious qualities, of someone like him."

"You'd come to like her too?" asked Harry.

"I must say I didn't think you'd pull it off," replied James evasively.

"Neither did I."

The next time de Coburrabias put off from the shore, the chest that had been out of their sight for so long took a prominent position on the deck, with him standing over it. Harry called de Chigny into his cabin.

"Lieutenant. You are to be taken ashore and there is something I would like you to do for me." He handed the youngster a package. "Please put this out of sight, and hand it to the Barón de Carondelet personally. It contains information that is vital to his future well-being."

"What is it?" he asked.

"It is enough to ensure that you are not censured for the casualties you suffered last night." That made him blush, and drop his head. "Put it inside your coat and give it to the Barón as soon as you see him. He is waiting for you on the quay."

"It's heavy."

"And important, remember. Now you'd best get up on deck."

Harry followed him out of the door. The breeze had freshened, cooling the sweat on his face. He stood watching as the *Navarro* repeated the earlier manoeuvre. De Coburrabias crossed the gangplank again, this time followed by two struggling sailors, the chest between them.

"Pender, look to that, if you please, and check the contents."

His men grabbed it off the Spaniards and laid it down on the deck. Pender had his picks out and on his knees was working steadily.

"You have something for me."

"Yes. I have the location of your reward."

He handed de Coburrabias a piece of parchment, a map which he'd drawn from memory.

"Bayou Pierre. Why so far north?"

"I could hardly take de Guerin in Spanish territory. And it's not a place many people want to visit."

"Are you ready, Lieutenant?"

De Chigny came to attention. "Sir."

"Then let us proceed."

He turned to walk away, but Harry restrained him, waiting till de Chigny was out of earshot. "Don Cayetano, would I be right in assuming that de Carondelet's safe conduct ends the minute you step ashore?"

"No, Captain Ludlow, the second."

"One other thing. Why did you lie to me about murdering your mistress?"

"Are you so sure I did?"

"Not positive. But I did wonder why you took all the food off the *Gauchos*."

"Do you miss anything, Ludlow?"

"I hope not," Harry replied, coldly.

De Coburrabias nearly lost control, such was the depth of his feelings. But only Harry, who was looking at him, observed this.

"Mademoiselle Chrétien loved society, Ludlow. She badgered me for years so that as my wife she could move in the correct circles. So I have made her a Queen. I admit her Kingdom is small, and barren. But it is all hers, if you don't count the millions of birds."

De Carondelet was waiting to greet de Chigny on the quay, his face set like a stern uncle. The boy had the package in his hand so swiftly it looked like a desire to deflect criticism. The Governor tore it open, his eyes so large they seemed to fill his face. The silver flashed in the sunlight and he read the message before turning to de Coburrabias, waving it under his nose. The crack of the musket ball came a split second after it had entered his head. The soldier crumpled to the ground. De Carondelet, stunned, looked once more at the writing on the inside of the wrapping paper.

> *From the man who recommended Captain Juan Baptiste*
> *   Rodrigo to your service.*
> *And for the memory of Hyacinthe Feraud.*

Out on the river, James dropped the nude sketches of Hyacinthe into the water. Innocent they might be, but Harry, he knew, wouldn't understand. Above his head, his brother raised Able Mabel and allowed the wind to blow the last residue of smoke out of the barrel.

"All hands," he said, in a soft voice.

DAVID DONACHIE is an avowed lover of
 naval fiction with a streak
of mischief. A best-selling
author well-known to
European audiences,
Donachie—writing as Tom
Connery—is the author of
the popular *George
Markham of the Marines*
novels, also set during the Napoleonic Wars
and telling the land and sea adventures of His
Majesty's Royal Marines. Under his own
name, Donachie is the author of a multi-
volume biographical novel about Lord Nelson
and Lady Emma Hamilton.

A Scot by birth, he lives in Deal on the
Channel coast of England, where he works to
keep his inspirations in motion.

The Royal Marines Saga

By the author of the Alexander Kent/Richard Bolitho Novels

NEW!

Travel through Britain's military history, from the bright morning of Victoria's Empire to its late afternoon in the Sicilian campaign of World War II with the proud tradition of a seafaring family called the Blackwoods, and the service in which successive generations make their career—the Royal Marines.

This is an era of Empire and an age of change, where tradition meshes with new technology to shape the destiny of men and nations. The Age of Sail gives way to the power of steam, and battleground muskets yield to sharp-shooting rifles.

Reeman presents a vivid saga spanning a century and a half in the life of a great family in this four-book series.

"**Masterly storytelling** of battles and war."
—*Sunday Times of London*

"If any author deserved to be 'piped' into book-shops with full naval honours it is Douglas Reeman, without question **master of both genres of naval fiction—historical and modern.**"
—*Books Magazine*

Badge of Glory
Royal Marines Saga #1
ISBN 1-59013-013-8
384 pp.• $16.95 paperback

First to Land
Royal Marines Saga #2
ISBN 1-59013-014-6
304 pp.• $15.95 paperback

The Horizon
Royal Marines Saga #3
ISBN 1-59013-027-8
368 pp.• $15.95 paperback

Dust on the Sea
Royal Marines Saga #24
ISBN 1-59013-028-6
384 pp.• $15.95 paperback

Available at your favorite bookstore, or call toll-free:
1-888-BOOKS-11 (1-888-266-5711).

To order on the web visit **www.mcbooks.com**
and read an excerpt.

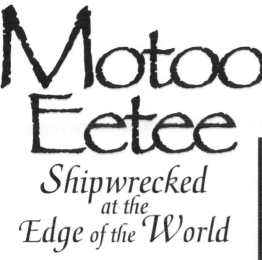

Motoo Eetee

Shipwrecked
at the
Edge of the World

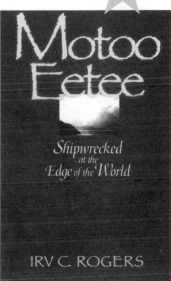